Do We Not Bleed?

The first James Enys mystery

Patricia Finney

GALWAY

First published 2013
Copyright © 2013 Patricia Finney

ISBN 978-1-909172-50-0

More about James Enys and his world may be found at
www.climbingtreebooks.net

www.patriciafinney.com

Published by Climbing Tree Books Limited,
Truro, Cornwall, UK

Cover design by Grace Kennard

Typeset by Grace Kennard

*M*aliverny Catlin was drunk, which was unusual for him. It wasn't his fault. He wasn't used to aquavitae and it had only taken a couple of horn beakers' full.

He was drunk because he knew he was damned, utterly and finally, without any possibility of remission. After all, why should a good, a just God deign to help someone as damned as he was?

He staggered along the alleyway, feeling the roughly plastered walls of the houses. Bits of them had been built with pieces of old Whitefriars abbey and filled in with wattle-and-daub. For most of them the only thing holding them up was the weight of other houses on either side. You couldn't see it in the silver darkness but the walls were pink with the bulls' blood in the plaster to help to hold it together – as Christ's blood held the World together. A pretty metaphor. He must have heard it in a sermon somewhere. Anyway, everything was blue in the moonlight but you could still smell the blood.

He wasn't exactly lost either. He knew the alley was going the wrong way – he needed to be heading uphill away from the Thames and towards Fleet Street and his house. This alley was leading him parallel to the river.

At a corner, he paused. Another man was squatting in the corner of two houses where there was a small rubbish tip. He must have been caught by a flux.

The man swore, turned his face away. Maliverny slurred an apology, also turned politely, coughed, staggered blindly against a wall and found a tiny narrow gap between houses which he thought might lead up to Fleet Street.

A few steps along and he trod on something horribly squashy. Then his foot stubbed on something soft. He looked down.

A face looked up at him from her veil of hair, eyes staring and set, the mouth quite peaceful, a dark hole hedged with teeth. The head was towards him, the body was confined by the alley walls, stretched out with her legs apart, her arms propped against the walls, all at awkward angles.

She was naked. Catlin gulped as his eyes bumped

on her breasts, gulped again. Down the centre of her body, starting at her breastbone was a huge black slash. Inside it were glistening things, some pale, some dark. All about her were shining snakes of flesh and removed neatly was a red fleshy pear, with arms, draped on her white leg, shining wetly in the moonlight.

Catlin thought his heart had stopped too. He couldn't breathe. He put his hand to his mouth, staggered backward into the alley he had come from. His heel crushed a rat skull; he retched a couple of times and then jack-knifed into the splattering foulness of vomiting.

He was helpless for a moment, his stomach clutching and cramping until every drop of the accursed booze he had drunk was wasting its fumes from a stinking puddle. He blinked at it. When had he eaten carrots? He had only had a slice of a raised pork pie and bread.

"Sir," came a quiet voice beside him, "May I help you?"

It was the man he had caught relieving himself, now decent again. The hat was pulled down slightly but Catlin recognised the badly pock-scarred face and light build.

"Mr Enys," he gasped, spitting and swallowing again, "I... I... forgive me... I am..."

A flash across his vision of the ruined body behind him hid everything and his stomach twisted again.

7

He leaned over with it. The man he had recognised as Mr James Enys, lawyer, deftly caught his hat when he knocked it off against the wall and waited for the vomiting to finish. He was breathing noticeably through his mouth.

"Be assured, sir," said Mr Enys drily, "Your distemper will be much the less in the morning for a trifle of suffering now."

The humour in his voice surprised Catlin as much as the fact that he was still there at all. With the plague increasing daily, most people would have nothing to do with someone taken sick suddenly, even if it seemed obvious what was the cause of the trouble. The alley did reek like a still-room. Perhaps Catlin had had more aquavitae than he had thought.

Nothing but bile was coming. Catlin coughed, spat. He straightened.

"Sir, I have disgraced myself," he said apologetically, flushing with embarrassment. "But... but I think I had cause."

Mr Enys lifted his eyebrows.

"Certainly, sir," he said affably, handing back the hat.

"No, I mean..."

It suddenly occurred to Catlin to wonder if Mr Enys could know about the horror in the tiny passageway only a couple of paces from them. His mind reared away from the thought like a spooked horse. He couldn't help

8

himself, he gestured at the opening.

Mr Enys looked surprised, moved to the opening and looked in.

There was complete silence. Then the man drew a long shuddering breath.

"Christ Jesus Almighty God," he swore.

After a long empty pause, Mr Enys took his hat off for respect. Catlin clutched his off again too. Enys moved closer and peered. Then he stepped back carefully, turned to face Catlin who saw he was shaking all over.

"It's Mr Catlin, isn't it, sir?" he asked softly.

Catlin nodded, looking shrewdly at the man's hands and sleeves which were quite clean of blood as far as he could see in the uncertain light. He was wearing a fashionable linen shirt with the linen turned over the sleeve-ends. All was clean of blood.

And Catlin knew from experience that no one could have done such horror without being splashed in blood. Then he realised that Enys was looking equally carefully at his own hands and sleeves.

He swallowed once more, against the bitterness of the bile at the back of his throat. At least his head was clearing now. Enys was speaking.

"I think this was done an hour or two ago for some of the blood has caked," he said. "I think the... the man who did it cannot be here still. Do you have any candles about yourself? I have no lantern at all nor anything but my tinderbox."

Catlin fumbled in his sleeve pocket where he had a candle end. Enys took it, stepped a little way along the alley where there was a small window with a stone ledge. He took out his tinderbox, struck flint on steel, soon the fronds of fireweed fluff were burning and Enys blew gently so he could light the stub of candle.

Catlin watched, hollow and light-headed, as if he had never seen a man make fire before. Mr Enys's fingers were thin and nimble, the nails bitten.

The candle light was a grateful yellow though puffing black smoke and a bad smell because it was a cheap candle, not beeswax but a mix of tallow and re-melted candle ends. Catlin could afford better but didn't.

Shielding it with his hand, Enys walked back to the narrow passageway and peered into it, then stepped carefully in. Catlin followed, feeling resentful that the younger man was showing more courage than he had, looking at such a thing twice.

Enys bent down, put his hand out to touch but didn't.

"Why..?" he muttered to himself.

"Why what?" Catlin demanded.

"Why anatomise the poor woman?" Enys's voice was a whisper.

"Woman?" said Catlin harshly, his jaw clenching at

10

the reminder of why he was damned. "That's no woman, it's a notorious whore." Then he stopped himself and clamped his lips tight.

From his squatting position, Enys turned his scarred gargoyle's face, the candle light making deep shadows of his eye sockets.

"Do you know her then, Mr Catlin?" he asked quietly.

Catlin hunched his shoulders "I... I have had occasion to question her for her notorious whoredom and her knowledge of... ah... of papistry and treason."

"Do you know her name?"

"I believe it is Ann," said Catlin as indifferently as he could, "Ann Smith or some such."

"And where does she work from? Who is her upright man?" asked Enys, showing he knew something of the ways of whores himself.

"I have no idea," said Catlin immediately.

"Hm," said Enys, with a cold look. He had edged alongside the corpse carefully so as not to touch anything. He did put a finger down to the whore's neck, though there was no possibility of life there. "Still warm," he muttered. He looked gravely at the ruin of the whore's belly and even peered up between her legs which was shadowed by her knees. Catlin heard a gulp.

Enys was coming back now, lips pale, face set. The candle had nearly gone and was guttering. It went out completely as he stepped back into the alley.

"We must find the Watch and alert them," he said.

"Why?" Catlin asked, genuinely puzzled. "What would they do save stand about and bleat?"

"Well sir," said Enys, with some edge in his voice, "Whom would you suggest? We certainly cannot leave the poor soul lying like this for dogs and rats to find her, it's indecent."

It was indeed, but more so. Somehow the whore was not just naked, Catlin felt, but more than naked, with the violent discovery of her innards an even greater obscenity of exposure than her mere bare flesh could have been.

"I know you're a pursuivant, Mr Catlin," said Enys softly in the darker night left by the end of the candle. "And that you serve a Privy Councillor. Mine own lord is at Court at the moment, or I would go straight to Somerset House. We must tell some man of authority."

"My lord is out of London too," Catlin said, not wanting to explain who it was. He thought for a moment. "Perhaps Mr Recorder Fleetwood should be told?"

"Yes, a good idea."

"Or Mr Topcliffe? In case... in case Papist priests did this?"

"Papists?" Enys asked, "Why in God's name should they do this?"

"Some evil superstition, some vengeance... Or the Jews perhaps?"

12

Enys's silence was a clear sign of his disagreement. Also of his good sense – who would want to defend Papists or Jews to so notorious a Puritan as Catlin? And Catlin had to admit that neither the Papists nor the Jews were very likely to have done it in fact.

"It could be a madman?" he offered.

"Of some sort, plainly," said Enys. "Come sir, let's go at once to Mr Recorder Fleetwood as you suggested."

"We should set a guard."

"Certainly," said Enys, "Who?"

Catlin thought it through, his normal cold sharp habit of thought returning now the fog of booze had blown away. "Yes," he said, "I'd not wish to guard her and nor would you, perhaps?"

"I wouldn't, sir."

"Her ghost..."

"I don't fear her spirit which is no doubt already facing Judgement," said Enys showing himself no Papist despite the rumours about his sister, "I fear her killer who may not want his handiwork known."

Catlin nodded. Enys led the way up the alley which he obviously knew well and through another narrow passage under an old stone arch still decorated with Papist images from the old Abbey – vines with full bunches, carried on poles by two men, bees and incongruous cows that made the bees relatively the size of dogs. Catlin recognised the quotation from the Book

13

of Joshua of the land of Israel, flowing with milk and honey.

On Fleet Street everything was quiet except for some beggars dossing down in the shadow of Temple Bar so as to be sure to have good pitches in the morning. Catlin took the lead, heading to the north of Ludgate so they could climb over London Wall where most of it had gone to more important purposes such as building houses. They took a shortcut through Poultry Street and Catlin looked up once to see a flickering light at one of the windows, unusual so late at night.

·

Bald Will Shakespeare saw the two of them pass by and sighed. He had sat staring at a blank sheet of paper for hours, completely forgetting how late it was and had used up an entire candle doing it, which was a waste of tuppence. His landlady would be annoyed as well, since she claimed that the light would keep the chickens in her yard wakeful and cause them to stop laying and furthermore was a terrible fire hazard, even though it was inside a glass holder. And she would charge him double for the candle as well.

He recognised one of the passers-by as the person who went by the name of James Enys, utter barrister of Gray's Inn. The other one he thought was a pursuivant,

14

although he couldn't remember the name which was quite a peculiar one.

What were they up to so late at night? They were walking purposefully and not even trying to take care for the Watch, which argued some kind of official business. The glimpse Shakespeare had seen from above of Enys's face had been of someone who had been shocked to the core.

Shakespeare shifted uneasily on his stool and wiped his unused pen, put the lid on his ink. He blew out the candle before it went out by itself, causing a stink. He sighed into the gleaming darkness, where the Queen Moon overwhelmed most of her starry courtiers in the cold sky. Maybe?

He shook his head. He had sat down intending to make a start on his first work for his new patron, the Earl of Southampton. He knew that writing for an earl was very different from writing for the playgoing groundlings. It was, in fact, what he was born to do as opposed to pandering to the mob. The earl was highly educated, or at least believed himself to be so and fancied himself a poet: whatever Shakespeare made would need to be elaborate, highly worked, smooth, classical and packed with allusion and simile obscure enough to please the earl's vanity when he puzzled it out, but not so difficult as to frustrate him.

And so Shakespeare had stared into space and at his

15

paper all evening. In his head he had another kind of space, labelled "th'Earl of Soton his poem" with certain things about it already shaped. However, in that space was nothing at all at the moment. He was stuck. In fact he had been stuck for a week, putting the damned thing off one way or another. He had got into a speed-drinking competition at the Mermaid before he sat down which may not have helped, although he had hoped it would. Mr Enys had been there too, he remembered.

Shakespeare smiled. He found the person who went about as the lawyer James Enys quite fascinating, because Shakespeare was one of very few people in the world who knew that the gentleman who was building a good reputation for himself as a man-at-law was in fact not a man but a woman. And as such could not even appear as a witness in court as her proper self, Mrs Portia Morgan.

She was getting better at aping men, Shakespeare thought. She had lost the habit of fluttering her hands from the wrist when anxious and she had much improved her walk – thanks, he thought, to his advice. She had learned to lengthen her stride and move from her shoulders rather than her hips. She now sat with her legs braced instead of tucked under as formerly. Her swordsmanship was still poor but vastly improved from a month ago when it had been comically bad. Shakespeare had arranged for her to have thrice weekly lessons from the man the Burbages used to plan their swordplay on stage and that was already giving her better-shaped arms and some power to her shoulders. As always, in the creating of an illusion, it was the detail that mattered.

What was she up to, going about with that pursuivant, whatsisname? Malvolio? Should be, but no. It was Maliverny Catlin. A notorious hunter of papists and a spy. Shakespeare shook his head, went up the ladder to his attic chamber, hauled his boots off and lay down on the straw pallet he used for a bed, still dressed to save time in the morning. He would have to ask her then. Him then. His head spun in emptiness, so he pulled out his little flask of aquavitae and took a gulp. Somewhere in the yard, a cock clucked quietly to himself, readying for his head-shattering greeting of the dawn. Shakespeare moaned into his pillow.

.

Mr Recorder Fleetwood's doorkeeper yawned at them from under a nightcap.

"I'm not awaking his honour for a murdered whore," he croaked flatly, "What the Devil..."

"Mr Beamish," said Catlin tightly, "Nor would I save for the manner of it. Also because the killer may remove the corpse before morning. We only came upon

17

it by chance."

The doorkeeper scowled at both of them as if they could have been up to no good themselves. Catlin scowled haughtily back. Beamish sniffed, called over his shoulder for the scrawny youth who was kipping by the fire.

"No sir," put in Enys firmly, "This needs two men full grown to guard the place for when the other whores find the body in the morning and more especially when the woman's upright man finds it, there is likely to be a riot."

"How do you know?"

"Because the body was... cut open and this is not the first," said Enys, "And because I would not have any youngster set eyes on anything so... obscene."

The doorkeeper seemed to wake up at last. He blinked a couple of time and then said, "Wait there, sirs."

It was a long wait. Catlin was thirsty again. Once the boy had put his head down again on his pallet, he licked dry lips and whispered to Enys. "Not the first?"

"At least one other," said Enys, also whispering, "It was all over the Mermaid last week that there was a woman found – as if the hangman had been practising on her for a hanging, drawing and quartering."

"I never heard that..."

Enys smiled. "You never speak to players. It was the

players who found her, inside the gates of their new building on Bankside."

"Ha," said Catlin grimly, "I never thought of that. It must be the players who did the murder..."

"They were very upset," said Enys coldly, "and very frightened that her ghost would walk and curse their new playhouse."

"Good..."

"... so they paid for a decent Christian burial for her."

Catlin sniffed. He hated all ungodly layabout players, poets and playwrights. Even the old pagan Plato had meant to keep poets out of his Republic and that holy man, John Calvin had had every one of the evil tribe whipped from Geneva for mocking God with their damnable lies and for leading the common folk astray.

"I would say that of all men in the world, the players are the least likely murderers," said Enys again, with that glint of humour which Catlin found unsettling. "Since the dead woman on that occasion was French Mary."

Catlin shrugged. "A notorious whore," he said.

"Certainly, a notorious retired whore who kept an alehouse where she was willing to give players credit, something hardly any other seller of booze in London will do. And she would commute the debts for playhouse tickets too which she sold on, so everyone was pleased. I hope Mr Recorder will..."

"God's blood, this is a bad business," boomed a

19

voice behind them. Both spun and made their bows, Enys a fraction deeper than Maliverny Catlin, as this was the Recorder of London who was in charge of the criminal Courts of London as well as the London Watch and the trained bands.

His broad florid face was frowning and he was fully dressed, booted and spurred with a soldier's old buff coat over his fur-trimmed doublet, his sword-belt buckled. He took an old-fashioned velvet cap with a feather in it from the doorkeeper and put it on over his grey hair.

"Second in a month," he growled at them, "The whores will be wild with rage. Do you know whose she was?"

They both shook their heads. Fleetwood led the way to the back of his house where was a stable-yard and a small building for his men-at-arms. Nominally they served as Captains and teachers for the London trained bands, but they also did Mr Recorder Fleetwood's bidding and were unofficially a much younger and more effective Watch for the City than the impending graveyard-dwellers of the official Watch.

The barracks clattered with activity, candles and torches lit along with a great deal of complaint. Four young men were yawning in the yard, buckling sword-belts and morion straps, while grooms brought indignant horses from their stalls including two for

Catlin and Enys.

Everyone was mounted before Mr Recorder nodded at Maliverny Catlin.

"Mr Catlin, tell me how you came upon this new outrage?"

Catlin sat stiffly in the saddle while his horse backed and sidled under him in the annoying way of horses. He admitted to being a trifle distempered of drink so no one would think he had been puking because of plague, and of needing to cut through the alleys from the water steps, so he had stopped in the alley and...

"I'm afraid I retched at once at the shock," he said primly. "Although I have seen executions, I have never..."

"Quite so," said the Recorder quickly, "Mr Enys?"

"I had been caught by a flux and was in a similar case to Mr Catlin," explained Enys smoothly, "although we were not together and not well-acquainted. When I realised from Mr Catlin's... er... reaction that something was badly wrong in the alley, I lit a candle and looked closer..."

"Were there tokens?" asked Fleetwood oddly.

"Of the Plague?"

"No... So Rumour is not so quick then. You say she was anatomised. How?"

Enys swallowed. "She had been... opened from above her navel to her... er... her quim. Her entrails had been pulled out and... er... arranged around her. Some

21

inner organs were lying on her thigh..."

"Oh yes? Which?"

"Ah... I didn't recognise them, sir, not being familiar with such things. Only perhaps it looked a little like a sow's pig-bed?"

"Yes, so, yes," said Fleetwood, his chin on his chest, "Her womb."

Enys paled further, if that was possible, put his hand to his mouth. "Sir?" he asked faintly.

"Her womb, sir," said Fleetwood, spurring ahead to go through the narrow gap of Ludgate which was being held open for him by an obsequious old watchman. "Organ of generation," he shouted back over his shoulder, "It's why the whores will be upset."

Cantering behind, Catlin wondered for a moment if Mr Enys might pass out and fall off his horse. For a moment he bounced painfully in the saddle as if he was a sack of meal, but then he straightened and kicked the horse back to a canter to keep up with the Recorder as he clattered down through the shuttered darkness of Tower Street, where the statutory lanterns had gone out.

It was the dead of night so deep that not even the bakers were stirring yet to light their ovens. Mr Fleetwood's men all carried torches and the clatter and thud of the horses' hooves and the blaze of light must have woken some of the people as their small cavalcade passed. Good, thought Catlin, why should they sleep when he was awake?

.

At the small opening between two slumping houses where Catlin and Enys had come out of the Liberties, they all dismounted. The youngest man was left to guard the horses from enterprising beggars and at Fleetwood's nod, Enys led the rest of them sidling between walls into the darkness.

To Catlin's relief as well as disappointment, she was still there. In the light of the torches her dark hair shone and it seemed as if her mouth moved. The eyes, however, said nothing. From the traces, rats had begun their own investigations but run at the arrival of men and lights.

Fleetwood sighed and took his hat off, his head bowed for a moment. Perhaps he was papistically praying for the whore's soul, Maliverny wondered? He hoped not. Anyway, the creature was certainly burning in the fires of hell for all eternity now.

Then the Recorder leaned down and closed the whore's eyes, turned to the older of the men he had brought and nodded to him. The man took out a notebook and stick of graphite and began to draw the corpse as it lay.

Fleetwood had them both repeat their stories of the

discovery. "Do you know who it is?" he asked.

"No sir," said Catlin, far too quickly as he immediately realised.

"I believe it might be Annie Smith," said Enys, giving Catlin a hard look.

Fleetwood nodded. "Known to all as Kettle Annie. I think so too though it's harder to tell without her clothes. Where are they, by the way?"

Enys shrugged. There was no sign of them nearby, but two of the young men were sent off to search nearby alleys and one came back with a large bundle of a striped kirtle and secondhand brocade petticoat and a tawny velvet gown that was worn down to the cloth. Kettle Annie had liked to dress fine. Enys bent gingerly down to the body and pointed out something under it – the remnants of her stays and shift lay there, soaked in blood.

"I think the cutting was done before she was dead," he said, "for the amount of blood..."

"Yes,"

It was clear the shift and stays had been cut, not ripped, with a sharp knife or shears and peeled back as if skinning a kill. Enys touched the edges of the linen. "And yet not in a frenzy," he added.

"Clearly not," said Fleetwood, "Look how carefully he worked. The stomach is still entire, the guts have not been breached. He has taken out the womb but not cut

24

into anything else. I know few butchers that could have done this so neatly, and fewer barber surgeons."

"Wasn't he afraid of discovery?" wondered Enys.

Catlin pointed to a rough screen of wattle that was tilted innocently against the wall in the wider alley. "If he put that across, nobody would see him."

"Wouldn't they see the light from his lantern? He must have needed light to work so neatly."

Nobody answered, but the fact was that in the Liberties if you saw a light behind a screen, you were wise not to pry.

"Hm," said Fleetwood, "The thing is... the really interesting thing here, gentlemen, is how did he get her to do it? How did he get Kettle Annie of all people into so narrow an alley on her own and then kill her?"

Kettle Annie had been a large strong woman and afraid of no one. It was something of a puzzle although Catlin thought the answer was obvious.

"He fooled her into it by pretending he was after her trade," he said.

"In only her shift and stays?" asked Enys.

It was a good point. Why would Kettle Annie take her clothes off? Most whores that worked outside the bawdy houses never did, they never needed to. The whores that worked where there were warm fires and curtained beds charged extra for the show and wore linen breeches which they charged even more for

25

shedding. No decent woman ever wore anything under her shift except during her courses.

This line of thought was making Catlin uncomfortable and he could feel his ears going hot.

"Did he knock her out and drag her here, then strip her?" asked Fleetwood.

Nobody said anything but they all thought, Kettle Annie? A woman that size? Enys looked carefully at the back of her head, then shook his own.

"I think not." When he laid her head back down again, something caught his eye on the side of it and he touched it with his fingers, rubbed them together, frowned and sniffed.

"More blood?" asked Fleetwood.

"No. Hair oil."

Fleetwood said, "But the true riddle is how did any man get Kettle Annie to lie down in the dirt in nothing but her shift and stays and then allow him to slash open her belly and rummage around in her innards. Why didn't she fight? There are no cuts on her hands, no bruises on her wrists."

"He must have been boltered in blood," said Enys.

"Not necessarily," Catlin told him, "If he was careful with his cutting and did it from behind... I've seen it done in the hunting field in such wise that the courtier was not even speckled."

"So have I, but that's for the first cut after the kill,

26

when the humours have stopped." objected Fleetwood, "You couldn't undertake this sort of butchery without an apron."

"Then perhaps he wore one," Enys put in.

Fleetwood sighed, shook his head again and peered over his man at arms' shoulder at the drawing. "Well done, Gideon, excellent."

The man certainly was a good limner. He had made several drawings of the woman: one from above, one from the foot end, one from the head. He had done a delicate drawing of her face as well, as if he was a court painter preparing to make a miniature of a fine lady.

"All right, lads," Fleetwood said, beckoning the other two, "Let's collect her up and take her to St Bride's crypt ready for the inquest."

The other two young men set their faces sternly, rolled their sleeve cuffs up and set about gathering the entrails and putting them back where they came from. Whether from superstition or the normal male disgust at such things, the younger of them used his dagger to prick up the woman's womb and put that back too. Although it was all higgledy piggledy, thought Catlin who had seen several Papist priests disembowelled, he had never before thought what a miracle it was so orderly to pack so much into the little space of a belly. Surely God was the greatest of Craftsmen?

The young men shifted Kettle Annie onto the litter

they had brought and covered her with a canvas roll from one of the horses.

It was still deep chilly night and Orion was tilting towards the horizon again. In the distance there was a bang of a door and the sound of someone yawning mightily on Fleet Street, perhaps a baker starting work. It was a tricky matter to squeeze the obdurate length and width of the litter up onto Fleet Street and then along it as quickly as possible before they could go down riverwards again to St Brides in the main part of the old Whitefriars liberty.

The beggars at Temple Bar at the other end of the street sat up at the torches this time, and squinted with interest at the procession moving away from them. Then they began scratching and making water against headless saint statues on the Bar and rearranging the plasters that kept their sores open.

"Sir!" called Enys, holding his hat on his head and running past Catlin to keep up with the litter and the looming Recorder of London. "Sir, was it the players themselves found the other one at the new theatre site?"

"Yes, it was, Mr Enys," said Fleetwood heavily. "One of them even drew a picture of it for a ballad about her, though he had not Gideon's skill. There were two or three of them that found her."

"Who were they?"

"Ah... Mr Burbage, Mr Henslowe and young

Shakeshaft..."

"Shakespeare? Bald Will? I thought he was in Oxford?" asked Catlin, who liked to collect intelligence on subversives like players and poets.

"Him? No, he's back. I heard Southampton's taking him on as his house poet."

Catlin scowled. They passed by a tavern where a sleepy-eyed woman in her stays and petticoat was standing on the threshold watching. Back up the street at Ludgate they could see the large cart and patient horses of the night-soil men who were clattering around with buckets, whistling loudly and occasionally dropping turds behind them. The woman had a covered bucket beside her and an irritated expression on her face so perhaps she was waiting for the night-soil men to rate them about something: however she stared with interest at the litter.

"That's never a plague death," she shouted over her shoulder into the house, "So stop your grizzling. Mr Recorder's there which he never would if it was plague."

They ignored her as officiously as they could, taking a wider lane towards the church door. Gideon had run ahead to wake the Reverend, who turned out to be waiting on the steps of his church for them, still in his nightcap, an old furred dressing gown over his shirt and his bare feet in his pattens. He was shivering in the sharp air.

29

"Mr Recorder," said the churchman, bowing his head slightly.

"Reverend," rumbled Fleetwood. "Good of you to meet us. I'm afraid this is a very shocking case and no one is to view the corpse until I have had a barber surgeon examine it myself. You can still lock your crypt, can you not?"

"Yes sir," answered the reverend, his eyes gleaming with curiosity. "I shall need to know who it is for the Register."

"Mrs Annie Smith," said Fleetwood.

"Kettle Annie?" asked the Reverend, shock on his face. Catlin wondered if he was another of the redoubtable Annie's band of old suitors and customers. "No? Is it? Lord above, how sad, God rest her."

Catlin snorted. Kettle Annie was an obdurate and renowned old whore and that was all there was to it.

The Reverend took off his nightcap in respect as the lads hefted the litter into his church and down the steps to the crypt. They all followed inside the cold church, colder than the churchyard, pitch dark in the night time with the torchlight catching whitewashed papistical vine leaves and grape bunches and a strange looking face made of leaves looking from the top of a pillar. Catlin averted his eyes from the papistical idolatry. At least they had painted over the old pictures of superstition.

They heard Fleetwood locking the door and coming

back up the stairs, followed by the clopping of the Reverend's pattens.

"I'll keep this," he rumbled, "Tell Nan not to worry about cleaning the crypt until Mrs Smith's properly buried."

The Reverend smiled faintly. "I'm afraid she rarely does since she finds the steps too much for her old knees. Do you know when the funeral may be?"

"Not until after the inquest which I will be calling at the Old Bailey tomorrow or the day after, depending on the lists."

Fleetwood came over to them. "Sir," asked Catlin, "Who was the other whore that was found at the theatre?"

"French Mary the Elder," said Fleetwood.

Catlin shuddered. This was getting worse and worse. Neither were young whores, being in their thirties at least, as far as anyone knew. Kettle Annie in particular was senior amongst the London whores, especially in the Whitefriars and especially since the incident of the kettle. Catlin had heard four different tales, each more unlikely than the last.

"Mr Catlin, Mr Enys," said Fleetwood formally, "Thank you for bringing this to my attention so promptly. You may have saved me a great deal of trouble. I am grateful but I wonder if I may propose something to you gentlemen?"

Enys's face was wary, a sentiment Catlin shared.

"I need this matter investigated," said Fleetwood, "Would you, Mr Enys, be prepared to assist Mr Catlin in finding out who did it?"

Catlin stepped forward hurriedly. "Sir, sir... I..."

"I know, I know, you hardly want to do it," said Fleetwood patiently, "But I know you served Sir Francis Walsingham for many years as one of his best pursuivants and I am willing to pay forty pounds between the two of you if you can clear the matter up for me."

Enys and Catlin stared at each other.

"Sir, my skill is in finding out papistry," said Catlin between his teeth, "And I am not in such need of money..."

"Are you not?" said Enys with some humour, "You must have a pretty package of confiscated lands then." He turned to Fleetwood. "I need the money, Mr Recorder, and I'll do it without Mr Catlin."

"No," said Fleetwood, "I want you both. You, Mr Enys, because you have been asking good questions and you are a man learned in the law, and you Mr Catlin in case there is any matter of treason here."

"I fear I am in service to another lord...

"I'll talk to his honour," said Fleetwood, "Or I will when he gets back from Oxford. I think Mr Heneage will not object..."

"He is no longer my lord," said Catlin, stiffly.

32

"No?" Fleetwood's bushy eyebrows went up, "Well done. I hear he has lost some favour with the Queen since the trouble at his house on Bankside." He stuck his thumbs in his sword belt and his eyes narrowed. "I want the two of you and either I'll pay you twenty pounds each or I'll take you both up as chief suspects in the murders, whichever you choose." Fleetwood's face was hard, though his bluff voice was still quite even.

There was a shocked silence, Catlin heard Enys swallowing.

"But... we..." began the lawyer.

"Were in the right place at the right time to do it and I need the killer taken and hanged as soon as may be. So it can be you two who hang for it or it can be the man who actually did the crimes, whichever you prefer, gentlemen."

More silence. Catlin spotted the lads who had carried the litter exchanging knowing glances behind Fleetwood's broad back. Enys cracked first.

He bowed to the Recorder. "I must have a warrant from you, sir," he said, typical lawyer that he was. "Otherwise, I cannot do anything to the purpose."

Mind, it was clever to ask for that so they could not be denied by Fleetwood if something went badly wrong with the investigation.

"Certainly," said Fleetwood after a considering pause. "You, Mr Catlin?"

33

"Likewise," croaked Catlin.

"We'll do it this morning. Should I speak to my Lord Chamberlain, Mr Enys, since I believe you are acting for him, aren't you?"

"Yes sir, but my duties are not onerous and the cases are unlikely to come to court for a while," said Enys, who seemed to be warming to the idea of finding out the killer (or killers, thought Catlin) of two mere whores. No doubt it was the twenty pounds he could bung that was helping, Catlin thought, being a typically greedy lawyer. "Though I think it might help if Sir Robert Carey, my Lord Chamberlain's son, were able to come back to London."

"Certainly, certainly," smiled Fleetwood who had probably expected to have to pay more, "I'll write to m'lord, he's attending Her Majesty, isn't he?"

"I believe so," said Enys, cautiously.

"Mr Catlin?"

Catlin too bowed to the Recorder. "I am at your honour's service," he said neutrally, his heart thumping with fright and fury. He wanted nothing whatever to do with the matter and was enraged at being blackmailed.

"Excellent," said Fleetwood with great good humour, "I'm sure you gentlemen will find the wicked recreant immediately. Come, we'll break our fast and then go and do the paperwork. God damn all paperwork."

.

It was certain that very few places made a better breakfast than the Cock on Fleet Street. The mild ale was sweet and nutty, the bread fresh from the baker on Ludgate, the butter cool and not even slightly rancid, there was curd cheese and honey, there were fat slices of ham fried on a griddle with a mess of eggs and good black pudding.

Mr Recorder Fleetwood sighed happily as the loaded pewter plate was laid respectfully in front of him. There was a moment of doubt over who was the junior in the mess, as Fleetwood divided the food into three equal portions, but Enys good-humouredly took the serving spoon and knife and served Mr Fleetwood first and then Mr Catlin, taking the smallest portion for himself.

Court customs having been observed as they were at the Inns of Court, Mr Fleetwood bent his head to mutter a speedy grace, then drew his eating knife and spoon and waded into the breakfast with gusto.

Catlin normally had no more than a penny loaf with cheese and perhaps a heel of a pie from the night before, but he was sharp set from being up all night and emptying his guts as well. Mr Enys looked at the feast before him and played with it. His pock-scarred face was still pale.

"Come, come, Mr Enys," boomed Fleetwood,

35

brutally, "You're not upset by the whore's end, are you?"

"Especially as no doubt she deserved it," added Catlin with his mouth full of egg. Enys's face was a mask and unreadable even when he was not being cautious, but there was a flicker of something fierce in his eyes.

"Hm. Certainly in the opinion of the man she famously kettled," said Enys, "Could it have been him?"

"Possibly. Though why would he have started with French Mary? And why anatomise both women?" Fleetwood helped himself to some of the ham Enys hadn't wanted.

At the next table, Fleetwood's men were having their own breakfast – minus the expensive ham, but with the eggs and black pudding. They seemed quiet and subdued. Fleetwood waved his knife at them.

"Come, come, goodmen, are you troubled at the whore's end as well?"

The oldest of them, Gideon the limner, looked up and nodded, his round snub-nosed face troubled.

"Well I am, sir, to be honest. I know she was a whore but she was a good woman too."

"Impossible!" sniffed Catlin, his mouth sour.

Gideon's face hardened. "With respect, sir, she was a good woman. She was kind to the young 'uns and she's fed ten of them at a time before now, nor she doesn't... didn't pander 'em neither. And she pays her rent prompt and she don't filch none of her customers and didn't say nuffin against none of the other morts around."

The younger of them looked up too. "She was kind to me an' my sister when me mam died," he said softly.

Catlin turned away. It stood to reason that a woman who sold herself was damned and that was all there was to it. It made no difference whether she was kind or not – to believe that anyone could earn their Salvation by good works was a papistical heresy that denied the sufficiency of God's Grace. As John Calvin and his Scots follower John Knox had so clearly shown. And he wished it wasn't true, indeed he did, but logic clearly showed that it was.

"Shouldn't fink the King of London will be happy about it, either," said the third man thoughtfully. "'E liked her too."

Enys turned sharply to the man. "Where's his game now?" he asked.

"Ah," said the man vaguely, "I wouldn't know that. Though a waterman might."

Enys nodded.

"Know the King of London do you, Mr Enys?" Fleetwood asked shrewdly.

"In a manner of speaking," said Enys, looking very uncomfortable, "He did me a great... er... kindness a month or so ago."

"Be very careful of Mr Pickering's kindnesses," said Fleetwood, "None of them are unpriced."

37

"Yes sir," Enys didn't meet his eyes, "I know it."

There was a moment of silence while Fleetwood washed down the last of his black pudding with ale. He banged on the table as he stood up and headed across the common room for the door. Catlin and Enys stood to follow him, but then stopped.

A woman was coming through the door, her chin high, walking as if she owned the place. She stood squarely in front of Fleetwood and blocked him. He stopped and watched her cautiously. She was a magnificent creature, in a high-crowned feathered hat, a yellow-starched ruff, a low cut bodice with a stomacher embroidered with hawks, a gown of dark blue velvet and a forepart to her petticoat that must have been made especially on a Huguenot loom for it was a new red and yellow striped brocade of silk – an outrageous brazen advertisement of the fact that as a notorious whore and the Madame of the Falcon, she was legally obliged to wear a striped petticoat. Mistress Julia Nunn made her stripes a badge of pride.

She had her hands on her broad farthingaled hips and in her pattens stood as high as Fleetwood's shoulder, though he was a big man.

She fixed him with a glare.

"Is it true what I hear, Mr Recorder," she said, without curtsey or greeting, "That Kettle Annie Smith has been murdered?"

Fleetwood paused, eyeing her coldly. "Yes, it is," he said curtly.

"And is it true that she was cut up like French Mary the other week?"

Catlin had to admire the speed and accuracy of the whore's intelligence network. Someone must have taken a boat across the river immediately to the Falcon on Bankside to tell the Madame about it. He wondered who.

Fleetwood paused. "Yes," he admitted.

Mrs Nunn shut her eyes for a second and Catlin saw her fists clench. "God damn him to hell," she whispered and then looked up at Fleetwood again. With the stateliness of a duchess she curtseyed to him "Sir," she said, "Is there anything we can do to help you find the evil man who killed her?"

"I doubt it," said Fleetwood, still affronted and chilly.

At that Mrs Nunn very surprisingly curtseyed again and smiled. "May I pay my respects to her corpse, sir?"

Fleetwood had inclined his head stiffly at her belated respects. "She is in the crypt of St Bride's," he told her, "until the inquest has convened and been adjourned or given its verdict. In the meantime, I have appointed Mr Maliverny Catlin and Mr James Enys of Gray's Inn here as my pursuivants in the matter."

Julia Nunn swept her glance over both of them and it seemed to Catlin that she found something amusing

39

about them.

"I see," she said. "My offer stands, gentlemen. If there is anything we can do to help you find the killer, simply ask."

Catlin would not acknowledge her, but Enys bowed shallowly in thanks.

"We are just about to draw up warrants for them," added Fleetwood. "Please tell your... ah... associates that I will do everything in my power to find the monster."

Mrs Nunn swept another curtsey. "Thank you, sir," she said and finally moved out of his way. The innkeeper served her aquavitae in a silver cup rather better than the pewter ones Enys and Catlin had been drinking from. Beer was carried to the two men at the door who had been attending the madame.

Catlin and Enys followed Fleetwood and his men out to the street which was full of noise and people as always, paid the spiky-haired boy who had been minding their horses and rode back up to Ludgate and the City.

·

The warrants were penned by one of Fleetwood's busy clerks, signed and sealed by Fleetwood with a flourish and handed over before Catlin and Enys were firmly escorted out the door by his steward. Happily, the steward also gave each of them a purse with five pounds in it as the first part of their fee.

In the street, Catlin stood looking at his warrant for a moment, fighting memory. In his work for Walsingham, he had not always had a warrant but he had always felt more comfortable if he did. Of course he had no need for twenty pounds. He had collected a very pretty parcel of property from the many Papists he had arrested and sometimes questioned, and he lived off the rents of five good houses scattered about the City, whilst he lived in the sixth with a couple of manservants to attend him. He kept thinking he should find a respectable wife for himself, but he always shuddered at the prospect of sharing bed and board with some feather-brained woman who would prattle all the time and spend his hard-earned money on hats and stomachers. Although bearing in mind St Paul's admonishment on the subject of marrying rather than burning, perhaps... He really didn't want to re-open old wounds.

On the other hand he didn't want to be arrested for the elaborately horrible murders of two well-loved whores and he certainly didn't want to hang for them either. He sighed.

"I must be on my way, Mr Catlin," said Enys, tucking his warrant into the breast pocket of his doublet, pulling his hat forward at an angle which would hide the worst of the pock-marks on his forehead. Catlin wondered why he was so anxious to hide them.

41

"Where are you going, Mr Enys?" Catlin asked.

Enys paused. "I want to ask the players what happened," he said, "before they drink away the memory of it."

Catlin sneered. "No doubt they'll lie," he said.

"No doubt they will," agreed Enys calmly, "But as I'm sure you know, Mr Catlin, when you question carefully and measure one lie against another, it can be possible to find out more of the truth as a result. What will you be doing?"

None of your business, was Catlin's first thought to this. He couldn't let Enys do all the work, no matter what his inclinations, or Enys might find out too much that should stay hidden.

"I shall be visiting some old friends," he answered cagily. "Shall we meet again for supper?"

"Certainly," said Enys, taking his hat off to Catlin, "I shall have been at the sword-schooling this afternoon and will likely have a better stomach to my meat than this morning. Good day, sir."

Catlin nodded to him and watched him go. Suddenly he felt bone weary and his eyelids made of lead and sand. Be damned to investigating, he would go home and sleep.

.

Bald Will was sitting in his favourite nook in the Mermaid, drinking double beer and watching the other men in the common room.

He liked to sit quietly and watch what people did, listen to their conversations if he could. Yes, that was part of what he had done for Sir Robert Cecil while working as a manservant in a great lord's house, but he enjoyed doing it anyway. It was fascinating. Sometimes he would talk to the more interesting ones, especially anybody with a non-London way of speaking. Thank God Marlowe was out of London at the moment, on some shady piece of business. At least Marlowe had delivered his long-overdue play of Edward II to the Burbages. Not that there was any use for it, with all the theatres shut because of the plague, as Shakespeare knew to his cost. The bearbaiting and the cockpits were still open of course. According to the authorities, he thought bitterly, a man was at terrible risk of Plague from the man standing beside him in the pit of a theatre whilst golden words and thrilling play carried him to France or the Americas or the far past. He was at no risk at all of Plague, however, whilst roaring at a bear that was fighting off eight mastiffs or laying down more money than he had on the prettiest of two cocks in a cockpit. Alternatively the owners of the cockpits and bearbaiting could afford better bribes. Shakespeare had heard that Henslowe had been quoted an eye-watering amount to keep the Theatre open which he had refused to pay. So they had even had to stop the building of the new playhouse on Bankside because Henslowe was now frightened they would run out of money.

Bald Will took a bite of the bread, having balanced a hunk of cheese and a quarter of a pickled onion on top of butter. It was the best breakfast he could afford as a way of getting started on his poem. He drew the line at the extravagance of meat for breakfast. He needed to be careful with his money so he could stretch it out.

He crunched and swallowed, drank more double beer. Nothing. Still no poem. Not the tiniest fragment of a notion of one. If he could just pick a subject he could at least begin. Nothing appealed. It was taking a lot of his willpower to stop himself calling for aquavitae and start the process of getting drunk for another day, just so he wouldn't have to feel that painful internal void.

He also knew what had really caused the trouble and he was doing his best not to think about that at all. So he was quite glad of the distraction when he spotted James Enys, whom he had last seen just before cock-crow that morning. Enys came and sat down in front of him.

"By your leave, sir," asked Enys politely.

"Mr Enys," Shakespeare said, "How are you, sir?"

It occurred to Shakespeare that Enys was looking even uglier than usual. The pocky face was pale and had deep bags under the eyes.

44

"Middling," said Enys with a smile, "How are you, Mr Shakespeare?"

Shakespeare beckoned the pot boy. "Aquavitae?" he asked, "You look like a man who needs it."

Enys gave him a cautious look and Shakespeare smiled to show he meant no irony. "I saw you in the street this morning, well before dawn."

"Ah yes," said Enys, rubbing his... her face.

The boy came scuttling over with the two cups and Shakespeare even paid for both since he had not yet run through enough of the Earl of Southampton's largesse to feel poor yet. And there was such a thing as investing for the future. God, he wished he could be rich so he could stop calculating pennies all the time. Enys took the horn cup and sipped.

"Bad night?" Shakespeare asked, hoping he... she? Blast it, he for mere convenience... would feel like talking to someone.

"It was a hell of a night," Enys answered. "Christ, I..." He shook his head and rubbed his eyes again. His voice was trembling and he gulped more aquavitae.

Shakespeare put his elbows on the table and propped his head on one hand. "Go on?" he said in the low gentle tone he used when he was particularly consumed with curiosity.

The person who normally called herself James Enys but was really named Portia Morgan, leaned back on the

45

bench and shook his head. Her head.

"You remember French Mary, that you told me about last week?" he said.

Shakespeare tensed. Damn it, this was supposed to distract him from the horrible thing blocking his fountain of words.

"Last night I... we... that is Maliverny Catlin the pursuivant and I, found another one."

For a moment Shakespeare didn't understand. "Another French Mary?"

"No," said Enys very quiet, "Another woman killed the same way and cut up."

"Jesus Christ," swore Shakespeare. The foul images from the week before broke down the walls he had put around them in his memory and stamped out to leer at him from behind his eyes. He gulped down bile and drank more aquavitae as quickly as he could. "Jesus God. Who..."

"Kettle Annie," Enys told him.

"Oh no," said Shakespeare, with a genuine internal swoop of sorrow, "Not her,"

Enys gave a weary nod. "It was only chance we found her."

Neither of them spoke for a moment as Shakespeare finished his aquavitae. Enys was staring into space, no doubt as plagued by memory now as Shakespeare was.

"You and Catlin?" Shakespeare asked slowly. He had

met Maliverny Catlin through Anthony Munday who was an occasional pursuivant as well as writer; Catlin had an ugly reputation. "How..?"

Enys's face twisted in a lopsided cynical smile. "It was funny really. Quite a joke. You know I drank too much last night?"

Shakespeare nodded, forbearing to comment that getting into a speed-drinking match with players and poets had perhaps not been the best of ideas, because Enys had probably worked that out by now.

"So I was going home when I... ah... I needed urgently to piss." Enys's face was red as a boy's. "So... as you know... ah..."

Shakespeare leaned forward. Of course, he thought, there would be a problem, he hadn't considered that. Normally answering the call of nature was easier for women than men. All a woman had to do was find a gutter, stand across it with hips tilted and she could let fly under the tent of her farthingale and petticoats with no one any the wiser. Men, being trussed up by fashion in tight hose or cannions, had to find somewhere more private and untie their codpiece before they could piss. However, a woman in breeches...

Shakespeare shifted on the bench and coughed. Interesting. His ears were treacherously hot. He wished they wouldn't go pink every time his imagination began to work on things like that. Or at least that he could

47

have more hair to cover them with.

Enys coughed as well and avoided his eye. "So... I'd managed to find a corner of an alley where I thought no one would come and I'd... ah... undone my points and so on and squatted... Then I realised my courses had come on."

Shakespeare blinked rapidly. And that might be difficult too. How did you deal with it? He remembered his wife back in Stratford making a great fuss about the matter, with pads and secretive washing of stained petticoats and so on. She was also a dreadful shrew before, he'd noted, and tended to eat more sweetmeats during. Almost as bad as when she was with child.

"So I was... er... trying to sort it out when that bloody man Catlin comes staggering along, sees me, turns aside, thank God – I don't think he saw anything – then stumbles into a little side-passage I had not even noticed. And then he stumbles out with his face whiter than his collar and pukes all over the place, nearly splattering me with a hit direct and splashing my boots."

Shakespeare grinned. "Oh ay?" He loved the way farce and tragedy hunted side by side. Even Enys looked rueful.

"So I managed to arrange myself whilst he was busy and then he gasped something and I looked where he had been and... I saw her." Enys was sober-faced now. He dropped his husky voice further. "Will, it was awful.

He had taken all her guts out and... and... he put an organ on her thigh which was her womb."

Shakespeare beckoned the potboy for more aquavitae since somebody seemed to have drunk his.

"Guts in a spiral pattern?" he asked.

Enys nodded. "Was French Mary's womb..."

"Between her legs and cut open very neatly," Shakespeare was whispering too now. The potboy was refilling their horn cups from a flagon.

"Kettle Annie's was entire," said Enys. "So... ah... so we went straight to Mr Recorder Fleetwood because I thought, if the whores find this on top of the Plague and the theatres, they'll riot."

Shakespeare grunted. That was certain. French Mary had made them very angry already.

"Fleetwood's a better man than I had thought," Enys continued, strengthened by aquavitae, "Once he knew what had happened, he came out with his men at once and took up Kettle Annie's corpse – it's in St Bride's crypt now. But then the bastard hired Catlin and me to investigate and find the killer."

Shakespeare swallowed a laugh. "How did he persuade you?"

"Offered twenty pounds each or he'd arrest the two of us for the murder."

"Ah," said Shakespeare.

"Quite," said Enys. "So I thought I had best agree

but now I'm stuck with a Puritan pursuivant who could as well be the man that did it for what people say about him, and I'm supposed to find out and capture a monster that kills women and then cuts them up."

"Catlin's a good pursuivant," said Shakespeare judiciously, "Even Marlowe respects him."

"I'm amazed Catlin would give Marlowe the time of day, he hates players. And as for what he'd make of Marlowe's other habits..."

"Well Marlowe can be discreet when he wants to be. He only admits to poesy to Catlin. Which is quite bad enough by the way."

Enys put his arms on the table in a very manly gesture for a woman. "So," she said, "As I have no knowledge whatever of... of pursuiving, Mr Shakespeare, I was hoping to treat it as I would a court case and begin by learning everything I can about the matter in hand. Would you be willing to show me where you found the other body? And tell me what you saw?"

Shakespeare considered this. He was completely certain he didn't want to be involved in any way. On the other hand, the playhouses were shut, the aquavitae was singing a siren song to him and he would do almost anything to avoid dealing with the ugly hole lurking inside him where normally a poem would already be growing like a mushroom... In the dark and on a rich bed of horseshit. He smiled slightly at his own metaphor.

50

But what good was it when he needed something a great deal less pungent and more polished than the groundlings could understand? Above all he needed something to do.

Decision made, he stood, knocked back what was in his cup and offered the remainder of his meal to Enys, who gratefully stuffed the cheese and a couple of pickled onions into the side of the penny loaf and took a large bite as they headed out the door.

They walked towards the Bridge, which was a two mile detour because neither of them felt rich enough to throw two pennies away on the mere convenience of a boat without an emergency.

Ludgate Hill was choked with people as usual, passing the Belle Sauvage Inn where a public sword fight was being advertised. St Paul's was also full of folk and Enys quietly manoeuvred Shakespeare away from the churchyard where the booksellers cried their wares. It seemed Enys knew not to let a poet get in among the stalls, because he would stay there for the rest of the day. They took Watling Street through the City, past St Anthony's church and into Budge Row where the furriers had their shops, They weren't supposed to do any tanning within the city but of course they did, so the streets behind the respectable buildings always stank with their vats of piss and oak bark until the City fathers cracked down on them again.

"Mrs Nunn of the Falcon knows," said Enys, as they passed the London stone. "About Kettle Annie's death, I mean. She challenged Fleetwood about it in the common room of the Cock this morning."

Shakespeare's lips pursed in a soundless whistle.

"Mr Recorder was not pleased," added Enys.

"What's Catlin doing?"

Enys shrugged. "How would I know? Probably hunting down his normal informers and blackmailing them. Can you tell me how you came upon French Mary at the new theatre?" he asked as they sidled down Crooked Lane which had the smellier overspill from New Fish Street. At the end of New Fish Street was the great clock paid for by the fishmongers' guilds, allegedly to show how quickly their fish had been brought from the sea. The street was even more choked with people, carts, donkeys, barrels, horses, messenger boys, serving men and broad-beamed women buying salt fish by the barrel at high prices. At the end of it was the entrance to London Bridge.

Shakespeare paused as, in the theatre of his mind the images lined up into a good story. He didn't want them to, they just obediently did. Perhaps telling the tale might help get rid of them. It occasionally worked for particularly annoying sonnets.

"We were there to inspect the works and talk about how big the stage should be and where to place the pillars."

"Why? Is it important?"

Of course, Enys wasn't a player. "Yes it is," Shakespeare told him, "If the stage is bigger of course it means you can do more with battles and sieges and suchlike, but then you can fit in fewer groundlings in the pit, which means fewer pennies. And vice versa. So if Mr Henslowe could have his way, there might be hardly any stage at all other than a painted ledge whereas Jemmy Burbage is on fire for a stage as great as the world whereon he can strut and fret." He had to pause to elbow his way through a group of high-coloured Kentish women with large baskets ambling along like cows in the middle of the street that led down to the Bridge towers. They could hear the waterwheels already.

"I was between the two of them trying to keep the peace."

"Not on Burbage's side?" Enys smiled but Shakespeare shook his head seriously.

"God no," he said, "Never trust a player with architecture nor money. Especially not money. And especially if they are good."

They were under the heads on pikes at the gate. The smell was no longer so bad since the crows and buzzards had pecked them clean and eaten the brains of the newest some weeks ago. They had to pause again because the crowds were thick with women taking up twice as much pavement space as they needed with the fashionable width of their farthingales.

Enys had to sidle apologising past two large ladies admiring the display in the first draper's shop on the Bridge. The window was barred like a goldsmith on Cheapside, a roaring boy standing at the door with his thumbs in his sword belt, busily guarding the delicate brocades that came all the way from the Land of Silk. Also tumbled from their bolts in artful display were the silk velvets, woven in Flanders by the best weavers in the world who first unravelled the silken threads of the less fashionable brocades from the east. Shakespeare had heard a rumour that silk came from giant worms that required to feed upon entire trees. He doubted it. Unquestionably that was as much a fantasy as the lamb-wort – the magical plant that grew fluffy puffs of wool which eventually grew together to make a vegetable lamb that hopped and skipped like any lamb until it died without ever becoming a sheep and mating, and from its corpse grew the new plants for next year. Besides, how would you catch such a giant worm and how much damage would they do and where on a worm could silk come from anyway? Much more likely that another rumour was true and that silk was the fleece of the unicorn which could only be shorn by virgins... Hm. Perhaps? As an opener for the poem..?

No, too quotidian. Mr Enys was talking again. He

had paused to look a little longingly in a milliner's window to admire the new high-crowned hats with their elaborate hat-bands and feathers. Enys pointed at one.

"If I can find the murderer and collect the fee, perhaps I shall buy my sister that hat to go to church on Sunday."

Shakespeare smiled. Mr Enys's sister was, of course, Mr Enys herself. It occurred to him that Sundays must be a problem as well. The church wardens would be keeping a count and while they would let Enys's sister miss Divine Service on Sundays, they would insist on seeing her occasionally in case she was a Papist. Shakespeare thought that might involve some quick changing and considered offering Enys lessons in the art. Purely to be helpful of course.

They had to push and excuse their way through another knot of women gathered around one who was having a fainting fit. Shakespeare spotted it was Mollie Stone and hissed at Enys to be careful of his purse... Yes, there were a couple of small children darting among the crowding kirtles, harvesting purses from their strings.

As they finally won to the other end, the carrion smell was fainter, because these were older heads, some dating back to the early 1580's harvest of Jesuits before the Spanish Armada. Once through the Great Stone Gate they were in Southwark and could turn right to thread through the alleys to Bankside and the great circular landmark of the bear-baiting ring. They threaded cautiously around the Clink prison and crossed the stream to Dead Man's Place by a rickety wooden bridge. The new theatre was being built in some fields that had been full of peasant huts, since cleared away.

At last Shakespeare opened the gate in the fencing around the new theatre. Somebody was already starting to steal the scaffolding, he noted, thinking it might be as well to take it down until they could start building again. He had heard that Henslowe was planning to call it the Swan in honour of the badge of the courtier who had made it possible with his investment and influence. Shakespeare was very proud of that connection because he had made it. A watchman came out of his hut to check on them: Henslow had hired him to stop their theatre being pilfered as an embryo. He nodded to Shakespeare who glared back because the man had obviously been bribed or asleep a great deal of the time.

"Who's that?" asked the watchman of Shakespeare, tilting his head at Enys, after swallowing a mouthful of pie.

"An investor," said Shakespeare. "Perhaps."

Enys was attempting to look haughty. However the watchman's eyes flicked over the worn velvet trim of Enys's respectable but out-of-fashion woollen suit and sniffed.

"Looks like an unfee'd lawyer to me," he muttered.

56

Hand on his sword hilt, Enys stalked past the man looking quite authentically offended.

They crossed the bare trampled earth which would eventually be the pit and went down the rear passage to the future tiring rooms where Shakespeare had found the corpse. He actually had to pause to gather strength as his memory hit him with full force and colour. And smell. The colours were particularly hard. Most of the time Shakespeare was grateful for the memory God had given him and schoolmasters had trained without much need of the birch. But on occasions like this and in his dealings with women, memory could be a treacherous friend.

The wood of the tiring room passage was raw and unpainted and now stained brown in splashes. The earthen floor had soaked up the blood in the forgiving way of clay. There was still a powerful smell of old iron though. There had been a lot of blood, Shakespeare recalled, he had been shocked at how much.

Enys was squatting down and looking carefully at the stains. "Tell me what you saw as exactly as you can," he said.

"It was French Mary, you know that," Shakespeare began, "So she filled the whole passage."

It was in fact an unusually wide passage because two players in full costume had to be able to pass each other in a hurry without tangling. Or in this case, one French

Mary and her barrel of slightly stale hazelnuts. Enys was waiting patiently for him to continue.

"Well," said Shakespeare hearing the reluctance in his voice, "Her head was here, looking up, back. She was lying on her back, legs bent up and apart. Her kirtle was off but not her farthingale, that had been pushed back and flipped over her head so at first... we didn't know her."

It had looked very odd indeed. Like a small tent filling the passage. The larger the woman, the larger the farthingale, of course.

Shakespeare paused. Henslowe had made an off-colour joke about who might be distempered of drink until they saw... He took a deep shaky breath. What was it about it that upset him so? He had seen dead bodies, he had killed and gralloched deer once upon a time, long ago, he had even managed to get up early enough to be in the front of the crowd to watch a screaming Jesuit being disembowelled and quartered.

Get it over with. "Underneath her stays and shift were sliced open down the middle." Enys nodded, intent. "Her stomach was cut from here to here." Shakespeare's hand started just under his breastbone and swept down to his codpiece." He had pulled out the guts and laid them in a spiral around the body, and so also with some of the organs. The hysterum..." Shakespeare coughed. He wasn't showing off his classical learning, for some

58

reason he was unable to say the word womb. Perhaps it was too intimate.

"How did you know what it was?" Enys asked. "I didn't."

"Ah. We guessed. For where it was."

"Which was?"

"Between her legs, cut open and... ah... spread out. As if someone was looking for something."

"Anything else?"

"The liver had been opened as well..." Shakespeare blinked as his inner sight gave him the pictures again, indifferent to his feelings. "It was white in many places and speckled. Perhaps if I were a Roman haruspex I should cry dole and misery upon all the Republic."

"Perhaps." Enys seemed a little puzzled. Of course, he... she was self-taught. She would never have gone to school and learned that the pagan Romans would prognosticate the future, not by astrology from the stars in a proper scientific way, but by sacrificing an animal to Jove and looking at the liver. "Her face?"

"Her face was hidden by her farthingale..." French Mary had been like a ship in full sail. "When we flipped it down again to make her more decent, we saw her face was not touched."

"How was it?"

"It was dead."

"No, I mean, what was the expression?"

"Calm," Shakespeare told her thoughtfully, "As if she had been sleeping."

"What about her hazelnut barrel?"

Carefully Shakespeare examined the pictures behind his eyelids. He shook his head. "I didn't see it, though surely she wouldn't be selling hazelnuts in a half-built theatre."

"So what was she doing here?"

"Well... ah..." Shakespeare knew his ears had gone red again. "I imagine she was working. She knows Mitchell the man that guards the place and if she had a customer this might be the place to come."

Enys had gone pink too. "A customer?" There was surprise in her voice. So she had really been a very respectable matron before the smallpox had destroyed her children, husband and face, thought Shakespeare, and that made him feel better.

"French Mary still had customers who liked her... um... size."

"Was her kirtle still on?"

"No," said Shakespeare, "We found it in a heap nearby. Her best, the velvet-trimmed tawny."

"Kettle Annie too," Enys told him, "Her kirtle was off."

"Hm. Yes," said Shakespeare, "So we have here a villain that allows the whores to lead him astray and then..." He gestured. "It must be a Puritan."

"Why?"

"Think of it! Think how they hate the whores."

"Surely this must be someone utterly astray in his wits, perhaps even possessed of a demon..."

"Of course, of course, but why else attack whores? It must be a Puritan like Catlin, full of bile and hatred and preaching against whores and players... Why else would he do it?"

Enys smiled. "Because whores are easy to attack?"

Shakespeare blinked at him. "French Mary?" he asked, "Kettle Annie?" They were probably the two most redoubtable women in the sprawl of London and Westminster together. Apart from Mrs Nunn at the Falcon and a few others that worked at the stews and Paris Garden.

"Perhaps not. Then perhaps it is a Puritan."

"Must be. Perhaps it's Maliverny Catlin himself. That's a bad bastard... Or so I hear."

"He was drunk. When he saw the body, he puked..."

Shakespeare dismissed this. "He was acting. He had finished his evil deed and then he saw you too near it, followed you and...."

Enys shook her head. "No, he came towards me, not from behind. And in any case the woman was cold."

"It must be a Puritan for they're all mad, touched in the head."

Enys grinned. "Catlin is certain sure it must be a

61

player."

"One of us? Killed Kettle Annie? The only alewife in London that would give us credit?"

"Owed her too much beer money perhaps?"

Shakespeare waved this ridiculous notion away. At least he knew now what had what had upset him so about the killing. It was the coldness of it, the consideredness of making patterns with innards. He had always assumed that deliberate murder must be hot, but neither of the whores' murders had been hot killings, they had been cold as clay. It was true, he knew that once he had acted with that kind of coldness – and that was one of the things that still kept him awake at night – but never like this. Not to stab and gut like this. What kind of man could do it? Unwillingly, he was fascinated by the idea, he even wanted to meet the man, gaze into his eyes and perhaps try and understand why he did it. And then find a place for him in a play and perhaps exorcise his own crime too.

Not a poem, unfortunately. That should all be smooth and sparkle sweetly like sugar-plate. Damn it. This was not working.

Enys was pacing slowly up and down the passage. Her nose wrinkled and she bent to touch a different damp patch with her finger, sniffed it. "She was sick here," she said, "This isn't blood, the smell is too sour."

Much of it had soaked away but there were bits of

carrot on the mud. Enys was frowning at her finger as if it could tell her something. Then she shivered and yawned mightily.

"Can you recall anything else about what you saw, Mr Shakespeare?" she asked.

Shakespeare shrugged. "If I do, I'll be sure and tell you," he said.

Enys yawned again, shook her head. "I must go to my chamber," she said, "I was up all night and still have to prepare some pleadings that should be with the clerk of the court by the end of this week."

So Shakespeare and Enys left French Mary's last traces, her last lying place. Shakespeare shivered as well when they crossed the empty and unfinished wooden 'O', as round and unfurnished as the Arab number.

"Do you think her spirit will walk?" he muttered, finally mentioning the thing that really worried him. "Dying such a death?"

"I heard you had her buried and paid for a decent funeral?" Enys said.

"Of course. Even Mr Henslowe agreed to do it. Very respectable too, we had four paid mourners in black gowns and the undertaker put most of the... innards back and sewed her up so she could be whole on Judgement Day. It cost a lot." The guts hadn't all fitted.

"No doubt God can arrange all that as it should be,"

said Enys with a distant expression on his hollow-eyed face.

"So do you think she'll walk?" Shakespeare persisted as he locked the gate again and tipped the watchman a groat.

Enys paused. "I am no priest nor expert..."

"Yes, but do you think...?"

"No," he said flatly, "I'm sure she won't."

It wasn't satisfactory but there was no sense asking any more. Besides, why would Enys know any better than Shakespeare? They were outside the scaffolding now, where the bear-baiting enthusiasts were now queuing for the afternoon's fight. The famous bear Little John had tragically died and so they were crying a new bear, by name Henry Hunkson, who had been sired, allegedly, by Harry Hunks, the most famous bear of the 1580's. The red-faced man backed by a trumpet was bellowing of Henry Hunkson's ferocity and courage while the man who kept the dogs shouted out the canine virtues with another trumpet as counterpoint.

Working the patient queues – fattened, Shakespeare noted bitterly, by many play-going regulars – there were jugglers and sword-swallowers, each with their followings of child pickpockets harvesting from any fool that had brought spare money or jewellery. One tiny urchin had a little knife and was busily cutting the buttons off fashionably decorated sleeves that hung from fashionably shoulder-slung embroidered jackets. Shakespeare smiled and said nothing.

Hazelnut sellers and orangeado sellers moved up and down busily hawking their wares – a ha'penny for a handful of nuts to crack and a penny for an orangeado. Shakespeare didn't recognise either of them.

"New and fresh from Seville," shouted the square-faced middle-aged woman with her tray in front of her in a slightly hoarse voice.

"Nuts, fresh cobnuts from Kent!" shrieked the other woman.

Enys blinked red-eyed at them and paused.

"What time did you find French Mary?" she asked of Will.

"About 7 o'clock in the morning," said Shakespeare, "But she was cold and stiff. It took the whole company to move her to the church and my shoulder is still aching."

"Had there been a baiting the day before?"

"I think so. Yes," said Shakespeare.

Enys immediately stepped towards the two women who were ostentatiously ignoring each other.

"We're busy," sniffed the hazelnut woman.

"This concerns the tragic killing of French Mary last week," added Enys. "Did either of you see her on the..."

"The Monday," Shakespeare added helpfully.

The hazelnut woman shrugged and moved away

quickly. The orangeado woman paused for moment, rearranging her tray with its orange balls, each with a hollow reed sticking out of the top. Like many women who had to work in the crowds where someone might have plague, she had a scarf pulled up over her nose. She nodded. "I saw her," she said, "She bought an orangeado."

"She wasn't selling hazelnuts?" Enys asked with a glance at the new hazelnut woman who now had her back to them.

"Yes she was, she traded some of them for one of my orangeados, like she usually did, said she wanted something sweet. Will you buy one, kind sir?" The woman's voice had a wheedling sound.

Enys hesitated, then paid a penny for a small one that the woman gave her from the centre of the tray. As he sucked on the sugary liquid from inside, Shakespeare reckoned that it was all London to a dog's turd that these were at least nine months old and very far from being fresh from Seville as the woman claimed. According to the Portuguese doctor and merchant he had talked to once, the Seville orange harvest would only now be happening and it would take at least a month before any ship bearing them could arrive in the Pool of London, just in time for Christmas if the investors were lucky. No doubt these were hulls that had been packed in sugar since last year, then soaked in water before being stuffed with broken bits of sugarloaf to resurrect them again.

Enys was still sucking bitter orange syrup from the hull making disgusting noises. It did at least look like a grenado, with the straw sticking out of the top and the two hulls stuck together with toffee, that small Spanish bomb for throwing. No doubt the pulp had originally gone to the confectioners kitchens to make wet marmalada suckets for children and pregnant women, perhaps even the Queen and her courtiers in Whitehall. But the hulls were a confectioner's perk and were sold on to the orangeado women. It was a respectable trade for a married woman since you needed capital for the outlay on hulls and more expensively on sugar loaves.

Enys offered his to Shakespeare, who sucked. It was delicious although he didn't have a very sweet tooth. When watching a play rather than appearing, he preferred hazelnuts because you could throw the shells at idiot groundlings who kept talking. He wasn't sure which he preferred when playing on the stage, since either set of noises were equally annoying: busy cracking and crunching from the hazelnut eaters and loud slurps from the orangeado drinkers who sometimes threw them at villains on stage. Philosophically Shakespeare, who often played the villain, took that kind of missile as a compliment and had got good at ducking.

"So French Mary liked orangeados, did she?" said

Enys conversationally to the orangeado woman.

"She did," said the woman, "She often bought them, said her teeth couldn't crack hazelnuts any more, even though she sold 'em. I think that was the day she said she was going home to put her best kirtle on just as soon as the gate shut and the bait began, because she had a client to meet when he came out."

"Oh?" said Enys neutrally, "Did you see him?"

"No sir," said the orangeado woman, her broad brow wrinkling. "Only French Mary said she was pleased at it for none of the bloody players at her alehouse were paying up their tabs because they were all utterly poverty stricken with the playhouses being closed and the ones that weren't were taking advantage."

Shakespeare coughed. That sounded like French Mary. His conscience was clear: he had paid his tab as soon as Southampton gave him his gift. Which, in retrospect, was a pity.

"Did she mention that man's name or tell you anything about him?"

The woman frowned and squinted abstractedly at her tray, moving the oranges about. "Now she did say something, sir. She said something about him being a noted gentleman and very important and a fine figure of a man." The woman coughed and looked down. "So I laughed at her, sir, God forgive me and I said, why's he going with you then and French Mary, she said, well some men have the good taste to like warm flesh and plenty of it and she was warm enough, she could turn any man to sugar plate or syrup, just as she chose."

Enys blinked and Shakespeare felt the whole back of his neck as well as his ears going red. That was certainly true and prettily put.

"Ah," said Enys.

"So I gave her an orangeado to give her strength and sweetness and off she went to change her duds." The woman looked down. "Last I saw of her," she added at a mutter.

Shakespeare suddenly realised what had been worrying him about the woman. "I wonder... where's Betty Warren?" he asked. "You've got her very tray; I recognise it for the pictures of the Moorish palace on it."

The woman blinked at him. "Ah... Betty. She's my cousin, sir. Had you not heard she died of the Plague in the summer and I inherited her tray and her pitch?"

"Oh."

"Goodwife, will you tell me your name?" Enys asked, "If I can lay hands on French Mary's wicked client, there may be a reward."

The woman hesitated. "Yes sir, my name is m... Goody Mallow, Judith Mallow." As an afterthought she gave a little bob.

"Thank you, Goody," Enys was on the point of

throwing her empty hull away but Goody Mallow stopped him.

"I'll take care of it, shall I, sir?" she said confidingly. Enys gave the hull back to her and it went into a bag hanging from Goody Mallow's belt. Shakespeare thought cynically that thence it would no doubt re-emerge that night to be miraculously resurrected again with more water and more broken up sugar loaf until the new crop had arrived. Possibly forever.

They wandered away from the queue which was starting to shorten as the bear-fanciers and the dog-fanciers entered by their separate doors. Behind the walls that surrounded the dog-sheds, the excited baying, growling and barking was deafening. Then from somewhere in the bowels of the ring came a loud angry roar, which silenced the dogs for a moment before the baying started up again, louder and more boastful.

"Will you be watching the sport?" asked Enys.

Shakespeare shook his head. "I must write a poem for my lord of Southampton," he said. "If I make no start on it, I'll never have it ready for him to hear when he comes to London."

Enys raised her hat to Shakespeare who bowed shallowly in return. They parted, watched by the shrewd eyes of Goody Mallow, as Enys turned wearily towards the Bridge again.

·

Maliverny Catlin was in the Fox & Hounds on Fleet
Street where the beer was better. He had gone straight
home and slept for half the day before rising and going
to visit some of his more reliable tale-tellers. All four of
them were full of wonderful stories about Jesuit priests
and looked highly offended when Catlin told them he
wanted instead to find the assassin of two whores.

"Whores?" sneered one, known as Peter the
Hedgehog because of the way his hair stuck up
permanently, "Nobody cares about whores."

"Other whores do, and their upright men and so Mr
Recorder cares and so I care," Catlin said coldly. "I will
pay for useful information as I see fit, as always."

"And the certain sure Jesuit what I seen sneaking in
at Mrs Crosby's two nights gone?"

Catlin paused, seriously tempted. Mrs Crosby was a
well-known Papist and harbourer of Jesuits but this was
too pat. "What was he doing?"

"He was carrying in of Newcastle coals," piped Peter
the Hedgehog, confidingly, "But 'e was in disguise, see."

"And did you recognise him?"

"Werll," said Peter, rubbing the back of his head
again, "I fink it was that traitor John Gerard, he was a
tall man and bony-faced wiv black hair and..."

Catlin came closer to Peter. "How interesting," he

purred, "When Gerard was seen leaving London two weeks ago."

"Ah," said Peter, not concerned, "Well, that was a feint, see and..."

"And Gerard is always habited as a gentleman or very occasionally as a gentleman's falconer and would no more have to do with Newcastle coal than you would since it is all entirely in the keeping of the Coulter family and Old Man Coulter is a fine upstanding and religious man who never misses his Divine Service," snapped Catlin. The urchin flinched back a little and his wizened old man's face screwed up with anger.

"It was him, I seen him, he was skulking about..." There was a whine in the child's voice now.

"Carrying a sack of coal, no doubt," sneered Catlin. "I don't think so." He reached and grabbed the back of Peter the Hedgehog's grimy sleeve and propelled him out of the Fox & Hound's common room and into the street, pinching the tender spot just above the lad's elbow.

Peter the Hedgehog yelped. "Well he talked like a priest..."

"Find me Kettle Annie's upright man," said Catlin, "I know you know him, Kettle Annie was feeding you and your sister last month."

Peter spat on the ground. "Ain't got one, none of the old whores in the Whitefriars do. They're upright men for each other, everybody knows that."

Catlin resisted the urge to punch the boy for his insolence and just cuffed his ear. "It stands to reason they must have someone. Who panders for them? Who brings them customers?"

Peter shrugged his bony shoulders. "Us," he said, wiping his nose on his sleeve, "Cos the upright men don't want to cos they won't be told an' they're all scolds so we bring 'em customers, see."

"And Kettle Annie's upright man? The one who got hit by the kettle?"

"I fink he works out of the Bridewell or the Fleet," said the boy, "I fink e's some kind of screever or similar."

"I want to know about all the customers Kettle Annie had in the last week. There can't have been that many; she was thirty-five if she was a day."

"Wot all of 'em?"

"All of them. Even the ones who were disappointed."

Peter the Hedgehog snortled his nose, then wiped it with his hand and rubbed the snot onto the back of his head. Catlin stepped back a little from him.

"Wot'll you give me?"

"A penny for each customer you remember and that turns out to be true."

"A ha'penny when I tell yer and..."

"No. Then you get rewarded for lying."

"Yer might not pay me."

73

Catlin shrugged. In fact he was better than most pursuivants that way and he knew it, because his conscience would not allow him to cheat even a mere kinchin. Not for concern but for disdain.

"I'll talk to the boys," Peter said at last, "I dunno many of 'em, I'm a bringer-in for the Falcon and Paris Garden, not the likes of Kettle Annie."

Neither Mrs Nunn at the Falcon nor Mrs Swanders at Paris Garden were at all likely to employ a child as filthy and scrawny as Peter and Catlin sneered. "You? They'd never use you to find their gentry clients."

"Do too," muttered the boy as he shambled off, rubbing his elbow.

Mrs Crosby knocked cautiously on the door of her smallest and highest bedroom and entered when she heard the quiet invitation "Come".

Scowling, she came in, shut the door behind her and crossed her arms to stare at the young man standing in front of her. How could he possibly be a priest, he looked no more than a boy, not very tall, not well-built, with a remaining youthful gangle to the set of his shoulders and the way his fingers tangled together. His face was quite round with a dimpled chin and light hazel eyes, but he had a habit of smiling at nothing which Mrs Crosby found irritating.

He was one of the Bellamy brothers as well and that

74

fact made her very nervous.

"And that can stop too," she said, "How do you know I'm not one of Topcliffe's pursuivants come to take you?"

Young Bellamy blinked at her. "Because I know you're a good and holy woman, Mrs Crosby?" he said mildly.

It was all she could do not to spit. Did they teach these boys nothing but religion at the seminary in Rheims?

"That's as may be, Father," she said frostily. "But I can be tricked or surprised just like anyone else. And I didn't know anything about you coming? Eh?"

He looked down at the rush mats.

"Er... well..." he said.

"Does Fr. Persons know about this? Or Fr. Gerard?" she asked with dread, knowing the answer from the boy's stance.

"No," said the boy, with less equivocation than she expected. "I came as a quite independent person, only a friend at the seminary gave me your address as a place to find refuge."

No friend of mine, thought Mrs Crosby. "You're not on mission, then?"

The boy coughed. "Well I am, of course, as a man of the cloth, but really I came... er... to try and find my sister Ann."

Mrs Crosby had to stop herself from spitting again. "I know nothing at all about that girl," she snapped. "And you'd best forget her as she's a wicked traitor and a heretic."

The boy's eyebrows rose. "Is she?"

"She betrayed poor Fr Southwell this summer," she said, "Gave the place where he was hiding and everything – at your parents' house too. Didn't you know?"

The boy didn't answer.

"The bitch sold him out completely to Topcliffe."

The boy must have heard some of it already because he didn't flinch or look angry at this description of his sister. He just nodded.

"That is what I heard from my parents," he admitted, "But I don't believe it, Mrs Crosby. I'm sure it can't be true."

"It can. You'd best forget her."

"No, Ann is my sister," he said quite gently, "I don't care what you or my parents say she's done, I've come to help her wherever she is and whatever people think of her."

Mrs Crosby uncrossed her arms, went through the door and paused. "Look at the skulls on the bridge," she said, "One's still got a bit of hair on from the summer. They're luckier than that poor man, Southwell. He was tortured for days, they say, didn't give anything away, not a name, nothing, and then they put him in the Tower at the end of July and that's the last anybody's seen of him or likely to."

She slammed the door and went to see to the burning of the clothes the priest had turned up in, which would probably burn well thanks to the large amount of coal dust in them. She could use the coals at the top of the sack he'd been carrying full of his gentleman's clothes and other stuff. She had to admit it was clever of him to come by way of a Newcastle coal barge – a less direct route but much less well-guarded by the tunnage and poundage men.

What would the boy do when he found out what had really happened to his sister? Mrs Crosby wondered.

On a thought she opened the door again without knocking and found the boy on his knees by the window, smiling stupidly as he prayed with his eyes shut. His hair still had coal dust in it but the rest of him was quite clean after a wash down. Mind, the basin she had brought was charcoal black with it.

Mrs Crosby took the basin herself, then put it down again.

"I'll knock tap tap tap, tap tap, tap. Three, two and one, like that," she told him, "That means it's safe to open. If I reverse the order or knock differently, then hide."

The boy – well, he must be in his mid to late twenties if his sister Ann were younger than him – stood up immediately.

"Where do I hide?" he asked.

She showed him a panel in the wall which slid open. He smiled. "It's very good," he said, which showed he knew nothing. "I hide there?"

"Yes, get in." Meekly, he did and she shut the panel. "Now then, Mr Nick Owen built this. While the panel is shut, press hard at the right side of the wall made of bricks." There was a moment of fumbling and then a faint creak and a soft chuckle from Bellamy.

"I'll bring a tallow dip to grease that hinge. Can you see where it goes? Can you fit down the ladder?"

"Yes," said the boy after a couple of grunts and a rustle, "This was a house of easement, was it? Where does it come out?"

"Chimney," Mrs Crosby told him, "You can't use them, they're too narrow. There's a passage at the bottom and then a door in quite a surprising place. I'll tell you later. For now, you stay here in this room and well away from the window."

There was the faint creak as the boy put the brick wall back in place and slid back the panel. He had a smudge on his chin and his hair was on end.

"Thank you, Mrs Crosby," he said nicely, "God bless you for all your help. Would you like me to say Mass for your household?"

She hesitated. It was the Month of the Virgin Mary

and it would be a good thing... but could she get the use of the crypt in Walbrook that had been raided the month before? She thought hard, calculating.

"Are you sure you don't mind the danger?" she said.

"It's what I'm for really, isn't it?" said the boy seriously, "Not just rescuing my sister, in a way that's quite selfish of me. I'm here to say Mass for you and hear your Confession and bring you the miracle of Christ's Presence and all the Sacraments. They come first."

Mrs Crosby nodded as a solution to the whole stupid problem suddenly occurred to her. It might be possible. And it might be a good idea at that.

The lawyer known as James Enys wearily climbed the endless flights of steps to the top floor of the tottering building made of scraps of old abbey in the courtyard recently bought as an investment by the Earl of Essex, or so it was rumoured. If the talk was true, then it was certain he'd only done it to annoy his great rival and enemy at Court, Sir Robert Cecil, who was equally busy buying up the Inner Temple.

Yawning and rubbing her red eyes, she unlocked the new door and went in, taking care to shout "I'm home, sister," for the benefit of James Enys's neighbours.

There was nobody else in the pair of chambers. The larger one was Enys's main chamber and study, with full

79

book-presses and piles of papers, pens in various stages of making and ink in bottles from different St Pauls stationers.

Beyond the next door was the bedchamber with a large and ancient four poster bed and the trundle that fitted under it for a servant to sleep on. Hanging on pegs around the walls were... Portia Morgan's clothes and James Enys's clothes and all of them now fitted the lawyer.

She unbuckled her sword, hung it on a hook and rubbed her arm muscles which were aching from sword-schooling – on the whole she was glad she had kept the appointment with the Master of Defence that afternoon, because it had tired her body and mind and made the sight and smell of Kettle Annie's body less pungently in front of her thoughts. She had bread and sausage and a flask of ale for her supper but was now too tired to eat, so they would do for breakfast.

She set to taking off the uncomfortable clothes she must wear to be a man: first the high boots, then off came the green woollen doublet with black velvet trim she had carefully altered and strategically padded to even out her hips and waist, off came the waistcoat she kept tied to her canions and then the long hose she wore underneath. Damn, there was another little hole beginning on the heel that she would have to darn since she couldn't afford to buy any more knitted hose yet.

Underneath it all was her plainest shift that she had cut down to get the bandages that she now unwrapped from around her breasts. She wore a man's under-breeks which was just as well. She thought the kerchief she had wadded up to save her modesty during her courses was now ruined. Hopefully she put it to soak in a bowl of cold rainwater that was under one of the dripping places in the ceiling, found her usual pad and made herself more comfortable. Scratching vigorously at the fleabites, she pulled on a clean linen shift that went to the ground and had her own blackwork on its collar and cuffs, then a comfortable old English-cut velvet gown on top. She sniffed the used shirt – perhaps it would do for the next day but would need laundering after that.

Then with a linen cap over her short hair, she could sigh and relax onto being a mere woman again. She opened the window and called.

A large grey striped cat came jumping across the complicated corners of the nearby roofs, thatch and shingle alike, miaowing excitedly. She cut the end off her sausage and the cat graciously deigned to eat it and be stroked and have his head scratched. Sometimes in cold weather he would come and sleep against her stomach and defend her against the cold empty expanses of the four poster with the curtains shut. He also kept the rats down in numbers and occasionally brought her one in triumph to pay the rent.

81

She yawned mightily and drank some of the mild ale in the bottle. It had been an exhausting 36 hours and she wished her brother could have been there to talk to her and dispute with her. Alas, he had disappeared in September and she could only hope that once again he would pop up somewhere like a Fool at the playhouse, unexpected and disgraceful. If he was alive, of course. It was quite possible, by all accounts, that he wasn't. She still wasn't sure what she felt about it: on the one hand, her heart ached that yet another person she loved was taken from her. On the other hand, she no longer needed to worry about her brother's gambling habits, recklessness and general unreliability.

She sat down and took her workbag out, found her darning mushroom and started repairing the hole in her hose. The cat curled up on her lap under the rest of the hose and settled down to a steady rumbling purr. She wondered vaguely what Shakespeare was up to and Maliverny Catlin as well. She had already decided that, thanks to the merciful inconvenience of her courses and as she wasn't in court, tomorrow was a day for being herself, not James Enys.

.

Shakespeare was drunk again. He was sitting in a booth at the Mermaid, playing dice and drinking aquavitae and wishing that he wasn't. Somehow he had got himself into a particularly stupid game of dice with Anthony Munday in his tidy grey doublet of double worsted fine wool. He didn't even like dice-play nor Anthony Munday who insisted on showing him his latest attempt at play writing.

It wasn't just that Munday was bad at play writing. It was that Munday was utterly cloth-eared to the music of language and completely devoid of imagination. However he was a very diligent worker. As a result he wrote plays that were dull and badly written but he didn't know this because he wasn't good enough to realise it and wouldn't listen to anyone who tried to tell him. After all, didn't the playhouse owners pay him for his work? Wasn't he an expert at turning a plat into a play? Hadn't his lurid youthful account of life in the Roman seminary been an instant hit many years ago?

Shakespeare himself had had to play some of his boring characters which involved the hideous effort of committing to memory his stupefyingly banal and stupid dialogue, in which Kings explained to Lords that they were attacking someone and the Lords explained to the King that someone was the King's brother and so on and so forth.

In Shakespeare's opinion, Anthony Munday was too incompetent to have any idea of how incompetent he was. He was convinced that he was the outstanding poet and playwright of the age, a dubious honour that in fact belonged to Marlowe. Still, Anthony Munday was well-connected, tenacious, shameless and busy and people were frightened of him because he was a pursuivant. So he had no trouble getting paid well for his dull work, never got into trouble with the Master of the Revels who particularly loathed imagination in a work, and added steadily to his pot of properties and money. Which he boasted about with the false modesty of the typical tailor, his original trade.

In fact, Shakespeare decided blearily, he hated Munday with a passion that shocked even him with its ferocity.

"You see, Will," Munday was presently lecturing him with a wagging forefinger, "you've got to give people what they want. If they want a love story, give it to 'em. If they want a comedy, make sure plenty of people fall over and the dog bites someone."

To be fair, other people had told him this but Shakespeare had to drink another cup of aquavita to avoid punching Munday's round dull face.

"What abou' poetry?" he muttered, without meaning to.

Munday nodded sagely. "Of course, scansion is important so the players can remember their lines. But you don't want too much poetry because it's harder to write and it puts people off."

84

Shakespeare blinked at the man. Harder to write? Was he serious? Poetry was much easier to write than prose, it just flowed out once you got it going. Ha! Once you got it going. He felt the tide of melancholy reaching for him hungrily and finished the drink.

Munday was in lecturing mood. "Nobody wants to have to work out what you're saying. If you compare a woman to ... oh... I don't know, a flower perhaps..." Munday's moon-face was full of proud complacency at his originality. "...then it's better to use a rose so you get the blushing cheeks and the thorns, you see? Then people know what you're talking about."

"You can compare a woman to... to almost anything," Shakespeare protested, unable to help himself. "A... crow... a summer's day..."

"No, no," said Munday, laughing tolerantly, "That's mad, Will. How can a woman be like a summer's day?"

Shakespeare knew that his forehead was overlarge. Right now it seemed to be one big wrinkle. "S'obvious," he said with difficulty, "Warm, changeable..."

"No, go with a flower," insisted Munday, "You've got to choose your metaphors carefully..."

"...golden, fruitful, could be storms..."

"Mind you, I did compare her Majesty with a sunbeam once," said Munday, "I think she liked it."

"Like this summer, it was awful," added Shakespeare deciding that arguing poetry with Munday was like

85

arguing the value of precious jewels with a red pig and that the weather was safer, "Wind, rain. And as for fruitful, they say the harvest's the worst it's been for years."

But Munday was a Londoner through and through and wasn't very interested. "Just an excuse for farmers to put the prices up. You see there are some subjects that are poetic and some that simply are not, Will," he said, wagging a finger again, "War can be poetic. A fight in an alehouse or a dead whore can't."

"What?" said Shakespeare, almost shocked into sobriety.

"Whores can't, virgins can. Beer can't, wine can," added Munday, drinking some of the Mermaid's dreadful wine which he felt showed he was a cut above beer-drinkers because it cost twice as much.

"You can't make a poem out of a pig," Munday added, "Or be romantic about a rape. It's impossible."

"Well I can."

"Anyway," added Munday with finality, "There's no demand for it. D'you want another one?"

.

Bald Will rolled home to his lodgings in the Poultry, with a kind of dull iron constriction around his heart. Anthony Munday always did this to him because the bloody begotten banal bastard of a man was so utterly certain he was right, so utterly blind to beauty, so... so...

He had to stop and hold onto a house corner for a moment and the boy he had paid to light his way stopped solicitously for him.

"You drunk, then?" he asked, not gloating too much.

"Urgh," sighed Shakespeare as he waited for the street to stop rocking.

"You the player wot found French Mary's body, done in like Kettle Annie?" asked the boy, wiping his nose on his sleeve and scratching his hair.

"Ah," Shakespeare had to stop and think. Had that been him? Yes, it had. He wouldn't have imagined something like that, that someone who had been so thoroughly killed could have such a peaceful expression on her face. "Yes," he said.

"That man Mr Catlin wants me to find out about Kettle Annie's clients," said the boy meaningfully. "Shall I tell 'im you was one of 'em?"

Aquavitae was making serious thought impossible. "Wha'?" asked Shakespeare, "But I wasn't." Kettle Annie was pretty much the opposite of the kind of woman he lusted after.

The boy shrugged. "I don't care, do I?" he said, "You're a player, 'e don't like you so he'll believe it when I give 'im yer name. If I give him yer name. He just wants a big list of names, like always. Fing is, if they're not people 'e already suspects, he gets annoyed and then he dun't pay, so what's the point of it? So there's no good giving 'im names of Kettle Annie's real clients cos 'e wouldn't believe me, so you'll do."

Shakespeare pushed himself upright and blinked.

"You want me to pay you for not putting me on a list of Kettle Annie's clients?" he said clearly and carefully because rage was starting to cut through the booze.

"Yerss," said the boy, picking his nose.

"Or maybe..." said Shakespeare, "I'd pay you and then you'd forget I'd paid you and put me on the list anyway and tell Mr Catlin that I'd tried to bribe you not to put me on the list and so get me taken up for the murders. Eh?"

The boy squinted at him for a moment, then said, "Oh."

Shakespeare wagged his finger at the boy in a very Mundayesque way.

"If you're going to get someone with more than half a brain to pay you for something it better not be for not doing something because then he'd have to keep paying you not to do it and he'd know that. Wouldn't he?"

The boy nodded, transfixed by Shakespeare's finger, the torchlight shining on the snail-trail down his upper lip.

"Sho," continued Shakespeare, "it'd be a lot shimpler just to kill you and have done with it, wouldn't it?" His voice was flattening and becoming more Midlands with anger.

The boy's mouth was open and he was backing away. It looked as if he hadn't thought this through properly. And perhaps Shakespeare was too hasty. He didn't want the boy to run off. And he really wasn't going to kill him.

"What you do," he said, continuing carefully on his journey and managing miraculously to avoid the large pile of pig guts and chicken heads that told him he wasn't far from home, "is you get paid for doing something and you do it and then everybody's happy. Ain't they?"

The boy stopped backing up, his ugly little monkey face transfigured by hope.

"Are they?"

"Fr'instance," Shakespeare continued, "If you give me the list of names you give to Catlin and the list of names who really were Kettle Annie's clients and another list of names of people who were French Mary's clients, then you might get some more money for it. If they were true names."

"A shilling," said the boy instantly, naming the largest sum he could think of, probably.

Shakespeare patted his purse which was in his doublet pocket because it was flat as a pancake and not worth the stealing.

"Two groats a list," he said, "And I'll feed you as well. Understand?"

The boy's eyes gleamed in the dark. "Yerss yer honour," he said, "But I don't tell nuffink to Mr Catlin."

Shakespeare narrowed his eyes with the effort of thinking straight. Not all the booze had burned off.

"That's for you to decide," he said. "Lift up that torch or it'll go out."

The boy held it up. Shakespeare shook his head muzzily again and hoped he could find some pennies somewhere... oh yes, he did have a penny for the boy firmly gripped in his hand. Good.

They got to the little chicken-breeder's house in a very slimy alley. Shakespeare paid for the light home, discovered that the boy's name was Peter the Hedgehog and watched him go round the corner. Then he let himself in carefully so as not to disturb the hens roosting on the house beams in the downstairs room. His bedroom was up a ladder in the roof, but he was used to climbing it in the dark and drunk. He wasn't supposed to leave a watch-candle there because of the feathers everywhere, in case he set light to the place while he was out. He thought wistfully of the Earl of Southampton and the secure place that could be his as a rich man's house-poet, with his own bedchamber and no feathers or chicken shit on the floor.

At least his pillow was soft, thanks to the chicken

down in it. He snored into the darkness within seconds
of falling on it.

·

In the alley, Peter the Hedgehog put out the torch and
grabbed up some of the pig guts and chicken heads just
lying around, only a little gnawed – they must have been
dumped only minutes before. There was good eating on
them, once you'd roasted them, some people even made
a stew out of them.

He felt obscurely that the poet had somehow bested
him but Peter wasn't too upset. He had a penny that he
had stored carefully in his crotch, the promise of some
pennies for giving the poet a few lists of names and one
could be re-used for Catlin, so that was all right.

He wiped his nose on his sleeve again, feeling the
crackle of previous swipes. It was no good crying after
spilt milk, but he did miss Susie so much. She was all
he'd had for a long time and she'd gone to work for
them both as soon as she could. She'd just been making
some proper money from the gentlemen now her tits
had grown. Well she could have done it earlier, but she
said it hurt too much. She'd said he could go to school
and learn his letters and be a lawyer and make them both
rich. She'd made a chickenhead stew for them once with
potherbs Peter stole from the gardens and she told him

stories about being rich.

They knew about lawyers because they had served one once, him as the lady's kitchen boy and Susie as a tiring maid to her daughter. Then something went wrong and the lawyer's mother-in-law told them both to go and so they'd gone. She was a good sister. It was a pity she'd ended as dead as French Mary and Kettle Annie and with her innards cut into just the same way, disgusting it was. He couldn't bear to think about it. A long time ago. Maybe mid-September before it got cold and wet. Everything had gone wrong after that so it was hard to remember beyond the constant griping of hunger in his guts.

Peter the Hedgehog crept away down the street and found some beggars sheltering in a crypt from the frosty night. Because he had some food with him they let him sleep behind one of the graves and they even let him have one of the roasted chickenheads to chew which was nice of them. Tomorrow he'd buy the penny ordinary somewhere and fill himself up to bursting and hope he wasn't sick like the last time he'd had a penny.

.

Portia looked out at the dawn and smiled because it was promising a fair day, for once, if cold. She was still tired but had slept from just after sunset until the new light woke her again, sliding past the curtains of the bed. The grey cat had given her a few more fleabites but it was a small price to pay for the furry warmth against her stomach which meant she didn't need to light a fire. Coals were desperately expensive in London and so was firewood. The coals still in the fireplace were stone cold and there was no other fuel at all in the room, apart from furniture which she was loath to use. And she certainly wasn't going to leave turds there to dry out and burn as her brother had once suggested because that was disgusting.

She pulled on a dressing gown against the cold, collected her slightly stale penny loaf and the sausage which had been in the food-box. There was the end of a wedge of cheese there too which had some blue mould on it – it would have been nice to get the fire going because she could have used the dish-of-coals that stood by the empty fireplace and toasted the bread with the cheese. But there wasn't so she couldn't and she was too ravenous to wait until she was dressed so she munched away on the bread and cheese and sausage, washing them down with the jug of small beer.

Sometimes she thought of her old household and her kitchen, in the completely other world she had lived in before the smallpox came. Her husband had delighted in the sweetmeats she made, especially the fruit preserves like the spiced apple cheeses that went so well with bread and butter and would add to stews and give them an extra tang. Her children had loved them too, in the way of children who always love sweets.

She now had neither the money nor the time nor the equipment to make things like that. She didn't even have a flitch of bacon hanging in the chimney because she had finished it and finished the pease pudding she made with the ends as well. And she had decided overnight while sleeping that she definitely couldn't wear her shirt or her hose again and so would have to get them washed, along with the other two shirts she had inherited from her brother when he disappeared. As soon as she could afford the linen, she would make herself a new shirt or two with blackwork on the collar and some kind of better arrangement to hide her breasts as well.

She spent some time hanging her doublet and cannions up on hooks and putting springs of rosemary, rue and wormwood inside them to cleanse them a little. She would like to buy a stick of incense to burn inside as well but that would have to wait for another influx of money. The money Fleetwood's clerk had given her had almost all gone to pay arrears of rent and her tab at the Cock. She had never realised before how hard it was to be on your own, even in a great city like London where you could simply buy things like bread or bacon without having to make it yourself.

Then she pulled her stays on over her head and laced

them up. Jesu, she was rattling around inside them, she would have to take them in at the sides. She had knitted woollen stockings which she gartered at the knee and put her old boots on. It was lucky she had big feet and had been able to go and buy a secondhand pair of man's high hobnailed boots, since her brother had taken his own boots with him when he disappeared. Which in any case would have been far too big for her. Her bum roll went on next and her old-fashioned modest farthingale with her petticoat over the top of it. And then she took a deep breath, dived into her cramoisie wool kirtle with the tawny velvet trim and the doublet-style bodice for winter, struggled it down and around her and started fastening the buttons down the front. She had had a fur-trimmed gown of black velvet once but that had long gone into pawn and nor did it presently look at all likely to be redeemed.

She put on a plain falling band because they were a lot easier to launder than a ruff and she washed and starched them and her caps for herself, using the soapwort she had found growing unexpectedly out of a stone wall near Whitefriars – a rare instance of there being a real advantage to doing what she was doing. A man wouldn't have recognised it, a woman could not have dared go there. As James Enys she had been able to pull up the roots and leave some for others as well. However laundering shirts, hose and sheets was a very different problem as she had no buck or copper or fire to do it in. For the last lot she had paid a woman inflated London prices to do it and had not been impressed. She had come up with a different solution which she hoped would work since she didn't have the money for a laundress again anyway. And she hated wearing dirty linen.

At least her modest white married woman's cap was clean and went on easily over her short hair, then the hat on top which was old, small and plain and very dull beside the high crowned beaver creations that were all the rage at the moment. But then she didn't have the new barrel-shaped farthingale either and didn't much care. Once she had cared about such things which accounted for the bright tawny velvet trim on her kirtle, but no longer.

She picked up her bag of dirty linen and put it in her marketing basket, found the sixpence she had put aside for this and a couple of pennies for her dinner.

As a woman alone she couldn't just walk into any alehouse on her own and order food or the men there would make assumptions about her that she couldn't afford. But she could go into and eat at one of the better inns if she had another woman with her and that went along with her plan for the day.

All she had to do now was brace herself for going outside as herself, as a woman. For some strange reason, she could do it without trouble when trussed up in doublet and breeches as her brother James Enys. Somehow wearing a man's hat and sword made her into a different enough person that she was numb to the horrors of eyes that had come on her after she got better of the smallpox... Well, it was still there but it changed. She felt superior as James because she was fooling them, they didn't know her and besides, a man with a pocked face was nothing strange nor pitiful. It was different as a young woman. She could well understand how Lady Sidney refused to leave her house.

She knew her heart was already beating fast and her mouth was dry. Her hands shook as she pinned her hat firmly to her cap and took the stiff-backed black velvet mask she had bought on impulse a few weeks ago. Forcing herself to face her small silver mirror, she lifted it to look. Her cap was straight. Her face... (oh God, her face...).. was clean. She eclipsed the moon with the mask and bit firmly on the button at the mouth to hold it on without need of strings. Her face suddenly was a darkness under her hat, not a shock. Yes, that was better. Her heart steadied, despite the stink of the thick glue the maskmakers used to stiffen the velvet.

She picked up her basket, slipped her pattens over her shoes, opened the window and shooed the cat out. It took a while, the cat was very reluctant to move from the warm bed into chilly sunshine and clung to the coverlet with all his claws. At last, she shut the window against hookmen. Then she unbarred her front door, pushed sideways past it and locked it behind her. On the landing she steadied herself, breathed deep, let it out. Holding your breath helped, she knew that, although sometimes she forgot and found herself fainting again. At least it felt wonderful to have space around her legs instead of the clothy confinement of hose and she wondered how men could stand it, poor loves.

She went down the stairs slowly and carefully and out into the sunlight where she paused on the step for a moment. The sunlight glittered on the edges of the eyeholes and she couldn't actually smell the fresh air through the small air hole but... Still. She felt like a prisoner released upon license for the day.

.

It had taken her a long time to breakfast and dress so the street was full this late – past eight of the clock, she thought. Some of the gentlemen in lawyer's gowns who were walking up the lane to Fleet Street near her, raised their hats to her. A few bowed, knowing her by her kirtle as her brother's widowed sister. She smiled and bobbed her curtsey back, almost dropping the black velvet mask and feeling a swoop of panic. Seeing through eyeholes reminded her very much of a fashionable masqued ball she had attended last Christmas with her brother at Gray's Inn, which had ended badly. She had forgotten that.

"Mistress Morgan," said one man, with a good stomach to him and his lawyer's robe hanging casually off his shoulders. "How are you? Mr Enys told me you had a severe megrim."

Damn it. She couldn't actually speak with the mask on since she had the button between her teeth – a detail she hadn't considered before. She put her hand up to hold it in place,especially as she was always worried about speaking to someone she knew as James Enys. This was William Craddock, a brother lawyer of Middle Temple, and a very pleasant man – though married. He had what looked like a nasty cold sore on his upper lip. Had she met him as herself or only as her brother? She couldn't remember.

"Thank you, sir," she said in a high voice, compromising with a curtsey, "I am much better of it although I find the sunlight often hurts my eyes."

Craddock tutted and chivalrously began to walk beside her.

"Then that brother of yours should take better care of you than to let you venture out without an escort."

Oh God, did he suspect? She looked sidelong at him through the eyeholes. His broad face seemed kindly.

"He does take care of me, sir," she said, "But he is

much pressed with business for my Lord Chamberlain Hunsdon."

"Then I'm delighted for it," said Craddock. He clearly wasn't – no fellow barrister could be entirely happy to hear that a competitor had landed such a wealthy and powerful client – but he was polite. "Perhaps he will be able to find a woman to attend you as well?"

"Yes, I am in hopes of finding someone suitable today," she told him, "But it is difficult and expensive in London."

"Ah, but with my lord Baron Hunsdon as his good lord, be sure your brother will prosper," said Craddock with another kindly twinkle, "The Careys are constantly suing each other and everybody else – a wonderfully litigious and open-handed family."

Portia smiled back at him although he couldn't see it. "My brother says that my Lord Hunsdon is a most kindly and wise lord."

"And indeed he is," said Craddock, "But his many sons... they're wonderful men... for injuncting each other."

"My brother has told me very little about you, sir," she said, needing to change the subject before she let slip what she knew of Hunsdon's youngest son. "Do you serve my lord Hunsdon as well?"

"Occasionally," said Craddock, offering her his arm as she had to pick up her skirts and step over the gutter

100

and into Fleet Street itself. "I have had to do a little with some of his purchases. The Earl of Southampton is also my very good lord and so on, a little dusting of equity and church court work, court of Requests and so on."

Portia was sure she had never been against Craddock in court yet, but he had a good reputation as a solid drafter of correct pleadings. However, this had to stop or the women at the conduit would talk.

"Mr Craddock," she said, "Thank you for your company, but I pray you will not go out of your way with me."

"Of course, of course," said Craddock, bowing and looking concerned, "Until you have a woman with you, I quite understand. Quite right, quite right. Besides, it wouldn't do to make my lady wife jealous."

That was sweet of him, she thought, considering no woman would likely be jealous of her. He smiled and tilted his head as she curtseyed to him. She hurried up the street, very relieved to have got rid of him.

So far the mask was working. She had conversed in the open air, she could walk up a street full of people without feeling the yawning lack of air and roaring in her ears that presaged a faint, something she was horrified and frightened by. She knew very well, with the rational part of her brain, that nobody was really staring at the ruin of her face, that even when she wasn't

101

wearing a mask, most people were content with a quick glance and a wince and that was the end of it. Her old nurse had scolded her long ago when she agonised over minor adolescent whiteheads and blackheads that it was plain sinful vanity to think anyone was more interested in herself than they were in themselves. Which was perfectly true. But. Somehow she felt burnt up by people's most glancing looks, as if she could actually feel the invisible rays coming from their eyes that that Latin writer claimed enabled everyone to see.

Mind, she wasn't the only woman in the crowds hurrying to and fro who was hiding her face: many women had similar vizards to her own to protect their complexions against the sun, others had a neckerchief high over their mouth and nose and their hats pulled down.

Hm. The sun. That was a thought. She was hardly brown like a peasant but inevitably when she went about as James Enys, she couldn't veil her face to keep it a ladylike white.

Perhaps she could visit an apothecary – she knew of one in the City that was reliable, although she had heard he had taken the Plague from trying to save others with his medicines. No doubt he was dead now but someone might have taken over his shop. Everyone knew that Mr Cheke, apart from being a dedicated alchemist, sold good quality face paints.

She changed direction and speeded up until she was heading down a street that had two or three shuttered and sealed shops in it. Mr Cheke's shop, however, seemed to be open again – his forty days of quarantine must have passed.

An utterly cadaverous man in a doublet two sizes too big for him sat on his doorstep. Portia had to look twice before she realised that it truly was Peter Cheke, with bandages around his neck.

"Mr Cheke," she exclaimed, having to catch her mask quickly, "... I am so happy to see you are saved, thank God!"

He turned to her and smiled. "Is it Mrs Morgan?" he asked slowly.

"Yes, yes, of course, I am sorry, this mask is..."

He nodded. "Does it answer to your previous malady of fearing the public forum, mistress?" he asked in his rich deep voice.

"Yes, I think it does."

"Then I'm glad," he said, "Forgive me for not standing, mistress. The plague finders have only this day released me from quarantine and my legs are still weak."

No surprise there, the knees under his robe looked to be as bony as a carter's donkey.

"Do you need food or drink?" she asked, "The baker's is still open..."

"No, thank you kindly, mistress," he said quietly,

holding up a pennyloaf of manchet spread with fresh butter in a hand so thin it was nearly transparent. "I have been... I have been most generously cared for by my family."

"I thought your family was in Kent?"

"It is, in Canterbury. I mean rather the family of... of... well, my patients." His voice sounded puzzled. "I must say, I'm still a little astonished at it myself since I do not think I have ever been able to help anyone that caught the plague with my physic, not even myself." His smile was very rueful. "It's a tale in itself."

Portia nodded encouragingly. She liked him and he was willing to sell face creams on credit, or had been in the past. He steepled his fingers. "When I came down with the high fever and had a nosebleed and realised my armpits and groin had been aching for a day or two, which I hadn't noticed for being so pressed with work, I sent my neighbour's boy to fetch the plague-finders to lock up the shop. I thought I was sure to die since all my precautions had clearly been to no avail and I had had no time to lay in stores. And of course, I had no one to nurse me since I could not risk the lad who normally helps me. So I lay down on a pallet in my shop to be nearer the bucket of water and another bucket to void myself and also..." He looked a little sheepish, "... nearer an important experiment that was still proceeding in my laboratorium at the back of the shop. At least, I thought then that it was important. That was all I knew for many days, I think, except once I thought I heard a loud voice I knew calling out my name. 'Mr Cheke!' it said, 'Mr Cheke, is there anything you need?' The voice was familiar but I couldn't remember the name.

"I couldn't answer either for the buboes gripped my throat and it was all I could do to breathe at all, and my fever was very high. But in my heart I answered, 'Save me, forgive me!' thinking, you see, that it was really the voice of God."

"Yes?" said Portia, putting down her marketing basket so she could listen better.

"Perhaps it was," he added thoughtfully, "Or perhaps it was only a friend or acquaintance who shouted, but you see it broke through the fever and my aloneness and... He did. God did come to save me. In my fever and desperate need, He... saved me."

"He did?" said Portia, sceptically.

"In my fever, with all my wits disturbed, there was suddenly a clarity, an understanding... I saw... I understood just as St Paul teaches... I saw face to face." There were tears on the man's face and Portia felt the sad stirring within her of envy for his certainty. "I saw that it was I in fact who was the base metal to be turned to gold and that God was indeed the True Stone which maketh the transmutation of all the changes of this world. But in all my alchemical striving to understand base matter, the stuff of this world, to master it and force it to become gold, I had misunderstood completely."

"Amen," said Portia softly, wishing this could be true and not just the product of fever. Cheke's face always had a hungry searching look to it, but now for the first time in her memory, he looked happy.

"It was so simple. I understood that everything is made of God's Love which is to say, God's Light. Everything in the world is made of Light, alchemised to solidity by God's Word. I found myself laughing at such clarity and although the fever and pain came back, I remembered what I had understood." Portia wondered if Cheke had strayed into what a Divine would call heresy or possibly even lunacy, and then thought that it didn't matter.

"Then I knew there were people with me," Cheke continued quietly, "giving me water and bathing my wounds where the buboes had burst. I was afraid for them that they would take the Plague themselves but then one brought the candle near his face and I saw bandages on his neck too and that he was a poor man that I had tried to help when he had the plague in August. Alas, I could not save his baby son. Behind him were two others of my quondam patients and at the door, another keeping watch for the plague-finders."

Portia smiled. Cheke still looked puzzled.

"And yet, you know, Mrs Morgan, I hadn't been able

106

to help any of them very much at all. I tried to speak, to push them away, but they said... they said it was time for them to help me and wouldn't be told no." There were tears on Cheke's face again. "They said it was only right."

Portia swallowed the lump in her own throat as Cheke blew his nose on a stained kerchief. "Forgive me, Mrs Morgan," he said, "I'm still as weak as a baby and weep like one at the least thing."

"Mr Cheke," she said, "Why wouldn't they wish to help you? Any decent person would. Apart from the Jewish physicians like Dr. Nunez and Dr. Lopez, you are the only medical man that has tried anything at all against the Plague. The Christian doctors and apothecaries all ran away."

Cheke put his hand on her arm.

"You don't understand, mistress. None of them were decent persons. They were not men of property nor even respectable. One was a beggar, the women who came to help later were whores, the man who guarded the door was a notorious upright man." He shook his head in wonder.

Portia was silent for a moment. "Well," she said, remembering what someone – she forgot who – had said to her once. "After all, who did Christ go to dinner with?"

For a moment Cheke frowned but his smile

was radiant. "Of course." Then his eyes narrowed. "Mistress, I cry you pardon, I have kept you standing on my step listening to my maunderings and not even asked how I may serve you." He struggled to stand up and without thinking about how she was a weak woman at the moment, she offered him her arm to lean on and braced so he could do it. He looked surprised.

"I was wondering," she said, a little embarrassed at her errand now, "Um... do you have anything that could serve to whiten my face and... er... hide it a little?"

He frowned. "The ladies of the court use white lead and cinnabar in a grease or wax to whiten their cheeks and lips," he said, "But I have always seen their complexions and their tempers become much worse after a few years of using face paint and I think it may have something to do with that. Perhaps I could make something better for you that could answer the scarring better? I will think about it, perhaps try a few things."

"Thank you, Mr Cheke," she said. "Are you sure you need nothing?"

"Thanks to my friends, I have bread, cheese, ale, bacon, a barrel of hazelnuts, even some money they gave me."

Something jogged her memory. "Did you know the names of those who helped you?"

"Not all, but the upright man was Gabriel Nunn who serves the King of London – and one of the whores was

French Mary. Not a respectable citizen among them."

Portia nodded, glad of her mask. She wouldn't tell him just yet what had happened to French Mary and she certainly wouldn't mention how she had come to meet Gabriel Nunn as well. Although... Could Peter Cheke have done the killings? It occurred to her that being locked up in your house with Plague made a good alibi – so long as you didn't in fact have it. No. Nobody, not even a lifelong clapperdudgeon, could fake that degree of skinniness, that pallor. It would take too long.

"Mr Cheke, I am off to visit a woman I am hoping will come to serve me and if I do not go now I may not catch her at her house," she said, "But I'll be back another day. I am so glad you are well of the Plague, thank God for it." she added conventionally, although as always she had to fight the little spurt of rage she felt whenever the god who had killed her children and left his knife stuck in her heart saw fit to save anyone else. Then she walked on down the street, enjoying the rocking of her skirts and the anonymity of her mask.

.

Shakespeare woke with a chicken roosting on his head and the suspicion that it had just shat in his mouth. There was sunlight filtering through one of the gaps in the thatch and driving nails into his eyes so he batted

109

the bird off his head and it flapped squawking to sit on a rafter nearby. There was something round and hard behind his neck and just in time he felt there and found a warm smooth egg. Well at least she had paid rent for the use of his head, he thought, and smiled despite the pounding behind his eyes. On reflection she probably had not used his mouth for a jakes, that was just the result of giving in to aquavitae yet again and served him right.

Sighing deeply, he sat up, reached for the jack of small beer and found there was only a little left in it so he would have to go out. Still, he had the egg. He had no fire nor dish of coals to cook it on, so he put it in the angle of one of the beams for safety.

He washed his face in the bucket of water that stood under the largest hole in the thatch, risked drinking some of it because he was so thirsty, tried to straighten his doublet and after some thought put on his last clean falling band because his other was disgusting. When he felt his chin, he decided he would have to go to the barber soon and wondered how the devil he was going to pay for it since he had lost all his money to that bloody man, Munday.

Inspiration struck. There was one option to gain quick money and so he sat down rubbed his eyes, yawned, dipped his pen and used one of his precious sheets of paper to write a close-packed letter to his unacknowledged lord, Sir Robert Cecil. He ciphered as he went, his memory having easily learnt by heart the figures that Cecil preferred for his correspondance. Cecil was very like Walsingham had been and very unlike the other pretenders to Walsingham's network of contacts; he valued intelligence for its own sake and was willing to pay for it.

And so the matter of the dead whores was packaged up in pithy phrases and pinned to paper in a pretty pattern, which Shakespeare devoutly hoped would make him some money and postpone for a little longer the necessity to stand by the serving man's pillar in St Paul's and try and look humble and helpful and hale and hearty. What with the Plague, his chances of finding a master were very poor anyway. Nobody was saying what the mortality bills were, but from the numbers of houses being shuttered in the City even though the weather was chilling, Shakespeare thought the theatres would stay shut for a while. The Burbages were planning a tour of the provinces to begin in the spring to try and stave off bankruptcy themselves. Would he go with them? Not if he could help it. He hated touring the provinces. Besides, he needed money now, not in the spring.

The letter finished, he sealed it and put his hat on, climbed down the ladder and nodded to his landlady who sat in her living room at her constant task of plucking a chicken. From the yard at the back where the

111

cockerels lived came a raucous crowing as the younger one again challenged the older one for possession of the dunghill and the hens.

"Ah, Mr Shakespeare," she said, scowling at him, "The rent..."

"You shall have it, Mrs Taylor, no later than the end of the week," Shakespeare said hurriedly as he slid round the door and shut it behind him.

The sunlight and chilly wind hit him like a mallet. He staggered but kept going, aiming for Cecil's house. Cecil himself was probably in Westminster at the palace of Whitehall, but in any case Shakespeare had dealings with Mr Phelippes, who was the finest artist of the age in the mysteries of the cipher and code.

With a standard fee for a report of a crown tucked in his crotch, Shakespeare got himself a quart of mild ale at the next alehouse he came to and downed it in one. Breakfast over, he went back to his house and shocked his landlady by actually paying her the couple of shillings of rent that he owed – you had to keep landladies on their toes, Shakespeare believed – and then went for a walk along Cheapside to cheer himself up. He liked staring at the silver and gold plate in the barred windows and letting his phantasy roam over what he would do when he finally got rich, how he would buy a house in Stratford and show them all, how he would have land, how he would be a sharer in every theatre in the City, how...

The aquavitae was singing to him again and he knew it was because he was bored. When the theatres were open, he didn't have time for boredom. If he was rehearsing a play in the morning for performance in the afternoon whilst also needing to learn a new play for the next day, he never had any trouble writing. He could sit down in any corner with any piece of paper and pen and ink – even a stick of graphite – and scribble away and out of every one of the inexhaustible warehouses of his mind poured forth wealth in tropes and pentameters. Now the stores seemed to be shut and sealed.

He had to think of the poem and he had to have some at least of it ready to recite to the Earl within the next couple of weeks, or Southampton would repent him of the money he had already given Shakespeare and which Shakespeare had already spent. He had to do it, had never before found it difficult. It didn't need to be all new – in fact it was better not. He could pick any tale from Ovid, most of which he knew by heart, but which one? He could use any verse, had no limitations placed on him by the demands of Henslowe or Burbage or Alleyn or the groundlings... He had what he had always chafed after, he had ultimate liberty of creative thought and... It was impossible to write anything.

.

Eleanor and Timothy Briscoe had a small house in the city near the Three Cranes in the Vintry. Ellie Briscoe was one of the few who knew of Portia's double life and Portia was very much hoping that she might do her washing for her. Not today perhaps, Portia's plan was different for today: but eventually, once Ellie had been churched of her baby who had been born on a wild night in September that Portia did her very best not to remember... Perhaps she might even come and serve Portia as her tiring woman as well. She might be glad of the money or even the entertainment. And as herself, Portia desperately needed a woman to go with her to market. As Craddock had pointed out, not to be attended was unseemly for a respectable widowed sister of a barrister. And Ellie wouldn't ask questions if she saw bloodstains on the bottom of a man's shirt. The Curse of Eve was mainly a terrible nuisance as well as an unneeded reassurance. Although Portia had a particularly old linen shift she kept for those times and had always washed out her rags herself, one of the reasons she kept Mrs Morgan around was to be able to be a woman when she needed. It was like the old stories of werewolves: she transformed into a different creature with the phases of the moon.

In the meantime, Portia was certain that Ellie Briscoe would at least have a big washing buck and a copper for linen and she would probably be willing to lend out the use of them.

As she lifted her hand to knock on the door in the respectably tidy little street, she heard a sniffling noise from inside as if someone was crying quietly to themselves. Portia knocked harder and called out, "Mrs Briscoe, Ellie?"

The door was only on the latch so when the sniffles got louder and there was no answer, she opened it and poked her head round the door.

Little Ellie was sitting in the tiny living room next to her small fireplace – Portia thought Mr Briscoe was probably very proud of renting a house that had an actual chimney in it, since neither one of their parents had had any such thing. Ellie was hunched over the swaddled baby, crying and crying as if she would never stop.

Portia froze with fear that the babe was sick of the plague, or even dead. Babies died constantly. The least ill-chanced puff of bad air could carry them off in an instant.

She came through the door and shut it behind her to stave off the bad airs, then hurried across the old rushes and crouched down next to Ellie, her heart hammering.

The babe was fast asleep and scowling, but definitely breathing. Gently Portia felt his forehead, it was cool and velveted like a peach, no fever, no cobbling of smallpox... Oh God, to feel the little pebbles of pocks

115

under the skin of your fretful child's hot forehead and know... and know... Portia drew in a breath, held it, crushed the memory. This baby was in fact sound asleep and a very large plump child for six weeks old. It was nothing short of miraculous to think that it had not long come out of the tiny person who cuddled it and continued to cry.

"My dear," Portia said, "what's wrong?" Ellie shook her head and carried on crying. "Are you sick? Is it the babe?" It was late for a childbed fever but still possible, so Portia felt one of the bird-boned wrists and found it to be cool and the beat of the heart next to the bone, quite slow. Ellie managed to nod her head.

Portia carefully took the baby who opened his dark blue eyes, already on the turn, and looked up sleepily. He shut them again since he had seen Portia before in his short life and was a bold child and not in the least frightened of women with caps and hats.

"Why? He looks lovely and strong and healthy."

Ellie snortled and turned a square mouth full of woe to Portia. "He's so hungry all the time, I keep feeding him and feeding him. My milk must be drying up because there just isn't enough and... and... he'll starve and d...die of plague and it'll be my fault..."

Portia's eyes narrowed. "Has Mother Briscoe been in?" she asked, knowing the normal effect on Ellie of her mother-in-law. Ellie nodded dolefully and sniffled again. "Yesterday," she whispered.

The swaddling bands around the baby were tight and secure, he looked nice and straight so his bones wouldn't grow bent. There was the warm smell of cinnamon which told that he needed changing, which meant he must be feeding and Portia had in any case taken an instant dislike to Mother Briscoe.

"She says... I'm too small to do it right and sh...she'll get a wetnurse in but we can't really afford it and... and... I don't want one..." wailed Ellie.

Experimentally, Portia put her finger on the child's cheek and stroked. He did the baby thing of turning and opening his mouth but it was a lazy turn, nothing fretful or desperate about it.

"Well, I think it's amazing your mother-in-law doesn't know this," said Portia, "I expect she didn't bother to feed her babies but had a wetnurse from the start. When are you going to be churched?"

"This Sunday."

"Well then, he's a little early but he's just growing strongly. All babies get hungry just before you're churched, my old nurse told me all about it. You have to keep them close to you and feed them as much as you can and drink plenty of mild ale possets with eggs and cream so you keep your teeth."

"Oh?" Ellie's red-rimmed swollen eyes were doubtful.

"My old nurse knew a lot about it for she had four of her own and then she wetnursed me and my brother and she was no bigger than you." No taller at least. Goody Janner had been as wide as she was tall.

Ellie nodded tremulously. She looked smaller than ever and had big circles under her eyes.

"Come come," said Portia, "You look exhausted. Are you still soiling your linen?" Ellie shook her head. "Well you shouldn't even be out of your bed in any case until your churching."

"I had to get up," sniffled Ellie, starting to weep again, "I have to clean before Mother Briscoe comes or she'll start scolding me again..."

"She'll what?"

"Sh... she says I'm lazy and... and..."

Portia thought quite seriously about strangling the bloody women when she did turn up. She felt Ellie's forehead. It wasn't feverish, thank the Lord, but no thanks to her appalling mother-in-law.

"I never heard anything so shocking in my life," she snapped, interrupting Ellie's tale of woe, "Expecting a woman who hasn't even been churched yet to do housework? It's outrageous. What does the silly cow think churching is for? You're not strong enough to clean so soon after the baby and if you do, you'll get sick. Is that what she wants?" Portia stood up, took the baby who made an interested little squeak as she tucked

118

him under her arm, and crooked her other arm for Ellie to stand and follow. "You are going straight back to bed so you don't get a childbed fever or worse a milk-fever."

"I can't..." wailed Ellie, "I've got t...to sweep out the rushes and change the baby and... and... "

"Where are your gossips? Isn't anyone helping you at all?" As soon as she had strangled Mother Briscoe, Portia decided she would go down to the nearest conduit and give the women there a piece of her mind as well.

"Jane Brady took the plague last week so they're all locked up and the Long family have gone all the way to their parents in St Albans for fear of it and... and..."

Perhaps she would simply kill the mother-in-law. "Ah, I see. Well, I'll do it then. Up you go."

"B... but you can't, you're a lady."

Portia smiled grimly. She had spent her teens learning huswifery at Arwenack House from the redoubtable and terrifying Kate Killigrew who believed that no lady could properly command a household if she knew nothing of how to sweep, mop, polish, wash and cook. It had been a very tiring adolescence and she had hated Lady Killigrew's guts with a passion, but... blast it, the woman had been right. Lady Killigrew also held that no man could command troops who had never fought, no matter how high his blood, but regarded herself as exempt from that rule and commanded troops herself as well as ships. She was rumoured to have laid a Spanish

nobleman out cold with a belaying pin during the
boarding of one of her prizes, but she also knew how
to sweep a floor. She contended loudly and often that
running a household was a great deal more difficult than
mere generalship or leading a privateering expedition,
and enraged every man in Cornwall by showing that this
was in fact the case.

With the baby-parcel securely under her arm,
Portia helped Ellie up from her crouch by the fire
and practically pushed her up the narrow stairs to the
bedroom where it smelled quite badly of birth-soiling
and old milk. And what had that bloody woman been
doing herself when her grandson needed her to help his
mother? Ellie clambered into the four poster bed that
filled the room and settled down again in the pillows,
took the baby in to lie next to her.

Portia found a jack with some mild ale in it, poured
it out for Ellie and watched eagle-eyed to see that she
drank all of it down. "What are you going to make milk
with if you don't drink enough or eat anything?" she
demanded, but Ellie winced back from her so that she
felt sorry for it and patted the girl's hand. "It's all right,
I'll make you something nice for your breakfast. Have
you had anything?" Ellie shook her head, of course.
"Tim tried to make a mess of eggs but it burnt," she
explained.

Portia snorted, unlaced her sleeves and took them

off, rolled the sleeves of her shift up to the shoulders and tied them there with her points. There was a not too grubby apron lying on the floor which she picked up and put on, then checked under the bed and found a truly horrible jordan brimming there.

"Godsakes!" she growled, just as Goody Janner would have.

She dumped the jordan out into the jakes in the back yard, found a rainbutt and tapped out some water so she could rinse the thing clean. There didn't seem to be any lye anywhere. There were a couple of hens poking around in the overgrown vegetables, so she poked around after them and found that for a miracle they hadn't quite stopped laying and there were two small eggs nestling in a leafy corner. There wasn't much growing anywhere and it seemed Ellie had been growing flowers rather than useful things like cabbage, but there were a few onions that hadn't been lifted.

Shortly after Portia had the dish of coals filled with some hot coals from the fireplace, more wood on the fire to build it up and provide extra coals for the copper she had found in a shed out the back. She got an earthenware dish that wasn't too dirty, scoured it with sand, rinsed it, melted some butter on the edge of going off and fried the onions with the eggs for Ellie to eat. When she took it up to her, she found Ellie had dozed off with the babe still on her breast, so ruthlessly woke her since she would wind up with a sore nipple and milk fever if she did that. Ellie protested that she wasn't hungry, then ate every morsel of the mess of eggs. There had been no fresh milk and the only beer in the shed was too strong for someone who was nursing, so Portia diluted it with some of the rainwater and hoped for the best.

You simply couldn't carry on ignoring the ripe smell from the baby. Portia took the child who was dozing off again, laid him on her lap by the fire with a linen cloth underneath and started unwrapping his swaddling bands, rolling them up deftly as Goody Janner had first shown her with her littlest brother who had died of something when he was three.

Sure enough, the clout between his legs was soiled with the swirl of yellow cream that a healthy baby made. She cleaned him off with the clout and some spit to protect him from a swaddling rash, put on a new one while his pink arms and legs waved and his fingers clutched at air and he made the surprised offended noises that most babies made when you dared to take their swaddling bands off. His shirt was in not too bad a state since the bog-moss sandwiched between the folds of linen had soaked up most of the damp. The moss went in one bucket, the cloths in the other. For a wonder, there was a pile of more of them, neatly rolled, so Portia wrapped a sheet around him and bound him up again, rolling round and round from feet to shoulders and tucking his arms in last. Ellie didn't use a board to keep his legs straight which Goody Janner would have tutted at, but that was thought old-fashioned now. He was quite a soft little package once she had done. She let him suck her finger afterwards but he wasn't at all hungry and his eyes were drooping with the little chirrups and sighs of a happy baby. It soothed her but it also made her own breasts prickle and ache. She hadn't held a babe since... Since... She wouldn't think of it. She couldn't think of it.

She put the baby carefully between the sheets where Ellie sleepily put her arm round him and smiled at last. Poor love. Not churched yet and expected by her hag of a mother-in-law to sweep the floor and clean up with no gossips to help either thanks to the Plague. Although Goody Janner was far away in Cornwall, Portia could practically hear her tutting. There was no quicker way to a dead mother and a sick baby than doing housework of any kind before the forty days after the birth had passed and you had been received back into the safekeeping of the church.

Portia's lips tightened down to a severe line with a rage that was also partly for the wicked god who stole children like Moloch, but she said nothing of that even to herself. It was very obvious what needed doing in the place and nobody around except herself to do it, so that

123

made it simple. At least it meant she could get her own washing done while she was at it and it would cost her nothing but considerable effort.

She went downstairs with the moss bucket and the clout bucket, both very full, went into the yard and dumped the moss and turds into the jakes as well. Tim Briscoe needed to bring in the night-soil men to dig it out soon, the rate it was filling up.

The laundry buck was hiding behind some badly overshot runner beans that had died back. It had filled up with rainwater which looked clean enough, so Portia dumped all the linen she had with her into it and added some more from a pile by the hut where the copper was. There was a useful stick against the wall that she used to stir it up and then, blessed be, she found an old barrel which stank of lye, nice and strong. There was a lye dripper on its side near it as well. At least someone had thought to provide Ellie with most of what she needed, even if she hadn't got to grips with it yet, so Portia put a good measure of lye into the rainwater buck and piled up firewood under the copper, brought a shovelful of coals from the living room fire and left the fire to catch and heat up the water in the copper. Soapwort was no good at all for soiled breechclouts and stained shirts, you need to boil them and scrub them with strong lye if you didn't have grated soap, something which made your hands red and unladylike. No help for it.

While she waited for the water to boil, she swept out the nasty old rushes and piled them next to the shed ready to burn, looked at the floorboards which clearly needed scrubbing but she was only one woman and didn't have time for that as well as the washing which was far more urgent. Tim would have to order more floor-rushes from the market or invest in rush-mats which could be cleaned by beating. Rushes for the floor were now out of fashion because the Queen used mats. One Portia's first acts when she and her brother had taken over the old top-floor chambers in the Earl of Essex's court, was to pay a man to dig out and cart away a foot deep litter of ancient rushes filled with bones and petrified pie crusts, revealing floorboards and enough dropped shillings and pennies to pay for it and more. She had got a woman in to scrub the boards with ten day old piss to take the stains out and perhaps kill a few fleas as well. Then she had bought white rush-mats for the whole chamber and never regretted it.

That shed had a neat shingle roof which looked to have been done recently – perhaps by Mr Briscoe who had even filled the copper with clean water. You couldn't fault him – he had done all that he could and more but you couldn't expect a man to launder, they knew nothing of the art.

The water hadn't boiled yet, so she tidied the sitting room, found a food-safe with some ham and cheese in it and very old bread, looked at the sun, scowled that it was already noon and no sign of the old harpy who should have been helping her daughter-in-law with her grandson. So she grated the bread, fried the ham on the dish-of-coals, grated the hard cheese and mixed it with the breadcrumbs, piled it on top of the ham and made a sort of pudding which she took upstairs and shared with the still sleepy Ellie. The baby woke up at the smell of melted cheese and sniffed hungrily, demanding more food, so Portia left him to feed, took the bowl downstairs to clean later and hauled the linen out of the buck into one of the scoured buckets, transferred it to the copper and boiled all of it at once as hard as she could get the fire sharpened up, which she stirred with the useful stick which she now realised must be one of Tim Briscoe's veney sticks for practising of swordplay.

The original buck needed emptying but was too heavy for her. It was now two o'clock for she could hear the drums for the bearbaiting clear across the Thames. At that point the door opened and in walked the hag, a broad red-faced woman in a red gown with murrey trim that didn't suit her and an expression of disapproving stupidity.

"Good afternoon, Mrs Briscoe," said Portia with killing politeness, "How lovely to see you."

Mrs Briscoe senior had small suspicious eyes and a truculent expression.

"Where's that little Ellie?" she demanded.

"Oh I'm one of Ellie's gossips," Portia said in the most disgustingly sweet voice she could manage, "I'm sure you wouldn't expect her to be out of bed so soon. I'm afraid I found her downstairs, trying to clean up this morning when I visited. Of course I sent her straight back upstairs."

Mrs Briscoe sniffed. "She's running out of milk and I have gone to some trouble to find a reliable woman to nurse the boy..."

"Dear me," said Portia, "Do you think so? Perhaps it is her having to run around and do housework before she is churched?"

Mrs Briscoe senior stared at Portia. Slowly but surely what passed for her brain was catching up with the implications of what Portia was saying and the way she was saying it. "She..."

"After all, your grandson is a lusty young man and he's growing fast. I'm sure if Ellie gets plenty of rest and food and drink she'll have no trouble feeding him and so no need to put yourself to any trouble or expense to find a wetnurse. Besides, with the Plague about, I'm surprised you'd dare bring a stranger in to feed him."

To be fair, Mrs Briscoe senior did look worried at this idea, which clearly hadn't occurred to her.

"At least she's done the rushes at last," she said to which Portia smiled brightly.

"No, Mrs Briscoe, I swept those out – they did need doing, didn't they?" Even Mrs Briscoe could catch the implication there. Come on, thought Portia, I dare you, I dare you to say that the floor needs scrubbing. I've got a scrubbing brush and some lye just waiting for you.

"I was delayed at the market," the hag said defensively, "You didn't have to..." She gestured at the floors and bright fire.

"I did, Mrs Briscoe," said Portia, "Of course I couldn't let Ellie exhaust herself doing it all herself. In Cornwall we say a tired cow makes no milk." They didn't in fact, but Portia felt they probably should since in her experience of dairying while her children were small, she had found it to be true.

"Now Ellie needs fresh rushes for the floor, more bread, butter, cheese and mild ale, collops for supper, more moss and I'm afraid there's a great load of washing to do. I just started boiling it all up."

Mother Briscoe frowned and settled her tall hat on her cap. "I've only just arrived..."

"And how lucky that you did," said Portia with iron in her voice, "If you go now you might catch the rushes man before he runs out."

Mother Briscoe stood up and haughtily straightened the hat again. Very fashionable it was too, Portia hoped she had enough money left to get supplies in. She swept to the door and then turned heavily. "How many rushes?"

"Three faggots of the freshest," Portia told her, "Bad airs are so dangerous for a small baby, aren't they?"

Mrs Briscoe got that hint too. And he wasn't small, he was large and beefy and already made Ellie look frail, but so what? He was still a baby and just as likely to die of bad airs.

Mrs Briscoe left, very much on her dignity, while Portia set about fishing out linen and scrubbing the worst stains with soap.

.

Mother Briscoe came back followed by a small procession including the rushes man carrying the faggots on his back and two street boys holding the food she had bought. The two of them worked together to spread the rushes in the living room and upstairs, sprinkled with dried ladies' bedstraw and rue against fleas. Ellie was sitting up in bed, looking much less hollow-eyed and feeding the great greedy baby again. Mrs Briscoe chucked him under the chin and clucked at him, but he wasn't interested and went on feeding with the little "glug glug aaahhh" sounds that babies made, while his little ears wiggled. Portia's breasts ached again so she refilled the flagon with some very good mild ale that Mrs Briscoe had found somewhere and made sure

129

Ellie drank it and had some bread and cheese.

"He's not nearly so cross with me," Ellie said, "Look,"

"You're resting now and making more milk for him," Portia told him, "You see, I told you."

"I've bought some double beer for Tim when he comes home," put in the mother-in-law, "and a great raised pork pie for his dinner so he can do for himself and you needn't leave your bed."

"Oh Tim wouldn't let me," Ellie said with an artlessness that was a credit to her, "He even tried to cook me some collops last night but I couldn't eat them because they were burnt too much."

"Dear of him," Portia said, "What a kind husband you have, Ellie."

Ellie shot a suspicious look at both Portia and her mother-in-law which Portia returned blandly. Perhaps she had overdone the sugar. Clearly Mother Briscoe had had time on her marketing trip to think about what it would do to her reputation if Ellie's gossips found out she had expected her daughter-in-law to do housework before she was churched.

Together Mrs Briscoe senior and Portia got all the dirty linen boiled, scrubbed, rinsed in the buck, after bribing the largest of the next door children to go to the conduit four times for the rinse water. By the late afternoon the clouts and baby shirts and shifts were festooning the little living room because it looked like rain outside and anyway, if you put out linen on a hedge or wall in London, you were simply offering a free gift to whichever urchin happened to pass by first. Ellie settled down to feed the baby again while her mother-in-law cooked the collops with mushrooms, ale and mustard to her own recipe, as she boasted.

Portia put her wet shirts and cloths into her marketing basket in a bundle and headed home, feeling tired and hungry, but somehow refreshed. She had never particularly enjoyed the minutiae of housekeeping, much preferring to command others. She had been her husband's steward for the small farm. Indeed, that was how she had first found out her gift for law when there had been a dispute over some land taken from Glasney College in Penryn in the Dissolution of Good King Henry's reign. But now there was a strange kind of refuge in being wrapped up in the subtler business of women, after the rough and tumble of the Inns of Court and Westminster Hall.

She had even hooked into the latest gossip, which was, as usual, juicy. An alderman had been caught by his wife in his mistress's arms, a prominent churchman found at the Falcon's Chick (the notorious boy-brothel on the South Bank), a series of thefts by hookmen had all the women in the city locking their shutters every time they went out, two women of the town had been found foully murdered, probably by the Jesuits who were back in London again, a barrister had made a contract with the Devil and wriggled out of it, so the Devil had possessed him, the Earl of Essex had supposedly got dead drunk at a banquet and fallen out of a boat taking him back to Essex House, there was definitely and for certain sure a witch's coven in London, an alchemist had been saved from the plague by the Philosopher's Stone...

"What?" Portia had asked, wringing a shirt against Mrs Briscoe's vigorous twisting.

"It's all over the city, there have been evil spirits and poisonous plants seen in many places and a woman ran wood from wicked spells..."

"No, no, the alchemist? Was it Mr Cheke?"

Mrs Briscoe shrugged. "I don't know. Perhaps it was, only they say he found the Philosopher's Stone by accident and it cured him of plague."

"Hm," said Portia.

"Only of course, the Philosopher's Stone has a wicked ingredient so it is the most unChristian thing to seek, almost as bad as witchcraft," said Mrs Briscoe.

"What ingredient is that?"

"The blood of a whore."

Portia's eyes stretched at that. "What? I've never heard of that?"

"If you're not an alchemist, you wouldn't," said Mrs Briscoe, fishing for the last tiny shirt and squeezing

132

it vigorously, "but they say that just as some harmful spells need the blood of a virgin, so the Philosopher's Stone, being beneficial, needs the blood of a whore..."

"And that's good?"

"Of course. It has the right virtue at least."

Portia had also tried to find out which barrister it was that had been possessed by the devil but Mrs Briscoe didn't know.

"How could they tell, seeing it was a lawyer?" Portia had asked sarcastically, knowing that nobody likes lawyers. Mrs Briscoe had laughed.

"Raving and disputing with the devil last week, he was," she said, "Such a speed and dripping with sweat, Mrs Corbett saw him and said his face was red as the flames of hell so it must have been the Devil possessing him."

Which settled the matter. Portia quite enjoyed that element of lawyering, of being the villain of every piece. Other lawyers swaggered out their disfavour too. Let one of the men who so loudly spoke against the plague of lawyers in the realm receive some writ or pleading against him, and he was into the Temple fast enough, looking for a champion to fight for him in court.

There would have been no point in telling Mrs Briscoe that poor French Mary had helped look after Mr Cheke while he had plague, because like all respectable women Mother Briscoe hated whores with a passion and

133

that was that. Who cheered and laughed loudest when a whore was whipped at the cart's tail? The respectable women in their white caps and high hats and damask aprons, always.

·

As she walked down the street with her slightly dripping basket, Portia was thinking so hard about the dead whores that she walked straight into one of the pie women who had been at the bearbaiting. It was another of the stout crew of French Mary's ilk, and Portia was embarrassed because while masquerading as her brother James, she had actually found herself flirting with the woman.

"I'm sorry, goodwife," she said.

"Three pies for a penny," said the woman with no look of recognition, Dorothy her name was, or something similar. "As they're cold now."

They had also been pawed about a bit by the bearbaiting crowds, but no matter. This was a bargain and Portia had never been able to resist one, even if she hadn't needed to count every penny.

She munched one of the six she bought as she continued westwards in a hurry, needing to get out of Ludgate before it shut at six o'clock. As James she could just go north and clamber over the stones of the old

134

wall, as Portia, she couldn't. It was very annoying in its way.

At least Tim Briscoe had been pleased to see her when he came home and had promised her a load of Newcastle coals as thanks for her help. From the way he looked at his mother, it was clear that he was not at all fooled by her. Portia put to him the idea of Ellie coming to attend her when she was ready – as Portia said, she would be able to bring the babe and do just light work and perhaps a little cooking to start with. Tim Briscoe had nodded thoughtfully about the idea.

There was some kind of commotion on Fleet Street, she saw, as she came down Ludgate Hill. A crowd of people were gathered near Temple Bar, craning their necks to see something exciting at the first floor level. To her shock, Portia saw it was William Craddock, that she had spoken to in the morning. Did he have Plague, perhaps?

Almost certainly not, there wouldn't be a crowd of people watching, they would all have run away. Craddock had his head out of the window from his chamber which overlooked Fleet Street, and had half climbed out of it, only somebody was holding his belt. His face was puce and he was shouting at something invisible which might have been standing near the big dunghill in Fleet Street.

"You'll not catch me out, you foul fiend, Prince of Darkness, no, you'll not murder my soul, no, no, no... I refute you utterly, there is a God as is shown manifestly in the Bible, yea, a God that hath holy angels that will utterly trample upon you!"

It was hard to understand what he was saying, he was gabbling his words so fast, sweat dripping off his nose. Then he caught sight of the people in the street who were pointing and laughing at him.

"Gentlefolk, have a care please," he called waving his hands, "Some of you are standing between his evil feet, surely you can see the claws, step back I pray you!"

Portia narrowed her eyes. William Craddock was the lawyer who called up the devil? Surely not. Some other people looked about nervously and a few stepped back. Behind Craddock was the vicar of St Brides who must have been called for – he looked very tired and anxious and was ineffectually trying to pull the man back from the window.

"I refute you, sir, a fortiori in conspexi coram Dei..." Craddock's speech turned to a frantic babble of lawyer's Norman French and Latin. He seemed to be citing a great deal of case law against the Devil standing in Fleet Street, most of which Portia thought was quite cogent and well-argued. For instance, it seemed that Craddock was accusing Mephistophiles of a breach of the old statute of Praemunire of Henry VIII which was almost certainly correct, since that was the statute which forbade an Englishman to give loyalty to any authority other than the English monarch – such as the Pope of Rome or indeed Satan, in this case.

Portia shook her head. It depended on whether the Devil Mephistophiles was an Englishman, though, didn't it? Praemunire didn't apply to foreigners... She caught herself. What on earth was she thinking? She smiled, she couldn't help it, although she didn't normally find the mad Bedlam beggars funny. But this was something you had to smile at or be terrified. Certainly it was the right statute and for choice, she thought that Maliverny Catlin would be the right pursuivant to arrest Old Nick for treason.

Poor Craddock's friends managed to pull him back from the window at last, his Latin raving still audible through the open window until they slammed it. Portia was about to go up the stairs and ask when the fit had come upon him, when she remembered that she couldn't do anything so direct and bold whilst she was being Ms Morgan the respectable widow.

So she sidled up to the tight knot of women watching avidly from near the conduit and stood quietly hilding her mask with her teeth so she could see them through the eyeholes. Nobody recognised her though she knew most of them.

Mrs Garret was blinking and squinting and craning her neck to see up the street.

"Well, I can't see anything," she said, "If there was

a Devil in the street I'm sure you could at least smell him."

"I don't know how," said young Mrs Coke pertly, "what with that stink from the dunghill."

Other women tutted. "Maybe he's seeing the miasmas."

"It isn't Plague, is it?" asked a woman Portia didn't know, "The fever makes people run wood too..."

"Like poor Jemmy Jones the other day," said a different woman, "Came roaring down the street and nobody would touch him for he had the black tokens on his face."

"He's dead now," said Mrs Coke with a shiver.

"And his family still shut up in their house," said Mrs Garrett, "Two of the children gone last night," she added absent-mindedly.

"Where is Mrs Craddock?" asked another woman, "Couldn't she calm him?"

"She's afraid of him when he takes this fit," said Mrs Coke, "And who can blame her. Her mother tried every physic she knew when it happened last week, but nothing worked."

"That's how it can't be plague," said Mrs Garrett definitively, "For if it was he would be dead and the plague searchers would have shut the house."

There was a rustle of assent at this. It seemed to Portia that every woman there seemed to close up

138

on herself at each mention of Plague. Many of them
had little posies tucked in their bodices or dangling
pomanders, withered oranges stuck with cloves. There
was always some plague in London but this year had
been bad, despite the shutting of the theatres, and
the winter was still quite mild, no heavy frost yet and
it was the middle of October. And the cases were
still increasing. It was everyone's nightmare, the worst
nightmare, the thing she had always feared herself. It
had never occurred to her to fear smallpox in the same
way and yet...

A window slammed open again and a candle and a
book came sailing through to land on the ground near a
startled man who was selling ballads about the Lawyer
Possessed of the Devil. It seemed the vicar had tried for
an exorcism and been rebuffed.

"Could it have been something he ate?" asked
Mrs Coke shyly, "I saw him coming home from the
bearbaiting yesterday and he told me he had a pain in
his guts then."

"What could do that to a man?" said Mrs Garrett,
gesturing as the frantic babble came through the open
window and there was a series of thuds.

"Or perhaps it's the French pox," said Mrs Town
with a spiteful leer, "That makes you run wood as well."

"But not at once, you get sores first and have to bathe
in murkery, don't you?" said another woman Portia

139

didn't know. She was about to tell them that she had talked to Craddock that very morning and he seemed perfectly sane then, when she saw Mr Cheke hurrying along the street, still no more than a walking skeleton, carrying a heavy bag and looking ready to drop. His anxious face scanned the women, and he inclined his head to them collectively since many of them were his customers for face paints and other salves. There was a plague-searcher behind him which made the women mutter and move away. One who lived next door to the Craddocks left the group and hurried down the road to a grocer's shop as quickly as she could.

Portia nodded at that and thought she would like to get a few barrels of herring into her chambers just in case. If you were locked up in your own house for forty days' quarantine, plague was only half of your problem. There had been many cases of men dying of hunger and thirst because they had no friends to bring them food and drink.

Mr Cheke knocked on the Fleet Street door of the house and was admitted by Mrs Craddock herself, a pretty young blonde woman in a smart black kirtle trimmed with rose and a rose brocade forepart to her petticoat, very fine indeed. Behind him was the plague searcher who leered at Mrs Craddock, conscious of his power. She flinched from him.

The ranting increased for a time then calmed a little.

William Craddock leaned out of the window again and pointed.

"I see you!" he screamed, "Butcher, killer of women, I see you!"

There were prickles up Portia's back and she looked around. Did he know? Was that what he was talking about in his frenzy? Could he be speaking to the devil that had killed French Mary and Kettle Annie? The women looked around them as well.

"Is he talking about the plague?" one of them asked.

"No," sniffed Mrs Towne, "Plague kills everyone. Maybe he's talking about the whore-killer?"

So the word had got to the respectable women already? Portia wasn't surprised. Not all respectable women were as respectable as they pretended. Now there was a struggle by the window again. It seemed Craddock was trying to climb out to attack the Devil – at least he had no want of courage. Mr Cheke was briefly in view as Craddock's friends held him, pouring the contents of a bottle down the lawyer's throat. The ranting slowed and finally stopped. The street was quiet for a second and then people started a babble of talk and nervous laughter.

Still followed by the plague-searcher, Mr Cheke came out of the house and the hare-lipped serving girl shut the door after him.

The women moved towards him in a body, Portia

following at the back. She felt sorry for the man – he looked transparent with weariness.

"Is it plague then?" asked Mrs Garrett anxiously.

"I think not," said the searcher, who was a weaselly faced man in a black stuff clerical gown, his seals and papers hanging from his belt and no doubt the paint in the large leather bag over his shoulder. "He has no tokens on him, nor any buboes, nor any bleeding from his nose or ears or other orifices. He has a fever and has complained of great thirst so it could be a jail fever.

All the women visibly relaxed. The Plague hadn't come to their part of Fleet Street yet and so they wanted to believe that it wouldn't. Jail fever was normal, even if it killed you just as dead.

Mr Cheke rubbed his eyes. "I hope the gentleman will sleep for a while. I gave him a large dose of laudanum. His mother-in-law says he has been up all night disputing with the Devil and must be exhausted. Perhaps the sleep will help him."

Portia frowned. She had seen no sign of madness on Craddock only that morning. Had he hidden it to talk to her?

Mr Cheke took his hat off to his customers and they bobbed him a communal curtsey in return. Portia went down the alley behind the Cock into the Temple, past the round church, through the crumbling cloisters and up to Essex's Court. She was thinking all the way. Could

the Devil have done the killing of the two whores?
It was possible. While she now found the myth of a
merciful God quite impossible to credit, she found the
Devil much easier to believe in. Perhaps the Anabaptists
were right and the Devil was the god of this world.

She went up to her chamber, got a bucket and went
down to the fountain in Fountain Court to get water.
She made several trips with all her bowls and then
checked her money to see if she could afford a barrel of
herrings. She couldn't so she went down to the grocer
with her marketing basket and found he was crowded
out with anxious women. For a mercy he hadn't put his
prices up much. She bought what she could: some dried
sausage from last year, a crock of pickled eringo roots
and cucumbers, a lump of leathery salt cod, a lump of
cheese and, on impulse, some salty ship's biscuits. It was
the best she could do and cleaned her out completely.

She still had no firewood or coals and was too tired
to go scavenging for wood in the Whitefriars. Then she
realised she had two sets of pleadings to write out in
fair copy and so she lit a couple of tallow dips and set
to work as she munched another of the pork pies and
drank the last of her ale.

.

Maliverny stared at the repulsive creature in front of him.

143

It was a notorious player and worse still a playwright.

"How did you know it was French Mary?" he asked.

"We all know French Mary. She sells hazelnuts at the Theatre," said Shakespeare uncomfortably.

"Do you remember anything else?"

"No. I have spoken to Mr Enys about it and shown him the place where we found her body."

Catlin scowled. "Oh. Why?"

"Mr Enys says he wants to know as much as possible about both killings so as to make a beginning as he would with a court case."

Catlin shrugged and then leaned forward to prod Bald Will's chest hard with his forefinger.

"Listen to me," he said, "If it was only up to me, I'd have all of you Godless scum taken up and whipped at the cart's tail from London town."

Shakespeare said nothing. There was sweat on his nose and he was staring hard at Catlin.

"I know that, Mr Catlin," he said.

"So when that lawyer finds out something, I want you to tell me what it is."

Something disquieting went across Shakespeare's pointed face. "Oh?"

"Or I'll have you and all your friends thrown out of London and whipped as vagabonds." The finger prodded again. "I'll have you whipped as a vagabond. And not a word to the lawyer either."

Shakespeare's face was smooth again.

"Very well, Mr Catlin," he said, "I'll be your spy with Mr Enys. What will be my reward if you catch the killer first?"

Catlin smiled nastily. "Freedom," he said.

Shakespeare nodded. He stood and made his bow, left Catlin sitting in his booth at the Fox and Hounds. Catlin felt obscurely dissatisfied. The player had treated him with perfect respect, but Catlin was sure he had seen contempt cross his miserable player's face as he left. It really didn't matter. This was how Catlin always worked: he collected information from his informants, cross-checked by collecting the information they were giving to any of his colleagues and then nipped in smartly and caught the priest first in the act of Mass-saying so he could have the credit and whatever money was going. Since he was doing God's work, it didn't matter how he did it. The system worked for Papists and it would work for murderers. He could use Enys's work and then perhaps take all of the fee, not just half of it. He had an important use for it, after all.

Outside in the street, Shakespeare was quietly punching one balled fist into his palm again and again. He kicked a stone with all his strength and bruised his toe. A scared-looking urchin blinked at him from behind a barber's pole.

"Sir, sir," said the boy, "I done it, I got the lists."

Shakespeare stopped and breathed deeply for a moment. "Follow me," he told the boy and marched up the road to Fleet Bridge and the little pawnshop there.

Senhor Gomes, at the foot of Fleet Bridge, knew him as he knew every one of the players and poets in London. Shakespeare went to the desk where Gomes sat peacefully reading something in Hebrew – Shakespeare stared at the book with its alluring, mysterious letters, wishing he could understand what was in it. Perhaps he could ask Snr Gomes for lessons? It was so frustrating: when he had the time to learn something like Hebrew, he didn't have the money and vice versa. Gomes stood up and nodded at Shakespeare.

"Senhor Shakspee, forgive me, but I fear your young page must stay outside."

Shakespeare whisked round to find the boy in mid-grab at a kerchief which was pinned on display to the wall hanging – also for sale, a fine tapestry of Jacob's ladder.

Shakespeare grabbed the grubby paw, cuffed the boy's ear and shoved him outside.

"You stupid kinchin," he snarled at the boy whose head seemed to be trying to disappear into his shoulders. "What the devil are you up to? I'm bloody pawning a ring to get money to buy you food and you're trying to lift something in plain view."

Peter the Hedgehog wiped his nose on his sleeve.

146

"Sorry sir," he muttered dolefully, "I'm hungry, ain't eaten today, I fort you wouldn't mind seeing 'e's only a Jew."

"Even if he's a Jew, he's got eyes in his head. Don't steal while you're with me, understand? It's embarrassing."

Peter nodded. Shakespeare went back into the pawnshop, sighed and took off his last gold ring which he had only redeemed the week before with Southampton's largesse. Blast Munday to hell and beyond, the smug bastard.

Gomes had seen that ring many times before. "Ay yes, the usual arrangement?"

Shakespeare nodded. He still felt pale with fury from the interview with Catlin, and wondered if he was, his heart was beating slow and hard as if he was about to get in a fight or go on stage in front of an audience of unhappy groundlings, well-armed with eggs.

He took the twenty shillings in silver and his ticket which required him to redeem the ring for 21 shillings, went outside into the street. Peter the Urchin was nowhere to be seen.

Shakespeare crossed his arms, scowled and waited for a minute or two. Then he shrugged and headed back down Fleet street, heading for the Cock.

Some prickle in his back warned him and he felt himself slightly jogged, then stealthy fingers at his codpiece where many people thought it was wise to keep their money. He caught the arm attached to the hand and lifted the scrawny creature up by it. There was hardly any weight there, you could hardly blame the boy for thieving.

"Listen to me, Peter," he hissed, while the boy writhed in front of him and a couple of passers by grinned, "You don't nip purses from people who are going to buy information from you. It's stupid."

"I saw that Mr Catlin go by, I had to hide," snivelled Peter.

"You didn't have to try and stick your thieving fingers in my crotch, you wittol,"

"I fort you wouldn't want to talk to me cos of Mr Catlin."

"You don't know me, do you?" snarled Shakespeare, letting the boy down, "I'll give you a chance this time, but don't be stupid again, understand? I don't mind a lot of things, but I will not tolerate stupid."

He kept hold of the boy's bony wrist and hauled him into the Cock and out the back into the yard.

"Listen," said Shakespeare, "I'm going to ask the landlord of the Cock if he'll give you a job here. That way you'll be easy for me to find and not starving. Understand?"

The boy was still muttering something about Mr Catlin. Presumably the pursuivant had bullied him to give the Puritan anything he got first, the same as he had Shakespeare.

"One of the reasons why you're here at all is because Mr Catlin doesn't like the Cock. For some reason, no matter what he pays, he never gets good beer here. It's a mystery. So you probably won't see him here."

:Peter nodded and wiped his nose on his sleeve again. His little red-rimmed eyes blinked hopefully – and squintily – at the poet. The fact of the matter was that there was no point him even trying to sell his arse, since nobody would be interested in buying it.

"You'll be washing up pots and mugs and you'll do as you're told, you'll get scraps to eat and any time you put a foot wrong he'll cuff you, but you won't be trying to sleep under the Bridge when the cold weather comes and you will have food. And I know he needs a scullery boy because his last one died of... of a fever." It had been Plague, but there was no sense telling everyone. Particularly not Peter who had to sleep in the boy's bed. The landlord had kept it very quiet, but Shakespeare had seen the tokens on the boy when the small body went into the plague wagon some way from the Cock. Outside the Fox & Hounds, in fact. "So keep your mouth shut, do as I tell you and don't you ever steal anything ever again or I'll turn you in to the bailiff and I'll nail your ear to the pillory myself. Understand?"

Shakespeare was nose to runny nose with Peter as he

said that and the boy trembled at his flat Midlands hiss.

"Yers, but will 'e want me?"

"Yes, he will, because you're too ugly and ignorant to cause trouble with his customers," said Shakespeare brutally. Peter stared at him with his mouth open, bewildered.

"Wot?"

Shakespeare sighed and shook his head.

"Quod erat demonstrandum," he said.

"Wot's just been shown," said Peter absent-mindedly.

Shakespeare stared at him, quite shocked. "How the devil do you know what it means?"

Peter shrugged. "Me sister'n me used to serve a lawyer and he said that sometimes and told me what it meant. It's foreign, innit?"

"Latin,"

"Yers. I fort 'e was a Papist praying and I told vat Mr Catlin but 'e said lawyers use Latin too."

Shakespeare nodded. "Why don't you serve him any more?"

Peter looked up and squinted at the sky. "Dunno, really. Somfink went wrong wiv my sister and the lawyer's lady and we got told to go so we went."

The landlord came out of the scullery and into the yard, looked narrow-eyed at the boy, nodded and went back to bring out a wooden platter piled up with food. It was the ordinary for the day of the Cock Tavern's far-famed steak-and-kidney pudding, steamed as it was just above the double-ale wort. There was a chorus of pot-herbs with it and gravy. Peter was actually dribbling as he sat down on a bucket and started shovelling food into his mouth with his filthy hand.

"Slow down, or you'll be sick and waste it," Shakespeare advised drily. The boy ignored him but did stop a minute or two later, both cheeks bulging with suet pastry.

"Me sister used to say that," he said through the food, "I fort it was just wot girls say."

"Where is your sister now?"

"She's dead, master," said the boy with quiet sadness, "Two weeks gone."

"Of plague?"

"No sir."

"You're sure."

The boy nodded vigorously and his face was bleak. "She was killt, sir."

"How?"

Peter shrugged and went back to shovelling food in his mouth. "Don't wanna fink about it."

"I'm sorry for it," Shakespeare said after a heavy pause.

"Me too," said Peter, with his mouth full again, "She used to work the gentlemen wot like kinchin morts and we'd eat regular as anyfing, every day sometimes.

Maybe it was one of 'em killt 'er. I wish she hadn't of got killed," Peter confided, as Shakespeare stared at him narrow-eyed, "She was good, my sister, good as... as...."

"Gold?"

Peter shook his head. "Nah. Steak and kidney pudding," he said with a gleam of humour in his eye, "You can eat that," he explained, still munching.

"How was she killed?"

"I don't wanna fink about it..." said Peter, with his head down, "It was horrible. What'd 'e want to do that for?"

There was a feeling like the fingers of a ghost running up Shakespeare's back. "Was she anatomised?" Peter's face was blank. "Cut open."

The dirty gravy-smeared face hardened at once. The boy nodded convulsively.

"Don't wanna fink about it."

"Where?"

The boy shrugged. "Dunno, don't remember." He'd finished the pot herbs and was running his finger up and down the plate and licking it. Then he stopped doing it the polite way and just licked the platter.

Shakespeare decided he'd better leave the subject or Peter might run away. "All right, can you tell me the list now? Of Kettle Annie's clients and French Mary's clients and customers as well."

Peter burped. "Yers," he said. To Shakespeare's

complete astonishment, he fished out a crumpled bit of waste paper, squinted at the smeared charcoal on it and started to read names out. Shakespeare noted them down in his own notebook, completing the clerkish cycle. Who would have thought the boy could actually write? It was extraordinary.

Mrs Crosby went down the steps that led to the small crypt they had used before when they had been miraculously saved from a raid by Topcliffe and his men. It had been blocked off and sealed with the Queen's Customary Seal, which made it an ideal choice.

The little crypt backed onto an alehouse in the next street. She went back up the stairs and round the corner, to the alehouse called the Bull. The landlord met her in the commonroom and led her to the the space at the back where the big oven had been built against the garden wall. Down some steps again and through a small door and there she was in the dark crypt which somehow smelled faintly of blood.

She went back up the steps, picked up a candle and lit it with a spill from the coals in the oven.

Maybe it really was a church. Once it had been used to store barrels of wine that had no tunnage and poundage stamp. The sturdy round pillars and round arches looked like some of the older churches you saw, though there was hardly any Papist decoration. Just the

153

odd blurred statue of the young bullfighter on one of the walls. She'd heard they did that in Spain instead of proper bear-baiting, perhaps this place had been built by Spaniards. Never mind, it was still perfect and it still had its amazing secret exit under the floorboards, the square pit with its drain where the priest had hidden the last time. It was a difficult place to escape from but you could do it by squeezing along the drain downhill and emerge on the other side of the street behind in a courtyard.

She shivered a little. The place gave her the creeps in the darkness, but you couldn't deny it made an excellent underground chapel. Father Campion himself had consecrated the place underneath where they put the table that made the altar, had hidden some sacred relics there and a splinter of the true cross. The landlord could still deny all knowledge and he was well-paid.

Mrs Crosby paid him again. She had her own interests to cover and she had made a decision after talking to the boy: after all, she had no husband now, no resources bar an inadequate jointure and her property. She had looked after many of the young idiots who came from the Continent after their priesting and she had gained nothing for it except danger and suspicion, expense and sorrow. She had to do for herself, since it was plain that God wasn't really interested in looking after Catholics. Once she had truly believed that He would protect His people, but no longer. Not since Fr Southwell had been taken. And so she spoke quietly to the landlord and rented the place for the next day.

.

Catlin had arranged to meet with James Enys at Ludgate. His plan was to go down to Blackfriars steps and take a boat to the Falcon on the South Bank, with a view to questioning Mrs Julia Nunn as to her knowledge of the whore-killer. Enys was vehemently against the idea when Catlin proposed it.

"Sir, if you cross-examine Mrs Nunn, you will only infuriate her," he protested. "Besides, if she knew anything to the purpose, the killer would probably already be dead."

"So we arrest her for running a bawdy-house," said Catlin.

Enys stepped back and stared at him. "And infuriate the Bishop of Winchester, the King of London and half the worshipful gentlemen of London?" he said, "Why? Why make our lives so difficult?"

Catlin began to consider that what you could do when you were hunting Papists on a charge of treason might be different from what you could do when merely seeking a whore-killer. "For her notorious whoredom," he said, colouring.

"Obviously she is a notorious whore," said Enys through his teeth, "She is also highly respected. What will Fleetwood say when he finds you have provoked the riot he has been at such pains to prevent?"

Catlin shrugged. "Why would they riot?"

"Because two of their company, two senior and respected women, have been very foully murdered," said Enys, separating each word as if talking to a foreigner.

"Their arrogance knows no bounds,"

"Nonetheless, if they stir their upright men to it, the apprentice boys and watermen will start shouting "Clubs!" and the whole of London will be in chaos from dawn to dusk. Is that what you want? Or, more to the point, what the City Fathers want? Or Mr Fleetwood?"

Catlin looked down. Two highly painted women walked by, in striped petticoats, wide farthingales and bodices so low, their tits were almost exploding out of the top. They had fine tall beaver hats and were arm in arm as they smiled at the passers by. One of them smiled at him and hitched her hip, to his horror.

"Look at them," he hissed quickly to Enys, "See their arrogance."

"I see they're walking in pairs now," said Enys neutrally.

Catlin stared longingly at the women, then turned aside, burning with shame at the way his unruly sinful brain rioted beyond his control at the whores' wantonness. They should cover themselves up and not walk abroad so he wouldn't have to try and not sin with them in his mind.

Enys was watching him with an ironic look on his face. He seemed better able to control himself. But then he put his hand to his sword-pommel and hurried after the whores in plain daylight.

"Goodwives, may I speak with you?" he said.

The two women stopped, smiled and hoisted the sides of their petticoats to show a bare ankle each under their farthingales and white under-petticoats. Catlin swallowed hard as he followed the legs upwards in his imagination, into the very hell-mouth itself.

Enys bowed slightly, very courteous. "It concerns the terrible murders of Mrs Smith and Mrs Mary de Paris," he said, according the whores far too much honour.

Both whores stopped smiling and one scowled.

"What of it? We don't know nuffink."

"The thing is, goodwives, I need your help. I have been ordered by Mr Recorder Fleetwood to find out the murderer so he may be brought to justice"

"Mr Recorder Fleetwood hisself?" asked the older of the two, with a jiggle of her hips. She must have been at least 21 and had a nasty sore on the side of her face, a certain sign of the French pox as Catlin knew well. "What does he care?"

"He doesn't," said Enys with a cynical smile, "But

he doesn't want trouble about either so I'm supposed to find out who did it or I'll probably end on a rope doing a jig myself."

The older one grunted, the younger one tutted.

"What about 'im?" she said, gesturing at Catlin. "'e your friend?"

"No," said Enys, "Although he is perforce my colleague."

Catlin gave him a dirty look. "Where do you want to meet us, then?" asked the younger whore with a leer.

"I would like to meet with you and as many of your friends as possible..." The two were elbowing each other knowingly. "Ladies, I promise you, I have no intentions of venery."

"Why not?" demanded the older one, "Ain't we good enough for you?"

Enys seemed at a loss for words. "Ah..." he stuttered, clutching his swordhilt as if it offered a clue to dealing with this, "Ah... I'm afraid I could not afford such services even if I... um... did not have a malady preventing me."

The girls elbowed each other again and sniggered. "S'alright," said the younger one, "We can get it up for you, specially if you have both of us."

It gave Catlin great satisfaction to see Enys had turned ruby red. The lawyer coughed and tried again.

"All I want is to hear what your thoughts are about

158

the killings, who might have done it and perhaps even why."

The whores looked at each other and then the older one nodded.

"I've been saying it was that lawyer what saw the Devil on Fleet Street yesterday," she said. The younger one shivered.

"Stands to reason it was the Devil, considering," she said.

Enys nodded. "But probably in human form. If you saw the Devil, you would run wouldn't you, not go into an alley with him and take your clothes off?"

The younger one sniggered while the older one frowned in puzzlement. "Why would I take my clothes off?"

"Exactly," said Enys. "There are other points like that for which I... I would be grateful for your expert advice."

"'e talks nice, don't 'e?" said the younger one to the older one.

"I could see Kettle Annie clouting Old Nick with a kettle," said Enys, "But not taking her kirtle off on a cold night."

"Witches take their clothes off and lie with Old Nick," said the older one, "And it's a certain fact there's witches in London. Everyone knows about it. Otherwise, why the plague? Eh?"

"Maybe the witches called up Old Nick and did what they do, you know," said the younger one, "Lying wiv him and wapping him and then it all went wrong and 'e cut 'em up?"

Catlin was astonished at such good sense from the girl. Enys seemed impressed too. He nodded seriously. "That's certainly possible," he said, "And it would account for the lawyer seeing him."

"Maybe it was lawyers wot done it all," said the older one flintily, "You know, as warlocks or wizards. Eh?"

"All of this may be true," said Enys, "Or none of it. At the moment all I want to do is find out as much as I can, as many true things as possible and for that I need you and your friends."

"Besides," said the older whore, continuing a thought and ignoring him, "Kettle Annie was a God-fearing woman, always going to church and that. She sang psalms as well as anybody I ever heard. So she couldn't've been a witch cos they can't go into churches, everyone knows that."

She turned and smiled at him, which would have been more attractive if her teeth had not been brown. "So that settles it. Must have been the lawyers."

Enys coughed again. "As this meeting is not to be for purposes of venery, I should like to meet at the Cock this evening..." That produced a gale of giggles from the youngest whore and a snortle from the older, while Enys went red again, "... with you and any of your friends you can persuade to come along."

"Will you pay us for our time?"

"No," said Enys flatly, although Catlin would have been willing to do it. "I told you, I have very little money. Besides, bought information is less trustworthy than what you tell me willingly so I can find out who killed Kettle Annie and French Mary."

The two of them nodded reluctantly and the older one put her hands on her hips. "Best get to work then," she said with a toss of her head.

"My name is James Enys, barrister-at-law," he said, taking his hat off to them as if they had been ladies in fact, "My chamber is at the Earl of Essex's new court."

Both of them curtseyed to him. "Isabel," said the younger one. "Eliza," said the older one.

Isabel turned to Catlin and raked him up and down with her eyes. "Morning husband," she said softly, "You coming with me?"

Catlin turned and almost ran in the opposite direction. He hadn't wanted to to talk to her, he'd desperately hoped she wouldn't.... He was a fool, as always. Oh God... Might Enys guess?

Enys hurried after him also quite red. "Kettle Annie, God-fearing," Catlin sneered, more to have something to say.

"God-fearing," said Enys firmly, "Everyone says it

of her. I'm going to the inquest now, if you want to come."

.

The inquest was held in the crowded crypt of St Bride's and it was short to the point of perfunctory, with a jury of solid well-dressed men clearly well-experienced in bringing in exactly the decision Fleetwood wanted. Catlin and Enys testified as to how they had found the body, the Fleet Street barber-surgeon testified that it had been mutilated, nobody wanted to view the body which lay between the old knight's tombs and the jury found they could come to no verdict except that of murder by person or persons unknown.

"I therefore adjourn this inquest pending further enquiries and the discovery of the the killer," said Fleetwood who was also, usefully, the London registrar. Catlin found that he and Enys were at the end of a stern look by Fleetwood and his pet jury, which made him feel very nervous.

Mrs Nunn was in court, flanked by an attendance of hard-looking young men who included her younger brother Gabriel.

"May I claim the body to bury, sir?" she asked with a deep curtsey.

"Is there any kin of Mrs Annie Smith present in the

court?" Fleetwood asked.

There was silence although some of the younger women and upright men clotting the steps at the back may well have been quite closely related to her, since successful whoredom tended, like so much else, to run in families. Or like the French pox, thought Catlin, that terrible vengeance on sin that made the children's children's mouths to set awry when their grandparents had eaten sour grapes.

"Any objections to Mrs Nunn being given possession of the body?" asked Fleetwood. There were no objections. "Very well, Mrs Nunn. I would appreciate due warning of the date of Mrs Smith's interment."

Julia Nunn curtseyed to him again. "Thank you, sir, it will be in two days' time."

Fleetwood nodded grimly, no doubt already mentally re-arranging the Watches of London.

It was interesting how Mrs Nunn had chosen to handle the matter of transporting Annie's bulky corpse in its blurring of cerecloth. Six men, two of them whom Catlin recognised as important upright men of the city, including Gabriel, brought in a litter draped in black. With some difficulty, Kettle Annie's wide body was shifted to it from the bier and draped in black cloth.

While they did it, Enys had moved quickly to the back of the small crypt and slipped out the door and up the stairs. Catlin missed this and watched as Mrs

Nunn using considerable ceremony, placed a large brass kettle with a dent in it at Kettle Annie's feet – it looked positively pagan.

Realising Enys had already slipped away and feeling exposed amongst the scum crowding the little underground chamber, Catlin struggled through the press at the door and won his way up the crowded steps. Enys was watching from the other side of the street, where a crowd had mysteriously formed.

The place was even fuller of beggars and street traders than normal – the ballad sellers were already singing out the Sorrowful Tale of Kettle Annie's Murther (only 3d per copy) – but there were others, whores and upright men and many urchins with swollen eyes, no doubt nips and foists amongst the respectable citizens who had turned out for mere curiosity.

As the litter came up the steps, a dirty boy fought his way to the front of the crowd, carrying a drum nearly as big as himself. Nobody was in a mourning cloak and yet this was looking very like a funeral procession. Gabriel Nunn whispered fiercely to the boy and the boy nodded, gulped, wiped his nose on his sleeve and started banging the drum hard.

Catlin recognised his informant, Peter the Hedgehog, which seemed appropriate. He at least had some colour in his cheeks and somebody had given him a cloak that was too big for him. With Gabriel holding his shoulder he found the two step beat and started forwards, muttering audibly, "One two, one two."

Catlin was surprised to see how much dignity the boy had, as well as the tears carving tracks down the dirt and dried gravy on his face. Gabriel and his sister were behind him, then the litter with the body and its eponymous kettle, then upright men and Whitefriars whores in a loose throng. There was an eery quietness about it: no psalms, no music, not even the wailing of paid mourners. Just the sound of feet on cobbles. Most of them had some black about them but nobody was wearing a veil, just a shawl or hat or neckerchief wound round the wrist. There seemed a lot of them in their bright petticoats although most had pulled up their bodices to be decent.

Catlin saw that balding weasel of a poet hanging around near the Cock as well, watching with fascination.

The procession headed for Ludgate, clearly aiming for the City – highly provocative since no whores were supposed to set foot inside the walls. Catlin wondered if the City Fathers might dare try to stop them.

"Was she so important?" Catlin asked Enys, staring at Julia Nunn, magnificent in black damask and wheel farthingale, her painted face stony under her high beaver hat.

"Everyone liked her, I think," Enys said judiciously, "But this is a message to Fleetwood and the City

Aldermen from Mrs Nunn and her people."

Catlin nodded. When you looked at who was in the procession, it was very clear. First came the various whores who worked out of the Whitefriars liberties and their upright men and the beggars that had taken refuge in the old Blackfriars cloisters until they fell down and the land was bought by a rich courtier who cleared them out. Some of the scabbier players who had visited her alehouse were there, but not the famous ones like the Burbages or Alleyn, because they were too respectable, in their own estimation at least. Then came the better dressed and perkier women of the Falcon from Upper Ground. Then the highly coloured pretty boys and the gentle gazelle-like black youths that some at Court favoured, from the Falcon's Chick. Then another contingent wearing roses. In fact, looking at them, Catlin thought that every bawdy house and stews in Upper Ground and Bankside must have sent a party to follow Kettle Annie's corpse.

Suddenly Enys nudged him and pointed. There at the back walked another silent group, some carrying brilliantly feathered fighting cocks in cages, and all the whores in their finest trademark fleur-de-lis stomachers above their striped petticoats.

"Paris Garden," Catlin said, "Good God!" He hadn't meant to swear but he was shocked. Paris Garden and Upper Ground were at daggers drawn usually. Often literally, since they were in such hot competition and had different landlords – the Bishop of Winchester for Upper Ground and the Lord Chamberlain for Paris Garden. Mary de Paris, or French Mary, had worked there in her youth as her name revealed. Behind them came well-ordered ranks of mostly older women, walking two by two, some wearing battered nun's veils and radically altered black habits inherited from the original nuns who had dealt with the long-ago Dissolution of their notorious nunnery by turning it into a business.

"Clerkenwell Convent," breathed Catlin, "Jesu, with one rank of arquebusiers here today we could clear London of all whoredom and venery."

Enys snorted. "I doubt it, sir. To be sure the trade would only spring up again somewhere different since there is such demand for it amongst the Godly men of London."

Catlin winced and scowled. What did he know? Did he know? He was talking nonsense, of course. Without constant temptation, Catlin and other men like him who were naturally hot of temperament would be virtuous and godly.

Also amongst the silent walkers were the traders that lived off the custom the whores brought in – the pork pie sellers, the water sellers, the oystermongers, the whelkmen and the hazelnut women, all with their trademark trays and barrels, stout women mostly with

167

boot faces – often the survivors of the trade from years before who had neither the faces nor the heart to sell their quims any more. After all, if you were not a Madam by the time you were thirty-five then you would simply not be able to find enough trade to live and that was that. Men preferred youth to experience, of course. And an old whore was inevitably poxed.

Catlin decided suddenly that he had better things to do with his time than watch the scum of the city, the congregation of the damned, parade to London Bridge and Upper Ground. He would go to his house and occupy himself reading a book of sermons. One reason was to pass the time. Another reason was to buttress his will against the stealthy encroachment of more sin, triggered by all the lewd young women who had marched so wantonly before him. Well, perhaps they hadn't been obviously wanton, they had all been covered up respectably, but they still had their striped petticoats, they still had their dyed bronze or red hair tumbling under their expensive hats, they were still...

They were still women, creatures of darkness and desire, still Jezebels, Liliths, Eves. Still... still...

In his reading chair with a lit candelabra of wax candles to help the dull and cloudy daylight coming through his windows, Catlin sighed, shifted, tried to focus on the Godly paragraphs. He would have to get him a wife. Hadn't St Paul recommended marriage

168

rather than burning? For all the disadvantages of a wife, there were some advantages.

Or he could carry on sinning the sins of the flesh, since he was damned anyway. At that moment there came a knock at the door.

.

Shakespeare was walking along through the crowds that had stopped to stare at the procession brazenly marching through Cheapside, warned by the beating of Peter's drum. The whores had passed to the north of St Paul's, along Paternoster Row and into the wealthiest street in London. The Cheapside goldsmiths had taken a gloomy view of the matter and their men and often they themselves were outside, busy boarding up their windows. Other shops along the Poultry were shutting early and the apprentices were out, hanging about on the street corners, watching with sticky eyes and sullen expressions, wondering if there'd be any excitement.

Through the swiftly clearing Lombard Street marched the procession, still silent, still with Peter the Hedgehog at their head banging his drum slightly off the beat, snot beading his upper lip, his face defiant. Shakespeare thought better of him for it and felt the ready tears prickle his eyes because of the power of it, the hard-faced anger in every one of these outcasts.

Would there be a riot? Part of him hoped not, another part, steeped in original sin, hoped there would. It was exciting and fascinating and for those who could see... the shapes of what men do, it was like watching a great wild animal. Or perhaps it was like what happened when you led black ants and red ants into battle with each other by the judicious creation of sugar trails. He had spent an entire truanting day from school once, watching just such a war. The birching that followed the day after from the schoolmaster who had known exactly what he had been up to despite his elaborate explanations, had seemed a perfectly fair payment for the drama.

He still kept pace with them as they came down Gracechurch Street and New Fish Street to the Bridge and marched over it where the boy's drumming faded in the distance. Nobody had barred their passage, everyone had got out of their way, the Aldermen had been conspicuous by their absence. What had they done with their time, Shakespeare wondered cynically, since the stews and bawdy houses must have been shut?

He jogged back through the City, determined to catch a few hours in an alehouse somewhere and make a start on his poem. Perhaps he could re-use Pyramus and Thisbe? He couldn't go back to his lodgings until nightfall because his landlady had made it clear that she didn't want him disrupting the chickens with his dangerous writing habits. He had to find somewhere else to live and soon. Please God, let it be Southampton House. Somewhere with no chickens.

An hour later, he watched as Peter came back into the common room of the Cock, made his bow to the landlord and was given a tray and told to go around collecting pots. He had managed to make one cup of aquavitae last a long time, which was an improvement, but he had wasted tuppence worth of paper on doggerel so bad, he thought he might as well keep it for the jig at the end of a play rather than burn it.

No matter how hard he tried, it wouldn't come. The burning in his stomach, the clouds of ideas rushing together in his head to make rainbow coloured pictures and jewelled words flow out of his pen... Nothing. Oh God. Had he lost it? Had he drunk, gambled (sinned?) it away? Surely not. Maybe. He didn't know where the poetry came from in the first place, from the Greek Muse or Elfland, and he had no idea where to look when it stopped.

So he leaned back in his booth and stared at the fire, while watching young Peter scurrying around picking up pots and cups and running to the scullery with them. Once the landlord caught him by the ear and growled into it, "When you've picked 'em up, boy, you go wash 'em, see?" Peter looked shocked and surprised for a second, then wiped his arm across his nose with a determined look and rushed into the scullery. The landlord came by Shakespeare's table.

"Well, at least 'e's willing and none of the buggers bother 'im," he said. "What about plague?"

"He's already had it," Shakespeare said with great confidence.

"Hmf. We'll see."

Luckily, or perhaps unluckily, and before he had got properly into the aquavitae, he saw Enys coming into the commonroom and looking around purposefully before coming over and putting his hat down firmly on Shakespeare's table. Shakespeare quickly put away the appalling doggerel he had wasted his time on, in case Enys should read it.

"Mr Shakespeare," said Enys with a smile, "Would you like to bear me company today? I have to do some work on papers in a case and then I need to question the men on Peter's list and I had rather not do that alone."

"Where will you be working on your papers?" Shakespeare asked.

"Gray's Inn library, as I'm a member. I'm afraid it's a fairly dull place but the work will not take me very long..."

Shakespeare was already on his feet, his hat on his head. "Can you get me in there?"

With a little emollient silver for the Librarian, Shakespeare finally got into Gray's Inn Library, a place he had chafed after for years. It was disappointing to look at, being full of dusty books, scrolls and parchments in a storage system by size that only lawyers could make head or tale of. But still, it was a library, a treasury. While Enys consulted his lawbooks and precedents, Shakespeare wandered happily, screwing up his eyes to read the Latin and Norman French in cramped Secretary hands of the clerks recording cases between long-dead litigants, once full of sound and fury and now turned to mere scratchings on a page, and perhaps a couple of deeds in an archive or a chest somewhere.

There were large glass windows but no fires and candles were utterly forbidden, of course. Even pipe smoking was not allowed because of the risk of fire. This made the room chilly but quite bright and above all it cost nothing to sit there and no aquavitae was available. So, after Enys had finished his legal work, and Shakespeare made copies of Peter the Hedgehog's list, they sallied forth to question the people on it.

After the first one, they retired trembling to a small alehouse for a quick beer to check for broken bones and to try and rescue Shakespeare's beaver hat, which the gentleman's servingmen had trampled. At least the mud had been fairly dry where he landed. Enys had a wrenched shoulder and a bruise on the cheek.

"We should have thought of that," Enys said, coming up for air and putting his half-empty leather jack down.

Shakespeare had his wounded hat in front of him on the table and was brushing it gently and prodding the large dent in the crown. The hair he carefully combed over the sparse top of his head was coming down at the back of his head.

"There was no call for them to throw us out like that," Shakespeare said sulkily.

"Well, there was if you think about it," said Enys, irritatingly judicious. "We were accusing the gentleman of fornicating with a notorious whore and then possibly of killing her in a particularly loathsome way."

"The men wouldn't even let you show the warrant..."

"No, because that means they could say truthfully they hadn't seen it."

"But..."

"At least they didn't beat us up."

"What about my hat?"

"It'll recover. We'll have to come up with something more tactful."

And so was born the man who had been robbed of a particularly fine dagger near Whitefriars and thought he had seen whoever they were talking to thereabouts and was willing to give a reward if they had noticed anything amiss.

"It establishes an alibi," Enys explained to Shakespeare, "If they can say for sure where they were, then they will. If they can't, they'll say they might have seen something or that they didn't see anything."

It was elaborate and time-consuming, but it kept them out of armlocks and ditches.

By the time the sun set they had nearly finished the list of men who knew both French Mary and Kettle Annie and had got some very good alibis and a couple of unconvincing witness statements to a robbery that never happened.

They hadn't been able to find Maliverny Catlin who was the last name on the list, according to Peter the Hedgehog, even though he was supposed to be helping with the work. Enys was looking grave as they sat down to the ordinary at the Cock as usual, which they split between them. Shakespeare was filled with unseemly glee.

"It's obvious," he insisted, practically opening Enys's nose with his eating knife, "The bastard is a Puritan and a whoremonger. He gets the taste for blood and mutilation when he's working for Walsingham and Heneage and that foul creature Topcliffe. Whenever he thinks he can get away with it, he lures a whore he knows into a quiet hidden place and then he..."

"Then he's a better actor than Alleyn and Burbage put together," snapped Enys. "I saw him when he found the body. He was white and he puked. You can't fake going pale."

"Ha!" said Shakespeare, "I'll tell you what you do,

175

you think of something that utterly frightens you and that makes you go pale and then..."

"Don't be ridiculous, he was drunk."

"Or playing drunk."

"It could just as easily have been me," said Enys, "I'm as likely a suspect as Catlin,"

"With respect, Mr Enys," said Shakespeare evilly, "You have many faults, but you are neither a whoremonger nor a Puritan." He let the other thing Enys was not hang in the air between them. To his surprise Enys started to laugh, shaking his... her head.

"What a recommendation. I'm touched by your faith, sir. So how do we get him arrested for it? Without doing the same to me?"

Shakespeare scowled. "It stands to reason, it must be him."

Enys shook his head. "We'll have to hope that if he does it again, which God forbid, we can catch him without an alibi and arrest him before he can do the same to me and then find enough evidence to accuse him."

Shakespeare shook his head. "Better if we catch him at it and kill him in a fair fight."

Enys looked shocked at his venom and Shakespeare coughed. "Or something," he amended. "I hope it is him, it should be, the poxy bastard puritan."

176

.

Maliverny Catlin lifted up the floorboards over the pit and looked about. He had a couple of good candles lit and a small watchlight in a lantern beside him although it was full daylight: the tiny high windows had been blocked off some time in the past or perhaps there had never been any. He had told the landlord he was from the Tunnage and Poundage men, checking for contraband and shown his warrant as proof, which the landlord had luckily been unable to read.

In front of him was a mysterious rectangular pit set into the stone-flagged floor beneath the boards. It was something quite like a grave, a little less than six foot long and about four foot deep, lined with very old coloured tiles that showed pretty designs of stars and flame-shapes. The floor of it tilted down to one end. When he checked that end he found a tightly fitting hatch that lifted up on grooves and moved easily. This then was the priest's escape that had mystified Topcliffe the month before, but you couldn't blame him for not taking the floorboards up. They sounded solid and you had to know where to look.

"This is how you bring in the contraband," Catlin said to the landlord who was standing patiently behind him.

"No sir," said the landlord, his voice a mixture of

177

caution and contempt, "This bit don't belong to me really and while I'll not deny it's been used for storing unsealed stuff before, I've never used it for that. I was thinking of letting it to players until Mrs Merry rented it off of me."

"Oh? Who's she?"

"A respectable lady," said the landlord, "But she's stopped paying the rent now and I don't know where she's gone. Anyway, that little passage is too small for a barrel though you can get through it if you're not too big a man."

"So excellent for Papist priests?"

The landlord shrugged. Catlin looked at the square opening and felt sweat pop on his nose. There was only ever going to be one way of finding out exactly where the passageway came out, which he needed to do if he was to flip a finger at Topcliffe. A pity he hadn't thought to bring that boy with him, but he hadn't.

He sighed, bent and lifted the hatch and propped it with a piece of wood clearly there for the purpose. Then he went down on all fours and crawled into the conduit.

It smelled of damp but was not too dirty. In the light of his little lantern he could see scuff marks all along it and it continued straight ahead for a while, 100 yards at least.

At the other end was another hatch, this one hinged

at the top so you could push it upwards and come out, just above a weed choked round pond in the middle of a courtyard, filled with a family of pigs and a curious goat. Directly behind him was an old wall which overlooked an alley and he didn't fancy challenging the pigs on their own ground. So Maliverny turned, climbed the wall carefully, sat on the top and then dropped down into the alley which was mercifully only tenanted by a beggar. He dusted himself off, smiled threateningly at the beggar and hurried back along the alleyway where he found himself looking at the alehouse again. Perfect.

Back in the commonroom of the alehouse, he gave the landlord back his lantern along with an angel to keep it company, smoothed down his hair and brushed mud off the knees of his cannions. It had been undignified but very well worth it. What a treasure. And what on earth had the place been originally? Surely not a church, despite the peculiar saint's statue and pretty tiles.

The landlord was looking at the gold coin and then at him with his eyebrows raised.

"For your future assistance, Mr Siddons," said Catline, "And your present silence."

The landlord nodded.

Next Catlin caught a boat to Southwark and hurried to the house where builders were still working to replace the fire-damaged roof and destroyed front door of Heneage's property, caused by the mysterious riot in

179

September. He was actually hoping to find Heneage but instead came upon Topcliffe, sitting balefully in a chair with carved wooden arms in the kitchen, his walking stick planted on the floorboards and his fur-trimmed gown up around his ears. As always, although the man was in his late 60s at least, his hair and beard were dyed coal black as if he had been an aging whore. It made him look strangely withered with his face unnaturally at odds with the rest of him. As always, something in Catlin's guts crawled away and tried to escape at the sight of him.

"Hah! Mr Catlin!" boomed the man, "What have you got for me?"

Catlin paused and considered, his lips thinning at the man's disrespect. "I was looking for Mr Heneage," he said.

"He's very busy," said Topcliffe, "Heard anything about the new batch of Jesuits?"

"No sir," said Catlin cautiously.

"What are you doing here then?"

Catlin got control of his innards and forced himself to relax. Above all, with Topcliffe, it was essential to show no fear.

"Perhaps I should talk to Mr Vice Chamberlain Heneage about it."

The walking stick lifted and prodded at Catlin. Topcliffe was in fact extremely healthy for a man his age and had no need of a stick, except to beat people with of course.

"He's not the Vice Chamberlain any more," said Topcliffe with a nasty grin, "Her Majesty said he needed to have a rest and recover his wits after some recent tomfoolery. Her blessed majesty is utterly displeased with him, she told me so herself."

Catlin eyed the man. Topcliffe always spoke like that, as if he and the Queen were kissing cousins, as if she regularly took him into her confidence. Sometimes Topcliffe would claim extraordinary mad things, that she had allowed him to put his hand on her breast or her arse. And yet he seemed to have complete impunity in all he did and was in fact Her Majesty's unofficial torturer. It was hard to know whether there was any truth at all lurking in what he said, given his licence. He had never been given any kind of warrant. Nobody was quite sure who he considered his lord although he would assist any of the Queen's privy counsellors against traitors and Jesuits, doing what they preferred not to have a hand in. In fact he had had the torturing of Robert Southwell, although apparently he hadn't succeeded in getting anything out of the man. Some said all he said was true and he reported directly to the Queen in private.

On balance, Catlin hoped this was a lie as well, but didn't dare assume it was. He bowed shallowly to

Topcliffe.

"I have heard from divers sources," he said delicately, "That Mass is to be said in London again."

Topcliffe's eyes were intent, the focus of a falcon on his prey. Or a snake, perhaps.

"Who's the priest? Gerard? Garnet?"

Catlin shook his head. "I think he's young and newly arrived by a different route than the usual ones." After Mrs Crosby explained it, he had been annoyed to find that Peter the Hedgehog's eye had been good and he had been right about the priest.

"Ah," said Topcliffe, "Where's the Mass?"

"The crypt behind the Bull alehouse," said Catlin. "Where there was a Mass in September and you just missed them because someone tried to move in too fast."

"I still don't know who it was," grunted Topcliffe, "I'll thrash him if I find out."

Catlin waited. Topcliffe reached into his purse and put down a couple of angels. Catlin looked at the paltry sum and smiled.

"I don't need money," he said, "I'd take it if I did, but I don't. What I want from you, Mr Topcliffe, is a promise."

"Oh?"

Catlin explained carefully what it was and Topcliffe roared with laughter. "Done!" he said, took the money back and waited. Catlin told him that the Mass was to be the next day at two of the clock, during the bearbaiting.

"The priest's name?"

"Felix Bellamy," Catlin said casually, not having heard the name before. But Topcliffe clearly had. His face froze. In the instant before it turned to stone, Catlin had glimpsed a look of feral greed, of absolute delight. It made him feel quite cold and he was not one who normally felt sorry for Papists, far from it.

"Excellent," purred Topcliffe, "Now that deserves much better than a simple promise. Let me know, Mr Catlin, if I can do anything at all for you by way of privy petition with the Queen or other good lordship?"

Once again Catlin's skin crawled at the thought. Surely the old man was lying about his influence. "Thank you, sir," he said quietly, "But luckily I am in no need of good lordship at the present. Do you know Felix Bellamy?"

Topcliffe sniggered. "Not yet. But I know his sister. I know her all right."

Catlin bowed and took his leave. He had no need to sit and listen to Topcliffe laughing and gloating over some other poor woman. Catlin had heard the stories.

Suddenly Catlin paused between steps on the threshold, then turned back. Could he be the one who mutilated whores? Was it possible?

"Have you lately come from Her Majesty, sir?" he

183

asked, "Are you returning to court?"

Topcliffe never missed a chance to boast of how close he was with the Queen.

"From her very closet," he said, "I rode from Court only yesterday."

So he was out of London on the night when Kettle Annie died and there would be witnesses as to whether he really was at court. Besides, now he thought of it, Topcliffe might enjoy raping a woman after torturing her – or indeed before – but if he wanted to anatomise one of them, he had no need of back alleys. He had his own private torture chamber at his house and access to the Thames at all times.

Catlin nodded, trying to look impressed, tilted his head politely and left the house. It occurred to him to wonder if Topcliffe realised he was damned as well? Certainly he could take no harm from questioning and torturing evil Papists but what about his dealings with women? Fornication was fornication, no matter who it was with. And if Topcliffe wasn't damned, then nobody was.

Catlin shook his head as he walked back down Upper Ground to find a boat. He had no intention of being at the Bull alehouse for the raid – but he would wait quietly in the yard where the priest's escape came out, with perhaps a helper or two, and take the real prize himself.

·

The commonroom was filling up and Shakespeare's brain was getting nicely fuzzed when a girl he recognised from Bankside came in, her ruff perky and her facepaint nearly as thick as a courtier's. She had a worried look underneath it and she went to the separate table where James Enys was waiting quietly, contemplating his usual pint of mild. Her. It was a her.

Shakespeare unfocussed his eyes and concentrated on eavesdropping as unobtrusively as possible.

"I dunno where Eliza's gone," said the girl, "We follered Kettle Annie all the way to Upper Ground and then we come back and she went off to see someone she knew, she said. She was supposed to be here. Have you seen 'er?"

Eny shook her head. "Is she usually late, Isabel?"

The girl shrugged. "Not usually, she's that frightened of the Devil. 'e's going for the old whores, she said."

"Perhaps. Now are any of your... ah... your other colleagues coming to speak to me?"

Isabel settled herself on the stool which was all her farthingale would allow and eyed the ale-jack hintingly. Enys signalled to the older potboy and got her a pint of what she wanted, double beer.

"I passed the word, but I don't fink they will, they're scared of lawyers anyway."

185

Enys nodded. "I understand that, and also of strange men who want no venery of them but to talk."

Isabel eyed him. "Werl, yes," she said.

"Would it help if I asked my sister, Mrs Portia Morgan, to speak to them on her own? Would it be easier for them to speak to a woman?"

Isabel shrugged again. "Might be, dunno, I'll ask. Would your sister do it, being respectable?"

Enys smiled. "I'm sure she will if I ask her nicely and promise her a new hat."

Isabel giggled a little, looked around the common room again and then stood up restlessly and went and talked to the landlord. She came back still worried.

Shakespeare yawned, sipped some more aquavitae and pulled a small edition of Ovid from his pocket which he leafed through restlessly. His eye rested on Venus and Adonis, a rather pointless tale, he'd always thought. The familiar Latin started parading through his brain as his ears worked as hard as the Thames waterwheels.

Another brazenly dressed woman approached their table. Her taffeta striped false front and her stomacher with a falcon embroidered on it, told of where she normally worked. The landlord was eyeing her cautiously, especially as she was better looking and less-painted than Isabel.

"Mrs Nunn said we could talk to you," said the

186

woman, "I'm Kat from the Falcon,"

Enys courteously half-rose from his... her bench, gestured for her to sit down and crooked his finger at the potboy to bring another pint of double. Then he brought out a notebook and a stick of graphite like the ones Shakespeare carried.

"We're all sad about Kettle Annie and French Mary," said the new girl, "and we're all scared, no matter what Mr Gabriel says about protecting us. 'e can't, it stands to reason, can 'e?"

"Can't he?" asked Enys neutrally.

"Not against the Devil."

Enys put his graphite down sharply enough to break it in the middle. "If it's the Devil truly and not some evil person possessed by him, then there is nothing I can do and no point to your speaking to me," he snapped. "You would be better going to church and praying for God's protection."

Kat and Isabel exchanged glances. "Yers, well, we tried that but the beadsmen wouldn't let us in, would they?"

"Do you truly think it's the Devil and not a wicked human?" Enys asked.

The two girls looked at each other again and shivered. Shakespeare realised that Kat was younger than she seemed.

"I fink it'd be better if it was the Devil," said Isabel

and her lip trembled, "Cos then we wouldn't have to think about it being some man done it, what we might of wapped already, somebody we knew."

Enys nodded while Isabel took a long drink of double beer.

"I agree with you," Enys said unexpectedly, "That is the frightening part of it."

"Or it might be witches," pointed out Kat, "Mrs Nunn says it can't be witches cos they help whores get rid of their babies and her own granny was one and so on, but then I fort maybe it was ghost babies..."

Kat clutched her arms. "Ooorgh, that's horrible," she muttered.

Once again Enys put down his bit of graphite stick, more carefully this time. "Listen to me, goodwives,for what it's worth, I think whoever did it was human, not ghost nor Devil. Ghosts can't touch the living, everyone knows that, and the Devil must make men do his work. A man working for the Devil, certainly, but not the Devil himself."

The two girls considered, then nodded slowly. They weren't convinced but they were being polite.

"Now tell me, has anything like this ever happened before in any other place?" Enys asked, "No matter how far away nor how long ago?"

It has, Shakespeare thought to himself, a little muzzy, it may have happened to Peter the Hedgehog's sister.

Both girls shook their heads. "Not like this, no," Kat said definitely, "Not wiv being cut open and that. Course you do get killed sometimes in this trade, sometimes by a husband or a wife or even a son or sometimes by one of them reformers. There was a vicar a while back, used to do it wiv a Bible."

"What?"

"After 'e'd wapped his whore," said Kat, "e'd hit her on the 'ead from behind wiv a Bible while she was sorting out her petticoats and down she'd go."

Shakespeare coughed to hide a terrible urge to laugh. He wondered who it had been and if the man was still alive.

"Didn't want 'er to tell nobody, o' course," said Isabel, "And 'e always did have a big Bible handy, used to like to read to 'em from the Song of Songs to get 'is yard ready."

Enys's face was ruby red at this and Shakespeare knew his own ears had gone treacherously pink.

"How do you know?"

Isabel looked puzzled but Kat was pleased. "Oh one day a girl turned and saw 'im at it, and realised what was going on, so she hit him. Then her upright man come in, what she'd had waiting just in case, and they toasted the vicar's bollocks with a hot kettle until 'e told 'em all about it and then the upright man killed him for it. Caused no end of trouble cos he was missed tho they

189

put 'is body in the Thames. He was found in the end but by that time it had come out he was a whore-monger and so everyone thought it was suicide."

Shakespeare blinked at the smooth pebbles of Latin before him, well-rounded by his eyes. He suddenly knew exactly who that young whore had been.

So did Enys. "A kettle? Was it Kettle Annie?"

Both whores rolled their eyes at him. "Course it was, a while back, before she got fat and she was still doing a good trade."

"So," said Enys, "Do you think it's another vicar, perhaps, revenging himself?"

The girls looked at each other. "We all fink it's someone wot hates whores but that's all."

"Why would someone hate whores?"

Both girls shrugged. Isabel was peering around the common room again. "Caught a dose off of one of us, maybe? Got robbed one night? Or beaten up by an upright man? Or just some youngster giggled when 'e couldn't get 'is tool to work."

"Or perhaps he hates all women?"

What a ridiculous suggestion, Shakespeare thought. Why would a man hate women? They were fantastic wonderful creatures and you could never ever get enough of them.

Surprisingly the girls considered this. "Maybe," Kat said doubtfully.

"But there's plenty of women easier to do than a whore," said Isabel, "I mean, look at all the women in the Fleet wot undercut us? And some of the wives of London, they go off wiv any fancy man they meet at the theatre."

"Well but they don't walk abroad at night."

Kat and Isabel considered this. "Kettle Annie and French Mary didn't go out at night much, either, they was retired. Kettle Annie had her player's alehouse, even if she didn't make much money and French Mary had to sell hazelnuts cos she couldn't get many customers once she was fat."

"Do any of you have any notion of someone who hated them enough to kill them?" Enys asked.

"We've all been finking about it," said Kat, "All of us, we've been flogging our brains to come up wiv someone. There must be someone."

"Not even Bill Smith, that was Kettle Annie's upright man?"

Both of them giggled. "Nah," said Kat, "'e loved Annie, it was 'er didn't want nuffink to do wiv him after 'e drank 'er savings."

"Where is he now?"

"Dunno. I 'erd he got the plague a month ago, so maybe he's still shut up in ve Bridewell. Poor Annie was ever so upset about it, even though she'd told 'im to go and jump in the Thames before."

Peter came past, industriously gathering pots.

"So nobody else has been killed and anatomised like that?" Enys said again, "Not even a while ago?"

Both girls shrugged and shook their ringlets. "No," said Kat, "We'd've heard."

Shakespeare noticed that Pater paused with his arms full of dirty tankards and jacks, mouth open as if about to say something.

"We'll tell you if we fink of someone," confided Kat to Enys, "And it could be the Devil. A goodwife saw Old Nick near Temple Church too."

Enys's eyes half-closed while Peter ducked his head, sniffled and scurried off to the scullery.

"Who saw it?" asked Enys, making notes.

"Betty Sharples," said Kat, "She saw him, plain as plain, next to the Temple Church, tall as the church wiv cloven hooves and all clouds of brimstone around him too and the heat of hellfire coming from 'im. The fright nearly killed her."

"Oh," said Enys but Shakespeare was interested. Didn't Enys know that Betty Sharples, who had a linen shop at the end of Fleet Street, was Kettle Annie's cousin and they always went to the bear-baiting together.

"Course," Kat allowed, "She could've been delirious cos she come down wiv a flux the day after."

"What day was that?" Enys asked conscientiously, scribbling away.

192

"Ah... the same day you found Kettle Annie's body, probly."

Enys made another entry in his notebook. Suddenly Isabel stood up. "I wish Eliza would come," she said, "She's never normally this late."

Enys frowned. "Did she say she had a customer?"

"She said she had to meet someone..." Isabel trailed off and stared at him, stricken. Then she put her hands to her mouth and started to wail. "Oh no, you don't fink... Oh no, not Eliza..."

Seizing the opportunity, Shakespeare put his book away and came hurrying over with the remains of his aquavitae.

"Good wives," he said, tipping his cap to them, "Mr Enys, I think we should move fast..."

Enys was ahead of him, already on his feet. "Yes, let's try and catch this creature."

The whores clutched each other at the idea.

"We want him red-handed," insisted Shakespeare, "otherwise he'll only deny any bad intent. It's no good finding his handiwork when he's finished. Where would Eliza go – was she meeting a customer? Did she have a regular place?" He glanced at the windows. It was dusk already, helped by a cold grey sky.

Kat and Isabel looked at each other. "Not really, she'd go round the back of the Temple or places like that. There's a little nook there, quite private and a bit of a shelf as well to hitch your bum on."

Shakespeare crooked his finger at Peter. "Bring us a good dark lantern," he ordered, "Not a torch."

The boy stood with his mouth open for a second and then ran for the back of the common room.

Moments later, he was back, with a jerkin hitched over his skinny shoulders and candle already lit inside the lantern. Shakespeare pulled the shutter across.

"Listen," he said to all of them, "Be guided by me. This is in the nature of a hunt by stalking, not par force de chiens nor by ambush."

"And she might be all right and just seeing to a business husband," Isabel pointed out. "Nobody's going to turn down money in these times."

"Precisely," said Shakespeare, "So we should creep up on them quietly and if this is merely trade, leave them alone. God forbid I should play the damned puritan like Catlin to meddle in someone's livelihood." Isabel snickered knowingly at that.

The whores supported at each other as they hurried out of the Cock, the girls going first, arm in arm for safety, despite being from rival factions, then Peter with his lantern and then Enys and Shakespeare.

They took a short cut down the cloisters and wound their way through the narrow alleys that had grown up in the wreckage of the Whitefriars abbey. There was no sign of anyone in the nook, but there was a sound of quiet voices next to the church itself, both women and one of them very drunk.

"I'm hotter'n hell... it'sh all shwimming..."

"Then sit yourself down, my dear," said another woman's voice, "Rest."

"Hot."

"Well undo your collar, cool yourself."

"Gi's a drink."

"I think you've had enough..."

"That's her!" hissed Isabel, "That's bloody Eliza, she's just gone and drunk her takings again. I'll bloody kill her..."

They came around the corner in sight of the round church and there sat the two women in the porch. One stood up in fright at the sight of them.

"Jesu, who are you?" asked the other woman's voice sharply.

Isabel rushed forwards to hug Eliza who was swaying on the bench, hiccupping to herself. "Oh fank God for it, I fort the Devil had got you for sure..."

The other woman's teeth flashed as she smiled. "Ah, you're friends of hers. Good. I found her wandering about here quite distempered and in drink and was afraid the Fleet Street Devil might find her in that state."

Shakespeare suddenly knew who this was – the new orangeado seller who had taken over from Betty. Though there was something odd about the way she

195

spoke.

"Goody Mallow?" he asked.

The woman curtseyed to him. "I'm so pleased her friends are here. I'll go to my house now."

Peter the Hedgehog was blinking and staring at Good Mallow with a scowl on his face as if she were his enemy. He wiped his nose anxiously on his palm, then wiped it on his jerkin.

"Thank you, thank you, Goody," said Isabel, catching the woman's arm, "I'll always buy orangeadoes now, I'm sure you saved her from the Devil cutting her up."

The woman smiled. "I'm sure..."

"I sheen 'im..." slurred Eliza, "I sheen him, wiv hairy legs and eating pork pies too. I sheen him."

She burped and nearly fell off the bench, caught at Isabel and Kat.

"She's hot as fire," said Kat doubtfully, "Feel her forehead. Do you think she's got plague?"

Goody Mallow shook her head. "No, I think it's only the drink she's had. Look after her well, gentles."

She turned and walked sedately up the alleyway, her pattens protecting her figured leather boots from the mud under her woollen kirtle.

Shakespeare had a sudden awful thought and ran after her. "Goody!" he called, "Wait! Aren't you afraid of meeting the Fleet Street Devil yourself?"

Goody Mallow paused, then turned.

196

"No goodman, I am not," she said.

"Why not?"

"Because the Devil comes only for his own," she answered.

"And have you too seen this Devil?" Enys asked, coming up more slowly.

"No sir," said Goody Mallow, "Though I am sure he goes about guised as a man."

"What if he is in fact only a man?"

Goody Mallow shrugged.

"And forgive me, Goody," added Enys, "How will he know that you are not a whore?"

Goody Mallow drew herself up haughtily. "I wear no striped petticoat," she said, "I am safe."

"Perhaps he only looks for women who are out late?"

Goody Mallow lifted her shoulder again and smiled wryly. "Then I shall be protected by my face which has never been my fortune," she said which was undeniably true as she was square-jawed and boot-faced, "And I am too old for him."

She curtseyed again and carried on up the alley, then turned right onto Fleet Street and speeded up, walking so fast she was waddling a little. Perhaps she wasn't as certain about the Devil as she pretended.

Shakespeare and Enys went back to Kat, Isabel and Eliza where Eliza had opened her bodice, unhooked

197

her stomacher and flapped herself with it. Her elbow knocked over a small flagon beside her on the bench and it made an oily mark on the wood.

Isabel scooped it up and sniffed suspiciously. "What's this? Hm, it smells like nit-killer," she said, thriftily stoppered it and put it in her petticoat pocket, then lifted Eliza onto her feet. Eliza was singing something very lewd.

"We'll get her home," said Isabel resigned, "Thanks gentles for your help. We didn't catch 'im but at least she's all right."

"We'll come with you a little," said Enys gallantly, "Just to be sure there's no devil running about."

Down the many alleys and back into Alsatia they went, to the little room that had been used by a whore for as long as Shakespeare had been in London – unmistakeable for there was a bit of salvaged stained glass window doing its duty in a very different place, a fine head of the crucified Christ. The door banged as Isabel and Kat half-carried half-dragged the singing Eliza into the room.

Enys glanced at the picture and smiled a secret smile.

"Come this way," he... she said to Shakespeare, then slipped down another steep alley that went to Temple steps then sideways and down again. She hoisted herself up on a stone and pointed at the top of the wall that had plants growing out of it. Most of them were in their withered winter state, brown and sad, although there was some aromatic evergreen there from the smell. Enys looked around furtively in the moonlight and pulled off a couple of twigs, sniffed hard. There was a small gap, filled with trampled greenery, and then another wall, a yard thick, another remnant of the monastery. On the other side of the second old wall, a door slammed in the darkness.

"Rosemary and thyme," said Shakespeare, "Sovereign against the plague,"

"Good against fleas too," said Enys, split them and gave some to him. Then she frowned at the other plants. "I thought this might be someone's little garden," she said, "But there are weeds here as well."

Shakespeare nodded, not much interested although Enys seemed pleased. "I got soapwort from here a week ago, very useful." She slid her posy inside her doublet front.

Shakespeare smiled back and thought to his own surprise about kissing her, because in the dusklight her scarring didn't show and opening her doublet casually like that, as if she were a man, had given him the scent of her undeniably being a woman, that sweet spiciness. Her arse was well-shaped and nicely close to his face as she tiptoed on the stone, her tits under her shirt flattened but there for the observant, her legs... Long legs were good too, she was as tall as he was which some men might find offensive. Not him though. And there they were, those secret female legs in canions and hose, not yards of brocade and linen, nonchalantly standing on a stone right next to him and...

Shakespeare shut his eyes, frowned and breathed deep. No. Under no circumstances. Never again. There was about women a strange magic which sucked your Muse away from you... then gave it back, admittedly, strangely shaped, as he had found with Mistress Emilia and his rapidly growing collection of sonnets. But he had no time for such complications, he needed to write a poem for the Earl of Southampton.

"Come on," said Enys, with an impish smile, only a little twisted by the pockmark next to her mouth, "Let's go down and look at the Thames from Temple Steps."

She jumped down like a boy and did up her doublet again, then strode ahead of him. Shakespeare's body was paying no attention at all to his practical and virtuous thoughts and he had to limp awkwardly for a moment before he could follow her. God damn it.

·

At dawn next morning, Maliverny Catlin found Shakespeare and Enys peacefully eating breakfast at the Cock as usual. He scowled at them, disliking the idea that James Enys was getting on so well with the player.

200

"Have you not heard yet?" he sneered, "There's been another one found."

Both of them stared blankly at him for a moment, then Enys jumped up, quite pale.

"What...?"

"But we..." stuttered Shakespeare.

"Where and who was it?" Enys asked.

"Hard by Blackfriars," sniffed Catlin, "Mr Recorder Fleetwood sent me out to find you."

Both gulped their mild ale and followed him out.

The woman's body lay crumpled awkwardly on its side in the pungent lee of a respectable merchant's jakes, close to the remains of the London City wall. The house itself had clearly been built with stones from the old Blackfriars priory and the Wall itself and was a handsome building with shining diamond panes of glass. Henry Bailey, the merchant householder, was at that moment being questioned very carefully by Fleetwood.

Enys went into the yard and touched the body – it was an old woman, one of the beggars who eked out a living selling stolen linen and scavenged firewood, a bony old woman with a pinched face. She was fully-clothed this time, her white hair matted with dirt and heaving with lice and fleas abandoning ship as if she were a hedgehog.

A ragged gash opened her belly and the guts were

spilled all over the cobbles. From the house came the sound of hysterics as the merchant's wife reacted to the problem.

"Hm," said Enys, stroking his chin, "Odd."

Shakespeare pulled his eyes away from the broken old woman. He'd never get down to his poem today, he would have to spend it drowning this picture.

"Why?" he croaked.

Enys' expression was cold. "Her face isn't as peaceful as the others and this isn't at all tidy."

Shakespeare could think of nothing to say to that because although it was true, that thought too made him feel sick.

"So the Devil was abroad again last night," he said in a low voice, "Only..." He stopped. They had talked about the killing of "another one" and here she was. It made his blood run cold. Had the killer been listening? Or the Devil?

Enys said nothing but shook his head, headed for the house. Fleetwood was questioning the merchant in his own parlour with its cup-board laden with shining plate and the walls lined with costly Flemish tapestries of the Queen of Sheba. Bailey was a pouchy-faced man whose plump and pregnant wife wept into her satin apron behind him.

"You didn't know the woman?"

"No sir," said Mr Bailey, drawing himself up.

Enys cocked her head slightly. Shakespeare had seen it too – Mrs Bailey had twitched her swollen eyes and looked down.

"She never served you nor you never bought firewood nor linen from her?" Fleetwood's voice was polite but sceptical.

"Of course not," snorted Mr Bailey, "I would not allow some filthy old beggarwoman anywhere near my property."

"With all due respect, sir," said Fleetwood in the lawyer's tone which meant that respect was neither due nor offered, "How then did she come to die in your yard?"

Bailey puffed up his chest. "I have no idea, sir. Perhaps she climbed over where the Wall is tumbled down – I have been intending to have it rebuilt."

"Then she must have been killed in your yard. Did you hear...?"

"We heard nothing last night," insisted the merchant. "Nor any other time. I have never seen her and nor has my wife. Will this take much more time, I am expected at the Exchange?"

Fleetwood's craggy face drew down in a scowl but the merchant was wearing a doublet of magnificent murrey-trimmed black silk Lucca velvet and could clearly afford to be rude.

"Hm," said Enys again, quietly, his eyes narrowing

as Fleetwood bowed, Bailey bowed back, Mrs Bailey curtseyed shakily and Fleetwood turned to take his leave.

Beckoned by Fleetwood, they followed him to his house on the other side of the City, leaving Catlin to organise the removal of the old woman's body. For the whole walk of about half an hour, Fleetwood said nothing. Once at Seething Lane, Fleetwood sat down at once at his desk and began writing a report. He was writing it directly in a numerical cipher which Shakespeare thought was impressive and also interesting. Who was the report for? He squinted at it in case he could read it, but he couldn't.

"I'll call Bailey for the inquest," said Fleetwood to them, dipping his pen, "At least it wasn't another whore though I've no idea how I'll find out who she was. Did either of you know her?"

Shakespeare shook his head. It was odd that it wasn't a whore, but perhaps this Devil dressed as a man only preyed on women – and older women at that. Two matrons so far and now one crone. Ah but there was also possibly one kinchin mort if Peter's sister really had been killed by the same devil.

They reported on what they had been doing the day before and Enys handed over the amended lists with alibis and statements noted. Fleetwood grinned when Shakespeare described how they had been treated at the first place they asked.

204

"Ah yes," was all he said, "I can see that would be delicate."

"There's one name on the list we were not able to question because we couldn't find him," said Enys unhappily. Fleetwood's eyebrows went up.

"Oh?" he said. Enys pointed to Catlin's name in silence. The silence continued. "Where did you look?" asked Fleetwood.

Shakespeare shrugged. "His usual alehouses, his own house."

"Did you ask him where he was yesterday?"

"Yes," Enys said. "He told me to mind my own business."

"Did you try the Falcon?"

Enys looked down when Shakespeare glanced at him. "Er... no," said Enys. "Should we?"

"Next time," said Fleetwood drily. "He has an account."

It was Peter who came running up to them when they came back into the Cock to buy aquavitae to scrub away the memory. "I 'erd there was anovver one..." he stuttered, "Was it..."

"Only a poor old beggarwoman," said Enys.

Peter puffed out a big sigh of relief. "Fank God for it," he said fervently.

"Why?" rapped out Enys, "Do you think that because she was only an old beggar woman, it doesn't matter that she was murdered?"

As Shakespeare had been thinking precisely that, he could sympathise with Peter who looked bewildered. The boy's mouth was open with puzzlement.

"But..." he said.

"A murder is a murder, whether it's done to a young girl, a whore, a fine lady or a miserable crone," said Enys, "Isn't it?"

Peter's face suddenly twisted, he began to snortle and then ran away into the kitchen, wiping his eyes with his arm. Enys frowned in puzzlement.

"That boy has a tale to tell," Shakespeare told him, "I think his sister may have been the first to be killed and cut up a couple of weeks ago, at least that's what I gathered from him. Trouble is, he won't tell me any more."

"How old was the girl?" Enys asked.

Shakespeare shrugged. "I've no idea, older than him, maybe ten or eleven years."

Enys looked thoughtful, then he shifted uneasily on the bench. "I must go, I'm expected in court," he said. "Can you find out more from the boy?"

Shakespeare shook his head. He had an appointment with a lot of aquavitae. "He's frightened of me and of the memory," he said, "Won't tell me any more."

.

Catlin was sitting in his preferred Fleet Street alehouse, the Fox and Hounds which had better beer and a friendlier welcome than the Cock. He was working at his own various lists of names, customers of French Mary and Kettle Annie as supplied by the terrified and snortling Peter, currently potboy at the Cock. Maliverny had paid him a couple of pennies to stand there and recite the names, since he assumed the boy couldn't write. Some of his other informants had come up with lists as well, well-peppered with Catholic names either from habit or because the Papists were indeed the whoremongers everyone said they were. It stood to reason: because of their fiendish travesty of confession to a priest and indulgences, they could have no fear of eternal damnation and could wipe their sins out any time they chose. Hence they were whoremongers.

It was disgusting and unfair, Catlin thought, before he suppressed the thought. At least all Catholics would end in hell anyway, no matter what they thought, that was some comfort.

The mocking little voice inside him that never left him in peace for long said, and you'll meet them there, eh, Maliverny? Do you think they'll be pleased to see you?

Catlin shuddered and dipped his pen. He started going through all his lists, making one further list that conjoined them where they touched, featuring the names

207

that appeared on all of them. He had to fight the instinct to simply pick on one man who was the least popular and weakest in influence, ideally with the maximum amount of property. Unlike with Papist-hunting, he had to find the man who was actually committing the crimes if at all possible, so he could be stopped from doing them any more. If Catlin accused the wrong one and he was arrested, tried and hanged, presumably the crimes wouldn't stop and then Catlin would be in trouble with Fleetwood. The bastard might even demand his money back, assuming he paid out at all.

Mind you, some of them would be ripe for a little squeezing, he thought, before his appointment with the Papists later in the day. There was one wealthy merchant and one prominent barrister on the final list who would probably be very happy to pay for Catlin's silence. A little cheered, Catlin took his papers and set off to collect Young Daniel his usual henchman, ready to talk to the nearest one, Mr Craddock of all people.

.

James Enys paced out of Westminster Hall, feeling exhausted, exhilarated and as if her boots were a couple of inches off the cobbles. She had appeared in front of Mr Justice Whitehead again and had thoroughly enjoyed a hammer and tongs argument with her opponent, a

well-known older barrister called Paul Chapel, which
the learned Judge had adjudicated with great relish
and much dry humour. The clients on both sides were
locked in a decade long dispute over an orchard that
had once been church property and was now full of
squatters as a no-man's-land while the litigation dragged
on. They had watched in awe, happy to be getting full
value for money.

They had begun at ten of the clock and it was now
afternoon: there had been shouting, there had been
waving of pleadings, there had been quoting of statutes
– several of them fictitious, as the Judge had pointed
out – and a wonderful fowl's parliament of Norman
French, Latin, English and some farmyard cursing from
Chapel when a sweeping gesture by him had knocked
a jug of ale over his papers. The judge had genially
offered to lock him up for contempt of court until he
could dry them out again.

At the end of it all the Judge had found for Enys's
clients, comprehensively, fully and, short of busy letters
to the Privy Council, finally. Enys's clients had been
delighted, had put a very heavy purse into the discreet
bung hanging at the back of Enys's robe and shaken
her hand. Enys had warned them about the looming
likelihood of letters to the Privy Council or even a
petition direct to the Queen, if the opponents had the
money to bribe a few courtiers. Enys had to explain she

had no control over this possibility as her one court contact was not available at the moment. The matriarch who had been running the litigation, hurried off to marshall her cousins at court in defence.

Paul Chapel came out and raised his sandy eyebrows at Enys. Enys bowed slightly to him, he bowed back and they smiled their satisfaction at each other.

"God, my throat's hoarse," commented Chapel unsubtly.

"Double or double-double?" Enys asked, knowing that as the winner it was up to her to buy the beer.

A few moments later they were in the small alehouse hard by Westminster Hall, with its Tudor Rose sign splashed over a carved pig.

"God, that's better," said Chapel coming up for air after demolishing his pint of double in one. Enys sipped, knowing that she had far less capacity for booze, even after a couple of years' practice at Gray's Inn while studying for the Bar. "That was fun, eh, Enys?"

Enys laughed. It had indeed been fun – much more fun than the sword-schooling which she did conscientiously because she had to. In court she could fight with words which were far easier weapons for her to wield than a long bar of steel whose edge still frightened her.

"It was a pleasure to dispute with you, brother," she said to Chapel who snorted and poured himself another pint from the gallon-jack on the table.

"Bloody idiots, both lots of them," he said, "Why didn't they just divide the plot in half and get on with it ten years ago, instead of spending double the orchard's worth on the two of us and a solicitor as well?"

Enys raised her eyebrows. "I've very glad they didn't," she said mildly, "Thanks to today I might be able to afford a woman to attend my sister at last."

Chapel grunted. "Obviously. And I'm worth considerably more than any orchard but still... It never ceases to amaze me how much clients will spend rather than simply agree together. Thank God." Enys toasted the sentiment.

"Are you free next week?" Chapel asked eventually. "I have a very juicy little suit in the Court of Requests over a wardship and I'm unable to take it, alas."

Enys's heart thudded with delight. A much more senior barrister passing a case on was praise indeed – whatever would Chapel say if he knew it was to a woman? Best not to think about that. She asked about the technicalities and decided that she could do it with some hurried reading work on the law on wardships in Gray's library and possibly Lincoln's Inn, if she could bribe the man who guarded the books.

"I'll have my clerk come over with the papers tomorrow," said Chapel, "Or I might bring 'em myself and call in on old Craddock, see how he is."

211

"Is he recovered at all?" asked Enys tactfully, "I saw him in his... er... his fit the other day."

"Woke up in the morning, so I heard," said Chapel, his face avid with gossip, "asked why everybody was looking askance at him and called for his breakfast and beer the same as ever. Nor could he remember a damned thing about the day before, or so he said, nothing at all about disputing with the Devil."

"Lord above," said Enys, puzzled, "I... ah... my sister spoke to him that morning in Fleet Street before he took his fit, and he seemed well enough."

"Mrs Craddock said he was feverish all night, then seemed well enough for breakfast and went out. He returned with the fever again and after that it was all a ranting and a raving at the Devil until the apothecary managed to knock him out with laudenum."

"My sister said she saw him try to climb out the window to fistfight with the Devil,"

"Sounds like Craddock," said Chapel, finishing his beer, "I remember when we were at Inner Temple together, he was always first into the fray when the apprentices shouted "clubs". Took on one of the biggest roaring boys in Smithfield once and beat him soundly. It's a pity..."

"What is? The fit of madness?"

"Yes, and that his wife is seemingly barren. All both of them want is a son but..." Chapel shook his head.

"His old witch of a mother in law blames him for it, of course."

Enys shrugged, though she knew it was the woman who generally got the blame.

"I have to make one proviso in taking your case to the Court of Requests," she said to Chapel as they called for the Ordinary, "I'm presently retained in... an unusual matter by Mr Recorder Fleetwood..."

Taking pity on Chapel's naked curiosity, she explained the situation and Chapel listened with his head professionally cocked, stroking his court goatee beard. At the end, he pursed his lips.

"Jesu, brother, rather you than me," he said, "It sounds bloody impossible. Though keeping Mr Recorder sweet will do you no harm at all as far as a Junior Readership is concerned – all the Benchers think the sun shines out of his arse."

Enys smiled faintly. "I hadn't thought of that, more that I had no fancy to decorate a rope for..."

" A crime so snivelling and pathetic as the killing of a couple of whores and a crone!" said Chapel with a shouted laugh, "If you must hang, at least let it be for a duel or high treason or piracy...

Enys laughed too, part-shocked part-encouraged. It was something she thoroughly enjoyed about the ridiculous masquerade she had somehow found herself in: talking with men as a man, the world was utterly different. At least she was getting used to the sense of humour. A woman would have been all shocked sympathy at her predicament; but here was Chapel who found it funny because it was too trivial for the danger. It was strangely comforting in its roughness. Not that there was ever anything trivial about a murder, even of two whores or a crone, no matter how much she liked Chapel. But still...

"I think Fleetwood's main worry is how to stop the whores from rioting."

Chapel was fuelling up with steak and kidney pudding, that autumn constant when every inn had suet and offal in their larders after killing their beeves to salt down for the winter. He grunted, waved his eating knife while he swallowed a lump.

"Much more likely to stop them going on strike."

"That too," laughed Enys.

"It's not lawyer's work, though, is it, brother? It's more in the nature of a pursuivant's job."

Enys made a rueful face. "I know. Maliverny Catlin is my partner by order of Mr Fleetwood."

"Christ's guts," rumbled Chapel, "Watch him, Enys, he's a complete bastard."

"I know."

"Clever as well so he might well solve the case and steal all the credit."

Enys shrugged. "Good."

214

"Or find a way to blame you."

Enys stared into space. "I have wondered whether he... might be the murderer."

Chapel's eyebrows went up. He leaned back a little. "Go on?" he said.

"Imprimis, when we found Kettle Annie's body, she was still warm though it was a frosty night – and he was the one who actually found her."

"Ah."

"But he puked afterwards. Though that could have been the booze, he reeked of it."

"Hm. Was he bloody?"

"No. I looked at his hands. But he could have washed and changed his shirt."

"Did he look at your hands?"

Enys had to think carefully. "Yes, perhaps he did."

"Probably not then, if you think about it. If he knows who did it, why would he need to check if it was you?"

"Ah."

"Though he could have been faking, knowing you might suspect him if he didn't."

Enys sighed.

"What about the other time? The one at the part-built playhouse?"

"I don't know where he was or what he was doing that week. Obviously he could have done it, she was in

215

a building site that was boarded up and hidden by from sight. He could have stripped naked, done his work, washed and clothed himself and nobody any the wiser."

"Is he a whoremonger?"

Enys paused. "I have no reason whatever to say it," she said carefully, "But I'm certain he is. Mr Recorder Fleetwood says he has an account at the Falcon. He's a Puritan, a pursuivant, rich on Papist spoils, still a bachelor despite all the mothers of London could do to catch him, and the way he looks at whores..."

"We all look at whores," said Chapel with a grin, spearing a piece of steak with his knife.

"Ay, you especially, Chapel. But it's the way he does it..."

"Stripping off their pretty striped petticoats? Thinking of sucking their pretty pink boobies..."

Enys laughed at Chapel's dreamy expression. "No, not like you. It's as if he hates them and craves them at the same time... "

"Well, nobody likes to pay for..."

"No, really hates them... like... like a dog with rabies trying to drink..."

"Hm," Chapel was now eating pot-herbs at high speed –he seemed to do everything at the gallop. "Yes, but Catlin isn't a big man, is he? Wiry and ill-looking but not even so tall as you, I think?"

"No, an inch or two shorter."

216

"Now I am not under any circumstances prepared to explain how or why I happen to know, you understand, but Kettle Annie is a... was a very well-built and powerful woman with a particularly fine pair of..."

"Boobies?"

"Shame on you, Enys," grinned Chapel triumphantly, "No, I meant muscular arms. Yet from what you said, by the tale of her body, he got her into the alley and stripped her as well, then cut her up with no other damage to himself. There was no primary stab or throttling, was there?"

Enys had to consult the livid picture in his memory. He shook his head. There hadn't been either of those things, but something was niggling him about something else.

"So how did he manage it?" asked Chapel through some carrots, "Kettle Annie is the last woman on earth to lie down for that sort of thing. As it were."

Enys frowned. "You're right. She wouldn't be an easy kill. And nor was French Mary."

"So you first must ask, not what was done and then by whom. You must first ask, how was it done?" Chapel was waving his eating knife again. "You know, like Whiteacre and Greenacre in a moot. Not, who took illegal possession of the acre of commonland, but how exactly was it done – by force of arms? By illegal enclosure? By conspiracy? By false deeds? Or by

217

unlawful purchase?"

"Ay," said Enys slowly.

"How, then why, then who, if necessary, which it probably is in this case."

"You're right, brother, the how is very important... I don't see Maliverny Catlin overpowering either of those women, though the most recent body..."

The thought came to Enys in a flash, like unravelling a particularly darkly-drafted pleading to find it was actually in error. In front of her eyes she saw vivid pictures as if made by the most expert court limner in the world. Kettle Annie. French Mary, by Shakespeare's description. The scrawny old woman tumbled behind Bailey's house of easement, her belly jagged open and the innards spilled... It was utterly different. As cruel and abhorrent, but different.

Enys felt her heart thud and the excellent dinner turned to stone in her belly.

"Jesu," she whispered, "Christ Almighty."

"What's wrong Enys, you look as if you had seen a ghost?"

"In a way, yes. You've helped me remember something very important."

Enys was on his feet, clapping his hat on his head, fumbling in his newly fattened purse for the extra sixpence to pay for the meal on top of the eight pence for the gallon of good ale. Chapel waved his money away and grinned.

"Mine," he said, "I'll bring the papers myself, I'll need to hear the rest of this tale. Make sure you don't get yourself hanged, or at least not before you can tell me about it."

Enys was in such a hurry to get down to the river, she nearly tripped over the nuisance of a sword which she hadn't done for several days. Having saved the pennies for food, she spent two of them on a boat to go downriver quickly to the Bridge and thence ran, almost sprinted to Fleetwood's house. It could indeed have been Catlin, but more importantly, it might not actually have been the whorekiller who killed the old beggarwoman. It could be some... other twisted murderer copying what someone else was doing. Jesu. Were there two of them in London? Surely not. Yet... The things were different.

Fleetwood was not there but Enys found out where was the crone's body from Armitage, the secretary. She hurried to the nearby crypt and there she found Peter Cheke viewing the body as well. They bowed to each other, Enys reminded in the nick of time by the weight of her sword on her hip not to curtsey.

"I thought so," Cheke said, as if they were continuing a conversation, "Look here. She has been strangled."

It was true. The wrinkled scrawny old neck was printed with blue fingermarks and tongue slightly stuck

219

out.

"Her face isn't blue," Enys protested.

"But she's old. The mere terror of being strangled may have stopped the movement of her humours by itself."

The old woman's lips were drawn back in a snarl showing the brown stumps of her teeth. The smell from her was already bad though the undertaker had put back the innards. Though that was all wrong as well.

"I think it was not the whorekiller," said Enys.

"She was anatomised though."

"Not really, not carefully. The corpse I saw and the one I had described to me, was done out so neatly, like a pattern, with the guts circled round and the... ah... womb laid upon her legs."

Cheke looked taken aback.

"You saw her womb?"

Enys nodded. "Fleetwood told me what it was, I didn't know."

Cheke nodded. "It is supposedly illegal to anatomise men or women although they do it at Oxford and Cambridge," he said, "I myself have... er... never seen a woman's inward organs of generation. Did you see any homunculus within?"

"What?"

"Any babe?"

"What? No, of course not, Kettle Annie was not

pregnant. Anyway, it wasn't opened. It was only the size of a small pear made of flesh."

Cheke nodded, his face hungry. "Could you tell me what humour it was mainly composed of?"

"I would say the sanguine humour, since it was red. But that isn't my point, Mr Cheke. It's that all was tidy with Kettle Annie, a tidy cut, the internal organs tidily arrayed. Shakespeare told me the same of French Mary. But this one was done at hazard."

Cheke rubbed his top lip. He was still cadaverous but always had been as far as Enys could recall and had clean bandages at his neck. His normal paper pallor was gone a little and he had some colour in his cheeks.

Enys gestured at the ragged slash half-hidden by the undertaker's bandages. "And that mess there... Look how ugly it is, how jagged. Surely this is not by the same hand?"

"Yet surely William of Occam's philosophical razor forbids us to have more than one whorekiller that cuts up his victims in London at one time. Could it have been the same man but in a hurry?"

"It could, I suppose. But why?"

"Afraid of discovery, surely? Given it was in a wealthy man's yard and a servant could have come or let out the dogs?"

"Why do it there at all then?"

Cheke shrugged, then sighed. His face was very sad,

looking at the frail remnants.

"Did you know her?" Enys finally thought to ask, surprised at her own insensitivity. Jesu, was she turning into a boorish man in her head as well?

Cheke nodded. "Her name was Goodwife Barbara Harbridge, a creature that never did anyone any harm, so far as I know, although some called her a witch. I knew it was her when I heard the Crier give her description. She went to St Bride's church every Sunday, she lived in the Blackfriars until my Lord Chamberlain evicted all the squatters there and afterwards she lived with a family near the Cockpit and spun and knitted for her living." He sighed. "It was hard for her to get for she had severe arthritis. And so she would gather herbs for me for physic – very accurate she was and careful to pick the correct ones and at the right phases of the moon."

"Does it really matter what the moon is doing?"

"As above, so below, is the principle. For causing an illness to reduce, the herb must be picked at the wane, to build up strength it must be picked on a waxing moon."

"I know that," Enys said impatiently, "But I have always wondered if it really does matter?"

Cheke smiled sadly. "I know so little, Mr Enys, I really can't say. Perhaps it does. Anyway, what harm does it do?"

"How did she come to know about herbs?"

"So do many women of her age and er... origins.

Sometimes she did a little midwifery which was once her trade until her hips got too bad for her to bend down to the birthing stool." Enys nodded. "Alas for it, I should have listened to her..."

"Why?"

"Goody Harbridge was very troubled these last few months. She wouldn't tell me why, though I think it may have been connected with a little herb garden she found and wondered about."

Enys frowned. "There are places like that all over London, little waste gardens where weeds grow..."

"No, she knew it because of the combination of plants there, although it had been well-hidden and deliberately planted to look as if it were wild. She seemed to feel that some of the plants should not have been there, she even said she would grub it up as it was a witch's garden."

"Where was it?"

"In Alsatia, she said, in a wall near the Whitefriars, new planted this last spring."

Enys felt her face paling as a cold wind blew along her backbone. She hoped Cheke wouldn't notice. "Oh?" she managed.

"I asked her if she had found the gardener yet last week, joking, and she frowned and said she hadn't, but I think she was lying. What if she found the witch after all?"

223

"How do you know she was lying?"

"She was an old woman, Mr Enys, deaf and a little wandering, she often talked to herself without realising what she was doing. She was muttering about chickens and the witch's garden, but when I asked her she said she had forgotten."

Enys relaxed slightly. There had been no chickens nor traces of them in the little patch of plants she knew of.

"Do you think it was the witch that killed her not the..."

"The witch or the witch's familiar or the Devil or the whorekiller or indeed all three in the one – it stands to reason there must be a connection between the witch and the Devil, if there is a witch at all," said Cheke, frowning with puzzlement. "I would give a good deal to know what kind of frenzy fills him so he cuts them up? What for? Is he looking for something in their guts? Perhaps some kind of foul prophesying as the Romans did?"

Enys shuddered and changed the subject. "Which family did Goody Harebridge live with?"

"The Worthings at the sign of the little white boar, next to the Cockpits. Will you go and talk with them?"

"I might if I can, but I'm overpressed with legal work at the moment, I may ask my sister if she will do it."

224

"Her mask answers well, I think. And she may get answers from people who are afraid to speak to you," said Cheke, "Do you think Mrs Morgan will eventually be able to leave the mask off?"

Enys felt her stomach swoop. For a moment there she had actually believed that she did have a sister she could ask to do things like that. She flushed at how close she had come to giving herself away. Mind you, there was something in what Cheke said...

"I don't know, Mr Cheke, she has a megrim today as she often does but I will ask her," she said, "I'm... er... I'm in hopes of finding a woman to attend her as well."

That was becoming a necessity. What if somebody questioned why Mrs Morgan and Mr Enys were never seen together when she obviously needed an escort? Mr Cheke nodded and bowed.

"I think that would help as well," he said, "With a woman to accompany her, she need not feel lonely, a condition that always irritates the melancholic humour. Please call for me to attend her at any time she should need me," he added as Enys left him.

.

Catlin was heartily sick of the whole damned business, but had to continue. He was having to outface the same tedious sequence of outraged and suspicious denials and flanneling. He had hired a serving man he had used occasionally before, a large silent creature who would do exactly what he was told. On the couple of occasions when an outraged suspect had shouted for his own men, Young Daniel simply moved up behind Catlin and coughed. He was large enough that a wealthy householder considered the damage likely to be caused by a fight as probably not worth the satisfaction.

Occasionally Catlin thought they might be telling the truth and marked the name with a question mark, but normally he assumed lies and was rarely mistaken. Eventually they would tell him what he asked, but none of it had been really helpful. Most of French Mary's clients had long stopped visiting her for venery and most of Kettle Annie's clients had witnesses as to where they were on the important days, including the night before. None of them had any traces of blood on them or their shirts nor anywhere about the house.

There were only a couple left on his list. He knocked at the door of William Craddock, a smart house overlooking Fleet Street, with a stone frontage and carvings stolen from the old Whitefriars abbey fixed over the door. Catlin eyed them sourly, a couple of female Papist saints done in a fusty ugly old style, one holding a cartwheel and the other a girl wearing a beard, of all things.

A scared looking child with a harelip opened the

door and let him in without a word. She showed him into a hall that had a very magnificent but overlarge mantelpiece over the fireplace and black and white tiles on the floor. The child scuttled away to fetch the mistress and eventually a square-faced middle-aged woman in a good murrey gown covered with a linen apron appeared, wiping her hands on a cloth.

"Yes?" she said in an extremely unwelcoming tone of voice, eyeing Catlin up and down.

"Mistress Craddock, I would like to speak to Mr Craddock?"

"I am Mrs Ashley. My son in law is busy at his paperwork and the lady of the house, my daughter is unwell."

Catlin gave the tiniest inclination of his head and showed her his warrant. Behind him Young Daniel stood, silent and massive in his leather jerkin and statute cap. Young Daniel was one of the few lads Catlin had ever met who wore his statute cap completely straight on his head. It gave him an oddly determined air. Mrs Ashley eyed him and then the warrant, her lips moved as she read the words, which surprised him. Most women of her age could not read. "I'll wait," he said.

Her shoulders shifted in an irritated sigh. "My apologies, Mr Catlin," she said, "I have been at salting down our pork for the winter – the butcher delivered the side yesterday. I will finish as quickly as I can so I can keep you company. Mary! Fetch Mr Catlin some ale to drink..."

The little creature in her blue kirtle scurried off to the kitchen again, followed in a more stately fashion by Craddock's mother-in-law, leaving Catlin alone so he could be sure he was unwelcome.

The hall also had some bright honey-coloured oak panelling for warmth and light and an expensive Flanders tapestry showing the tale of Solomon's judgement of the two women disputing the dead baby. Everything was shining and clean with beeswax. As Catlin stood waiting a slender girl came slowly down the stairs, carefully polishing the bannister and the post at the end. She said nothing to Catlin and didn't even look at him, she seemed to be counting intently under her breath or possibly praying. She was wearing a fine wool kirtle of a rose colour that suited her fair complexion and a brocade false front to her petticoat so she looked a little overdressed for a lady's companion. Perhaps a sister to Mrs Craddock?

"Leave it alone, will you, Phyllida, for God's sake?" said Mrs Ashley's voice, an odd combination of weariness, impatience and something else... Concern perhaps? Sorrow? Catlin turned to look. "Go and rest."

The girl sighed and turned to the matriarch. "Now I have to do it again," she said in a fragile toneless voice, "from the start."

Mrs Ashley rolled her eyes. "Why? You'll only wear it away."

The girl shrugged as she went slowly up the stairs again. "It's worth it if I kindle," she muttered.

Mrs Ashley sighed heavily and watched the girl trailing her way from step to step. She had taken her apron off, he saw. Then she scowled at Catlin as if he had caught them in the act of doing something illegal or embarrassing. Young Daniel was standing by the fireplace, staring into space as usual.

"Come Mr Catlin, what must you think of us?" she said in a false high voice and led him into the parlour where there was a fine oak table with benches and two large chairs, a large cup-board displaying immaculately bright silver plate. "My daughter Phillida Craddock is not well as you see, she... Ah... Have some wine."

She poured more wine into his Venetian glass goblet and he drank, impressed at the quality of the wine. Catlin felt awkward. In fact he wasn't really used to being invited into the house of a suspect. Usually he went in behind a boot and a battering ram.

"That girl is Mrs Craddock?" Catlin asked.

Mrs Ashley's face was frosty. "She is married to William Craddock Esquire, barrister at law, yes."

"Ah..."

The girl drifted through the parlour counting under her breath, turned and went back again. Through the open door to the hall, he could see she was polishing the bannisters again. Catlin stared, burning with curiosity as to why the wife of such an obviously wealthy man should be doing her own polishing while the mother-in-law dealt with the far more important matter of salting meat for the winter. She was a slender little thing, ghost pale and hardly really filling her stays.

"So is Mr Craddock expected...?"

"I believe he is at the Inner Temple library," admitted Mrs Ashley, "I expect him home later."

"I can wait," said Catlin.

The woman's jaw set, she inclined her head with what was meant to be courtesy and poured herself a glass goblet of wine which she held by the stem with such force that Catlin wondered if it would break.

Phyllida drifted past again, counting, Catlin was sure of it. Mrs Ashley followed his eyes and her face was suddenly full of pain.

"My daughter has a... belief," the older woman said heavily, "She greatly desires a baby and alas... my son in law has given her... no baby. She believes that if she paces fifty steps and polishes the newell post of the stairs fifty times, she may conceive."

Catlin's eyebrows went up to his hairline, very nearly. "I never heard of such a thing," he said disapprovingly, "It sounds very Papist."

Mrs Ashly snorted. "Of course it's a stupid

230

superstition," she snapped, "But if I prevent her doing it, my daughter weeps and refuses to eat."

"And Mr Craddock? How is he after his... er... his distemper?"

Mrs Ashley had very sharp grey eyes and they looked at him a little fixedly. "He is a great deal better and is preparing papers with no ill-effects." The chill in her voice was strong. Catlin felt the familiar thrill of excitement: he was hitting the true ore here as he dug. Best keep digging.

"There's a great deal of talk about at the moment about Mr Craddock seeing the Devil in Fleet Street," Catlin pushed, "Does he..."

"He was disordered by a megrim," snapped Mrs Ashley, "I don't believe he could truly see such things and the whole nonsense stopped after Mr Cheke gave him a dose of laudenum."

The girl drifted back across the floor, still counting and Mrs Ashley's lips tightened to a hard bloodless line as she watched.

"Mr Catlin, may I ask what your business is with my son-in-law? Is it a legal matter..?"

"No, madam, it is related to the two women... three, rather, who have recently been hideously murdered."

The woman's face was stony. "I heard of it. Two notorious whores and a witch," she said. Catlin inclined his head. "Investigating? Why?"

231

"Mr Recorder Fleetwood is concerned because the other whores, of whom alas there are many in and around London, might riot or incite their upright men to riot if another is killed in such a fashion," he said. Mrs Ashley's grey eyes were chips of granite in her head. "And the means of it is so unnatural they are afraid it might be the Devil, perhaps the very one that Mr Craddock saw."

Silence. Mrs Ashley drank from her goblet slowly, her fingers bloodless.

"It certainly is a terrible thing,"

"The whores think so."

"And do you think Mr Craddock may have seen this... Devil the whores are afraid of?"

Catlin shrugged and smiled. He had no intention of actually discussing what he would say to Craddock once the bloody man turned up, especially not with a mere woman and the man's mother-in-law to boot.

Silence fell again. They watched the pale child in her self-imposed penance. At last she stopped her pacing and polishing.

"I'll rest now, mother," she whispered, heading wearily for the stairs.

"Can I make you something to eat, my dear, perhaps a posset...?"

The girl shook her head. Mrs Ashley sighed again as her skirts rustled from sight.

"All will be well with her if she can only fall with child," she said, as if she had forgotten Catlin was not one of her gossips, "Her attacks of the mother will cease – it's always the way with a maiden, they are naturally subject to hysterical fits until their hysterum be properly anchored by a baby. Until then it is apt to wander all over the body, with the results you see."

Catlin was surprised at such learned speech from a woman – she sounded almost like a physician.

"Madame, have you consulted a doctor?"

"No need," said the woman proudly, "My own father was a physician, Dr Richard Garbrand in fact, and I learned a great many things from him of the humours and the teachings of Hippocrates and Galen, Avicenna and Paracelsus as well."

"Surely none of them ever prescribed such..."

"Of course not," snorted Mrs Ashley, "The silly little fool picked up the idea from one of her gossips who took a while to kindle with child. Some old witch told her to do this as a magical spell and of course, since Jane got her baby, nothing will do for Phyllida except to follow the spell until it works. She will not leave off – she says it's the only thing that stops her falling into her terrors again."

Catlin tutted as sympathetically as he could although he was both bored and revolted. The whole thing made hims shudder, this sort of mucky women's business. If he were to wed there would be no escaping it.

On the other hand, as St Paul said, it were better to marry than to burn in hell and he already burned. He winced away from thinking of the torments of hell.

There was a slam of the front door and footsteps on the tiles. Mrs Ashley stood and opened the parlour door wider, then curtseyed to the master of the house. William Craddock came in, smiling and holding a little bottle in his hand. At first he didn't notice Catlin.

"Ah, there you are, ma'am," said Craddock affably, "See, I've bought a new bottle of ointment here to replace the stuff I spilled, so Phyllida can still..."

Catlin stood up and made his bow to Craddock, who paused, then bowed back. Craddock's face was broad and pleasant, the kind of face Catlin thought of as stupid though friendly, but something sharpened in it when he saw Catlin.

"I am Maliverny Catlin, Mr Craddock," he introduced himself, "Her Majesty's pursuivant." He used the dull neutral tone of voice which he knew was far more frightening to the guilty and innocent alike than any amount of dramatic shouting could be. He proffered his warrant which Craddock took and read carefully.

"Ah," said Craddock, handing the bottle of ointment to Mrs Ashley, who took it with a wary expression.

"What's in this?" she asked.

"Mercuric salts of gold," said Craddock with a

proud smile, "It's very expensive and sovereign against all attacks or disorders of the mother," he added.

Mrs Ashley seemed transfixed in some way, looked at the bottle and there were white patches above her nostrils and sudden dull purple spots on her cheeks. For no reason Catlin could see, she was suddenly enraged.

"Indeed?" she said in a neutral voice, "How kind a husband you are. I'll take it to her." She paused as if she was trying not to say something, or perhaps measuring it carefully. "Although Mr Craddock, mercuric salts of gold are a better remedy for the French Pox than the Mother. I fear you were gulled by the apothecary again."

She curtseyed shallowly to Catlin and Craddock and set off to climb the stairs with the slow heaviness of a middle-aged woman – she must have been at least forty. Craddock looked taken aback at first, but then shook his head and chuckled.

"Now then, Mr Catlin," said Craddock, going to his sideboard and pouring himself a large silver cup of wine – he offered more to Catlin who shook his head. "How may I serve you, sir? Are you enquiring about Papist priests again?"

Catlin's lips tightened.

"I'm always interested in anything anyone can tell me about them..."

"Well, the word at Inner Temple Hall is that another boatload of Jesuits landed last week near the Isle of

235

Wight. Only hearsay of course, but you might find it useful."

"Many thanks," said Catlin, hiding his pleasure. If true, that was very useful indeed and he could pass it on to Topcliffe this afternoon. "However, I fear that at the moment I am more interested in the murders of some well-known... ah... women of the town." As if dead whores could ever be as important as the discovery of Jesuit traitors."

"Oh? A bit out of my ambit. Of course, I don't normally deal with criminal prosecution."

"We have no one to accuse yet, unfortunately," said Catlin.

"Well then I don't see how..."

Catlin stood and went to the door, checked outside for listening servants or wives and came back.

"Sir, this is a delicate matter," he began with a hint of menace, "I have been questioning all the clients of the two women of ill-repute who were killed recently."

There was a short very nasty silence. Catlin felt his heart thud. This was the moment of truth, when the killing blow went in. He had never hunted boar, not being of noble blood and so not entitled, nor indeed did he have the kidney for it, but he suspected that attempting a true blow to the heart in a hunting field must be something like this.

Craddock's face had become satisfyingly serious.

"You think it was one of the whores' customers?"

Catlin shrugged. "It's a place to start, after all." He left the ending open but had the sense that his blow had missed the sweet spot.

"Good God!" Craddock did seem genuinely shocked, "I could understand a man killing his wife or, indeed, the other way about but why would anyone want to kill a whore...?"

"To prevent her accusing him?"

"Nonsense. A woman and a whore? No one would believe her or even listen."

"Nonetheless there are two dead whores and their fellows are angry enough to worry Mr Fleetwood."

"Lord above." Craddock shook his head and tutted.

"You have been reported to me as having had... dealings with both of the women."

Craddock blinked, stared. Then he did something utterly unexpected. He laughed long and loud.

"Good God," he said, patting his stomach and drinking, "Well well, there's a good joke. You have it wrong, Mr Catlin."

"Really?"

"Oh yes. My dear fellow, it's perfectly true that I used to visit trollops many years ago when I was a naughty young student full of vim and vigour and indeed I paid many a woman to play the beast with two backs with me... Occasionally two of them in the

237

same bed, I recall..." There was a faraway nostalgic look in Craddock's eyes. "But that was some time ago, Mr Catlin, and alas my furnace burns much less hot than it did, which is apt to happen when you grow older as I expect you'll find. I've not visited any whores for several years. When I married my angelic little Phyllida, I swore to forsake all other flesh."

"Oh?" Catlin found the good humour and the casual admission of sin enraging. "So why are you still known to be visiting the whores?"

"Well, I drop in to see dear old Kettle Annie every so often, see how she is, and French Mary as well, bless her. They're both old friends. Why shouldn't I?"

"Surely you are respectably married and your wife might reasonably object..."

"None of her business, not that Phyllida would mind, I'm sure, poor little love."

"So you have no idea why the two of them Annie Smith and Mary de Paris might have been killed and cut open...?"

"What?" Craddock seemed uncommonly slow on the uptake, even for a lawyer. He was surprised again. "You mean it was Kettle Annie and French Mary that were the two who..." Catlin nodded. "I had no idea." Now Craddock was pale, which was very hard to fake. "Cut open? Why? Who would do a thing like that?"

"I don't know, Mr Craddock. Perhaps you can tell

me?"

"Eh? How could I know?"

"Some say the Devil is walking abroad and doing the deeds. Some say it's the Devil in the guise of a man."

"What... oh!" Again enlightenment dawned on Craddock's face, followed by another rotund laugh, which made Catlin feel like a fool. "My fit of distemper the other day?"

"Possibly. You claimed to see the Devil himself abroad in Fleet Street."

"Did I? Yes, they said I did. I'm afraid I can't help you, Mr Catlin, for I remember nothing at all of my strange humour."

"Nothing?"

Craddock spread his hands. "Nothing at all. You'd think if I had indeed seen the Devil, I would remember it, but although I understand I offered to fight him with my fists and needed a heavy dose from the apothecary to quiet me down, after I woke I knew nothing of what had passed and must ask why my hands were tied to the bed and everyone was staring at me so strangely. Poor little Phyllida was in floods of tears, bless her."

"Oh." Catlin very nearly sneered, how convenient, but thought better of it. Liars were easier caught if you didn't let them know you knew they were lying.

"You should ask my mother-in-law or my wife, although I don't know how much you'll get out of Mrs

Craddock – poor child, so many things upset her. As for me, I remember nothing which I am sure is just as well."

"And you are quite recovered?"

"As far as I know. All I recall is feeling very unwell and a sense of great heat and then nothing until I woke again."

Catlin contemplated Craddock for a while, who smiled briefly, sat down in his chair at the head of the table and drank his wine peacefully. There was no tension, no defiance in him. He seemed genuinely amused by his attack of raving lunacy – or perhaps his vision of the Devil. How could he take it so lightly? Did that mean he was in fact possessed?

"Of course I want you to find the murderer of poor Annie and Mary," he said comfortably. "It's a sad day for me to hear my old friends have been done away with." He did look sad, admittedly, though hardly grief-stricken. "I have some good friends that saw me in my fit," he added, "Why not ask them?"

"Perhaps you were the man who killed the whores? Have you thought of that, Mr Craddock?" Catlin burst out, goaded beyond endurance by the man's smug bonhomie. Craddock considered this as well, his expression suddenly changed. Not afraid, unfortunately, only intent.

"An interesting accusation," he said eventually, setting his goblet down with a little tap, "And one to which in principle I might have no defence. However, in my right mind I would never do such a thing, so greatly to my dishonour, and while out of my right mind I was in a raving fit and both audible and visible for miles, quite apart from being first surrounded by friends and then knocked out by laudanum and tied to the bed to boot." Craddock smiled a very charming friendly smile. "Your case would be extremely difficult to make, Mr Catlin, and I think I could supply several dozen witnesses to the contrary, including a member of Her Majesty's Privy Council."

The words hung in the air like the golden cloak of Pallas Athene which protected her favoured heroes. Craddock had made it clear he had good lordship available to him if he chose to use it.

Catlin swallowed. He hated this sort of case. Papists were so much easier and hardly ever had numinously powerful patrons.

"Perhaps you have been in such a fit before and killed without remembering it, thinking the women to have been demons?" he pressed.

"Hm, you have a point, Mr Catlin," said Craddock seriously, but not seeming worried at all. "It would be a terrible thing but I suppose it must be possible."

"You might not have been in your right mind?"

"Clearly not, but do you have any witnesses that place me at the locus in quo?"

241

Catlin saw no reason to answer that question. At last Craddock was looking concerned – not trembling, but his brow was at least furrowed.

"It is an appalling thought that I could have done such crimes and not known," said Craddock slowly, "and if, which is not admitted, I were indeed to have been the unknowing perpetrator of them, I can only say, Mr Catlin, that you must use every power you possess to find the evidence that will hang me."

Catlin frowned. He also hated lawyers and anyone who could speak fluently in deponent clauses. "You do not deny the charge?"

"I do, of course," said Craddock easily, "I deny it most vehemently. But you have most astutely pointed out that if I committed the murders whilst deranged I might not know I had done them – although it might be arguable that a murder committed in such a fit would not be a murder at all, since you would be in difficulty establishing mens rea, ergo it would be a manslaughter. The result would be the same, though, for I am sure that any man of sense would agree that if it were indeed shown without doubt to have been myself that did such a dishonourable thing as to murder two defenceless women, leave alone then mutilating their corpses, the sentence must be most infallibly to hang me and in fact I could not quibble with it."

Catlin blinked fast as he navigated the linguistic maze

and found that Craddock had in fact simply elaborately repeated himself. From the look on the man's broad smug face it was something he could do at will, at length and, as he would no doubt say, ad nauseam.

"In fact, I think you should question Mrs Ashley, my mother-in-law. Although as a woman she is not able to act as a witness, she may be able materially to help you." Christ, the man was getting more pompous by the minute. "I would prefer it if you did not question my dear little wife. Poor love, she is terribly subject to attacks of the mother."

Catlin shuddered at the thought. "Thank you, Mr Craddock, I think I shall indeed speak with your mother-in-law. Perhaps you would clarify to her that I have your permission to do so?"

"Of course." Craddock stood up, waited courteously for Catlin to finish his wine, then led through the parlour, out the back hall and across the yard to the kitchen and larders that were built against the back wall.

In the kitchen the girl with a harelip was busy peeling small onions and weeping, there was a strong smell of vinegar and salt and also the smell of meat and blood. A half pig's head hung from a hook by the door to the wet larder, and the wall was lined with chines and sides of pork. Mrs Ashley had a boy next to her, who was busy grinding salt in a mortar with peppercorns and allspice berries. The carefully emptied and washed pig's guts were hanging in neat spiral loops to dry, ready for turning into sausages. Mrs Ashley herself was vigorously rubbing salt and spices into the large piece of pork on the counter in front of her, a large barrel half full of pork and salt next to her on the stone flags.

"Mrs Ashley," said Craddock, "I'm sorry to trouble you but Mr Catlin wishes to question you about the whore-killings."

The woman paused in her work, then turned and laid the pork belly carefully into the barrel where she packed it with more salt and saltpetre. "Indeed?" she said as she took a large knife and cut the next piece from the hook in front of her.

"Yes, Mrs Ashley, I would like to know more about Mr Craddock's fit of distemper the other day and also whether he has suffered a like problem before?"

"I gave Mr Catlin permission to talk to you," said Craddock, "He has pointed out that if I remember nothing after a fit, it is not impossible I could have killed the whores in my fit and not known it."

"It is impossible," said Mrs Ashley at once, "You were at home all the time you were ill."

"I did go out to collect some papers," said Craddock, "As I recall, in fact I think I spoke to Mrs Morgan on the way. Then when I came back I was in my chamber for a little while and that was when the heat and frenzy came upon me."

244

"From which point we were with you and I sent for several of your friends to come and help as well."

"Has Mr Craddock had a similar fit before?"

"No," said his mother in law flatly, "Never." She took the mortar from the boy and poured it over the pork belly in front of her, started rubbing. "Don't just stand there," she said to the boy, "Fetch more salt and spices and start again. We have to fill this barrel tight before we stop. Forgive me, sirs, I am very busy."

Catlin took the hint and they left, Craddock sweeping him on from the parlour and out the hall door. "Mr Catlin, let me know if you find out anything to the purpose," he said, "Do you know when Annie and Mary's funerals will be?"

Catln shook his head. "Mr Recorder Fleetwood will know about Kettle Annie's funeral, but I doubt it will be before the matter is cleared up. Mary de Paris was buried by the players who found her, I'm afraid."

Craddock nodded, bowed courteously and ushered Catlin back into the street. He stood there blinking, annoyed with himself. There was something not right there, he knew there was, but he had no time to do anything. He was late for Mass.

Father Felix Bellamy was trying to prepare himself to say Mass but felt he had no time. He was in the back of the alehouse whose yard had the entrance to the crypt where

245

they would worship. He had no proper vestments, only his stole around his neck. He had a small crucifix that unscrewed to be hidden under his clothes but he was using an ordinary silver goblet and plate as his chalice and patten. Mrs Crosby had made the hosts in her wafer iron the day before. He had his breviary of course, but no matter how carefully he read the prayers to be said before Mass and the Gospel appointed for the day, he couldn't settle. The small print blurred in his sight while his heart made a drum beat that drowned his own voice. He knew the people were gathering in the crypt because they slipped past him occasionally. There weren't very many of them, it was at short notice. They were hoping he would bring them the spiritual sustenance of Our Lord's Body and he knew that he was there under false pretences. He hadn't come to England on a Holy Mission. He had come on a personal matter which had no place here.

The words blurred again before him, a meaningless babble of Latin. He hadn't wanted to celebrate Mass publicly like this, he had only wanted to rest a little and then start making enquiries, but once he had foolishly brought the matter up, Mrs Crosby had insisted. She had shown him the bolthole in the crypt, the square pit that he could use if necessary. He had nearly choked at the smell of blood that seemed to come from it although it seemed clean enough.

And now she was nowhere to be found. She had brought him to the cider cellar and then muttered something about needing firewood and had disappeared down a side alley.

He took his stole off and put it in his doublet pocket, wandered restlessly into the kitchen of the alehouse, pulled in by the cooking smell. He was sharp set since he was, of course, fasting. There were two large raised pies on the table there ready to be sliced and a large cauldron of stewing salt beef and carrots rumbling away on the main fire. It looked as if the alehouse was expecting a large number of hearty eaters that day.

A cook shoved past him to grind pepper into the salt beef.

"Who's the feast for?" he asked the man, more out of something to say than real curiosity.

The cook grunted. "Big party of Topcliffe's men coming in later to celebrate," he said, "He always wants the best."

For a moment, Felix couldn't understand what the man was saying but then his brain caught hold of the most hated name in his life.

"Who?"

"Mr Topcliffe, her Majesty's priest hunter," said the red-faced man, blinking at him, "Why, ain't you wiv him?"

"Ah... yes. No, not with him. I... have a message for

him," said Felix with the first thing that came into his head.

The cook grunted again, picked his nose and flicked his trophy into the stewing beef pot.

"Well, you won't find him here yet, so what do yer want?" said the man insolently.

"Of course not," said Felix brightly, "Thank you. If you see Mr Topcliffe, would you tell him that Felix Bellamy wants a word with him?"

The cook shrugged. "Not likely to see him, am I? I hope. Give me the willies, he does."

Felix felt his smile might crack his face, the way it was pasted over the top of boiling rage and terror mixed. His hands were shaking, so he crossed them and hid the wobbling fingers under his armpits. He walked on through the kitchen and into the yard where the chickens roamed. He went into the putrid jakes and sat there for a few minutes in the warm stench of manure, his brain tinkling thoughts over the gigantic cobbles of his fear.

His breviary and cross were still in the alehouse where the people were still coming in. If there was no Mass being said there was no breach of the law and even Topcliffe would have to let them go, probably. There was no gate in the yard and the wall was high and spiked.

He couldn't go back to Mrs Crosby either, that was

clear. He had no contacts in London, nowhere to go and although he knew there were safe houses in the Liberties and St John's Wood, he didn't know their addresses. He turned his doublet inside out as he used to do when he was a naughty schoolboy truanting, then slid behind the jakes shed. A large stand of nettles there was dying back with the frost. He waded through them carefully, climbed the slippery wall and very carefully lifted himself over the spikes on top. He missed his footing and fell into the alleyway, but was only bruised and a little winded. After dusting himself down he put his doublet back the right side out, then turned his back on the crypt and all his congregation and walked quite slowly out of the alley.

A very blackhaired old man was striding up the street, a silver shod walking stick in his hand and his henchmen behind him in a cluster. Felix lifted his hat to him and bowed slightly. He knew immediately that this was Topcliffe. It was a shock he was so old. How could he fight a duel then?

Felix made way for him. His rage and hatred and fright turned the cold sunlight into knife blades, he saw every detail with a strange feverish clarity. This man had never met him, knew nothing of him, didn't recognise him. Felix drank in his appearance. This was the man who had ruined his sister's life, broken his parents and tortured his friend. Just for a moment, Felix's hand

249

brushed his dagger hilt – a quick draw and stab when Topcliffe was unaware... came the thought. Felix shook his head. Honour would not allow it, even though the bastard had no honour himself. He could not do it. Not like that. In a fair fight, despite his calling, yes. But not like a footpad, not the way the Dutch prince William of Orange had been assassinated.

Felix sauntered on into the street, took a cupful of water at the conduit on the corner as the last of the henchmen disappeared into the alehouse, and then headed into the crowds of London. He had no idea where he would sleep that night, but somehow his rage had alchemised into delight. He had seen his enemy and his enemy didn't know him. He had escaped by the skin of his teeth.

Somewhere in the distant parts of his soul came an ironic thought: one minute preparing for Mass, the next considering murder? it said. Haven't you missed something about disputes with your brother and bringing an offering to the altar? How can you be a priest and say Mass with that black sin in your heart?

Felix shrugged. All right, then, he wouldn't say Mass. Mrs Crosby had betrayed him as his sister had been betrayed. He had unfinished business and if he couldn't be a priest until he had finished it, then so be it. There would be one less priest cluttering up England.

Topcliffe punched the cook in the face again, then rearranged his knuckledusters. The man's face was bloody and his nose a mashed blob.

"I do'd do, how could I do?" he wailed, "'e wodded to talk to you tha' all..."

Topcliffe took judicious aim and punched the cook's nose again. He felt another bit of bone crack and the man screamed. It was a little bit of satisfaction.

"His name?"

"He said Felix Bellaby wodded to..."

Punch. Blood and snot flew everywhere but Topcliffe wore a dull black doublet for good reason and it didn't matter. The cook seemed to be crying.

"I didden dow, how could I, dobody tol' be nod to tell..."

No doubt that was true, Topcliffe thought, finally pleased by the weeping and bubbling.

He left the cook and walked through to the commonroom where his men were standing around drinking his money. All of them moved away from him, out of punching distance. He liked it that they feared him, it made him feel safer. The Papists had scattered. They had been gathering simply for good fellowship, they said, nothing more. Mass? Whoever said anything about a Catholic Mass? Didn't His Honour know that

251

it was illegal? There had been a pathetic haul of a few rosaries and a few forbidden Agnus Dei, but nothing more and especially no promised priest. And Felix Bellamy had somehow flipped his fingers in Topcliffe's face, figuratively speaking. That could not be allowed.

He put his head round the door of the kitchen and the cook cowered away from him, trying to dab the ruin of his nose with an apron.

"Take him to the barber," he ordered his men who were helping themselves busily to pie. "Get the bleeding stopped, then bring him with us. He can identify Bellamy for me."

.

Shakespeare wished he wasn't where he was, but that damnable creature Enys had caught him again and swept him along to Mrs Betty Sharples' linen shop at the end of Fleet Street, as being the woman who had seen the Devil. The place was festooned, choked with napery of all kinds, some of the more old-fashioned shirts and aprons dating back to before the Armada when she had bought it off a woman who had been getting married late in life and quite suspicious haste. Her best-sellers were the handwoven linen sheets and pillowcases that came in by mysterious means and were often bought back by women who had carelessly failed

252

to watch their own linen drying in their yard. All was clean and well-ironed with the cold wild smell of the cloth in the air, and the woman was clearly prosperous despite the evident fact that her head was fuller of feathers than any of her pillows.

She was talking at incredible length. Shakespeare knew the type – male and female were prone to the malady. There were people in the world who were simply unable to get to any point quickly: if they wanted to tell you about a notable thing that happened in the evening, there was no help for it, they must start with what they had for breakfast that day. Any attempt to cut to the marrow of the matter quickly only made them worse. His eyes were glazing over and he had a terrible mad giggle under his ribs.

"No, I tell a lie, it was a very good beef stew, and with carrots and a bag pudding of herbs to it and I said to my gossip, I said to Mary, well, I said, I'm sure I don't know but if she says there's a gentleman who wants to speak to you, why not go speak to him and find out what he wants, after all, you're not a virgin, Mary, I told her and she did laugh, it was just my little joke, and hazelnuts won't do you forever so why not?"

He already knew that Betty Sharples had been born in the same village as French Mary de Paris and had travelled up to London with her to work for a fuller in Westminster who was a cousin, but alas, Mary had fallen for a rogue who left her ruined and the fuller's wife had turned her off, for all Betty could try and say and she had gone to Paris Garden where she changed her name. He learned these interesting facts again.

"The man she was to meet?" put in Enys, "Do you know his name?"

Betty Sharples' round pleasant face drew together. Well, she said, it was a problem, she wished she did know it, wished she could tell them right off for he must be the Devil of Fleet Street and once they had his name the gentlemen could take him up and hang him and no decent woman was safe with the likes...

"Did you ever meet him?" asked Enys, while Shakespeare rolled his eyes. Hadn't Enys worked it out yet? Betty Sharples' thoughts were a procession full of nervous horses and if you interrupted the procession or broke into it in any way, then the horses bolted and the litters upended and the whole had to be slowly reassembled from the start. From breakfast, in fact.

"You what?" Enys asked sharply.

"I did meet the Devil," said Betty Sharples with great emphasis, "I'm sure I did for I was all hot and bothered when the baiting ended and he was very kind and took me home, saying I was perhaps a little distempered and not to be concerned for he had had plague a few years ago and was well of it again but he didn't think that was what it was since I was only feverish and had no tokens

254

and..."

"Mrs Sharples, what did he look like? Did he look like a Devil?"

The Sharples thought procession halted again, bumping into itself as it did.

"I don't know you see, I can't remember, though I know I saw him and I knew he was the Devil because he was invisible." There was a distinct note of triumph in her voice, with its little crumbs of West Country under the sharpness of many years in London.

Shakespeare looked at a very well-embroidered tablecloth and counted the flowers and birds on it so he wouldn't laugh.

"Do you remember anything at all of the later afternoon?" asked Enys patiently.

"Let me see now, I know that the beer I had for my breakfast that day was quite sour and the bread was stale for I told Mary about it..."

Shakespeare turned aside and gently bit the knuckles of his left hand to stop himself screaming. This was the third time he had heard about the sour breakfast beer. Enys didn't seem to mind, curse him.

Slowly and inevitably, the Sharples memory procession approached and got lost in the same swamp at about the same point, just when she and poor Mary her gossip had had a good laugh at the monkey on the goat's back and Mary had needed a napkin for her hands were that sticky and then they'd seen that new bear, Harry Hunkson – he wasn't fighting that day but they were parading him out with his new keeper and she almost thought it was Harry Hunkson who was the gentleman who had helped her home except it couldn't have been him obviously because he was a bear kept safely in a cage at the bearbaiting and wasn't it sad that poor Tom of Lincoln had run mad for sorrow when his keeper died of plague, there was a good ballad about it, and... It had been a gentleman anyway, of that she was quite sure, since he hadn't tried anything with her although she had been so hot and muzzy she had opened her stays down the front to let some steam out and after meeting the Devil she had woken up in her shop wrapped in a sheet and none the worse for it only poor poor Mary...

At which point, for the fourth time, Mrs Sharples began to cry about how they'd tramped to London from their village back in the Sixties when the Queen herself was young and looking for a man and they were girls and it had been such fun and Mary was the best gossip she had ever had for all her trade...

Shakespeare went out into the street, away from the smell of linen and the fat old woman's sobbing, hoping the air would mend his headache. Eventually Enys came out, frowning.

"God, I thought she'd never stop," Shakespeare said

256

to him as they walked back along Fleet Street to the Cock.

"I'm glad she didn't," said Enys, "That was very interesting."

"Eh?"

"She went through it four times..."

"I thought it was only three..."

"In aggregate and each time she lost her thread at the exact same moment. After which somebody, probably a neighbour rather than a bear, guided her home. But not French Mary who was somehow lured to the new theatre and killed."

Shakespeare nodded. "Do you think they were working together, the neighbour who was not a bear and the Devil himself?"

Enys was fully scowling now. "I don't know. It's all too cloudy and vague and she's already told it too often."

Shakespeare was more than ready for a quart of beer. "It's almost like an enchantment or a spell, a cobweb of dreams that fell over her," he said. Enys was too deep in thought to answer.

.

Catlin had agreed to meet Enys the lawyer at the Cock and went straight there. He found the man sitting in the shadows of a booth at the back, aquavitae in front of him and a large heavy looking legal book in his hands. He looked up as Catlin sat down in front of him, and tipped his hat with the very barest of civility. But Catlin didn't care. He had spent a very chilly hour waiting like a cat at a mousehole only to find from Topcliffe's rage that the mouse had scurried away long before. However it had given him time to think about his present problem.

"Mr Enys," he said, "Is it possible to find out if a lawyer was really at court as he says?"

Enys put the book down open in front of him and marked the place with a scrap of paper – it was in a combination of lawyer's English and Norman French, neither of which languages Catlin knew well enough to read upside down.

"Certainly it is," he answered, "You ask the presiding judge or the clerk of the court and there is a written record kept as well."

"Oh. So if a man says he was at Westminster all day, it should be easy enough to find out if he was?"

"Yes, unless the hearing was in camera, of course. But even then a record would be kept. Why?"

Catlin hesitated but in the end decided to pass on some of what he had learned at the Craddocks and while working through his list. After all, he had a reason for wanting Enys on his side.

He told most of what he had done that day and Enys explained that he himself had been in court, but was victorious. "Did you not have problems with the gentlemen you were questioning?" Enys asked, with touching naivete, "Weren't they angry that you accused them of trafficking with whores?"

Catlin smiled. "Not with my henchman Young Daniel standing behind me," he said. "Not one manservant wanted to try his luck with him."

"That's Widow Creavy's enormous son, isn't it?" Enys said.

"Yes. He has very little wit but is a most faithful hound," Catlin said complacently, "Goody Creavy hires him out by the day as a henchman and once she has told him to protect you, then I suspect you could outface the Watch, the Trained Bands and the Queen's Gentlemen of the Guard together."

Enys smiled crookedly and chuckled a little, but didn't explain why. "So you think that Craddock's vision of the Devil was a sign that he's the man who killed the two whores?" Enys asked.

"Yes, I do. What could it be but a guilty concience?"

"It could be a mere overheated phantasy of his brain."

Catlin sliced his hand across the air between them. "Yes, it could," he said, "but then it turns out that someone... something has been doing devilish things in London. There must be a connection."

Enys nodded, staring into the cobwebs festooning

259

a high corner of the commonroom. "Do you plan to arrest Mr Craddock?"

"Not yet. Mr Fleetwood will want better evidence than a vision of the Devil to take up a respectable man like Craddock. He denies all knowledge of the crimes, of course."

"Of course," murmured Enys.

"And I believe we cannot simply take the man into the basement of the Tower and have him meet the Keeper's Daughter, as we could with a Papist."

"Most certainly not, Mr Catlin. The statute of Edward III 1368 forbids torture without warrant and I don't think Mr Fleetwood will give you a warrant for the putting to the question of one of his brother lawyers." Catlin scowled. Enys smiled cynically. "Besides, I have never known good intelligence and information come out of a torture chamber and I'm sure you have not either."

Catlin ignored the question. In fact he hadn't, but important people like Cecil and Topcliffe believed as the Spanish did that torture made truth more likely and who was he to argue.

"A little rough treatment will do the trick," he said, "Sometimes. If at all. That and waking."

Enys said nothing. From his face it looked as if he could have said a great deal more. A young round-faced man in a sober black wool doublet was sitting in the corner of the next booth, blinking into his beer as if it was his last and he hoped to find treasure in the depths. At Enys' silence, he looked up and stared hard, and then looked away quickly.

"I'll go to Westminster tomorrow," Catlin said, preoccupied with Craddock. "I'd like to find out if Craddock really is as busy at court as he says he is."

Enys nodded, glanced at his still open book.

Catlin decided to take the bull by the horns, as it were, and find something out.

"Mr Enys," he said formally, "I understand that you have a sister living with you to keep house for you, a respectable widow?"

Enys's face had become wary. "Yes, I do, Mr Catlin." He closed his book and laid it on the table.

"How old is she?"

"About twenty-seven like me," said Enys, "We are of an age, being twins."

"And what are her... her prospects?"

For a moment Enys looked baffled. "Her prospects..?" Enlightenment dawned. "You mean her marital prospects?" Suddenly he reached for his cup of aquavitae.

"Yes. Have you... ah... any new husband in mind for her?"

Enys seemed to have swallowed some brandy the wrong way, because he was in a paroxysm of coughing.

261

"I'm afraid, Mr Catlin, she is not much of a catch. She has very little jointure and no settlement from her late husband. That's why she is keeping house for me."

"No dowry?"

"Unfortunately not. Or... not until I can make some money at the law."

"I'm very sure you will. If I may ask, sir, with respect, can you tell me what kind of a woman your sister is?"

Once again Enys needed to drink some brandy to stop a coughing fit. While he was still doing it, the player, Will Shakespeare arrived at the table, looking expectant. He was also clearly quite drunk. To Catlin's annoyance, he sat down next to them without so much as a by your leave and took some dice out of the pocket in his sleeve. Catlin glared angrily at him.

"I'll give you a penny a point," slurred the revolting player. "Anybody feeling lucky?"

"I don't like diceplay," sniffed Catlin. "It's an offence against the Lord to try and foretell the future."

"Why do you ask about my sister's character?" asked Enys when he had recovered from his coughing fit thanks to Shakespeare pounding his back. "Have you heard anything against her?"

Catlin shrugged. There was no point giving everything away at this time, in any case, the idea had only just occurred to him. But she was respectable, could keep house, was no longer married and... He narrowed his eyes. "Surely she should be one of St Bride's congregation?" he said quietly, "Why have I not seen her with you in Church?"

Enys hesitated and for a moment, Catlin thought he saw a flash of guilt there. "She has a malady," he said, "A megrim that makes it very hard for her to venture out of her house. It came on her after the smallpox."

"Is she a Papist, sir? I understand that you yourself are not, but sometimes women prove obdurate..."

Enys' face was cold. "No sir of course not. She is simply often ill on Sunday. Are you considering arresting her?"

The whole interview was somehow going badly wrong. Catlin put his hands up, palms out. "No, no, sir, I only wondered... er..." What he really wanted to ask was why hadn't she found a husband yet?

However he couldn't exactly ask that right out, it risked a duel for God's sake.

"You've not met her, have you, sir?" said Enys.

"No. But Mr Enys, to be blunt with you, sir, I would welcome a meeting... with you as escort, of course."

"Two pennies a point. More!" said the player, tossing the dice from hand to hand.

Enys had suddenly gone red, which made his pocky face uglier than ever.

"Alas, I am... likely to be busy tomorrow," he said, "Ah... I'll ask Mrs Morgan. But... er... sir... if I may be

263

honest with you as well..."

Catlin nodded. Perhaps she wasn't respectable. If she wasn't she would be no good at all, he couldn't possibly have a scandalous wife. Nor a nosy one.

"Ah... my sister is..."

"Like the moon," said the player, making a conventional compliment and juggling all four dice quite deftly, given his state. Then he added, "Covered in pockmarks. Terrible really."

"Oh," said Catlin, taken aback. He looked at Enys. How would he take this kind of talk about his sister. Enys was coughing again.

"Mr Shakespeare, please," he said at last, quite mildly, considering. Shakespeare burped, shrugged, continued juggling. "Although I'm afraid he is right. She is scarred as I am by the smallpox that took her husband and children."

Catlin made conventional tut-tutting noises. "How terrible."

"Yes. She always says that the ruin of her complexion is a far worse thing for her than for...m..me."

Catlin considered for a while. Smallpox scars could be very off-putting – he had heard that even the Queen had a few which she covered with facepaint. But still. Of course that meant Mrs Morgan would not catch smallpox again and no doubt, although she was quite old, she could still have babies. And would be unlikely to stray. He nodded thoughtfully and smiled at Enys.

"I do hope I shall have the pleasure of meeting your sister, some time soon," he said to Enys and Enys, bright red from all the coughing, nodded silently.

After that it turned into quite a convivial evening, with the player acting the part of a fool extremely well, throwing dice, making puns and by the end, when they were all drunk, he took the Cock's hard-to-tune house lute, managed to tune it after half an hour of battle, and then sang to them in a good clear baritone. Before the end of the evening, Enys had called over Peter the Hedgehog who seemed somehow to have become the Cock's new potboy and gave him some money for something. Catlin was trying to learn a song from Mr Shakespeare and so didn't notice when Enys quietly slipped away without giving him any real answer about his sister.

Catlin wasn't worried. The more he thought of it, the more he liked the scheme, even though he had never met Mrs Morgan. Catlin himself was wealthy, respectable and all in all, aside from a slight shortage of hair along the sides of his head (much less serious than poor Shakespeare's at that), quite good-looking. Mrs Morgan on the other hand was pock-marked, poor, respectably widowed though with good prospects thanks to her brother. And it stood to reason that Mr Enys would want to have his sister off his hands so

265

he could be unencumbered to make a good match for himself.

Felix Bellamy hurried after the man he had been eavesdropping on while he drank his last penny in the form of beer. His head was spinning from not eating all day and from the nervous tension of needing always to keep moving and watch for Topcliffe and his men. Once he had glimpsed the poor cook who had given the game away, his face horribly swollen black and blue, his nose a bloody remnant that a barber-surgeon was attempting to stanch with a red hot iron while he screamed and struggled and three men held him down. Luckily, he thought the cook hadn't noticed him. He had hurried away, murmuring guilty prayers for the man.

It seemed as if the lawyer's sister might just be willing to help if she were faithful to the Church, despite her brother's apostasy. Perhaps God or one of his holy angels had led him to the Cock tavern to help him out at last, after a day spent praying for help. He had to find somewhere to hide for the night and if the brother and sister gave him up to Topcliffe, well, he would just have to sell his life dearly, that was all. At least, dressed as a gentleman, he had a sword at his side again – it felt comforting there, although it was a loan from Mrs Crosby. On a thought he drew it and checked the blade, which was blunt and pitted with rust. The thing was no more than a decorative metal club and of a piece of his experience of Mrs Crosby.

He sheathed the weapon and went up the last flight of stairs two at a time as he heard the key turn in the lock at the top. He wanted to appeal to the lawyer while his sister was there – the man would probably value his career over his immortal soul but the woman, if she was reluctant to go to an heretical Mass, perhaps she would be sympathetic...

The lawyer spun on his threshold and put his hand to his own swordhilt as Felix came up behind him.

Felix backed off quickly. "I'm sorry, sir, I was hoping to speak to your sister?"

"My sister is away from home at the moment, staying with her gossip," said the lawyer after a moment's pause.

Felix could have groaned. He was sunk. Again. Some of that must have shown in his face for the lawyer asked suspiciously, "Why? Do you know my sister?"

It was a reasonable question but Felix was stuck. What could he say? He'd listened to the lawyer's conversation with the puritan and dared to hope that his sister was a Catholic and might shelter a stray priest...

"It's all right," he said hollow with disappointment, "It doesn't matter," Out of sheer habit he lifted his hand in the gesture of blessing, then dropped it. What a stupid slip.

The lawyer's face hardened again. He had seen.

267

From the look of him, he wasn't a Catholic at all.

"Are you a missionary priest, a Jesuit?" demanded the man harshly. Numbly Felix nodded.

"Although..." he offered, knowing in advance how lame it would sound, "I'm not really here officially..."

"No?"

"I'm here trying to find mine own sister," he said sadly, "Her name is Ann Bellamy and she was foully dishonoured by Her Majesty's favourite priest hunter, Richard Topcliffe."

The lawyer hesitated. "What do you mean?"

"She was forced, sir," said Felix, the rage boiling up in his stomach again at the thought, "When she was arrested last spring by Topcliffe, she was a virgin. By summer she wrote to my parents that she was with child. Then somehow he got her to betray my dear friend Fr. Robert Southwell that my parents were hiding. Now my parents have aged ten years and they will not speak of her nor contact her though she is still in his hands. Nor will my other brother or sisters. They all say that it is her wicked lewdness that caused the trouble and that she is damned for fornication and her selling of Fr Southwell to her heretic lover."

The words had come tumbling out, stuttering with his anger. He didn't think he had been very convincing and no doubt the lawyer in front of him would think the same way as his parents – that if she quickened with child, then she was not raped, but was willing.

"And you?" asked the lawyer, "What do you say?"

Felix only lifted his shoulders. "I say that I know Ann, she is closest to me in age, a year younger. And she is a good and virtuous woman and has been wickedly treated. I say it is nonsense that a woman cannot fall with child if she is forced, or there would be no marriages arranged against the woman's will. Jesus Christ himself would not condemn the woman caught in adultery, why would he condemn a woman that was raped? And so why would I?"

The lawyer nodded as though Felix had made a good case which he was sure he hadn't.

"What was your plan?"

Felix shrugged again. "I came only to investigate, to try and find out where she is – she'll be ready to lighten of her babe soon – and help her in any way I can."

"Is that all?"

Felix coughed. "And also I have hoped to call out that evil man Richard Topcliffe and prove him a rapist and a liar in fair fight..." He looked down. "I know it makes me very unworthy to be a priest but I can't help it that I want satisfaction for my sister's ruin. I can only pray I'll have the strength to resist temptation and God's guidance to find my poor sister and bring her to a safe place with her child if they live through their hour."

The lawyer dropped his hand from his sword hilt,

269

opened the door wide and gestured for Felix to go in front of him. Hardly able to believe such a change, he went.

The room was dark and the fire out. The lawyer bent to the grate to start up the fire and take the edge off the chilly air in the chamber. As he used the tinderbox and the flames leapt up in the kindling, Edward looked around. It was a plain enough pair of rooms. The main room was lined and piled with books and papers and a door led to the bedchamber where Edward could see the outline of a fourposter bed with drawn curtains.

"Have you eaten today, Father?" asked the lawyer quietly and Felix spun on his heel to see the man hanging his sword on the hook by the door and going to the food safe next to the window for the cold. Felix shook his head.

"Well, have some supper," said the other man, and cut a hunk of bread which he put on a pewter plate with a couple of herrings, cheese and an apple.

Edward sat down at the small table, pulled out his eating knife and then remembered just in time and said grace. The lawyer turned aside and did not join in, pouring two horn cups of mild ale from a flagon.

The place was no bachelor hovel, Felix could see the woman's touch wherever he looked. All the surfaces were clean, the papers in neat piles, the rush mats had been recently swept and there were clean shirts and

270

shifts hanging up to dry near the fire. On a stand in the corner were a woman's linen caps and falling bands, neatly starched and drying on poking sticks.

"My sister is staying at her gossip's house to help with a baby," said the lawyer again.

"Forgive me, sir," said Felix, "I don't even know your name."

The man paused. "Enys," he said, "James Enys, esquire, utter barrister."

Felix had his mouth full of bread but inclined his head politely. "Father Felix Bellamy, SJ," he said in return. "Are you a Catholic, sir? Perhaps in your heart if not in your actions?" He was already thanking God in his own heart for the food and refuge.

Enys shook his head, his face darkening. "Once I was a church Papist, Father," he said, "But no more. I go to the Protestant church when I have to."

"And your sister?"

"Mrs Morgan is the same."

"Why did you change? Was it to become a lawyer so you could take the oath?" Felix wondered if he should have asked that, after all, it sounded bad no matter how you put it.

Enys smiled briefly. "No, sir, though I'll admit it was convenient to be able to swear the oath of supremacy without troubling my conscience. It was more that I had a quarrel with God and felt it best we not meeet for a while."

Felix managed to hold his tongue but couldn't help raising his brows in question.

James Enys sighed. "God took my... my sister's husband and my best friend and three fair children with the smallpox, leaving her too badly scarred to marry again. I was scarred as well, though it doesn't matter to me. I know others have come through such fire and worse with a deeper faith. But I'm afraid, I simply said to myself, would I remain friends with a man that did such a thing as to kill a husband and three children in terrible agony and sickness, as God does over and over throughout the world? And I answered myself, no, I would not. And so I attend where I must and agree where I must and let God go about His business, but I'll have no truck with him."

"'My ways are not your ways,'" quoted Felix softly, "'My thoughts not your thoughts, I am the Lord thy God, saith the Lord.'"

Enys shrugged. "I don't dispute His power, I just want nothing to do with the man."

"God is not a man," Felix couldn't help adding but Enys cut across him savagely.

"We are taught that He was a man, as Jesus Christ," pointed out the lawyer. "Come Father, I won't dispute with you or I'll end up repenting of my being moved to help you for your sister's sake."

"Do you not think it might be God Himself that so moved you?" Felix asked.

"I hope not," said Enys with finality. "I can offer you a bed for the night and a place to hide for the morrow. I'll tell my sister to stay at her gossip's... ah... no, damn it. No. You'll have to leave before dawn tomorrow. Damn it."

He busied himself with the fire until he had built it up well and warmed the chamber gratefully. After Felix had finished his supper, Enys immediately scoured off the pewter into the fire and cleaned it with sand and a cloth until it shone again. His hands were quick and neat in movement, he also rinsed and dried the cups and Felix found himself staring to see such huswifery.

"Does Topcliffe know you're in London?" Enys asked suddenly.

Felix coloured. "Yes, I was betrayed by the woman I sought refuge with..."

He told the tale of the abortive Mass and the cook and then that he had seen the cook at the Fleet Street barber-surgeon, which had been why he ducked into the Cock. Enys's ugly face drew down and became darker. After a moment he let out a heavy breath and scratched his eyebrows.

"God send that nobody saw you coming in here then," he said.

Felix nodded anxiously. "Perhaps I had better go..."

273

he said, not really meaning it.

Enys saw straight through him and smiled crookedly."We may need to take drastic measures," he said, "But I have a plan that may work and at least the door is new. You sleep in the great bed – the sheets are not fresh but not too bad. I'll sleep out here if you help me move the truckle bed against the door so I can hear them on the stairs if they come up."

Felix helped roll the little servant's bed across the matting and wedged it against the door. "Will you be well enough out here?"

"Of course," said Enys, taking his cloak off the hook and wrapping it round himself. "My sister and I normally take turns to have the truckle."

"You are truly kind..." Felix began.

"Hmf," said Enys, "Somebody has to give God a good example." The lawyer lit a rushlight from the coals in the fireplace, then banked them up and put the curfew over them.

Felix took himself into the bedchamber, shut the door. He undressed and knelt for a time in prayer to say the Office and to thank God for his mercy and pray for the poor lost soul of James Enys the lawyer. Then he climbed into the four poster in his shirt. It was flearidden but warm enough with the curtains shut and he tumbled headlong into sleep.

.

He was woken far too soon by a quiet scratch-scratching. His eyes blinked open, he froze for a moment, imagining demons led by Topcliffe and then heard a faint irritable miaow.

There was another one. And another. Nobody could sleep with that steady scratch scratch and the persistent miaow.

Muttering under his breath about bloody animals and hoping it was a rat he could simply kill, Felix hopped out of bed and went to the window. A furry face and two large green eyes reflected the moonlight. He opened the window to shoo the animal away but instead it jumped onto the sill from the thatch and then to the floor as if it owned the place.

"Out!" he whispered at it. The look the cat gave him was magnificent with contempt and Felix, who was more used to dogs, tried to pick it up and nearly had his face slashed. He caught the cat eventually and held it at arm's length to throw it out of the window and onto the roof when he froze on the spot...

There had been a flash of red light in the alleyway three storeys below. Only a flash but he knew immediately what it was. Someone had checked to see if a dark lantern was still lit. There was only one reason why anyone would be there with a dark lantern at four in the morning, which is what he thought the time might be, judging by the moon. Felix listened, poised, cat at arm's length and an occasional growl and struggle from his furry saviour. Yes. A quiet mutter, a chink of metal, movement of shadows passing through the archway leading into the courtyard.

He dropped the cat onto the mat and it immediately jumped into the bed as he padded through to the main room where Enys was snoring on the truckle bed against the door.

"Sir! Mr Enys!" whispered Felix, shaking his shoulder.

"Herkle! Grunmg!" said the lawyer, sitting up at once, "Wha...?"

"There are men in the courtyard with dark lanterns," said Felix.

Enys was still fully dressed. He crossed to the window of the main chamber which looked out directly over the courtyard giving onto their staircase. Gathered at the entrance was a dark clot of men in cloaks.

"God damn it to hell!" swore Enys. "Er... sorry, Father."

"Perhaps I should give myself up," said Felix, his tongue so dry and leathery he could hardly say anything at all. "There's nowhere to hide and you would be..."

"No," said Enys, "I told you, I've a plan. Besides you'll take me down with you."

276

Felix had seldom been more shocked and horrified in his life when Enys explained the idea to him.

"It's against the Bible," he said, "Deuteronomy says it's an abomination - "a woman shall not wear anything that pertains to a man, nor shall a man put on a woman's garment...""

"I know. In the same chapter 22, it says "You shall not wear a mingled stuff, wool and linen together," said Enys, "I checked. So does that mean we should execute the weavers?"

"But... but won't your sister mind?" Felix spluttered, desperately.

"She'll understand," said Enys with a grim smile as he pulled the woman's stays down over Felix's shoulders and started lacing them as tight as they would go. Two wadded cloths went under his shirt at the strategic points. "It's a good thing you're not big-built."

"But if they find me like this..."

"We'll all have something to laugh about in the Tower," said the lawyer, tying on the bumroll and engulfing Felix in a farthingale and then what seemed like a ton of petticoats. Felix tried to rearrange himself with the flounces of linen over the strange wicker cage hinging from his hips. He had not really had the chance to find out what women had under their kirtles, for all his fevered imaginings at weak moments.

Enys had already taken his discarded doublet, hose,

277

stockings and boots and tucked them under a blanket in a box by the bed. The sword he stuck out the window and pushed into the thatch of the next house. Now he advanced on Felix with an incredible amount of lined woollen cloth into which he had Felix dive, still sputtering about the shame of being discovered.

"Help me move the truckle again," snapped Enys, "And stop moaning."

Furious and red with shame, Felix tried to follow him and tripped on the heavy skirts. Enys steadied him, took a falling band from the stand and put it round his neck and then tied a neat widow's cap over his hair.

"Sit down here," said Enys, "My sister often acts as my clerk. Do you have a good Italic hand?"

"Yes."

"Try and copy it like that," Enys pushed some sheets of paper at him. Felix squinted at the writing which was small and neat and even more wild in spelling than most women's writing. Then he realised that it was in a combination of Norman French and Latin as was normal for legal papers.

"Here," grunted Enys, dropping a velvet face mask on the desk, "My sister is well known to be very shy about her pocky face – put the mask on immediately the door opens. If they see your stubbled chin the game will either be up or my sister's reputation will be utterly ruined."

278

Felix blinked at him and realised that Enys thought this was funny, which made him even hotter with embarrassment and anger.

And then the madman went and unlocked the door, even lifted the bar across it. For a moment Felix wanted to protest but then he found he couldn't speak. The leathery dryness had gone all the way down his throat and he couldn't even swallow. Somewhere inside himself he was beseeching God that if he had to be caught and martyred, could it please not happen while he was dressed as a woman?

Enys lit a good wax candle and a rushlight. He left the candle on a shelf so that the pale light would fall on the paper but leave Felix in shadow.

Then Enys cleared his throat and began to dictate something about a case to be heard before Judge Whitehead in Westminster Hall.

Felix bent his head and began to write, watching his hand shake and waver and then firm as he tried to copy the small Italic of the rest of the page.

There were feet on the stairs, quite quiet considering they were wearing hob-nailed boots. Enys clasped his hands behind his back and said in slow measured tones,

"In the matter of Land Sergeant Henry Dodd versus Sir Thomas Heneage, quondam Vice Chancellorius de Regina nostra in coram de banco reginae..."

Felix pressed too hard and split the nib, fumbled for

279

another pen. Enys reached over and put one in his hand, brought up the inkpot. Felix took a deep shuddering breath, dipped and wrote, struggling to write as small and neat as Mrs Morgan. His hands seemed a long way away from him and he tried to stop them trembling. For some reason he thought of the long hours he had spent face downward in front of the altar before his ordination, promising God everything. He prayed again wordlessly as Enys continued to dictate and he struggled not to blot the villainous lawyer's Latin.

Enys's voice was steady and quiet, he paced as if he really was writing an opinion or perhaps a pleading, Felix wasn't sure which. His ears were under his respectable starched cap, he stretched them to hear what was happening on the landing. A quiet muttering in the darkness and then...

Bang! Bang! "Open up in the name of the Queen!"

There was a scant second's pause and then the crash of a battering ram. Enys went to the door, waited a second and opened it at the exact moment when the battering ram swung at the door again.

The man wielding it stumbled over the threshold and landed on his face next to Felix's borrowed skirts. Something like a hysterical shriek escaped him, then he grabbed up the velvet mask and put it over his face, found the button to hold in his teeth. He shrank back as if he truly were a woman, that was the thought of an

280

amused and objective part of him.

Enys had grabbed his sword from the hook and drawn.

"Help!" he shouted, "Murder! Robbery! Fire!"

That got a response. Felix could hear answering shouts from the couple who lived one floor down and a banging on the wall from the next door neighbours.

In the centre of the gang of men on the threshold stood Topcliffe with his mouth open.

"We are in the service of her Majesty the Queen!" he bellowed, "You've got a God-damned Jesuit hiding in there."

Enys was standing between Topcliffe and Felix with his sword en garde before him. At least his blade was well-oiled and sharp and he looked steady and as if he knew what to do with it. Felix couldn't see properly because of the small eyeholes of the mask and he didn't dare move at all to peer past Enys' back.

"How dare you sir!" shouted the lawyer, "I am a loyal Protestant subject of her Majesty and I go to St Bride's church as often as my work allows. My good lord and master, my lord Baron Hunsdon, Lord Chamberlain and cousin to the Queen, he will hear about this outrage!"

Topcliffe stalked over the threshold.

"Your warrant, sir?" demanded Enys, moving to keep his sword between Topcliffe and Felix.

"I don't need a warrant," sneered Topcliffe, "I work

directly for Her Majesty."

"So you say, sir," said Enys, "Where is your proof? You could be a Jesuit priest yourself for all I know."

Topcliffe fairly snarled at him.

"I'll call you out for that insult."

"Certainly, sir, where and when shall we meet?" snapped Enys.

Felix put his hands in his lap because they were shaking so badly. He concentrated on breathing through his teeth and not dropping the mask.

Somebody pulled on Topcliffe's sleeve and Felix saw that it was a smallish well-dressed man with a sour tight-lipped face. He whispered in Topcliffe's ear urgently.

Enys obviously knew him for he tilted his head at the man.

"Mr Catlin, what brings you here?"

"A mistake, I believe, Mr Enys," said Catlin,"My apologies Mrs Morgan," he added with a little bow and then spoke again at length in Topcliffe's ear.

Topcliffe scowled at Enys. "You are working for Mr Recorder Fleetwood in the matter of the murdered whores?"

"I am," said Enys, "I think he would hardly employ me if I were a papist. And I have sworn on the Bible my allegiance to Her Majesty and to the Church in England before I could be called to the Bar. Why in God's name would I risk mine and my sister's lives to hide some fool of a Papist Mass-monger?"

Topcliffe spat. "What's there?" he demanded, pointing at the other door.

"My bedchamber."

"Share it with your sister, do you?" said Topcliffe, with an unmistakeable leer. Enys stepped towards him. Two henchmen moved in. Felix tensed for the fight.

It was Catlin who opened the bedchamber door. Topcliffe stalked to the fourposter, drew the curtains and found the cat with his back arched, spitting and slashing at him with a pawful of blades. He yelped and stepped back and there was blood on his hand. He drew and threw his dagger at the cat, but missed and had to pull the blade out of the headboard. Nobody laughed. The cat contented itself with swearing down at him from the top of the tester. Topcliffe looked under the bed, in the chest and ostentatiously tapped his way round the walls.

He came out of the bedchamber again. "I can smell Papists here," he hissed. "Are you going to challenge me then, boy?"

Felix could just see a crowd of neighbours, some holding candles, peering in from the darkness of the landing. He couldn't make them out at all and prayed they couldn't see him properly either. Enys and Topcliffe were nose to nose: Topcliffe had his dagger in his hand and Enys's sword was still out.

283

"You are an old man," said Enys quietly but loud enough to be heard by the crowd on the landing, "Above sixty years of age by what I hear, and a well-known letcher, fornicator and forcer of virgins. Why would I soil my honour and dirty my sword by challenging such as you?"

Topcliffe's old face under its thatch of black hair whitened and his lips lost all colour as well. His dagger twitched.

"I would however welcome a chance to kill you in self-defence, especially with plenty of witnesses," Enys added. Topcliffe's eyes moved slightly and took in the audience, a couple of whom seemed to be quietly laying bets.

He walked out the door after deliberately tipping the inkpot over what Felix had written as he passed the desk. The people parted for him and his men.

"Thank you for your intervention, Mr Catlin," said Enys, and Catlin nodded in response as he shut the door. Catlin's voice could be heard on the landing, saying that they would now search the next chamber down.

Enys locked the door, listened carefully to the noises of Topcliffe's men barging into the set of chambers just below his. He then finally sheathed his sword again, hung it back up on the peg. He sagged down onto the chest and put his head in his hands.

"Jesus," he said in a shaking voice, "Jesus Christ."

284

He looked up at Felix and his eyes were bright with slightly hysterical laughter.

"Lord, you make a terrible woman," he commented, "Thank God I could keep Topcliffe's mind on me."

"I fear you've made an enemy of him," said Felix in a whisper. He was dripping with sweat under all the cloth he was wearing and the stays were so tight under the bodice that he couldn't breathe, in fact he thought he might black out and caught the edge of the desk to steady himself.

"Use your stomach to breathe," said Enys, then shook his head and laughed again.

Felix was embarrassed. "I must look very comical..." he said stiffly.

"You do, Father," said Enys, "But then the whole situation is hilarious. And I would probably have crossed Topcliffe sooner or later anyway. The man is vileness incarnate and I seem to have a knack for making powerful enemies."

"Do you think it would be against my honour to fight Topcliffe?" Felix asked a moment later, once he had taken a gulp of the cup of aquavitae Enys had passed him.

"I never even thought of honour that way before," Enys said, swallowing, "But, yes, I think it would. A fight should be between equals, not a foul old man and a young strong man."

285

Felix nodded. He had a point.

"Anyway, aren't priests forbidden to shed blood?" Enys asked, "Isn't that why they used to carry a mace on Crusade?"

Felix felt the fire running down his throat relight something in him and found he could smile back. "A technicality," he said, "I'm sure I can get an indulgence to cover that. Anyway, I'm a very inadequate priest."

"I must ask you to go before sunrise," Enys said, "My sister will be back and I wouldn't want to worry her with this whole matter. Also I have hired a boy to help her with something today who I know works as a spy for Mr Catlin."

"But what about the searchers?"

Enys went to the door and opened it again, listened carefully. There was no one on the landing and he peered down the stairwell. A sound of crashing and angry argument came from the first floor chambers.

"You know," he said, "I think they're busy. If you go now and are quick on your feet, I don't think they'll catch you."

"What about the window in the bedchamber?"

"Well, I wouldn't try it especially not in the dark."

It took another twenty minutes for Felix to change back into his proper clothes and find his sword in the thatch.

"God bless you, Mr Enys," he said formally to the

lawyer who was looking sadly at the ink-blotted papers on his desk, "If there is anything I can do for you..?"

"Yes, you can get out of London, your sister won't be here any more. Topcliffe will have moved her away from wagging tongues," said Enys.

"I thank you from the bottom of..." He gripped Enys's hand.

"It was not your priesthood," said Enys, "Only that I honour a man that will understand his sister to be innocent in such a terrible case. I hope you find her."

He peered down the stairwell again and then beckoned to Felix. Heart in his mouth, throat dry again, Felix started down the stairs two at a time.

"Walk," hissed Enys, "If anybody says anything, say that you're due in court at eight o'clock and need to get to Westminster."

Felix slowed. The stairs seemed to go on forever, surely there could not be another flight. There was a man on the first floor landing, and Felix tensed to go past him, but then just as he came down the stairs the man was called into the set of chambers to help with lifting a chest.

He went past, head down, convinced they could hear his heart. At the arched entrance he paused and looked about. The courtyard had four horses standing there and a lad sitting leaning against a tree, clearly supposed to look after them but actually fast asleep.

Just for a second Felix thought of stealing one, but then thought better of it. He carried on, through the court, up through the little alleyway that led onto Fleet Street and turned right towards the City. He was at Ludgate when he suddenly found himself laughing under his breath like a boy. It was true. When you thought about it the whole thing had been very funny and a good story to tell later, though perhaps not to Fr Persons. And it showed God was not yet ready to make him a martyr, for which he was extremely grateful.

·

As dawn broke over the smoky thatched rooves of London, Peter the Hedgehog climbed the rickety stairs to the top of the old building in the Earl of Essex his court. That pocky lawyer had come along to the Cock and paid the landlord for his services for a couple of hours to serve his sister while he went to court this morning. Peter was a bit worried about it because he didn't like working for women; it's true they boxed your ears less often, but then sometimes they were offended about something and didn't tell you about it until they were so offended you couldn't calm them down. He went despite his worries in case there was a tip or food.

There was a whole bunch of men with pursuivant written all over them and that Mr Catlin among them too, just climbing into saddles ready to ride away. A very angry well-stomached man in a fur-trimmed dressing gown was shouting that Mr Topcliffe would be hearing from him again through the courts. Peter hung back to watch the show; Topcliffe said, "Put your writs up your arse, sir," and kicked his horse to a canter, followed by all the others. Mr Catlin hadn't noticed Peter and looked worried which was nice to see.

As soon as the coast was properly clear, Peter climbed up all the stairs. Everybody was up, some people were in their dressing gowns and some others were dressed and they were all shouting and raging and banging doors as if there'd just been an attack of robbers, which in a sense, Peter supposed, there had been if Topcliffe had raided them. He crept past them doing his best not to be noticed in case they thought he was a hookman.

When he knocked on the door at the top and went in he found Mrs Morgan putting things away in a chest. She turned with a squawk and picked up a velvet face mask like they wore at Court masques and held it over her face.

He'd seen much worse than that in the dear old gaol. And her brother's face was worse than that, definitely.

The woman fastened the mask's ties behind her head, put her beaver hat on and said to him in a kind enough voice, "You must be Peter. I want you to come with me and carry my shopping."

289

Peter nodded, his heart sinking. He hated going shopping. Never mind. She might buy him a sweetmeat or even a pie. Things were definitely getting better, he reminded himself, thanks to that funny balding young player. He actually had food every day now from the leftovers at the Cock, but still... Why did women do so much shopping? Even his sister had insisted on going down to the Bridge on good days so she could gawp and sigh at the bright cloths and silks and the hats in the windows there. They usually got chased away by burly apprentices – so what was the point? Peter and Mary had as much chance of buying something from one of the merchants on the Bridge as the Bridge had of breaking away from its starlings and walking out into the ocean like a sea monster.

"Yes we will," Mary had said when he'd protested about this, "One day, when you're a rich lawyer, yes we will."

A pie's a pie, he told himself. Mind, he'd never eat another orangeado after the last one but a pie... With gravy?

Mrs Morgan locked the door behind her, gave him the basket to carry and went down the stairs, swishing her skirts and he scurried after her. She stopped to commiserate with a flushed angry woman on the first floor about the wickedness of Topcliffe searching respectable peoples' chambers. Why couldn't he do it to

Papists, that was what he was for? Mrs Morgan agreed and tutted and finally got away down into the courtyard.

"Now Peter,"she said. From her voice she was smiling though she sounded tired. "I'm visiting my gossip Mrs Briscoe and we'll need to buy some supplies for her."

It wasn't far. They bought soap and raisins and half a sugar loaf which was heavy and smelled so sweet it made Peter's mouth water. When they got to the place it was a neat little house on a street that was full of rich children playing – the girls skipping and the boys at football. It reminded him of the good old gaol again, though there wasn't anybody dragging about in chains because of not paying the gaoler enough garnish, obviously.

Mrs Morgan knocked on the door and a small birdlike woman opened it and smiled. They went right in. He pulled his forelock to the lady because he didn't have a cap to take off any more. The innkeeper had been moaning about it, he was supposed to have a statute cap and he didn't. Well that was a problem for the innkeeper to solve, not Peter who certainly didn't have the money for even a second-hand one and wouldn't have wasted pennies that could buy him food in any case.

Peter looked around inside the house: it was big with a main room you could fit several chairs in and the kitchen at the back, all clean with new rushes and the walls covered in pink plaster and even the table was clean and there was an impressive fire made with those expensive northern coals that came from Newcastle. In front of the fire was a wooden cot with a swaddled baby in it, sleeping soundly. Peter remembered babies in the gaol with their cheesy smelly swaddling clothes and their red angry faces. He could never understand why any woman would want one though he supposed they couldn't help it really.

He'd better not stare at the baby, they might not like it or it might start crying. He put down the basket, wiped his nose and ducked his head nervously at the lady of the house who smiled at him.

Mrs Morgan took her mask off and put it in the basket. She certainly did have a big pockmark next to her mouth, that was sure. It made one side of her mouth lopsided because it couldn't move so much.

Mrs Briscoe was talking to Mrs M. "I don't know what you said to my ma-in-law," she said, "But she's been lovely ever since.

Mrs Morgan sniffed. "I made her feel thoroughly ashamed of expecting you to do housework before you were churched. Now, did you get the ale barm and the flour?"

Mrs B nodded excitedly. "Oh yes, and I got it bolted twice because little Annie from next door asked me if she could help and so I got her to do it rather than me, like you said. And I got the starter from the baker three days ago and I've been feeding it every since and it's all foamy and bubbly and smells of booze so I think it'll work. I'm ever so happy you could help, I've been so worried about the churching party on Sunday."

Mrs M smiled crookedly. "This is really a twelfth night cake," she said, "But it does very well for any party because it's so big. Did Mr Briscoe get you the spices and the dried fruit?"

Peter was staring with his mouth open. He loved cake. His old mistress used to make it too for special occasions and she made sweetmeats too, knew exactly how to boil up sugar and fruit together, all that. He stole a piece once that had been cut off because it was burnt and it was so wonderful, just thinking about it made him drool. Were they actually going to make a cake?

"And you've talked to the baker?"

"Yes, he said when we've got it kneaded and thrown, we can bring it along and prove it by his oven and he'll put it in right after he's baked his penny loaves tomorrow. He's baking a second batch now because there's a big banquet at the Guildhall this afternoon and we can use his oven after the penny loaves have come out."

"Splendid," said Mrs M, taking her sleeves off and putting on an apron. "Peter, I want you to go in the yard and wash your hands, then come back and help with grinding the sugar."

For cake, Peter would even wash his hands. He fairly

sprinted into the yard.

.

Two hours of measuring, mixing and kneading later, Peter and Mrs Morgan carried the big circle of dough along the street on a big slate, to the baker who was waiting at the door of his shop. It weighed a lot – it was as big as a barrel head because it had been cast inside a cleaned barrel hoop. The baker showed them into his shop, full of the wonderful smell of new bread, right up to his oven door at the back which was still glowing hot inside. The penny loaves were piled in baskets and were too hot to touch when Peter experimentally tried to pick one up. The baker took the big slate as if it weighed nothing and put it on a shelf by the oven, covered it with a napkin.

"It should be baked by nine tomorrow morning. Will Mr Briscoe come for it in the afternoon?"

Mrs Morgan had her mask on and nodded mysteriously at the baker. She paid him and he gave Peter a penny loaf which he immediately started to gnaw in case someone stole it, so he burnt his mouth. She bought some pies too from the counter, mutton pies with onion gravy from the smell.

Back at Mrs Briscoe's house, the two ladies sat down to eat the pies and started talking – amazingly they gave Peter his own pie to eat by the fire instead of just giving him the pastry from theirs, and he listened while he happily engulfed it. It was mutton, but with mint. They talked the way people did when there was a serving boy around. Sometimes they forgot you were there, sometimes they remembered. It seemed Mrs Briscoe was going to come and work for Mrs Morgan as her companion, he heard that. There were also hints about some secret but Peter was tired from being up late washing pots at the Cock and then from grinding the sugar and cinnamon and almonds to put in the cake and pulling the seeds from the raisins (although a lot of the raisins had gone into him, not into the bowl). He was sitting next to the fire, carefully picking pie crumbs off himself to eat, and his eyes got heavy and he fell asleep.

.

It was one of the dreams about his sister which he hated because she was scolding him and he didn't know what he'd done wrong. He woke up crying and found Mrs Morgan's ugly face close to his.

"What's the matter, Peter?" she asked and he snortled and wiped his nose.

"It's my sister Mary," he mumbled, still half in the dream. "She's so angry with me and all 'er guts is coming out and they won't go in again and... and..."

Mrs Morgan's eyes narrowed. "Is that what happened to her?"

"Yerss," sighed Peter, with tears still flooding down his face. Mrs Morgan gave him a handkerchief of real linen, worth as much as a penny, and he snortled into it. He was ashamed of crying like a baby but he couldn't help it, couldn't possibly stop now.

"Where did it happen?"

"Dunno," sobbed Peter, "somewhere near the river in Whitefriars. I found her once the Devil went away."

"What devil?"

"The one what killed her. I saw him. Hot as hell and a big Devil with horns and tails and a mouth full of teeth. I was so scared, I just fell down and then when I woke up, it was gone."

"Was that when Mary died?"

Behind Mrs Morgan's shoulder, Peter could see Mrs Briscoe quietly take the baby out of the cradle and go upstairs with it.

"Peter, was it..."

"I dunno!" he wailed, "She went off and I never seed her again and she said it was all right she could get lots of money for it and have a whole orangeado to be a good boy and she went off and I never seed her again, not alive, and..."

"Where did she go off to?"

"I dunno, I dunno, or I'd go and kill 'im for wot he

296

done to my sister, don't care if I hang for it or go to
Hell cos that's where she is anyway cos she was bad, she
was a... a..."

"Was it a customer she was going to?" asked Mrs
Morgan and her voice had ice in it that almost made him
choke on his tears.

"Probly, he was going to pay her a lot of money, a
whole pound and I don't suppose it was for her to sing
to him, do you?"

"No, I don't suppose so either," said Mrs Morgan.

"So he done it maybe thinking she was a virgin and
when she wasn't e cut her up, I fink."

"She wasn't?"

"Nah, course not, she was at least four years older'n
me."

"How old are you?"

"Dunno. First fing I remember is the Armada and
the bonfires when they was beat by Sir Francis Drake,
so I must've been about three then. We got extra meat
and wine in the old gaol too."

Mrs Morgan's lips moved as she did the sums. "So
you're about seven years old?"

Peter scowled. It was up to her to do adding up, not
him. He shrugged. "Somefing like that. So she was old
enough and anyway that was why we had to leave the
lawyer's house."

"What?"

"Well, the master was tupping her, wasn't he and the lady didn't like it and nor did her ma-in-law so out we went."

"What was the lawyer's name?"

Peter shrugged. "Dunno. I always called 'im sir."

"Could you tell me where he lives?"

"On Fleet Street, sign of the bearded lady. I'll take you there, if you like missus."

"The master was lying with your sister, you had to leave and that's when things went wrong?"

"Yerss. It's cruel hard to get a new place though we tried and tried and she was too skinny and small for most of the gentlemen. Falcon wouldn't have us... Well, they'd have had her, Mrs Nunn said, but not me cos Mary said I wasn't to go to the Chick cos I'd get poxed and it was against Scripsha and it wasn't right so that was that and we was just starting to get somewhere and she went out to get the money to put down on a room in the Whitefriars and... and..."

"Who was the pander?" asked Mrs Morgan, which surprised him because she was a respectable lady.

"It was that orangeado seller, Goody Mellow. She got Mary some clients before even though she said she was a cousin to the Missus wot kicked us out, she said she felt sorry for us."

Mrs Morgan shook her head. Peter was suddenly full of terror that she'd turn him off now because of his wicked sister.

"Mary said it couldn't be helped about her but I wasn't to be a punk like her. I'd've done it," he whispered, "I'd've let 'em do it at the Falcon's Chick, but Mary wouldn't have it, she said I'd got to be a lawyer and I couldn't if I was poxed, could I? I don't care if that's wicked, I'd do anyfing, but you try and get a master in London wivout any letters or friends. Mary said our mother said in the old days before the change, I could've been a monk or a priest but I can't now so it's got to be a lawyer."

Mrs Morgan's smile was rueful.

"What happened to your parents?"

"Oh they was rich once, Mary said, but they lost all their money and land and ended in the Fleet for debt or somefink worse and then they both got a gaol fever and died of it, see and left us alone. I liked it in the dear old gaol, see, and Mary was helping at the gaol but then the keeper got a new woman and she didn't like us so we went to work for sir and his missus. See Mary could read and I fink she read something she shouldn't of..."

"Can you read?"

"Yerss," said Peter, wiping his nose on his sleeve and then remembering and swiping with the grubby hankerchief. "Mary taught me and she said Mother taught her but I was too little for it then and she said if I worked hard and she could get me in a school and I

299

got to be a lawyer I could get rich and get her a husband, maybe."

Mrs Morgan narrowed her eyes and went up the stairs to call to Mrs Briscoe. She came back with a small new book of the gospels and psalms like you could get at St Paul's for the vast amount of several shillings. Peter squinted at it.

"Yerss," he said, "I can read from that."

She just opened it anywhere, the way sir did once and showed it to him. Peter narrowed his eyes to a squint because they were sore and swollen from all the crying he'd been doing and started to read.

"B...blessed are the poor, for they shall in-herit the king-dom of heaven..."

Mrs Morgan smiled ironically.

"Dunno about that," commented Peter, looking down, "Mary said it's wicked to argue wiv Scripsha but I fink it should be more like cursed are the poor for everybody will kick 'em, wot do you fink?"

Surprisingly, Mrs Morgan nodded.

"Peter," she asked without commenting on what he had said, "Can you write as well?"

"A bit, I never 'ad time to learn that proper but I can do me name and lists."

The look on Mrs Morgan's face was suddenly so fierce, Peter hunched back away from her with his knees tucked up against his chest and his arms wrapped around. She gently touched his shoulder. "It's all right, Peter," she said, "I'm not angry with you at all. Thank you for telling me about Mary, she sounds like she was a... a very good sister to you."

Well the tears started again after that, of course, but not so hot and scalding. She left him alone by the fire and went up stairs again to do mysterious woman things with the baby. Gradually the tears stopped, leaving him empty and strangely clear-headed. He dozed a little and there were no more dreams.

Mrs Briscoe and Mrs Morgan hugged when they left and Peter knew that she and Mrs Morgan had agreed on something so he went with Mrs Morgan and they stopped off at St Paul's for paper – a big expensive pile costing two shillings that Mrs Morgan said was also for her brother's work as a lawyer. She'd got a good deal on it though, she was sharp like that, she'd got thirty sheets, not twenty-four, for bulk.

In the large comfortable chambers she shared with her brother, Mrs Morgan sat down at his desk, cleared up some spilled ink and started to write. She did it very small so you had to squint to see the letters but you could still just make them out because it was still quite clear.

She wrote down all that happened, asking questions the whole way. Some of the questions made Peter cry again because it was about what he saw when he found his sister's body bundled into a gap behind a wall in the Whitefriars.

"Nah, it was a straight cut, not ragged, and 'er innards was falling out like a hanging drawing and quartering at Tyburn."

"What was her face like?"

"That was funny, you know, cos it was calm, like she'd been sleeping."

Mrs Morgan nodded.

"What was the weather like back then?"

Peter frowned. "Dunno, not cold. She'd started to smell a bit cos she went off in the night and then I saw the Devil and when I woke up more than a day had gone by but she wasn't back so I give it anovver day cos you never know wiv gentlemen and then I'd eaten all the food see, even the rainy-day cheese so I went to look for 'er and then it took me anovver day to find 'er..."

Mrs Morgan stared into space, biting her lip. Then she coughed, blew her nose and said sternly.

"What did you do with the body?"

Peter started crying again. "I tried lifting 'er but she was bigger'n me and I was tired so I couldn't so I left it."

"Two weeks ago?"

Peter nodded. "I done a terrible fing not burying her," he muttered. "But I couldn't fink how to, no money nor noffing to pawn and so I l...left 'er. I just left 'er. All alone, wiv 'er innards coming out. I left 'er."

Once again. Mrs Morgan coughed. Then she pulled out her purse, counted carefully, put it back inside her stays and leant over to him.

"I don't think you did anything bad, Peter, because you just didn't have the strength," she said, her eyes fierce and shiny, "But I think it would be a bad thing if I didn't help you give her a decent burial so that's what we'll do now. Can you show me where the body is?"

Peter gulped and shut his eyes, which never did any good to stop the pictures in his memory.

"I'll show you but I won't look cos it was scary enough before."

"Quite right," said Mrs Morgan, standing up and putting on her hat and her mask again. "I'm not going to look any more than I have to."

From her voice Peter knew she was smiling at him. She left the chambers locked carefully behind her and held out her hand to him as if she was a sister or something to go down the stairs which were a bit steep. He hesitated then put his grubby paw in her pocky hand, surprisingly brown and strong it was. He looked up at her face which gave him a bit of a turn because of the velvet mask.

"Do you fink she's in a nice bit of Hell?" he asked huskily, "Maybe not too big a fire or somefing? After Mother and Father died, she always looked after me as well as she could. Even though she was a little trollop

303

like the missus said."

"Well... er... the Papists say she would be in Purgatory which is like a prison where you..."

"Oh yes, I remember!" said Peter joyfully, "That's what it was, Purgy, we couldn't remember what it was called but she said we'd only go there. Do you fink so? Like a gaol?"

"Ah..."

"Cos it was nice in the Fleet wiv warm places and food wiv brown sauce and people to play wiv so long as you kept out of the Beggar's Ward... Specially before our Mother and Father died of the gaol fever."

They were walking down Fleet Street and Peter found himself suddenly skipping with happiness. He was sure that was where Mary was, and it stood to reason, if she could get into Purgatory, he might too if he tried hard enough to be a lawyer and everything and then he could be a proper brother to her and head of the household and get her a dowry and...

His brow wrinkled. "Do you still need dowries to get married in Heaven?" he asked.

"I don't know," said Mrs Morgan slowly, "I don't think so. Which lane should we take?"

He showed the way, past the window with the scary-looking picture of a dying man with a hat made of thorns and all blood on him, past the back of the lawyers' new hall which Mary said only in the summer he would go

304

and eat in one day, some chance, past where they were knocking down more huts to make way for gardens and down another alley, deep in Alsatia. Mrs Morgan looked nervous, as well she might. Peter looked around but didn't see anyone he knew was a nip or a footpad or an upright man. He held her hand tighter.

"S'all right," he whispered hoarsely, "I'll protect yer."

"Thank you, Peter,"

"I ain't got a knife, but I got teef," he told her seriously so she wouldn't be frightened.

"I do have a knife," said Mrs Morgan firmly, "So if someone needs sticking with one, you can borrow it."

Peter nodded. That was sensible. They came to the wall.

"Oh!" said Mrs Morgan, "I know this place!" She gathered her skirts, climbed up on a stone and peered over. "The garden's gone too, somebody's dug it all up."

"Is... is... Mary there?"

Mrs Morgan leaned to peer over carefully into the space between the two walls. "No, there's no body there and there hasn't been for at least a week because I'd have noticed. I was... my brother was here too with Shakespeare."

"It's gone!"

"Yes, Peter, I didn't think it would be here, really. People don't leave bodies lying around if they can help it."

"You fink he put her in the Thames?"

"Yes, or even gave her a proper funeral and put her in a grave – or most likely tipped her into a plague pit so she at least got blessed. There's a lot of plague around London now, it wouldn't be hard to get rid of the body. What's in that shed?"

It wasn't really a shed, it was a bit of monastery that had survived, so it had stout stone walls and a chimney but the slates had been stolen so it had a thatched roof now.

"That's Goody Mallow's shed, the orangeado seller."

"It is? What did she say about the body?"

"Dunno, she's not often there. It's all locked up tight cos she don't want nobody getting at her orangeados nor sugar wot's so expensive like you said,"

"Peter, I know we can't bury Mary, but could you get up on the wall next to me and tell me exactly what you saw?"

He didn't know why she wanted him to tell her, it was horrible, but maybe if he told someone it would stop getting into his dreams. He scrambled up and knelt on the double skinned wall and looked down into the little space behind the orangeado seller's yard wall where Mary had lain, all higgledy piggledy. He'd only found the place because of the crows and buzzards and dogs anyway.

"Did you see blood there?"

"There was some, smeared onna walls, but it's rained since then."

"How was Mary lying?"

He gulped. "On 'er back," The pictures marched in front of his eyes. His stomach was full of the cold terror that had filled him like that cold feeling you got before you actually came down with the fever. He started to shake with the cold. "Her face was all right but 'er guts..."

"Cut open?"

"Yerss, like I said, and all the innards in a spiral and a sort of bit of meat onna ground next to her and cut open, looked like ox heart."

There was the sound of Mrs Morgan taking a deep breath through her nose.

"Anything else that you thought was strange?"

"Nah," Peter shook his head, screwing up his eyes. "Only..." There had been something else but he couldn't remember what it was. "I don't fink so." The coldness overwhelmed him and he jumped down quick before Mary's ghost could get him.

Mrs Morgan hopped down too and he put her hand in hers again, so she'd know she was safe with him even in Alsatia. "Do you fink she'll stop getting angry at me?" he asked, "In my dreams?"

"Yes," said Mrs Morgan firmly, "She's certainly buried now. We'll go back to the Cock and you can go to work – I promised the landlord I'd bring you back."

They came out on Fleet Street but instead of going to the Cock right away, Mrs Morgan walked along it. "Tell me when we come to the house where you and Mary worked?" she said quietly.

They passed it not far from Temple Bar. "This one," he said, trying to keep Mrs Morgan's skirts between him and the windows in case the mistress was looking out. "Wiv the bearded lady over the door."

Mrs Morgan's eyes behind her mask narrowed. He could hear her suck in her breath again.

"Thank you, Peter," she said, the ice crackling in her voice. They crossed the street as a string of packponies came along, laden with cheeses from the smell. Peter's mouth watered and he wondered about nipping some cheese but they were in big round trucks and well-stowed. On the way back to the Cock, though, she stopped in front of one of the pie sellers and talked to him a bit and bought two whole pies that were full of gravy and he got a whole one all for himself again. He wolfed it down in about two bites, while Mrs Morgan took the other one in its waxed paper and put it in her basket for later. Amazing that. How could she do it? What if somebody stole it?

"Wot?" he said. She'd been talking again while he concentrated on the pie.

"I'll tell my brother James Enys the lawyer about

you," Mrs Morgan told him again, "He's helping Mr Recorder Fleetwood find out who's doing these terrible things so he might want to talk to you about your sister too. Now do you know where Goody Harbridge used to live? I heard it was near the Cockpit?"

He did and while he was telling her, he remembered the thing that was strange about Mary.

"She had her little cross on," he said, "She still had it, see, cos she wore it for luck. It was off of a long string of beads that Mother pawned one by one when we were in the gaol and then she couldn't pawn nor sell the cross because it had a little Jesus on it and that's dangerous because it was idolatry but she couldn't melt the little Jesus down, cos it was carved so Mary got it. She said it was good luck but it didn't stop her being killed, did it?"

"No, Peter." It looked as if Mrs Morgan was going to say something else but then she didn't. "That's very interesting. So whoever killed her wasn't interested in robbing her, as far as we can tell. I'm afraid that cross has probably gone for good now."

Peter shrugged. "Don't matter, it wasn't gold or anyfing and you couldn't sell it cos it was dangerous." He wasn't being quite truthful because he wanted it back as a remembrance of Mary, except he wasn't sure if he did want it after all because remembering Mary made him feel so sad. He had been too upset and overwhelmed to take it that time he found her but he wished and wished

309

he'd done it now.

They were at the alley that led to the Cock's courtyard and he knuckled his forehead to Mrs Morgan and trotted down to start work.

.

Portia Morgan found the Worthing's house – it was small and ramshackle and right next to the Cockpit so it must be a deafening place to live when there was a fight on.

The woman who opened the door had a permanent worried expression and a swaddled baby of about four months roaring lustily in her ear.

"Is Goody Harbridge here?" Portia shouted, "I asked her to knit me some gloves and I've heard nothing from her, which I've paid for by the way, mistress."

The woman's face fell. "Goody Harbridge is dead," she yelled back, "Died a couple of days ago after she went out to collect firewood. Very sad it was, mistress."

Portia stepped closer. "I'm sorry," she shouted, "What did you say?"

The baby's face was puce and the noise coming from his square mouth was amazing.

"I said..." shrieked the woman, "Oh, come in, missus, I'll tell you when I've got him quiet."

Or at least Portia thought that was what the woman

was saying, she had to read the lips.

The front room had a wooden cot hanging on ropes from the ceiling beams, a toddler with padding strapped on his head staggering about purposefully in his little shirt, clutching firewood, a little girl of about five busy carding wool from a fleece by the fire and two boys aged about seven or eight, punching and kicking each other as they wrestled in a corner.

Portia took her mask off once she was through the door, picked her way across the reasonably clean rushes and sat herself on the chest under a window while the woman perched on the nursing stool by the fire and popped a tit over the top of her stays to plug the baby in. The baby latched on like a starving wolf and started glugging. The relative quiet was delightful. Once again Portia's own breasts prickled at the sight. She smiled.

"Poor lamb," she said, "He was only hungry."

Goody Worthing nodded, her face looked tired.

"He's certainly a fine strong boy," Portia added politely, "Is he..."

"I'm nursing him for Missus Bailey," explained the woman, "but I've never known such a lusty babe."

One boy was now sitting on the other, battering him.

"Michael!" shouted Goody Worthing, noticing at last, "Will you for God's sake go and feed the goat like I told you an hour ago?"

The boy on top got up reluctantly, picked up a leather

311

bucketful of scraps and trotted out the back door into the yard, followed a moment later by his brother who seemed to have found a football.

"Poor Goody Harbridge," sighed Goody Worthing, "She was a lovely old soul and ever so helpful when my youngest was born and with Ted as well." She tilted her head at the toddler who was carefully piling firewood up to build a house. Suddenly his face became faraway and intent. Portia tensed, she knew the signs.

"Alice," shouted her mother, "Take Ted outside to the jakes, quick!"

The little girl dropped her carders, leaped for the toddler and hauled him bodily out the back door where he squatted and laid a remarkable pile of turds while his sister held up his shirt and made understandable faces.

"It's awful when you're just training them," said Goody Worthing to Portia, "Do you have any of your own, missus?"

As always, the knife permanently lodged in her heart twisted and she was shocked by it. This was one of the reasons why she had originally welcomed the idea of playing at being a man – men never asked each other questions like that. She had to pause before she could answer.

"I did once," she said quietly.

The woman looked at her pocky face and her eyes were full of sympathy. "I'm sorry, missus," she said softly, "It's cruel hard for us all. I lost my baby last summer with a fever, that's why I could take this one on."

Neither of them said anything for a moment.

"Goody Harbridge said it was God's will, she did her best for the little girl but it was just too little, you know? I don't see what God wants with babbies or children for that matter, but what do I know, I'm not a reverend?"

Portia said nothing since she had nothing to say that wasn't heresy and probably treason too.

Goody Worthing coughed and shrugged. "So... she was knitting you gloves. You can look at her things – they're in the chest you're sitting on, in case her family should come. But I don't think she had a family, poor old soul, she never spoke of anyone."

Portia knelt down by the chest and opened it. Inside were neat hanks of wool, some undyed and still greasy with sheep yolk and dirty with bits of leaf – she must have been gleaning the hedges near London for her wool. Her steel needles were rusting despite being wrapped in some sheep's hide. Underneath was a small cloth bag with herbs and lichen in separate pockets.

"I heard from Mr Cheke the apothecary that Goody Harbridge was upset in the last few weeks."

"It was the witch that murdered her, " said Good Worthing angrily, popping the baby off her teat and sitting him up to wind him. Portia sat back on her heels and watched her carefully.

"How do you know?"

"I don't know exactly, but she came home in a dreadful taking one evening, said she'd found a witch's garden in a secret place full of plants that shouldn't be growing there."

"What plants?"

"She said it was full of mandrake, nightshade and henbane..."

"Henbane? That won't grow on London clay," Henbane famously was what witches used on their broomsticks – or rather the poisonous seeds of it ground up and made into an ointment. Portia felt herself freeze in place, kneeling next to the old midwife's chest. Her spine had turned to ice, her knees to jelly. She suddenly knew where the garden had been and what Peter Cheke had been talking about – henbane, not chickens, mumbled by an old woman. Honestly! She should have spotted it.

"No, it won't. That's what Goody Harbridge said too. She said to get it to grow you had to bring in sand because it liked a sandy soil and that's how she knew it wasn't just weeds."

Portia nodded.

"When she found it, there were still flowers. Later she said someone had harvested the seeds and she said then that the Devil would be abroad in London because

314

of the witch for only a witch would have such a garden."

"The Devil?"

"Oh yes, henbane ointment mixes up the humours," she said, and so you see things."

"Goodness," said Portia because this was new to her, "But why the Devil?"

"Ah, that's because you get hot if you have too much," said Goody Worthing "You feel the heat terribly. Goody Harebridge said she knew about it because she used to use it as an ointment for mothers that were having trouble with a birth – she'd put a very little of the ointment on their privy parts and that would quiet them and relax them so she could get a hand in and shift the baby if it was breech – she was a very good midwife, you know, only the College of Physicians took her to court and prosecuted her for they said that she was ignorant and a witch herself. And her at church every Sunday."

Portia's heart was thudding. "I've never had henbane ointment," she said, thinking she could have done with it for her first.

"Yes and you spill everything in your heart, tell all your secrets. Goody gave me some when my little Laura came early, she was trying to stop my waters breaking so early and it was a cruel hard birth. I was telling Goody Harbridge all about when I was a girl – not that I remember what I said, you never do. It's a wise woman's secret – Goody only told me about it because of finding the plant, you know. She said all that knowledge was dying anyway as the Physicians drive out the midwives for their fees."

"Did she say where the garden was?"

Goody Worthing shrugged. The baby spat out her nipple and turned to stare boldly at Portia, then gave a one-toothy grin. She couldn't help smiling back despite what her insides were doing.

She looked in the chest again and in the purse. There were a few pennies there..

"Goody Worthing," she said, "Did Goody Harbridge tell you who the witch was?"

"She was going to. She came back the day before yesterday and she said she knew who it was and she was a wicked wicked woman. So she said she was going to accuse her."

"Ah,"

"And whoever it was, killed her," said Goody Worthing bitterly, laying a cloth on her lap and starting to unwind the swaddling bands parcelling up the baby. "That was the last I saw of her."

"Who did she tell?"

"She was worried she wouldn't get to talk to anyone, even Mr Recorder Fleetwood would tell her not to trouble herself with imaginings. She told a merchant's wife she knew but she said nobody believed her. Missus, would you pass me that changing basket..?"

Portia reached over and handed it to her as the ripe smell of a well-fed baby's bowels filled the room and Goody Worthing wiped and cleaned and changed the baby. He waved his arms and legs around and grinned happily up at Goody Worthing who smiled back. His little willy stood up and he peed, but she caught it with a cloth and laughed at him.

"Ah you won't catch me that way again, little John, no, you won't."

Portia climbed to her feet, feeling sick and shaky. She needed to get out of the place with its healthy babies and living children. Through the back window she could see the toddler, the little girl and the two older boys playing a complicated game with the tethered goat.

"Thank you, Goodwife," she managed to say, "I'm very sorry to hear about Goody Harbridge. Please don't worry about my gloves. If you find the money I gave her for them, use it towards her burial."

"Ralph," shouted Goody Worthing, "Open the door for Missus Morgan now!"

The oldest boy trotted through from the garden holding the usual stick essential to all boys of any age, opened the door for her. Portia put her mask back on and walked out of the house, remembering her own marketing basket just in time. Her heart was tight up against her ribs, throbbing from God's knife stuck in it,

317

but she ignored that. Her head was mercifully busy with ideas and thoughts, packed tight with them. She needed to make one more visit as herself and then she needed to sit in an inn somewhere and think it all out over a cup of aquavitae...

She caught herself. As the respectable though shy widow Mrs Morgan she couldn't do that, so she would have to change into her brother again. But first she had to visit the merchant's wife who owned the yard where Goody Harbridge's body had been found.

.

She found the woman unwilling to receive visitors. It was only when Portia sent in the warrant she had from Fleetwood as James Enys that she was admitted to sit in another golden oaklined parlour with a good display of plate.

The woman who came downstairs was well-dressed in a new brown velvet English-cut gown, over the rounding belly of early pregnancy. She looked tired which was hardly surprising. If the baby being wetnursed by Goody Worthing was born in summer she must have been with child again barely after she was churched. She looked anxious.

"Yes mistress?" she said, "how may I help you?"

"I'm so sorry to trouble you, mistress," Portia began

carefully, not quite sure how to proceed. It was all rather complicated. "My brother has been charged by Mr Recorder Fleetwood with finding out who killed the old woman that was found by your jakes. He asked if I would help him by speaking privately with you."

Mrs Bailey looked surprised, then afraid. Then she nodded and clasped her hands at her waist.

"We don't know her at all and... er... we don't know how she came there," said the woman in a high drone.

"He asked me to do it," Portia added carefully, "because you might be more able to speak to me than to him."

"We don't know her," repeated Mrs Bailey, her voice shaking.

How to put it to her without getting Goody Worthing in trouble?

"Mr Cheke the apothecary told me... my brother that she used to find herbs for him and that she had been a midwife. Is it possible she might have attended you..." The woman's face was scarlet and suddenly Portia realised why she might not want to admit that she knew the old midwife. "...or someone you know?"

Portia stared at the merchant's pregnant wife. Come on, she thought to herself, I don't care what you asked Goody Harbridge to do when you found out you were pregnant again so soon, especially as it seems she didn't do it. Come on, get the message.

"Ah... yes... a friend of mine, a gossip. Um... might have known her."

Excellent. The ever reliable anonymous friend. "Surely Goody Harbridge herself wasn't a witch?"

Again the flush. "No," said Mrs Bailey, "No, but she... er... my friend did ask her about charms to fall with child a while ago."

"Oh? And what did she say?"

"She said that for all the good they did, you might as well polish the banisters' newel post instead. So that's what I... er... she did with beeswax and linseed and then she did quicken." There was a rueful little smile on her face. "My husband was delighted."

With some difficulty, Portia kept a straight face. "Ah. Did she attend the birth?"

Mrs Bailey nodded. "She did but she made me promise not to tell anyone for the College of Physicians were after her to stop midwifery as it took money away from them, even though they know nothing at all about childbed, being men."

"What nonsense!" said Portia, outraged, "How can a man attend a woman in labour? It would be a scandal. Can you imagine anything more horrible?"

Mrs Bailey nodded vigorously. "I wouldn't have one though my husband thought a physician would be safer for me. Disgusting!"

"So you had Goody Harbridge. Was she skillful?"

"Oh yes, she made me feel ever so warm and comfy with a little of her magic ointment and after the babby was born and my husband didn't like the crying in the night, she found me a very clean and respectable wetnurse to take him. Only then..."

Mrs Bailey sighed and pressed her lips together and looked down at her rounding belly.

"Ah yes."

"But then... my friend thinks her brain took a turn, she was terribly worried about a witch in London, a real one who was doing terrible things, she said."

Mrs Bailey suddenly stopped, frowned, went to the door and checked behind it, then came back and sat right next to Portia.

"I don't care, my husband says we should say nothing about knowing her..." she whispered urgently in Portia's ear, "... she was only an old woman, but I think it's terrible and wrong what happened to her and it does matter if an old woman is killed." She smiled tremulously. "After all, if I live through my hour this time and all the other times, I'll be an old woman one day and I don't want to die as she did. It looked so awful..."

Portia put her hand on the woman's arm, which was trembling. "Of course it did, Mistress," she said softly, "But please don't think about it because you don't want another shock to the baby."

Mrs Bailey nodded seriously. "You don't think the

321

baby will be marked by it?"

"No, I don't," said Portia, "With my first, I saw a boy with a terrible mark on his face and I was frightened the baby might have one too, but he didn't." No, that mark came later when the pocks covered his face and broke and he screamed and screamed... Jesus, she had to stop this. Mrs Bailey was talking again.

"You see, I think she was right about witches. I think that she went to challenge Mrs... She said it was someone I know, you see, but it can't be. I simply don't believe it."

"Who did she say it was?" Portia asked softly. But Mrs Bailey only started to cry and shake her head.

"I don't know, she wouldn't say in case the witch found out, what if she puts the Evil Eye on my baby – it'll be my fault," she sobbed. Portia felt for her hankerchief then remembered that she had given it to Peter the Hedgehog. Mrs Bailey had one in the pocket of her petticoat and blew her nose like a trumpet. "I can't tell you, I can't, it's too dangerous... And I don't know. It's only a guess. I might be wrong and that would be terrible too..."

"Shhh," said Portia, stroking the woman's arm, "It's all right. Don't do anything you don't want to. Perhaps you could tell your husband..."

"I tried and he was very... a... angry with me, he said she's a respectable good woman and I was a silly jade with silly notions."

Portia sighed.

"Can you at least tell me where she lives? Goody Harbridge might have been wrong about it after all."

"F... Fleet Street, near Whitefriars."

Portia nodded grimly. She felt the loom of an answer in the crowd of thoughts packing her head. "Mrs Bailey, thank you for speaking to me," she said as she stood to leave and made sure her mask was on straight, "I think perhaps Goody Harbridge was mistaken about who was the witch. Men can be witches too, you know?"

Mrs Bailey stared. "You think it was a man who killed Goody Harbridge?"

"Yes, I do. If I'm right he's respectable and well-liked but he has killed at least two other women and a girl as well as Goody Harbridge and possibly more."

Mrs Bailey's mouth was round and open. "A man witch?" she said, "Good heavens, what a terrible thing... Almost as bad as a man-midwife."

"Indeed," said Portia, "Mistress, if you feel you could let me know the name of the person Goody Harbridge suspected, please send a message to me at my brother's chambers in the Earl of Essex's new court." She swept her curtsey to the lady of the house and went to the door.

Her heart was thudding again with anger and fear as she came down Ludgate to Fleet Bridge again. Paul

Chapel had once said over a beer, that if you were looking at a dangerous fight with more than one enemy, you should go for the biggest and ugliest one first and the same with arguing a court case. So before she could think about it, she marched down to the Craddocks' house and knocked on the door. After a while the door was opened by the girl with the harelip.

"May I speak with the mistress?" Portia asked.

The girl flushed and shook her head, turned and made a strange ugly cry. After a moment the young boy who seemed to be her brother came trotting up.

"Is the mistress of the house here?"

"No, missus, Mrs Ashley's gone to market."

"I meant Mrs Craddock," Portia said patiently.

The boy and the girl looked at each other in surprise. "Oh. She's resting missus, is Mrs Craddock," said the boy, "She usually is. Doesn't usually have visitors."

"Tell Mrs Craddock that I desire to speak with her on the subject of her servants Mary and Peter," said Portia, rage making her voice very frosty behind her mask. Both of the children looked frightened and the girl turned and ran up the shining polished stairs.

Without waiting for any more invitation, Portia pushed past the boy and entered the hall.

"She's busy, missus," said the boy.

"Then I'll wait until she is able to meet with me in a neighbourly way," said Portia, still frosty. In fact they were fairly near neighbours and sort of in the same line of work. In fact she was surprised she had never seen the young Mrs Craddock at the conduit in the days before the world full of staring faces became too much for her and she hid away in her chamber while James did her marketing for her and paid a boy to bring up water for her since a man obviously couldn't be asked to do such a thing.

"Where is Mr Craddock?" she asked as the boy came and stood next to the cup-board with the plate on it, quite tactlessly guarding it from her. She happened to find that quite funny: after all, what on earth would be the point of stealing somebody's silver ware? Everyone would know whose it was unless you could melt it down, which she couldn't.

"He's in court," said the boy, "he's got a big case on, a wardship, all the way upriver in Westminster. We won't see him back until after dark, I'd say."

Portia nodded. She sat herself down on the bench and prepared for a wait. All around her was quiet, the noise of the street muffled by the walls and the low sun slanting through the diamond panes and the smell of beeswax polish.

"She's very tired," said the boy, "She's tired from spending all night polishing the banisters and the stairs too, she thinks she'll fall with child if she does."

"Oh?"

"Don't see why? If that was all it took, every servant in London would be in trouble, wouldn't they?" The boy gave an innocent grin.

Portia thought of trying to explain how she thought the idea had got abroad, but decided against it.

At last there was the sound of footsteps on the stair, court slippers. The bony-looking blonde girl coming down the stairs was as ethereal as Maliverny Catlin had said. She was wearing watchet blue satin today, a very dangerous colour for anyone who wasn't pale and blonde, although this child could have done with being less pale. She had big rings under her eyes as well.

She frowned when she saw Portia. "I cry you mercy, mistress," she said, "My mother is at market and my husband at Westminster in court..."

Portia smiled, rose and curtseyed as she would to the lady of the house. The girl flinched.

"I know, your pageboy told me. I believe you are a friend of Mrs Bailey's, aren't you?"

For some reason a flush went up Mrs Craddock's cheeks. "Er... yes," she said, "I am, but I... I haven't seen her recently. She has a beautiful baby, hasn't she?"

"Yes," said Portia, "Very strong and lusty. She got some good advice from her midwife, didn't she?"

The colour was heading towards an unbecoming bright red. Mrs Craddock looked out of the window. "Um," she said, "Yes." Then in a whisper, "It hasn't worked for me yet."

Of course it hasn't, you silly girl, Portia wanted to say, do you not know the meaning of metaphor? Hm? She didn't say that. Instead she gave it a minute's sympathetic silence and then said brightly, "I really wanted to ask your opinion of the two youngsters who were your servants before last summer, Mary and Peter."

Now that was interesting. The girl didn't change colour this time, didn't look frightened, didn't look guilty. She blinked rapidly.

"My mother said they had found better places in a bigger household. I was pleased for them."

"Oh?" said Portia, "And what did you think of them? I might employ the boy as my page. Are they honest?"

The girl's milky velvet brow wrinkled. "I thought they were," she said, "I liked them, but I haven't heard anything of them since they left."

Was it possible she didn't know? Quite possible, Peter had kept his sister's death quiet out of terror.

"I've only seen the boy."

"His sister is a very hard worker, but he's a little simple," said Mrs Craddock, "I'm sure they're... honest."

Again that pure brow clouded.

"I didn't see them leave but I was sorry for it. Then I think my mother spoke to them at the door a week later but I don't know what she said. She wouldn't let me see them."

327

"Oh?"

"You could ask her about them," said the girl, walking to the plate board and examining a cup. She seemed to find something she disliked for she touched it lightly with her fingers. "Though my mother didn't approve of the girl at all."

"When will Mrs Ashley be back?"

"Soon perhaps," said the girl distantly, picking up the cup and walking away with it. "Sometimes she goes to see the bear-baiting with her gossips and doesn't come back until dark."

Quite a few stout matrons enjoyed bear-baiting and went in loudly-coloured groups to crack hazelnuts and suck orangeados. A few, greatly daring, might visit the playhouses as well, despite their scandalous nature, and watch plays – when the playhouses were open of course, and not shut for the plague.

"I'll wait," said Portia again, and Mrs Craddock nodded distractedly and went upstairs again, carrying the goblet, pausing every other step to touch one of the bannisters. She disappeared into gathering shadows.

It didn't take much longer which was just as well for Portia's patience. The door opened and Mrs Ashley came bustling in, carrying a market basket full of cabbage and pot herbs with some pork collops arranged in a napkin on the top.

Portia stood and curtseyed to her as well.

"Good day, mistress," she said politely, "I'm sorry to trouble you but I had hoped you would advise me."

Mrs Ashley's eyes seemed a little cautious. She smiled a stiff social smile. "I must put these in the larder," she said, "Boy, take this into the kitchen."

The boy trotted in and took the basket from her, trotted out with it held high. Portia told her story again. She thought the woman seemed a little familiar, she must have seen her around Fleet Street but not been introduced.

But as a lawyer, Portia was used to seeing the look in peoples' eyes as they thought frantically while trying to talk at the same time. She was surprised to see that exact look in Mrs Ashley's eyes.

"Let me see, Mary and Peter," she said. "Yes, I had to tell them to go a few weeks ago."

"May I ask why, mistress?" Portia said, "I'm thinking of taking on young Peter as a page boy."

"I'm afraid I can't recommend him, I think he's nearly half-witted."

"And his sister?"

There was a sour expression around Mrs Craddock's mouth. "A very bad character," she said, "I believe she ended as a whore."

The hair on Portia's neck prickled upright. Young Mrs Craddock didn't know that Mary was dead but it seemed Mrs Ashley did. How, when Peter had kept it

329

secret?

"Oh?" Portia managed to say, sounding as disapproving as she could.

"That was why she had to go," said Mrs Ashley, "Her behaviour... Very distressing to my daughter if she had found out. I'm sure you understand."

Portia allowed her eyebrows to rise in question.

"Mr Craddock was not dissatisfied with her but my daughter was and so was I," said Mrs Ashley, confirming the hint. "So she went and her half-wit brother with her. I haven't seen her since."

"I had heard that they were seen at your door about two weeks ago."

Mrs Ashley looked away and her hands began to make an odd movement, rubbing each other as if washing. They were quite big hands for a woman, with a reddish rash, the sort washerwomen got from putting their hands in lye.

"Oh yes," she said distantly, "They came begging at the door with some nonsense. I told them to leave."

Portia managed to shake her head regretfully. "I'm sorry to hear it. So you wouldn't recommend the boy?"

Mrs Ashley shrugged. "I don't think he is dishonest," she said, "Only stupid. Don't let him bring in his sister, she'll only cause trouble. A very uppity little madam, in fact."

So perhaps Mrs Ashley didn't mean "end" as in

"die" but as "finally became". That made better sense. Suddenly rage started filling Portia up, flowing outwards from the tight knot in her stomach. Stupid? The boy could read and quite possibly better than this woman. Or perhaps not – Catlin had said Mrs Ashley was surprisingly learned for a woman as her father had been a physician. It didn't matter, Portia must leave before the rage burst out.

Portia stood up. "Thank you mistress," she said, "You've been very helpful. I do hope I will see Mrs Craddock again perhaps. I haven't seen her at the conduit lately."

Mrs Ashley shrugged. "She really has no need to go out," she said, "Except to go shopping on the Bridge or visiting and at the moment.... She is distressed because my son in law has not given her a child in more than three years of marriage."

"If there is anything I can..." Portia began hesitantly. She suddenly realised it was getting late, the boy was trotting round lighting candles.

Just at that moment, the door banged and the loud footsteps announced the master of the house.

"Why Mrs Morgan," cried Mr Craddock, "How delightful to see you, ma'am, how are you?"

God damn and blast it, she shouldn't have stayed so long. Now she would have to be doubly careful if she met him as James Enys, now he had seen her face. As casually as she could, she put her black velvet mask back on and tied the ribbons she had sewn on it.

"I'm very well, Mr Craddock," she managed and curtseyed, heading for the door. He followed her and opened it for her.

"My regards to your brother, Mrs Morgan," said the man who had destroyed young Mary's life. "I hear great things of him from our brother lawyers."

All she could do was curtsey again as she passed him and head out into the street as fast as she could.

.

As she got wearily to the top of the stairs and fumbled for her key, a male figure emerged diffidently from the shadows. She jumped back with an inelegant squawk. Her hand fell quite naturally to her left hip where her sword should have been, only of course it wasn't, it was hanging on the wall in her chamber. Women don't wear swords.

Trembling, she rearranged her mask again. She knew who it was, it was that blasted Father Bellamy and she was utterly dismayed to see him. What had possessed him to come back? In the nick of time she remembered that she only knew him as James Enys. As her proper self, she had been with a gossip all last night. God, it was hard to keep all the lies straight in your head.

He had already started apologising in a low soft voice. "Mistress Morgan," said the idiot, "I cry you pardon, please don't be alarmed. Is Mr Enys within?"

She shook her head and stepped back again into the shadows. Damn damn damn it! Would could she do?

"Do you have no woman attending you so late in the evening?" he asked with a frown. God blast him, what business was it of his?

"I... she's busy with her babe and husband and I was delayed coming home. Who... who are you, sir? A friend of James's?"

He smiled wryly. "In a way, ma'am. In fact I owe him my life." He made a neat bow. "I am... er... I am Felix Bellamy."

"The priest?" she said, sharper than she intended.

He nodded once. "Your brother told you what happened?"

She fiddled with her mask to give her time to think. What would James Enys likely have told his shy, nervous sister?

"Um... he said that he had given shelter to a priest. I own I rated him for it but James said he did it for the reason that this one was not about any treason but trying to help his sister who had been attacked and ruined by that villain Topcliffe."

The priest nodded, looking slightly relieved. "Just so, mistress. Your brother was magnificent, a true hero.

333

He hid me very cleverly and outfaced Topcliffe himself with his sword."

So he wasn't too eager to explain exactly how he had been hidden. Portia started to find a stupid bubble of giggles rising up in the middle of her fright and her annoyance at the silly idiot for coming back, in God's name. Why? Though it was nice to hear that she was a hero.

She shook her head so as to try and stay seemly.

"I'm afraid my brother is often too brave for his own good," she said prosaically – and lord knew, that was the truth. She had been astonished herself at what pretending to be James had done to her – had she really almost challenged Topcliffe to a duel?

"Do you know where he is, Mrs Morgan?" asked the priest.

"Ah... he often stays at Westminster when a court case sits late or is likely to begin early because a boat is no more expensive than a bed at an inn." She was improvising wildly. "He would certainly be annoyed at me for coming home so late if he were here."

"So would I, ma'am," said the priest, "If you were my sister. The world alas contains wicked men."

"Hm," she said, looking narrowly at him through the holes of her mask. "So were you hoping to stay the night again?"

He nodded, looking miserable.

"I have not found any Catholics to help me," he said, "It seems Mrs Crosby has blasted my name among them as a traitor."

Now that was interesting. So the idiot priest was loose and friendless in London. Unfortunately, thanks to her ridiculous impulse of the night before and the terrifying stand off in the small hours, he now held her safety in his mouth. If he was caught and tortured, no doubt he would put James Enys among the first names he gave up.

"I'm sorry, mistress," he said again, his shoulders sagging, "I understand. I was hoping to impose on your brother's kindness but I can't..."

"But didn't my brother tell you to leave London?"

"He did," said the priest, "but every time I tried to hire a horse or get a boat upriver, I saw some kind of pursuivant or tunnage and poundage man on the watch."

Portia bit her lip to stop herself asking him why he didn't simply walk. Since the new Armada in the summer and more Jesuits caught in the spring, London had been full of informers and watchers and it would only be good sense to keep a watch on boats and livery stables. Probably he had just hunkered down somewhere, too frightened to move.

"My brother spoke well of you," she said, slowly and hesitantly. For God's sake, she had to do something,

335

they couldn't stand here gossiping on the landing, her neighbours would talk. "He didn't tell me what to do if you came back but I think he would wish me to help you if I can."

"Your reputation..."

"Is already in your hands, isn't it, Father? I'm a married woman, a widow, you a priest. Surely I can trust you?"

It didn't necessarily follow but she smiled and then remembered he wouldn't see it. She had to take the chance.

Decision made, she unlocked the door and waved him in. She looked carefully down the stairs in case someone had been listening, but they were dark and empty. She just had to hope that Topcliffe wouldn't bother to raid her chambers twice.

She had not had time to set any pot of food among the banked coals and so had nothing ready. Still. There was something pleasant about playing the hostess again, without having to remember to speak deep and do things carelessly. And Mr Briscoe had kept his promise to send her a load of coals so she had plenty in the coal scuttle, even if she didn't like the smell and dirt they made. Wood was much nicer but impossibly expensive.

Young Father Bellamy came in and looked round. Just as he did she saw her cloak and sword still hanging on the hook, which James would certainly have taken with him. It was in shadow, had Felix Bellamy seen? She wasn't sure.

"Do you have a jordan, ma'am?" asked priest in a strained voice, "I fear..."

Thank God, she thought. "Under the bed," she said, pointing, shut the door of the bedchamber behind him and quickly grabbed the sword, cloak and – oh Jesus - worse still, her brother's hat from their pegs on the wall. She stuffed them quickly in the clothes chest, probably denting the hat but no matter.

By the time Felix Bellamy had come back she had got the fire restarted and the flames were leaping up in the luxurious Newcastle coals, she had the dish-of-coals by the fireplace to warm up, she had looked in the food safe and found that the bread had gone mouldy but there were a couple of sausages and a couple of slices of bacon, more apples which had been on special offer because bruised at one of the market stalls, butter and cheese. She thanked the Lord she had laid in plenty of supplies when she had been paid. Fr Bellamy came out of the bedchamber looking a little less tense, followed by a certain miasma of bad bowels which she thought she would leave to clear before she investigated.

She ushered him into the chair with carved arms and fetched ale for him which he drank in the manner of one who hasn't drunk all day. She poured him more and he sighed.

"Ma'am, you are too good to me to be a Protestant. Are you sure you are not a Catholic and your brother mistaken?"

"I was baptised one in Cornwall," she said, "It was early in the Queen's reign, bless her, and everyone thought she would surely marry the King of Spain and we would all go back to Mother Church."

"And now?"

"I go to church when I can bear it," she said quietly in a voice that forbad further probing. At least he came off that tack.

"Do you wear your mask always?" he asked.

"When I am with people I don't know and when I go out of the house..." Oh Jesu, what could she say? He had worn her mask himself last night when she had ostensibly been out... "I have several, in case I lose one. For months and months I couldn't stir at all and my brother did everything for me and then... Well then cirumstances led to wearing a mask which answers well." Had she bought it as herself or as James? She couldn't remember? She'd better buy another one soon.

"Perhaps I could say a Mass for you and your brother as a small thanksgiving for your kindness to me?" asked Felix Bellamy. She felt herself colouring but with temper not modesty. Could he not get the point?

"I'm sorry Father, I dare not. I don't worry myself with the niceties of religion and I dislike going to church as often as I should because the place is full of people who stare at me – that is, I'm sure they don't, but I feel they do and it makes me ill and faint. I am not a recusant; my brother would hardly be able to practise as a barrister in her Majesty's courts if I were, I think."

Bellamy shook his head and tutted. God damn it, what could she do with him? She really didn't care about his precious religion since all the varieties of them she had ever heard of served the God who had robbed her of her children, but she did care about his safety since on it rested her own.

Perhaps he could be educated in logic a little?

"Did you wonder why the woman you were staying with before, why she spread it around that you were the traitor that brought Topcliffe down on the congregation?"

Felix shook his head. She used the tongs to pick out the hottest of the red coals to put in her dish-of-coals and shut the grill lid. "I was so shocked at the injustice of it," he said sadly.

"Hm. Well perhaps the traitor was Mrs Crosby herself, trying to get rid of you, especially as you say she wasn't there when the raid took place?"

He nodded. "I wondered if it was her, though I tried to be more charitable." She shook the coals and laid the sausages on the grill.

"Somebody's got to take the blame and it might as

339

well be you. You're on your own and unofficial to boot."

"She did say she was waiting for five of my colleagues when I came, in fact she thought I was their harbinger."

"There you are then, it was Mrs Crosby sold you for a certainty and blasted your reputation to protect her own."

He scowed at that and Portia fel the beginnings of a plan stir in her. Or something similar. She had to concentrate on cooking as the sausages started sizzling and she took out the bread and cut the bits of mould off, then sliced it and buttered both sides. The meaty smell rose up and she stood to open the window but young Bellamy forestalled her and opened it himself, staying well back as he did. Maybe he wasn't that young, he just seemed young.

"Perhaps you could go to Mrs Crosby," she said slowly as she set pewter plates by the fire to warm up. Those had been the first out of pawn. "Perhaps you could talk to her and say that you know she betrayed you and that you'll have to do likewise to her in the matter of the other priests coming to stay."

He frowned. "Why?"

"So she'll give you money, help you out of London to get rid of you?"

"Might she not betray me again?"

"Yes, she might. Make her give you three different routes and then choose one at random and take it immediately."

"Tonight?"

"Very early tomorrow morning," said Portia. "At least get some money from her so you can eat without coming back here."

"I don't know," said Bellamy and his whole round face drew down with unhappiness. "I don't think I should stay..."

"Phooey. Seeing my whole life is in your hands now... and my brother's, you may as well stay the night and I'll have to trust to your vows."

He inclined his head to her. She started the bacon and found a pan to put on the dish-of-coals to make a mess of eggs from some of the preserved ones Ellie Briscoe had insisted on giving her. With the fried bread as sippets there was enough for both of them.

He caught her out again when he said a Grace over his food. She had completely got out of the habit. She waited and when he had picked up his knife and spoon again, she poured him ale and smiled. It was actually a pleasure to sit over food with another human being, since the grey tabby cat had limited conversation. She almost said this before she caught herself. After all, according to the story she wanted Felix Bellamy to believe, she sat like this with her brother almost every night, didn't she – as she had when her infuriating brother had been here and in a way she had become his ghost. Even as a ghost, his existence had given her amazing confidence.

Well it was clear the boy hadn't managed to eat that day either, so she was glad she had the food. Poor little unshorn lamb, it was a pity his God didn't see fit to temper the wind to him. But perhaps he would see it as a salutary testing of his faith. And perhaps she was part of that Godly tempering which if true, she found irritating. She wanted no part of God's schemes.

In the candlelight as he concentrated on his food, she thought to her own surprise, he's a good-looking man. It was true his face was round and boyish and he wasn't big or strong or her stratagem of yesterday could not have worked. His brown hair was cut close though he obviously hadn't visited a barber recently and his beard was growing past the confines of its goatee trim. But he had a charming diffident smile and a dimple in the middle of his chin which she suddenly thought of putting her finger on.

She coughed and looked down at her food, stopped eating. She was a little shocked at herself. Since her husband had died, she had not really looked at a man in that way at all. It wasn't a forced chastity of principle, it was a chastity born of ... well, a lack of interest. And time.

He was clearly struggling to think of a way of opening some polite conversation, but of course, as she remembered from before, he knew she was a widow so he couldn't ask about her husband, and she had no living children so that was not a good thing to ask about.

She had taken her mask off to eat which she had done so naturally it only just occurred to her. She shifted back a little, more into the candle shadows. So where was he going to start with a question? Never mind, she would help him out.

"Tell me about your poor sister," she said to him, "James told me she had suffered terribly for her faith."

It wasn't an easy subject for him, of course, but at least it was a subject that he could just about discuss with a woman and it would be better than giving him nothing to do but look at her face and possibly make comparisons.

"My family was sheltering Father Robert Southwell in our house. Someone laid information and they raided the house. They didn't find Fr Southwell in his hiding place so they arrested Ann my sister, who was then a virgin and wanted only to serve God." He paused and she nodded, full of sympathy. She knew how terrifying it must have been for Ann, only too well.

"Topcliffe had her in his keeping for three months by which time she must have known she was with child for she wrote to my mother." Portia nodded encouragingly. "That was bad enough," Bellamy's young face was twisted with pain, "but the next thing I heard was that Topcliffe had raided the house again and this time he had a full plan showing where all of our priestholes were, including the one where Fr Southwell was hiding. Nobody else could have known, other than the man who built them who is utterly reliable."

"So Ann sold Father Southwell for..."

Bellamy shrugged. "For marriage, for Topcliffe's protection. We don't know. My parents will have nothing to do with her, my father has disinherited her, for her lewdness."

"James says you think differently."

"I know my sister," he said, "She is not a lewd woman. Whatever happened was not what she wanted."

"Of course it wasn't," scowled Portia, the anger rising in her again, ""How could it be? She was a prisoner, at the mercy of a man who has no mercy."

"Yes. I thought so but my parents will not listen. They say she should have held firm and died rather than be defiled."

"Hard to do when you're bound or chained and strong men are assaulting you," said Portia trenchantly, "Don't you think?"

He was staring at her wildly. "You think they did that?" God, he was naive.

"Of course they did. Why wouldn't they, when they enjoy it? Trust me, there was no scene of seduction."

"My parents say she must have been willing if she..."

"...fell with child. My brother approved the logic

344

of your point on unwilling marriages. Are you not convinced yourself, Father?"

"I... sometimes I wonder."

She could have shaken him by the throat. "A woman only needs to be...er... bedded to fall with child, she doesn't need to enjoy it. Which is just as well, really, or there would be very many fewer children born."

He flinched back at her vulgarity. "I thought..."

"Nonsense. Your poor sister! And I expect once she knew she was with child, she only wanted to protect the baby – no doubt Topcliffe threatened to kill it. Perhaps he even threatened to call in a witch and kill the baby in her womb."

Bellamy's eyes were like saucers. "Good God," he said and put down his spoon and knife. His eyes were full of tears.

"I would imagine she sold Robert Southwell for the life of her child," said Portia, who had tried to make some terrible bargains with God when her children were dying. "I know mothers are ruthless that way, with themselves and everyone else." God, however, had proven more ruthless still.

Bellamy nodded. "Yes, I see. I'm afraid you must think me and my family very naive."

"Yes," she snapped, then softened a little. "Well, no. I think you're a man who has not had many dealings with evil."

345

"And you have?" he asked, gently cutting through her patronage.

She looked down at her meat which she no longer wanted. "I suppose I have," she said after a careful pause, "Unwillingly... As a kind of clerk to my brother, I know some of what he has to deal with. And I know that as a woman with no man to protect her, no money, no property, I would be many men's prey, who would turn their lustful greedy eyes on me and then blame me for it."

"And yet you are still chaste?" said the boy, quite reverently.

"By luck and by what the smallpox did to my face," she told him tartly, "What happened to your sister was the fault of the man who did it, not your sister's. The superstition that a raped woman does not quicken and so if she quickens she was willing - is it not a very convenient lie for whoremongers and defilers like Topcliffe who can then turn a good and virtuous woman's family against her." To her astonishment, Portia found she was actually shaking with anger on the unfortunate Ann Bellamy's behalf. It was why she had been stupid enough to let the priest in the night before.

The boy's face relaxed. She chided herself – he must be about her age if he was a Jesuit, since it took extra study to join Loyola's Society of Jesus, she shouldn't lecture him, men didn't like it.

"That's what I believed," he said simply. "That's why I came, breaking my vow of obedience."

"Oh?"

He flushed a little. "My Superiors told me not to come and try and find her," he said, "But I have."

She toasted him with the last of the ale and they tapped beakers together. Then she found she was gripping his hand with hers.

"I honour you for it, your sister needs you desperately," she said.

His face suddenly creased with distress. She let go his hand quickly before he could misinterpret her.

"Yes, but where is she? What is she doing? How can I find her?"

"Your only link to her is Topcliffe himself," she said slowly, "You have to get close to him or his men."

"But without ending up in his dungeon."

"Ideally," she agreed drily.

They talked over how it could be done for an hour but they came up against the same blank wall each time.

"You need to be respectable," she said, "You need to be what you are not, a man of unimpeachable Protestant loyalty."

Finally he suddenly sat back and laughed. "Well, I can't solve it. I'll have to leave it to God, his holy angels and perhaps a saint or two."

"Ah,"

347

"Yes, I'll make an appeal to... oh.. St Jude should do the trick, the patron saint of lost causes."

She laughed too.

"At least sleep on it," she agreed as she rose to clear away the plates and remains of the food. She left her unfinished meat where the cat could find it – he liked eggs and bacon and his rough tongue made scouring the plates easier.

Fr Bellamy had already gone into the bedchamber and was pushing the truckle bed into the main room. "I had the best bed last night, thanks to your very hospitable brother, but I got not a minute's sleep last night for the pestering of a demon in disguise as a small grey cat."

"Ah," she said, "Yes. But he also kills mice."

"Splendid," said Felix, "You have him." Their eyes met briefly and she smiled at his wry expression. And they stopped for a moment as if somebody had stopped the world so that they could see the colour of each other's eyes. And then Portia shook herself and started digging in her blanket box.

The candle was burning down to its end and she had found a spare blanket for Bellamy to wrap himself in. She went into the bedchamber to change for bed and as she used the remarkably ugly-smelling jordan, she saw her furry minion sitting on the windowsill blinking at her as he waited to be let in.

"Were you jealous?" she asked with a knowing smile as she opened and closed the window for him,"Thank you for giving the alarm."

The cat gave no answer, only lashed his tail as he stared at the closed door into the main chamber.

.

She woke very early again as the cat left her side. Feeling confused and groggy, she wondered if it was James she could hear moving around in the main chamber and then remembered the young Jesuit.

She smiled as she remembered their talk of yesterday and his complete confidence that God and his holy angels would riddle out the problem for him.

It was freezing cold, far too cold to stay in bed now the cat had shoved the bed curtain aside. A whistling wind was coming into the cave of her bed from the window which didn't fit as well as it ought.

She got up, used the jordan again which urgently needed emptying and started dressing as a woman again. She might have been a man as her courses were nearly done, but there was the priest of course. Luckily she wasn't in court that day.

Once decent, she knocked and came out to find that Felix Bellamy had got the fire going again and the frost flowers inside the windows were disappearing into the

349

dark. The poker was balanced on the coals and after she had tapped them some morning ale, Bellamy mulled the ale so they had something hot to drink.

"Mistress, I'll be gone now," he said, "I thank you most heartily for your kindness and hospitality to me and I pray God you will soon find a kindly and suitable man to marry – or your brother will stir himself to find him for you, at least.

She inclined her head to him: God forbid her brother ever took it into his head to find a husband for her. "I hope you can find your sister," she said, "Do you have a plan now?"

"Not yet, but I know I will find one before this evening. If I am not further forward by then, I'll leave London on foot. I won't risk you or your brother again."

"So you slept well? Did you get any kind of answer to your prayer to St Jude?"

She had never known one despite all the many desperate prayers she had whispered over her children.

He smiled at her and she thought again what a pity it was that he was a priest. Not that she needed the trouble that would come of marrying a penniless Catholic.

"Only the usual answer: Be still and know that I am God."

"Oh," What kind of answer was that? But the idiot seemed happy enough with it.

"Good day, Mrs Morgan, God bless you and keep

you," he said as she opened the door and they both listened carefully for nosy people or pursuivants. He bowed to her and quietly pulled the door shut, leaving her to finish the hot ale for her breakfast.

Warming her fingers at the coals, she looked at the pile of paperwork waiting for her, some of which had been destroyed by Topcliffe's spite. She needed to get on with that, there were a number of pleadings that needed to be put in fair copy before they could be lodged.

So she sighed, set the best ink to melt by the fire, checked and recut two pens and drew clean paper towards her at her inkstained desk.

.

By midday her eyes were squinting and she was getting a headache, so she went out for a breath of air, not forgetting her now essential mask. Will Shakespeare was standing there, obviously waiting for her. Portia wanted to thank him for coming to her rescue with Maliverny Catlin two nights before. But that could wait. She only needed one look at the player's face to know at once what had happened. She heard his voice from a long way away.

"Mr En... Mrs Morgan," said the player, "There's been another murder."

"Jesu," she said. She was feeling sick and dizzy.

Another one. She fell into step beside him as he headed up the alleyway that led to Fleet Street.

"Will you come?"

"I must change first..."

"No, mistress, come please as you are, Eliza's in such a taking you might calm her better."

"What?"

"It can't go against your reputation to do a Christian kindness even if it is to a whore."

Knowing the harsh clacking tongues of London as she did, Portia thought distantly that it could, but if Eliza was so upset that meant...

"Not Isabel?" she breathed. Shakespeare nodded. She had to stop, she had that feeling of yawning emptiness in her chest that made her gulp air and feel that she was drowning. She couldn't breathe properly through the mask and she couldn't take it off... In a minute she might faint.

She put her hand on the wall next to her and stood very still, feeling the sweat run down her back under her shift. After a few long black moments, it seemed to be getting better. Her head was no longer spinning although she did feel very sick. What was wrong with her? She could not afford to be ill under any circumstances... Oh God, did she have plague?

Shakespeare was looking at her, very worried. "Mistress," he asked, "Are you all right?"

352

"I'll be better in a minute." The waves of blackness were receding. Her practical mind worked again. "I can't come by myself, I must have a woman or a boy with me." She stopped at the door of the Cock, longing for a cup of brandy. "Will you fetch out young Peter the Hedgehog to go with us at least?"

Shakespeare went briskly into the alehouse and came out a few moments later with a cup of something in his hands, followed by Peter who was scowling.

"Mistress, take some of this," said Shakespeare and Portia grabbed it and knocked it back in a quite unseemly way. The fiery spirit battled its way down into her stomach and started to warm her a little

"I want to see the body," she told him, "Before anyone else except Eliza."

"E done anovver one?" the boy growled, "I liked Isabel too, she giv me and my sister a penny loaf each once."

With Peter trotting behind her, Portia followed Shakespeare down the alleyway that led directly into the ancient black heart of Whitefirars, going straight to the little cell in the piece of old monastery to which someone had fitted a Christ window. Peter squinted at the stained glass.

"Brr," he said, "I hate that picture, it's too scary. Wot'd they want to do that for?"

Portia didn't try to explain. Clearly he had never

353

listened to the Easter readings at any time. "Turn away," she said, "Don't look at it. And leave the door open but don't look in."

She went ahead of Shakespeare who seemed to be in no hurry to see what had happened to the whore.

There it was again. The strangely calm face, the body laid out on its back, this time on a bed, well-used with a deep dip in the middle. The neat cut down the length of the stomach, the guts coiled neatly, the parts mutilated and... Not much blood. Portia held her breath and looked closely. The place where a woman's womb was hidden had been cut into but there was no sign of that small bit of meat that looked like an ox-heart.

She was sweating again, she knew it and hoped she wouldn't throw up. Bald Will had his hand to his mouth. She reached for help, any help from anywhere, and found a useful kind of coldness and distance in her that she worked with in court. There were no bruises on Isabel's throat – but there was one on the side of her head, quite a big one. Something greasy was staining her hair and the pillow she lay on.

Portia sniffed the stuff on the pillow, touched it with a finger. It was bitter-smelling. On an impulse she lifted the head – with difficulty because it was stiff – and took the pillow out, pulled off the greasy pillowcase, rolled it up and put it her petticoat pocket.

"Where's Eliza?"

354

"She's in the Fox and Hounds, drinking," said Will, "Christ, I need a drink too."

Portia agreed with him but hadn't finished yet and her stomach was settling a little. She couldn't see the womb anywhere – perhaps Isabel's had become unseated and travelled about her body as it was said to do. But the fact was that it wasn't there. Where had it gone?

Portia closed Isabel's calm eyes and turned to look at the little room. There was a crudely done painted cloth of Europa and the Bull, a polished mirror, various pots of face paint, some of which she recognised came from Mr Cheke's shop, some bits of sponge and bags of moss, old shifts cut up and a couple of rose-scented pots of goose fat for no purpose Portia could see.

She left the little room and shut the door behind her. "We must send for Mr Recorder Fleetwood," she said.

"I already have – or Maliverny Catlin has gone personally."

"Thank God for that. I think I had better change..."

"Stay as yourself, mistress. Come and talk to Eliza, she's saying some very strange things."

"Well then, get her out of that boozing ken and bring her to the Cock, it's a little more respectable." It was enraging how difficult it was just to sit and have a quiet drink as a woman, at least without an attendant. At least Ellie Briscoe's churching was today so she would be able to come out.

355

Maliverny Catlin paused for breath behind a conduit in Cheapside which had a handsome head made of leaves for the water to come out of. He had run all the way from Whitefriars, as much to get away from the sight of... the sight of...

He was damned. He surely was damned.

The sight of Isabel. The sight of Isabel. The sight of Isabel. The sight of...

The sweat was rolling down his face so he unbuttoned the neck of his black doublet, loosened the strings of his falling band, wiped his forehead with his sleeve. Some of the passers by were staring at him sidelong, wondering why he was running when he was clearly a respectable gentleman, and if they should run too.

He was damned.

Some of the sweat was tears, he knew that. Isabel... was dead. Somebody had... No, he wouldn't think of that or he might puke or howl or something.

Was it God punishing him? Perhaps for considering a respectable marriage with Mrs Morgan when the woman he loved was called Isabel? Of course not. Once he was married to Mrs Morgan, naturally he would no longer go to see Isabel... or only occasionally. Not often. And he couldn't possibly marry Isabel, she was a whore, she was...

She was dead. Dead and cut up.

He held his breath, took his hat off, bent over the conduit and put his head in the slimy cold water, pulled it out again with water splashing on his starched collar. He would have to send it to the laundress.

He had to hurry up. Fleetwood needed to know of this as quickly as possible – who knew what the whores of London would do when the word of this new atrocity got out.

Well, he rather thought he did know what the whores would do since that Eliza had been shouting about it loudly enough.

His hands were trembling and a big ball of tears half-blocked his throat, but he could breathe a little bit better, so he walked on again, breaking to a jog as he came near Seething Lane.

Fleetwood was not at home. Mr Jenkins, his secretary was and instantly understood the gravity of the situation, so he sent a boy on a pony to fetch Fleetwood from the Tower where he had gone to a meeting with the Master of the Mint about the quantities of forged shillings about London. Normally Catlin would have been very interested in that tidbit, but today he didn't care about bad shillings. The secretary offered Catlin some mild beer which Catlin took gratefully.

"This will be three whores and an old woman," said Jenkins, shaking his head, "How's he doing it? All the

357

whores are going armed at the moment, we've got one in the Bridewell now who stabbed a gentleman because she thought it was the Devil of Fleet Street."

Catlin didn't answer. He thought of Isabel and how peaceful and gentle her face had looked.

The ball of tears threatened to explode like a grenado so he drank some more. His hands were shaking so hard he could hardly hold the horn cup.

Jenkins was watching him wisely, head on one side. "Mr Catlin," he said, "Would you like pens and paper so you can make a report while you wait?"

Catlin nodded. He needed something to do. So he sat at the table with paper and ink and wrote down what he had seen after he went to Isabel's little room for his usual midday visit. The fixing of horror in black and white italic seemed somehow to lance the boil a little, to draw its poison. At least his hands had stopped shaking.

He was still damned. But now he could carry on without thinking so much about it. He was damned because of what he had done with Isabel, over and over again, sinning himself into Hell as if the Saviour had never come to rescue mankind, willfully delaying what he knew he should do which was to find Isabel a husband, give her a dowry and marry her off. He delayed because he wanted her for himself. That was why he was damned.

He found he had bitten his lip until it bled and had

to suck away the annoying metallic taste.

"When did it happen?" came Fleetwood's gravelly voice at his shoulder. Catlin flinched and looked up. Fleetwood's broad face was grim.

"I don't know, Mr Recorder," Catlin said softly, "I found her body about midday but it was already cooling and stiffening."

"How come the word is already out?" Fleetwood's normally kind blue eyes were freezing and Catlin realised the Recorder must think he had been blabbing. He pushed the paper towards the man who read it quickly.

"Ah," said Fleetwood, "Her door was locked and when you couldn't get in..."

"I asked Isabel's friend, Eliza if she had the key, which she did so there was no need to break the door."

"It's the Christ's head room, isn't it?"

Catlin nodded, feeling his face redden. He would have thought that the idolatrous Papist image of Our Lord would have put him off, but in fact it somehow perversely sharpened the sinful pleasure of being with Isabel.

"Hm. Expensive. She must be doing well?"

Catlin nodded again. That had been something he could do for Isabel, even though it damned him even more finally. The Christ's head room had indeed been expensive, especially when he was paying the rent.

"Or she was doing well," said Fleetwood heavily,

359

reading on. "Mr Jenkins, I've called out the London trained bands, will you make sure they muster under their usual Captains on Smithfield and then come straight to Fleet Street. Messages to the Lord Mayor, the London Crier, to the Privy Council, to Sir Robert Cecil and to Mr Hughes of course... I'll be in Whitefriars."

"Yes sir," said Jenkins, very calm, "I've taken the liberty of bringing out the official copy of the Proclamation against disorders – shall I call on the magistrates to read it..."

"No," said Fleetwood, opening a cupboard door, pulling a northern-style padded jack from its rack and putting it over his shoulders. From the way he hefted it and the grunt as it went on, the thing had plates of steel sewn into it. He shrugged a buffcoat over the top, buckled a gorget at his neck and strapped on his sword. "I'll read it." Mr Jenkins gave him the grubby parchment with a little bow, as if there was something holy about it – and there were in fact old brown stains of blood on it. Fleetwood shoved it in the front of his doublet under his jack without much ceremony though.

Catlin was feeling like a moulting crab and wishing fervently he had some kind of armour too. Not that he was a military man, far from it, but...

"Come along with me," said Fleetwood, over his shoulder.

He didn't want to, but he couldn't argue. Catlin

360

scrambled to his feet, finished his beer and scurried after the Recorder to the large stableyard. There had always been a big stables here, Catlin recalled, after all this had been the same house in Seething Lane whence Sir Francis Walsingham had controlled his spider's web of correspondence that reached throughout Europe to Istambul and beyond. Sir Francis had spent much of his fortune on good horses and dispatch riders, not on bribes as everyone thought. Walsingham seldom bribed: he believed honest conviction or plain blackmail were cheaper and longer-lasting. As a young man Catlin had served him assiduously, utterly convinced of the Godly righteousness of the Protestant cause and the vital importance of protecting the Protestant Queen. Perhaps it had been true. Perhaps it still was. Certain things had happened which sometimes made him wonder.

On horseback Catlin felt tense and unhappy as always. Horses didn't like him, as a rule. They came out of Fleetwood's gate in a bunch, with the Recorder's usual escort of four men. As they clattered down to Ludgate, they could see the merchants of Cheapside and their apprentices and guards stop and stare to see them go. Then, as one, the goldsmiths started shuttering their windows and emptying them of plate at breakneck speed.

Fleetwood's face by itself was a warning of riot. They had to come to a walk at Ludgate where the press of humanity clogged what was left of the great gate in London Wall.

"Damnit," said Fleetwood under his breath, "What did he want to kill Isabel for, of all people? What harm did she ever do anybody?"

For a moment Catlin nearly said what he usually said at such moments: that the woman was a whore, was a tool of the Devil to lead men astray, was damned anyway. But that made him long to howl again because he had been about to save her, he had, really, and make her respectable but now he couldn't. She was already in Hell, she was already doomed. And he didn't think Hell would be the sort of place where they would be able to meet again. In Heaven perhaps, but not in Hell.

"It must be the Devil, like they say," he muttered.

"No doubt," said Fleetwood drily, "But by the agency of man, of that I'm certain." They picked their way past two women arguing over a cabbage on a street corner stall. "Did you smell any brimstone near the corpus delictae?"

Catlin thought back. "There was a peculiar bitter smell, but it wasn't sulphurous."

"Oh? Of almonds?"

"No. Just bitter. But it probably came from her hair oil."

"Oh, that awful stuff, whatever did she want to put that on for?"

362

The horses were booming over Fleet Bridge where Senhor Gomes was already shuttering his shop. Catlin gulped. He hadn't realised that Fleetwood and he shared... an interest in this crime.

"Ah..." Should he tell? Perhaps Fleetwood might be jealous? Catlin certainly was. He hated the thought of Isabel with other men, no matter that it was her trade. She wouldn't leave it without a contract and a ring on her finger and that had been final.

"She spoke well of you, Mr Catlin, don't be embarrassed," said Fleetwood quietly and Catlin was indeed embarrassed as well as angry and flushed to the tips of his ears.

"I... um... she said it was good against nits," he explained helplessly.

Fleetwood grunted. "I'm surprised she even had any, the way she bleached her hair with lye and combed it every day."

Fleet Street itself was worryingly full of apprentices and young men, hanging around the corners and talking loudly. A knot of respectable women were still at the conduit as usual, also talking, including a number of redoubtable matrons. The whores were nowhere to be seen. Where were they?

Catlin spotted that player Shakespeare standing by the door of the Cock tavern with a very odd expression on his face. On the one hand he was nervous, as any

363

sane man would be with a riot brewing. On the other hand, Catlin got the distinct impression from the bright curious look and his half grin that he was thoroughly enjoying the excitement. He was also wearing a very new poinard dagger at his belt, 19 inches long and highly lethal-looking. Catlin wondered if he knew how to use it. Every so often the player's hand bumped up against the hilt and then caressed it, which argued that he was no more a fighting man than he looked.

Shakespeare saw Fleetwood and his men riding up and raised his arm, came over to where they were dismounting.

"Go and hold the Christ's head room," Fleetwood ordered his men, "Nobody goes in or comes out."

"Sir, Eliza's in here," Shakespeare said, gesturing at the tavern door, "but..."

Fleetwood nodded his thanks and went in, Catlin following. When he saw who else was there, he wished he hadn't. The common room of the Cock was full of angry frightened and highly painted women in striped petticoats, all arguing at the tops of their voices. In a corner, the centre of attention, sat Eliza, her face-paint running down her cheeks with her tears, spent aquavitae cups in front of her, sitting next to the only respectable woman in the place who was holding her hand. That woman was wearing a black velvet mask under a good beaver hat and linen cap.Catlin was shocked: he recognised her at once from her clothing: it was James Enys's widowed sister, Mrs Morgan. Next to her on the floor by the bench, like a bony little toad, squatted young Peter the Hedgehog who was gripping a paring knife in his fist and muttering to himself.

Shakespeare led Fleetwood over to Eliza who stood and curtseyed unsteadily to him, drawing the attention of any of the women who had been too busy arguing to notice the Recorder coming into the common room. Mrs Morgan also stood and curtseyed. She was wearing the same tidy cramoisie wool doublet-fronted bodice and kirtle and an unfashionable bell-shaped farthingale that she had worn when Catlin had seen her during Topcliffe's abortive raid. Shakespeare presented her to Mr Fleetwood as Mrs Morgan.

Catlin's mouth had dropped open. What on earth was a respectable widow doing in a tavern surrounded by women of... by whores? It was outrageous! Did her brother know where she was?

Fleetwood was clearly as shocked as Catlin.

"Ma'am, I would urge you to go home at once," he rumbled disapprovingly at Mrs Morgan, "I'm astonished to find you..."

"Mr Fleetwood," interrupted the player hastily, "It's my fault she's here at all – I asked her in Christian charity to comfort Eliza, which she did with only young Peter to be her escort and while she was talking to Eliza,

365

the other women came in and so she was caught here. I dared not let her go to her chambers without proper company and I could not escort her until you arrived for fear of Eliza running off."

"Ah," said Fleetwood, "Can you not send for her brother?"

"I have no idea where he is, sir," said Mrs Morgan in a low slightly muffled voice, "I'm sure as soon as he hears of my situation, he will come to find me. Believe me, sir, I had far rather be safely in my chambers. But first will you hear what Eliza has to say – she wanted me to be with her when she says it?"

Fleetwood looked around at the packed room and the painted faces all watching him. He sat down opposite Eliza on the bench.

"Eliza," he said, "Did you see who killed Isabel?" he asked quite gently. She shook her head.

"She had a message to wait for a gentleman who would be along soon," said Eliza, shooting a dagger glance at Catlin under her blue eyelids which made him feel very uncomfortable.

"Did she say who it was?"

"Yes," said Eliza slowly and clearly, "She said it was Mr Catlin, sir, 'im over there.'"

Catlin's stomach froze. What? It was true he often did visit Eliza at noon and indeed he had been on his way to her but...

"She was puzzled cos she knew that so she asked Goody Mallow who it was again. I went away then cos I had a business husband of my own to see to and that was the last I ever seen of her... I dunno what I'll do wivvout her, I'll never talk to her again, I'll never share a bed wiv her again and what if the Devil comes back..." Eliza started wailing and rocking herself on the bench while Mrs Morgan patted her shoulder.

"So Mr Catlin was the man Eliza expected."

Catlin was fervently wishing he hadn't come with Fleetwood and had simply gone home to bed. He was surrounded by angry faces and hostile eyes.

"Yes sir, and he's a pursuivant and he works for Mr Heneage and that devil Topcliffe. And he found Kettle Annie's body too..."

Catlin realised that Mr Jenkins was quietly moving away from him and that two stout women were barring the doors with their arms folded and their hips hitched. His heart started to thud.

"But I..."

"Mr Catlin, a moment. Eliza, are you accusing Mr Catlin here of being the Devil who killed all three women of the town..?" A calm and distant part of Catlin thought it was wise of Fleetwood to use a more delicate term than "whores" on account of being outnumbered by them.

"And poor Goody Harbridge, what's more."

367

"That's ridiculous," shouted Catlin, unable to bear this, "I loved Isabel, I would never kill her, never harm her... I...."

"And he's a Puritan and they're all whoremongers who preach against whores so nobody guesses wot they get up to!" shouted another woman.

"I... I was at the Tower all this morning, I was concerned on State business..."

Fleetwood was standing up, his hand on his sword hilt. Even Bald Will had a hand on his shiny new poinard, whilst young Peter was on his feet, teeth bared, waving the little knife in his fist.

"If 'e done my sister, I'll slit 'im!" shrieked the boy, "Lying bastard!"

The noise of shouting was getting louder and louder. Catlin looked desperately for the door to the yard but that was blocked too, by more women who were all crowding in on him, shaking their fists. Fleetwood shouted something but could not be heard. Catlin glimpsed Mrs Morgan sitting back in her booth, her fingers bone-white as they gripped the table, so she was frightened too.

Suddenly she surged to her feet. She looked very strange as she stood there, her kirtle vibrating, in her modest widow's cap and hat and the face a mere black shape. Although her face was muffled by the mask still, she looked quite frightening.

"Sirs... and ladies!" she said in a voice which was not raised to a shout but did carry through the noise, "If Mr Catlin did these crimes then he deserves to be burned for witchcraft."

That made them pause. A hanging was quite exciting, but a burning... Now that they would pay to watch.

"But I didn't..."

"However this is not Spain nor France full of papist foreigners, this is England," said Mrs Morgan, her voice strengthening, "And in this land we live under Her Majesty the Queen's rule of law! In this land a man must be tried for his crime. In this land we are honourable. We'll have no Papist inquisition here."

A few shouts of No, some muttering and scowling but at least they were listening. Would burning be worse than simply being ripped apart by enraged women?

"Mr Catlin must be given a proper fair trial as to whether he is guilty or not guilty of witchcraft and murder, by a jury of his equals."

Someone shouted that Catlin's peers should go to Hell with him, and the shouting started once more. Mrs Morgan held up her hand for quiet and to Catlin's amazement, she got it.

"There's something I don't quite understand," she said, her voice higher now and clear, "If, which is not admitted, Mr Catlin did the killing, why would he call you, Eliza, to help him get into the room where Isabel

369

lay?"

There was silence.

"Surely, anybody who had done such a foul dishonourable thing would slink away quietly and let the body be found by someone else when he was not nearby? Surely only a man who was woodwild would actually call on Isabel's best friend to open up the door for him to see the thing he himself had done? And Mr Catlin may be a Puritan but that does not necessarily mean he is a lunatic."

There was a little scattering of laughter then. Fleetwood was leaning back, watching Mrs Morgan narrowly.

"Besides," came another woman's voice from the door to Fleet Street, where the two large women had moved away. "He could 'ardly have killed poor Goody Harbridge when he was busy tupping my whores at the Falcon the day she died and the night before that as well."

Framed in the door was Mrs Nunn of the Falcon, fists on her hips above her very latest Spanish farthingale and her stomacher embroidered with a picture of naked Grecian gods and goddesses hawking. It was detailed and Catlin remembered it well.

There was another laugh and the other women parted for her; most of them didn't work for her since they were Whitefriars whores and proudly independent,

370

but she was nonetheless a power in their land. Behind her at the door stood Gabriel Nunn her brother, that had been the most dangerous young upright man in the City and now worked directly for the King of London.

Fleetwood looked highly amused and relieved. Catlin was hanging his head, quite purple with shame.

"Is that true, Mr Catlin?" the Recorder asked, "The night Goody Harbridge was killed, you were at the Falcon?"

Catlin nodded dumbly. Oh God. Why did it have to come out like this? Mrs Morgan knows I am not only a whorekeeper but also that I go to the bawdy houses on the South Bank. Oh God.

Mind, at least the whores who had looked ready to string him up a moment ago were now giggling and elbowing each other. Bright red and miserable, Catlin concentrated on the ale and spit-clotted sawdust between his boots. At least Mrs Morgan had sat down again. She put her hand on Peter's shoulder and whispered to him firmly.

"Then maybe not him, but the Devil did it!" shouted Eliza, "I knew it was that Devil, I knew it and it's that lawyer Craddock wot called him up in the night and then argued with him on Fleet Street. You saw the Devil too, din't you Peter?"

Peter the Hedgehog looked up. "Yers I did," he shouted, "I saw 'im afore he killed my sister Mary!"

"It's that lawyer!"

"It's Craddock wot called him up..."

"Even a lawyer should have a trial..." Mrs Morgan started to say but Shakespeare leaned down to her and muttered something. Catlin couldn't read her face because of the mask but she shrugged and said no more.

"It was the lawyer, he called up the Devil!"

"First we'll kill the lawyer!"

Peter was on his feet waving the knife in his hand. "It was 'im!" he shrieked, "First he wapped 'er and then 'e cut her up, he did!"

One of the younger whores hushed the shouting and caught his ripped sleeve.

"Is that what happened to poor little Mary?" she asked.

There were tears purling down Peter's face. "Yes, 'e did, that bastard, 'e done it wiv 'er and then the missus turned us out and then Mary was gonna go and get money from 'im and 'e killt her, 'e did. He's the Devil of Fleet Street!"

There was the ugliest roar Catlin had ever heard, made more frightening by being high-pitched. The women were shouting at each other again.

Fleetwood's man Smith pulled him closer to the Recorder, where Mrs Morgan had her face tilted up to look at the women shouting at each other. She was shaking her head and arguing with Shakespeare in a low voice, so Catlin couldn't hear what she said.

Mrs Nunn had a jewelled dagger in her hand. She shouted for quiet and got it. And then she led the women out the door and onto Fleet Street, with Peter at her side, jumping up and down, his face purple, screaming about Mary.

"I thank you for that, ma'am, but now would be a good time for you to go to your chambers," said Fleetwood urgently to Mrs Morgan, "Mr Shakespeare, will you bear her company? Mr Catlin come with me. We still have the body to deal with."

"What about the Craddocks?" Mrs Morgan asked.

Fleetwood's face was grave. "There is very little I can do for them until the trained bands arrive and they will only just be mustering now. We must hope that their house is securely shuttered as I'm sure it is. And I must view the body myself."

"Mr Fleetwood, I think I know how..."

"Please ma'am, go to your chambers and make yourself safe. If your brother arrives, send him to me. I shall need every well-affected able-bodied man I can get."

"My brother is a lawyer, sir, not a soldier."

Fleetwood smiled at her. "So am I, ma'am. But at the root of the fair tree of law is enforcement, the keeping of the law by deadly force. Therefore when riot breaks out, we must put it down at once for riot is the utter denying of law by the people. And so at a time like this, all lawyers are also men of war."

Mrs Morgan swallowed and nodded. "I shall tell him so, sir," she said.

"But you are no such thing, ma'am, and so I must command you, go to safety."

There was a pause, and then she stood up, bobbed a curtsey to him, took her market basket and went to the door with Shakespeare. She didn't look back.

Catlin watched her, sick and furious with himself. Unless he could somehow bribe her brother, or pressure him, there went his chances of a respectable marriage – not just with Mrs Morgan but with any woman of reputation in the city. It was not to be doubted that Mrs Morgan would not only tell her brother of his whoring but also all her gossips. And her brother might be insulted if Catlin pressed his suit. No doubt the pastor of his church would hear of it. In fact he might have to do penance for fornication... Oh God, what was he thinking?

And the pity of it was that he rather liked Mrs Morgan. It was true she was too thin and tall for a woman and certainly a great deal too bold and forward and had learned to ape the legal speech of her brother in a manner completely unsuitable for a woman. But at least she had talked the whores out of thinking that he was the Devil who killed their friends. And she had been kind to Eliza, Isabel's friend.

He sighed and stood next to Fleetwood. "I'd put you in protective custody, Mr Catlin, if I had anywhere to do it," said the Recorder, "But I don't, nor the men to do it with. You will have to come with me."

They went down the alleyway cursed with the Papist idolatrous abomination in its window. At the first opportunity Catlin found, he had decided to break it with a brick. But not today. Out on Fleet Street there was a lot of shouting. It seemed Mrs Nunn was making a speech.

At the door were the two men Fleetwood had sent to guard the place, looking nervous and visibly relieved to see their captain arrive. He shouldered past them into the room where Isabel still lay, unseamed and naked. It hadn't been visibly robbed by anyone else which argued a good deal of fear of the Devil. The place smelled of death. Catlin sniffed carefully: apart from that universal smell there was no stink of brimstone but there was still the strongly bitter smell he had noticed before.

Fleetwood stood by the corpse and took his hat off, stood reverently for a moment. He lifted Isabel's head which was turned to the side, her head was greasy with oil, put it back down on the pillow, looked carefully about the room.

Then he called his men and they brought in the litter

they had for such occasions and put her on it – Catlin helped them, squeamish that they might hurt her when they moved her, although nothing could ever hurt her again.

"Cut through Hanging Sword Court and Salisbury Court to St Bride's," Fleetwood said wearily, "I'll be on Fleet Street."

Somebody had brought the horses down from where they had been left outside the Cock. Fleetwood mounted up and raised his brows at Catlin. Catlin shook his head. He would follow Isabel's body to the church where he would pray forgiveness for his sins. There was no point praying for Isabel – only Papists did that. She had already met God's righteous judgement and wrath for her life and was utterly lost to him. But St Bride's church was respected and he might be safer there than on Fleet Street where the whores and their upright men were gathering.

Sorrow caught him shrewdly by the throat and he gasped from it. He would never again cup Isabel's beautiful soft breasts, so horribly split by the red chasm done to her by the Devil, he would never again laugh as he lay on top of her, never again...

He yanked his mind away from his sin and sucked in his breath as hard as he could, held it tight. He was weeping for a murdered whore. What was wrong with him? He walked behind the litter which the young men

376

carried quickly – it wasn't so very heavy. Hanging Sword Court was empty, no longer a carpenter's yard, it was built over with new houses now. Salisbury Court was full of the French Ambassador's men, keeping a wary eye on the entrances. Watching himself from a distance, he somehow spoke to their Captain, a young man with lovely black ringlets and lace on his falling band, showed the Frenchman his warrant. They passed through without any trouble to St Bride's churchyard. He looked sidelong at the men carrying the litter carefully down the steps to the cool church crypt. He helped them when they caught on the corners and they thanked him politely, calling him "sir." One of them casually gripped his shoulder. Catlin could say nothing. There was no deserved condemnation on the man's broad rough face, Catlin thought with surprise, only an unexpected kindness.

"Did you want to say a prayer, sir?" asked the man, "before we lock 'er up?"

"I... er... thank you," said Catlin convulsively, grateful for the chance to pull himself together.

That was right, in fact. He needed quite literally to pull himself together, for he felt as if the parts of himself were breaking apart, as if he were a thing made of clay and an arm was crumbling here and a leg there, leaving only a naked frightened worm behind. So he stood trembling in the little dark crypt with the

377

old knights lying on their monuments, some with legs awkwardly crossed, some with their feet on dogs or lions, with Isabel's body in front of him. He tried to get his thoughts to parade in a line as accustomed, instead of swirling round and round in circles.

There could be no sin, he thought, in confiding Isabel to God his mercy, nor in hoping that perhaps she was... No. She was judged and damned now. He had better face that fact, as Calvin had taught it by unimpeachable logic and scriptural authority.

In the end he said the Our Father. Afterwards he stood, wondering what to do now. He was alone in the crypt. He looked carefully around – was anyone watching? Since he was already damned... He was alone.

He went up to Isabel's body, pulled back the cloth that covered it and laid his head on her cold breast as he had loved to do, kissed her greasy bitter-tasting ear and her face, rubbed his face in her hair which she had always dyed out of its unbecoming red. Then he stepped back, covered her face decently again...

He ran up the steps where he nearly cannoned into Fleetwood's man coming down.

"We got to go, sir," said the man, still nothing but kindness on his ugly face, "I 'eard the boys shouting "clubs!" "

Catlin felt shaky again: it was the apprentice boys' warcry and it meant they were out. "Where should I

378

go?" he asked. The sounds of the key turning in the lock boomed like metal drums. For some reason his head was swimming and he was feeling feverish.

"Wouldn't come with us, sir," said the man, "The prentices might go for you if they can't find Craddock."

He had nowhere to go. So he sought sanctuary and went into St Bride's dark church and sat at the back on one of the benches by the wall and leaned his head back against the cool whitewashed wall to listen to the thundering of his heart. The door banged as the two men left him and trotted away uphill to Fleet Street where the trouble was beginning. No condemnation there still. Why not? Catlin wondered.

Neither do I condemn you, came a quiet kindly voice in his ear, so clear he looked around to see who it was, only there was no one there. Go and sin no more, it continued.

He was sweating with the heat of his sudden fever and his lips felt strange and swollen, still bitter from his frantic kissing of Isabel. Did he have plague? And so what if he did?

Isabel was standing in front of him, holding her guts in and shaking her head.

Catlin yelped with fear and reared back against the wall. Isabel changed to a man and then back again and the man was himself. The two went back and forth while the middle of the church was suddenly filled with

379

fireworks.

Catlin was terrified, he tried to hide from the ghosts and demons, burrowed his way into the corner of the church wall, panting with terror and whimpering like a child.

"Sir, are you well?" came a voice. Catlin yelped again and then saw through the swirl of Isabel's face that an old lady in a stout blue kirtle was looking at him. She was quite short and round and was carrying a broom in her hand. This terrified him even more. Surely witches were abroad in London and the demons were out to celebrate.

"I... I..." he gasped.

She came forward and helped him back onto the bench. As her rosy round face came close to his and he flinched back, she paused and her nose wrinkled as she sniffed.

"Hm," she said, fishing under her kirtle for her petticoat pocket and pulling out a coarse hemp hankerchief, "You wipe your face with that now, it's all dirty."

Her voice had a motherly command in it, so he did it and as he did the figures of Isabel and the swirling colours began to fade. He could see that this was only an old woman here, perhaps not even a witch since she was actually sweeping the floor with her broom rather than riding it.

"Hm," she said, blue eyes narrowed in their crumpled rosepetal beds. She took the kerchief out of his hand and bustled to the font in the corner of the church, dipped it into the holy water there and came back with it, then dabbed his face carefully clean of oil and tears with it. It was such a kindly thing to do, it calmed him.

"Are you the gentleman that came with poor Isabel," asked the woman.

"Y..yes, I... I... thought I saw her ghost and demons... That was why..."

The woman tutted. "Now my name is Nan and I clean this church and I'm a terrible old busybody, but I'm quite sure, sir, that you can see nothing evil in this Church because it is under the protection of St Bride and the Lord Jesus Himself and the water you just cleaned yourself with is sovereign against all such foolish phantasies."

The common sense and complete certainty in her voice calmed him though something very odd was happening to his eyesight again and his mind seemed to be whirling in all directions at once. He wanted to tell her about his sin, even though Confession was a Papist abomination, he had to tell somebody and it had to be now.

"I thought it was Isabel haunting me, walking to... to.. call for vengeance. She's in Hell, you know."

"Sir, I'm sure she's not, she was a good... well, she

381

was a kind woman, sometimes, and that counts, you know."

"She's damned and so am I," muttered Catlin.

Nan leaned her broom into the corner, sat herself down on the bench beside him and took his hand in hers. "Why sir?"

"For venery, for desiring woman, for fornication..."

"With Isabel?"

"And with the whores at the Falcon and the false nuns at Clerkenwell and at Paris Garden and..."

The little woman's eyebrows went up. "Dear me," she said, "You have been busy, sir."

"I knew that as I was assuredly one of God's Elect, I could fornicate and take no harm," said Catlin, "But then I... I liked it too much. And I began to wonder if I was really saved at all?"

Nan sighed and nodded. "To be sure, to think so is a kind of heresy though I forget which," she said.

"So I went to the Falcon for information, you see, only that but then I was led astray again and on that very day, the old woman was killed...

Nan's chin was on her chest. "Poor Kat Harbridge," she said softly, "I was so sorry for that. She never did any harm and tried to do all the good she could, for all the College of Physicians worked against her. There'll be more mothers dying in childbed in London now, you mark my words."

382

Catlin ignored this irrelevance. "And now Isabel..." he gulped out. "I was... I was even thinking of marrying her... so as not to burn... But how could I? She's a whore... or she was."

Nan's eyes were suddenly piercingly blue, as if they had turned to chips of ice. She raised her head.

"Did you kiss Isabel goodbye?" she asked and her voice was so stern and cold that Catlin answered.

"Yes," he said, flushing again, "I kissed her ear and her face and her... and..."

"Was there anything greasy?"

Catlin shrugged. "There was a lot of hair oil..."

"Ah," She reached out so suddenly that he flinched and felt his forehead. "Yes, still feverish. How are you feeling now, sir?"

"Better," Catlin admitted. His sudden sickness seemed to have mainly passed. Perhaps he had only been overwrought. He still felt hot and a little dizzy but the ghost of Isabel had gone and so had the strange whirling colours from the church's stained windows.

Nan nodded to herself. "Yes indeed. Who is searching out the killer, sir?" she asked, "Is it you, Mr Catlin? Seeing you are an old pursuivant too?"

"Not me by myself," Catlin said hastily, "Mr Enys is helping me and so is Mr Shakespeare, I believe, since he was one of those who found French Mary a week or so ago."

383

"I'd like to talk to Mr Enys," said Nan seriously, "Where is he?"

"Mr Enys has gone missing, Goody," said Catlin, "Or at least his sister Mrs Morgan says he is away from home and she doesn't know where he is. But she at least is safe in her Chambers now, I hope."

"Yes. Perhaps I'll visit her. Would you like to stay here? Near Isabel? Even the apprentices will respect a church, I think."

He nodded. He would. He might be able to pray as despite its Papist name, the whole church had been whitewashed and cleansed of the Papistical pictures all over it that even he remembered from his childhood. They had been quite scandalous, showing the marriage at Cana with drunken disciples and Jesus smiling over the vats of water as he worked the miracle, wearing a very odd-looking crown of vineleaves. It was still the church of the Guild of Vintners, of course, who were no longer permitted to put on their near-blasphemous mystery play of the Wedding.

Even the London prentices would respect this church. Perhaps. He could see why they might blame him if they couldn't get Craddock. He hoped they would, in a way. Perhaps he should go to Fleet Street and tell them what he had done, how he had betrayed Isabel. No. He would stay here and pray forgiveness for his incontinence and venery and cowardice.

384

Pray forgiveness for loving Isabel. He would do it but he could not mean it. He hoped that God wouldn't notice that. Now she was there no longer, he knew he had really loved her. He had.

He was still feeling sick and exhausted with emotion. So he dozed off where he was with his head tilted against the wall, not thinking to wonder where Nan might have gone to and why the door had banged shut. The church of St Bride seemed to breathe around him, bending a little inwards to protect him, as a cave might protect a crab that had been robbed of his shell.

Nan was panting hard as she climbed the stairs to the very top of the rickety building in the old courtyard of the Temple which had once held the houses for the lay brothers of Whitefriars monastery, the Dominicans.

She banged on the door, hardly able to speak. "Mistress," she gasped, "Mrs Morgan, please... let me in... I must... speak with you."

The door was unbolted and opened and Mrs Morgan peered out. She had her mask lifted to hide her face again but when she saw Nan was alone, she opened up and let her in.

That odd player Shakespeare was standing by the window, looking out anxiously The way he stood made Nan think of an argument, suddenly stopped. "Sit down Goodwife," said Mrs Morgan politely, "Did you

385

have trouble with the prentices? You look upset?"

Nan smiled at the thought. "No, I haven't been on Fleet Street." She sat down on the chest of clothes and caught her breath. She kept forgetting she was no longer a slip of a girl to scurry upstairs without paying for it after.

"I think Mr Fleetwood will have the trained bands guarding the Craddock house and the prentices will be waiting for the roaring boys from Smithfield before they take the Devil out of his house," said Shakespeare. His right hand fiddled with the pommel of his shiny new poinard at the small of his back.

"How may I serve you, Goodwife?" said Mrs Morgan, "I have some beer, will you take some?" Well, it was a pleasure to meet someone who still believed in the old ways that had badly gone by the board hereabouts in London. Nan accepted a horn cup of middling mild beer and drank it down quickly. It steadied her heart a little.

"Perhaps you could tell me..." Mrs Morgan asked, with only a little impatience in her voice.

Nan caught her hand and pressed it. "My dear friend Goody Harbridge said she knew there was a witch in London and there is." That got her attention.

"Did she tell you the name?"

"She didn't. But I can say it's certainly the witch that's been killing the women of the town."

"How do you know?"

Nan looked hard at Mrs Morgan. She was standing up, her mask forgotten on the table beside her. Jesu, the smallpox surely had made a mess of her face. But how much did she know about women's matters? It would have been better if the player were not there, but there was no time for secrecy now.

"What do you know of hebenon?" she asked carefully. She knew the player's ears were pricked, in fact if he had been a cat they would have been swivelled backwards to listen, though he continued to watch out of the window.

"Is it like witch's ointment?"

"Indeed it is. It's what you get from henbane seeds which must be extracted into an oil or a grease – the vital principle will only go into something fatty, not into water nor aquavitae for instance. Almond oil or goosefat are the best."

"Midwives use it?"

"The ointment, yes. It's a very powerful magic," said Nan, "And like most magics, it is also a poison if strong enough. Hebenon is the poison and it is always an oil. A little of it makes you feel hot and talkative. More of it and you see visions. More still and you become very cosy and fall asleep. And more than that... not a great deal more, mind, though it depends on the person and how big they are, whether they've eaten, whether they've had it before, many possibilities. All sorts of things."

"What happens?"

"You die."

Mrs Morgan was silent, her lips open. "But..." Something seemed to occur to her. She started delving under her kirtle for her petticoat pocket and pulled out a grubby pillowcase that was slick with grease. She held it out to Nan.

"I took this from under Isabel's head, I was wondering about her nit oil myself."

Nan took it and sniffed it while Shakespeare watched, fascinated. "Yes," she said, "This is hebenon. The thing about hebenon, mistress, and this isn't usually known, is that you don't have to drink it. It doesn't have to pierce to the blood. All you need is to rub it onto your skin, especially where the skin is delicate, that's why midwives use the ointment. It helps ease the child and the mother at the same time."

"Ah,"

"But it's possible to kill with hebenon by simply pouring it into someone's ear."

"I see."

"What you do is you give the person a small amount by mouth so they feel sleepy and then when they're asleep, you turn their head to the side and pour the hebenon oil into their ear and then... Well, you wait, mistress. And they'll die quite quickly. The poison goes into the humours through the ear, straight into the phlegmatic humour of the brain and stops it."

The player Shakespeare had given up all pretence of not listening and was staring at her. "Jesu, goodwife," he said, "Is that really true?"

Nan nodded seriously. "It's well known to poisoners and alchemists and even some physicians know of it. I heard that there was a man tried to poison the Queen with a saddle – that will have been a strong hebenon oil rubbed into it."

"Are you a midwife, goody?"

"No, mistress, I never had the strength of mind. I only clean the Church of St Bride and try and live a good life. But Goody Harbridge was my friend and she told me about hebenon and I know she was afraid of this witch in London, for there are such things as witches, ma'am. They are men or women who think that the wonders of the world put there to help us by God are theirs to take and use for their own desires and for dominion over others. They misuse the wonderful gifts of God in herbs and plants and they will kill because it is convenient to them. Of course, many of them become witchfinders and burn such as me."

Mrs Morgan snorted. "But they don't actually worship the Devil, surely."

"I think they do, mistress. Only they call it Money. Or Knowledge. Or Godliness."

"I don't think the women were killed for money, goodwife," said Mrs Morgan thoughtfully, "Not one of them was robbed."

"Perhaps they were killed for curiosity."

"What?"

Nan shrugged. "They were all cut open and their innards taken out – I've heard the stories. That's why they think it was the Devil, of course, but the Devil would have no need to do that. Perhaps whoever did it was curious to know what is inside our skins."

Mrs Morgan gulped and changed the subject.

"So how do you think they were killed, starting with French Mary."

"As I heard it, French Mary was not the first. There was a girl."

"Yes, hardly more than a child and poor Peter's sister. But according to him, the same happened to her as happened to all of them."

"Well then, somehow the witch got them to take enough of the hebenon to become confused, hot and sleepy. Mind you that would be hard to do – it's very bitter and would take a great deal of sugar to get down. Then, being hot they would take off most of their clothes. Being sleepy and confused, they would lie down to take a nap, as French Mary did in the part-built playhouse and Kettle Annie did in the alleyway and Isabel did in her room. And her business husband

390

Catlin did just now in St Bride's, which is what gave me the understanding, for he had rubbed his face in Isabel's hair that was greasy with the hebenon and it was strong enough for the vapours of it to have him see her ghost and demons as well."

"Good God," swore Mrs Morgan, somewhat to Nan's surprise.

"It's all right, I got him to wipe it off and wash his face with St Bride's well water which, as you know, mistress, is sovereign against all ills including warts." Nan smiled at the woman and the woman smiled shakily back. "He just needs to sleep and then he'll be well and have no memory at all of what he saw when he was...."

"It stops the memory as well?" Mrs Morgan asked sharply.

"Yes, indeed, which makes it a very good poison. If the thing goes wrong, the victim will remember nothing about what happened."

"Well then..." Mrs Morgan's fingers were working together as if she was kneading dough. "Well then... I know where Mr Craddock's Devil came from – he was hot, he saw phantasies and after disputing with the Devil and being calmed with laudenum by Mr Cheke, he woke up with no memory at all of what had happened."

"But how did he get hold of hebenon?" asked Nan.

"Perhaps it was in his bedchamber? I remember that Mr Craddock brought some new ointment for Mrs

Craddock after he wasted hers. Perhaps he spilled it and got it on his hands and...."

The player had suddenly started laughing. He tried to stop, but he was doubled over with it and his face went red.

"What?" said Mrs Morgan with a great deal of irritation, "I don't think this is very funny, Mr Shakespeare."

"No," gasped Shakespeare, wiping his eyes with his sleeve, "No, it isn't. Not at all funny. You're right. He must have got the ointment on his... er... on his hands. Or the hebenon oil. Quite so. Yes."

"Yes but this doesn't make sense," said Mrs Morgan, "I always thought it must be something to do with Mr Craddock because of the connection with poor little Mary, but if it was his own poison, he would know better than to get it on him..."

"Or rub it somewhere sensitive..." sniggered Shakespeare making a lewd schoolboy gesture.

Finally understanding what was making him laugh, Nan and Mrs Morgan both stared at him with great disapproval. He spread his hands and gave a smirk. "Sorry, ladies," he said. "And don't scowl at me, it wasn't me that did it."

Mrs Morgan coughed and Nan turned away. "He wouldn't do that if he'd made it," Nan said, "He would know what it would do to him..."

392

Suddenly there was a roar in the distance and the sound of breaking glass. Shakespeare flinched and peered out of the window but the courtyard was still empty.

"I must tell Mr Fleetwood at once," said Mrs Morgan, "Or... er... my brother must. I think he'll be back soon. Mr Shakespeare, would you bear Goody Nan back to St Bride's so she can keep an eye on Maliverny Catlin? I... er... I'll make sure my brother hears all about this when he arrives."

She was staring wildly at Shakespeare and he stared back with a very ugly scowl on his face. "Mistress, I told you that..."

"I'm sure Goody Nan wants to get home, don't you, Goodwife?" said Mrs Morgan loudly and Nan took the hint although the whole question of what was going on between the two of them was nearly killing her with curiosity.

"Yes, I'm quite tired and I haven't finished sweeping yet, nor put the candlesticks in the chest which I ought if there's trouble on Fleet Street. Come with me, Mr Shakespeare, it won't take long and then you can help Mr Enys."

He sighed and very chivalrously offered Nan his arm for to go down the rickety stairs with him, leaving Mrs Morgan alone. Nan hoped she would be all right. There was something about her that suddenly seemed to crackle with urgency. Just to be on the safe side she said a quiet Ave Maria for her and asked St Bride to help the young woman and her mysterious brother.

.

Shakespeare sprinted back to the courtyard from St Brides to find James Enys waiting for him on the steps. On his... on her... damn it, all right, on his face was a mulish expression that Shakespeare knew, from his experience as a married man, not to waste time arguing with.

"Fleet Street?" he asked resignedly.

"No," said Enys, surprisingly, "First we're going to find Goody Mallow."

"The orangeado seller?"

"Exactly. It came to me when Nan was talking about how bitter hebenon is and how it needs lot of sugar. What's the only sugary thing you can find that is also bitter?"

"But..."

"Peter was given an orangeado by Goody Mallow when she pandered for his sister. I think it's quite likely that French Mary and Kettle Annie had orangeados too. Didn't Mrs Sharples say that French Mary had sticky hands? And Eliza said that Goody Mallow had acted as the go-between for Isabel... And she was the woman

394

that helped Eliza that night she was drunk. Or drugged more likely."

Enys was already striding down into the alleyway that went past the Christ window and on down towards the river. At the bottom was the wall which had been planted at the top and then dug up. On the other side of it was the little space where Mary's small body had lain for a short time, and then beyond the next thick wall squatted a small stone hut that might have been a monastery cowshed or something similar long ago.

Enys climbed on a stone and boosted herself up with surprising strength, if you remembered her sex. Unable to help himself for curiosity, Shakespeare followed and forced himself not to think of how close he was to Portia Morgan and how if he tilted his head slightly he might just glimpse her breasts under her... No, Enys was modestly buttoned up. Unfortunately, Shakespeare's imagination was as rampant as ever. He was no boy-lover like Marlowe, although he had occasionally had lascivious thoughts about the women that boys turned into when they took parts at the playhouse. But here... Here by God, was the direct opposite and that was a very different thing because... because... He had to stop. He had to concentrate. This was absolutely not the time to think of things like that. He frowned, scowled with the effort.

"She was down there, poor child, just cut open and

dumped when Peter found her."

"Who was?"

"Little Mary, the serving girl Mr Craddock fornicated with because she was easy meat and who was then turned out of the household with her brother when Craddock's mother in law found out about it."

"Cut...?"

"Yes, and gralloched."

Shakespeare winced. The hunting term for disembowelling a deer somehow made it too clear: he had, after all, hunted deer once upon a time. He saw that, lawyer-like, Enys had used it deliberately to shock him.

"Pay attention, Mr Shakespeare," Enys growled at him. Shakespeare nodded unhappily, wondering if Portia Morgan had the same ability to read his mind that his wife Ann also had and which was one of the reasons why he had left Stratford. He supposed she must have since she had been married. "That over there is Goody Mallow's shed and we are going to break into it."

"We are?"

Enys jumped down quite nimbly. "Yes."

Shakespeare thought about jumping the other way and heading for his lodgings by the back streets, but the thought came that he might then never know if Goody Mallow was the witch who had killed the women and what connected them all together and also... Well, also he wanted to stay near Enys. Just in case. In case he... she needed help, of course.

He followed Enys across the small yard which was tidily swept and had a rope coiled in the corner on top of a trolley. Suddenly they both froze on the spot. The sound of crying was coming from inside the shed, a woman's voice.

They exchanged looks. Enys stopped, irresolute for a moment, and then reached out and knocked on the door.

"Who... who's that?" It was a young light voice, not like Goody Mallow's.

Enys's face frowned with puzzlement again. "Mr James Enys, barrister at law, and Mr Will Shakespeare, poet." He spoke slowly and formally. "Is that Mrs Craddock?"

The door opened and the pale oval face of Mrs Craddock peered out, made even paler by her white married woman's cap over her hair and her expensive beaver hat on top. She was wearing a very good kirtle of rose-coloured wool, trimmed with black braid and a Spanish farthingale and the whole of her was trembling.

"Oh sirs," she gasped, "Have they stopped? Are the prentices still fighting?"

"I don't know," said Enys, "We... er... we heard you crying and wondered if you were well. Why are you in Goody Mallow's shed?"

397

"It's not Goody Mallow's shed, whoever she is, it's my mother's shed, she inherited it when Betty Warren died, she said so. She sent me here to hide until things had calmed down and she gave me the key for the padlock, look."

The girl held up the key and a big heavy padlock which she must have taken off the door. Enys and Shakespeare exchanged looks.

"May we come in, mistress," said Enys gently, "We don't want anyone seeing us here in case they ask why."

After a moment's hesitation, the girl gingerly opened the door with the tips of her fingers and shut it behind them. "She said I mustn't touch anything in here, it was full of things that pertained to the confectioner's art which is a thing she is very expert at and that's why she had the shed, to make comfits in."

The girl's voice sounded as if she was reciting a lesson.

"She also said I mustn't do any cleaning or polishing in here since it is clean and I would disarrange things, but... but... it's too sticky. I have to stand so still in case the sugar touches me."

She was standing in the exact centre of the little shed with her arms wrapped around herself. Shelves had been built into its walls and despite looking tumbledown from outside, inside it was clean and neat. There were barrels along one wall containing Seville orange hulls packed in sugar with two large sugar loaves standing on a chest in the corner. Across the width of the shed went a closed confectioner's range, with a cubbyhole for the hot coals and the open holes in the stone counter covered with a grill of iron. In the corner was the main oven that had a chimney but the fire wasn't lit and the sugar-laden air was chilly. Along the third wall were knives, clean linen cloths and a flask that Shakespeare recognised from somewhere, but couldn't think where. A pottery jar smelled of almonds and there were two smaller jars of goosefat. In a hemp bag hanging from a hook were a small quantity of seeds and in pots all along the wall were more pots where the same seeds were soaking in oil.

Enys picked up the flask and sniffed it, offered it to Shakespeare. "Nit oil?" he said.

"You mustn't touch any of that. It's all medicine to make me fall with child. My husband spilled another flask and that's when the Devil came to Fleet Street. My mother said it was his own fault."

Shakespeare smiled a little. "Has any of it helped?"

The girl had her eyes shut. "I don't want to see what you're doing. I don't want to know. Men are always doing nasty things that hurt. My mother says she hasn't learned enough about the hysterum which is where babies grow but when she has, she is sure she can help me get with child."

399

Enys stood stock still for a long moment, gazing down at the flask in her hand. "What else did she say about what she was doing?"

Mrs Craddock shrugged. "She doesn't tell me anything, she only says that my cleaning and polishing is stupid superstition and a waste of time but it worked for Jane Bailey my gossip."

"Tell me, Mrs Craddock, where was Mrs Ashley early this morning?"

"She was out from before dawn for she said she had an important thing to find out. She came here first, though, she always does."

Enys nodded, put the flask down and started poking in corners. In the chest under the heavy sugar loaves she found a goodwife's clothes, along with a slightly sticky apron and also the decorated tray for the oranges. Underneath was a key that might have opened an old monk's cell with a Christ's head window. Beside it lay a small daybook, leather covered, the kind with blank pages that some of the more enterprising stationers at St Paul's had begun selling, for people to record their sins in. Shakespeare had a pile of them under his bed, full to bursting with poems, stories, ideas, plays and parts of a tragedy which concerned an old man who longed to be a knight of old and set off to become one. For no reason he understood, that had somehow petered out.

Enys grabbed it and opened it: the whole was written

400

in Latin, in a clear large Italic hand. "Whose writing is this?" he asked Mrs Craddock.

She looked at the book without interest. "My mother's, sir, she was taught penmanship and reading and Latin by her father who believed that women as the weaker sex are more in need of education than men."

Shakespeare nodded at this surprising good sense and found that Enys was looking annoyed. He thought that such a strange creature as Enys would appreciate the wisdom better than most.

"Can you read it?"

Mrs Craddock smiled a wan little smile. "No, indeed, sir, my late father was of a completely opposite opinion and felt that the less a woman's brain was unsettled, the less affected it would be by hysteria."

Enys took the daybook over to the light and opened it. Shakespeare peered over his shoulder to read the most recent page.

The Latin was poor, not classical, more a schoolman's Latin but what it said was clear enough.

"After I had killed subject vii mercifully by an application of hebenon to the auricular passage, the abdomen was opened and the intestines resected to uncover the hysterum..."

There were sketches as well. The first page concerned the killing of Betty Warren and her innards. Mrs Ashley had had some trouble to find the womb at all.

401

Shakespeare stared down at the book. He liked orangeadoes and sometimes bought one at the bear-baiting, if he could afford it and there weren't any hazelnuts. There was a pair of stays in the chest, on top of Goody Mallow's other clothes. Shakespeare and Enys's eyes met. Shakespeare couldn't speak.

"Ah," said Enys. Restlessly he went to the door and looked out of the yard. "The Thames was convenient, I think."

Back to the chest. At the very bottom of it, he found something else that made him sigh – Shakespeare came over to look, circling round the quivering girl in the middle of the shed with her eyes shut. It was a small jet cross skillfully carved in one piece with a figure of Christ, very obviously the last and most unsellable part of a highly illegal rosary, from which small jewels, perhaps rubies or garnets, had been levered out, leaving holes in the carving on the hands and feet and in the side.

Enys's face suddenly twisted and he clenched the cross in his fist, then put it carefully into the inside pocket of his doublet, allowing Shakespeare only the hope of seeing something of the woman under the man's clothes, not the reality. That was enough, though, despite the circumstances. Shakespeare had to concentrate on mentally reciting something very dull from the Aenid for a while in order to be able to straighten up without embarrassment.

Mrs Craddock was now muttering to herself as she clasped her elbows together, turning slowly on the spot with her eyes shut.

Shakespeare watched her for a while. Was it possible she didn't know what her mother had been doing – or was that one of the reasons for her lunatic behaviour? Was it possible to both know something and not know you knew? He thought it might be although it was hard to understand how the humours could behave like that. But he had seen things...

Perhaps it was nonsense. Perhaps her mother had been doing nothing but the most ordinary sort of superstitious magic to help her daughter conceive. Perhaps the daybook was only a murderous fantasy or...

Enys went and stood outside the door, still holding the flask, jerked his head so Shakespeare went out with him, shut the door behind him. "The cross belonged to Peter's sister Mary," Enys said quietly, "The key belonged to Isabel. The flask was in Isabel's room for she picked it up when Eliza was drunk... And that woman calling herself Goody Mallow was there supposedly helping her when she was drunk the other night."

A finger of ice went down Shakespeare's back as he recalled the scene. "We did save her from the Devil?"

"We did. And it's clear that Goody Mallow and Mrs Ashley are the same woman but what I really want to

403

know is... why?"

"Why?"

"What was the point of cutting the women open and rummaging about inside them? Why did she kill them in the first place?"

"To learn what is hidden, as her daughter said, as Nan said," Shakespeare said quietly, "Have you not seen Marlowe's play, The History of Dr Faustus? I had never thought a woman could have such a desire, but there again, why not?"

Enys nodded, his hands shaking. He opened the book in another place and there was a tolerably good picture of French Mary lying on her back with her guts spilling, pillowy lumps of fat escaping, except there was no face. None of the sketches showed a face of any kind.

"Here is the account of the day Goody Harbridge was killed. "It was necessary and right to put an end to an old witch that threatened me, but my hebenon being stolen from me by the whore, I was forced to do it by violence, wringing her neck. A quick resection was begun but could not go on as the place she had run to was overlooked by the merchant's house." Jesu. It's as if they are chickens she's killing."

"And poor Craddock is taking the blame for it," Shakespeare pointed out. Enys looked at him blankly.

"He should take the blame as well. He lay with little

404

Mary and caused her to be thrown out and I think he has not lain with his wife recently, perhaps he never has. Perhaps she isn't young enough for him." Enys's lip lifted with distaste.

Shakespeare shook his head. "But he didn't actually kill anybody. It may have been his fault, but he has not actually killed. Not... not like this."

Enys sighed. "No."

"We have to tell Fleetwood and we have to stop the whores from taking their revenge on him."

"We do, but..." Shouting was coming from Fleet Street and Enys looked up the alley that led that way with the whites of her eyes showing.

Shakespeare crossed his arms. His heart was beating slow and heavy, there was a lump of lead in his gut, and he knew that any sensible man would stay well away from Fleet Street but... But. It wasn't enough to be sensible, it wasn't enough to stay out of trouble. There was the matter of a man's honour as well. Would Enys understand it, being in fact of the weaker sex?

Enys was scowling at the flagstones between her boots. "We have to, don't we," she said. Shakespeare swallowed hard, which didn't at all clear his airway.

"We have to," he agreed.

Before either of them could think of a clever argument for avoiding it, both he and Enys started walking quickly up the alley that went past the Christ's head cell, the shouting and banging echoed down it and both of them started to jog. Shakespeare found himself doing what he often did, standing somehow apart from the action at the back of his head, watching in amazement as the emotions and pictures rolled out in front of him, both the hero and the teller of the tale. They were jogging because they very much wanted to run the other way, but knew they mustn't, and so they ran to meet the trouble.

They came out to find Fleet Street shuttered and the trained bands drawn up around the large house on Fleet Street where Mr Craddock lived. That too was as well shuttered and locked up as if there were plague inside.

The colourful mob of loose women was standing in front of the young men of the trained bands and behind them a less colourful, mainly blue-clad mob of apprentices and roaring boys, bravos and upright men. The City being what it was, the trained bands were full of the prentices' older brothers and fathers which was leading to a certain amount of banter.

Mrs Nunn was standing with her hip tilted and her arms folded while Fleetwood stood and read loudly and slowly from an old and stained scroll. Beside the conduit where the women had been gathered to watch earlier, lay a young man in a buff coat with a bloody head, and another one who looked as if his arm was broken. There was glass on the ground near Temple Bar.

It was a stand-off. The young men of the trained bands had bows but not many of them and polearms and clubs. They went out on Sundays to march up and down and play veneys with each other and most of them had probably joined in the Armada year and then kept on going because they enjoyed themselves and liked smart white livery coats slashed with red and the free beer after their meetings. Not one of them was anxious to fight off a crowd of lads and the upright men the whores had called in, but then the prentices weren't anxious to fight either. They didn't mind fighting each other, but they didn't fancy trouble with someone who was wearing a buff coat and carrying a spear, even if the point was a little rusty and blunt.

Some of the upright men at the back were shouting and throwing stones at Fleetwood while he read steadily through the Norman French of the old proclamation read by the Lord Mayor of London at the height of the Peasant's Revolt. He was taking his time about it as the long yellow light faded.

"We don't need to hear all this," shouted Mrs Nunn, "We know about it. Give us the Man-witch, the lawyer that called up the Devil to kill us, and we'll all go home." The women behind her growled and shouted and shook their fists. Some of them were drunk but all of them were serious.

"When you have all gone peacefully home," shouted

407

Fleetwood in measured tones, "I will make it my business to arrest Mr Craddock and bring him to trial for witchcraft and treason,"

"Hah!" sneered Mrs Nunn, "He's a lawyer, he'll bring all his friends as oath-swearers and he'll get off. You know he will."

"On a charge of treason, madam?" said Fleetwood, "I very much doubt it."

Mrs Nunn only narrowed her eyes and tapped her foot. "We want him and we don't go home until we get him," she said.

Fleetwood began reading the English translation of the proclamation, which was in the language of two hundred years ago and nearly as incomprehensible as the lawyer-French. He was reading slowly and pompously and Shakespeare had to hide a grin as he realised that the senior lawyer of London was doing his best to bore the mob into dispersing. It looked as if it might even work.

He stole a look sideways at Enys who was very pale and biting her lip. She walked straight out of the alleyway, still panting from the jog up the alleyway and across the street to where the Recorder of London still stood, now disputing with Mrs Nunn, her brother, the frightening thug Gabriel and the urchin with staring hair, Peter the Hedgehog who was bouncing up and down, waving a small knife and shrieking something incomprehensible. At the moment though he was being ignored while Fleetwood and the madam of the Falcon argued. They were watched narrow-eyed by all the whores, the prentices and the trained bands.

And then a rock came sailing over the heads of the London trained bands and struck Mr Fleetwood on his head, making a musical sound as it bounced off his morion. Fleetwood staggered and fell to his knees. The young men of the trained bands, shouted and raised their polearms, the ones who were old-fashioned enough to carry longbows nocked arrows and drew their bows, while the upright men started throwing more stones. The shouting women who had gone quiet by habit to listen to the proclamation, started shrieking and advancing on the front door behind the three ranks of men.

Shakespeare knew they couldn't have worked out where the rock came from, but he knew. He had seen it thrown. He started running for the nearest alley that went round behind the Craddocks' house. He heard Enys shouting but the sound of what he said was drowned out by the roar of the mob as the prentices also started forwards, pushed from behind by the upright men. Once he shouted what he had seen, to try to distract them.

Nobody was listening. Shakespeare put his head down and sprinted, down the alley, right, left and right again. He was sure it was the right alley, but he couldn't see anything useful except some urchins with cunning looks on their faces, clearly waiting for the rioters to break into the lawyers' houses where there would no doubt be rich pickings.

And then he saw a figure in a cloak, with a hood over its head, come out of the yard behind the Craddocks' house. He skidded to a halt, hid behind a corner. The cloaked figure paused when it saw the boys, then it threw some round orange things at them. They were orangeadoes which the boys caught, looked at and some of them began to eat. "Don't eat them, they're poisoned," he said to the boys as he ran past.

The figure hurried down through the alleys. Shakespeare went after it and wondered about trying to stop her, trying to arrest her... But she had managed to throttle the life out of Goody Harbridge and she had killed, by her own account, six other women and although he might have tried his chances with a man, he felt very alone and...

All right. He was frightened. The objective watcher at the back of his head sneered at him and he shrugged. She was a witch. Who knew what else she could do apart from poison people through their ears? He was berating himself for abject cowardice and at the same time he crept along behind her.

She seemed intent and was carrying something

410

cradled in her arms. Was it more poison, perhaps? Or a knife?

She came to the Christ window, paused a moment and then hurried past, down the side of the wall to a door that led into the small yard belonging to the monastery hut. This she opened and bolted behind her, while Shakespeare hid round the corner. When she had gone into the house, Shakespeare boosted himself up onto the wall, down into the small space, and up again onto the wall of Goody Mallow's yard. He lay full-length along it and waited. What would she do? Where could she possibly go?

.

Maliverny Catlin felt his brain must be melting down through his nose in an unending stream of phlegm. He had woken up crying, slouched in a corner on one of the wall-benches of St Bride's church. He was still crying, as if his eyes had somehow been connected to a freerunning conduit with fresh water from Hampstead Heath,

His kerchief was sodden and slimy by now. Then, suddenly, a not too grubby but dry one was slipped into his hand and he looked up in fright, fearing more phantasms.

It was only an ordinary round-faced man, in a dull

411

dark wool suit, his hat on the bench beside him.

"I cry you mercy..." Catlin stuttered, flushing with shame. The old woman had been embarrassing enough. This stranger with sympathy in his eyes was worse.

"I only came in to pray, " said the man, "for guidance and for mercy and thought you were ill when I saw you weeping in your sleep. If you like, I'll leave."

Catlin shook his head. Actually, he didn't care. Another wave was rising up from his belly, the desolation of knowing that he would never ever see Isabel again; the logic was unimpeachable. Either she was in Hell while he would be with the Elect in Heaven, or more likely they would both be in Hell and part of their torture would be never to meet.

After a moment, the man spoke again, looking down at the scraps of straw on the tiles. "Sir," he said, "is there anything I can do to help you in your sorrow? My name is... Edmund Goodfriend and I have been known to live up to my name."

Catlin shook his head again. Then he stopped. What did it matter what anyone thought of him? The fear of what people thought of him was why he had delayed so long over marrying Isabel when he realised now he could have done it easily. He was rich, had no need of a woman's dowry, could himself endow her with a generous jointure if necessary. Only the fear of what others would say had stopped him, really.

"I lost a woman I longed to marry," he said, his nose so packed with phlegm it came out distorted and bubbling. "Or... I could have married her and been happy but... but I delayed."

"Why?"

"For pride." The word came out without Catlin intending it, but in fact seemed surprisingly true. "I thought... I thought the woman not worthy of me." And that was true as well, although he had never actually thought it in so many words."

Young Mr Goodfriend said nothing and only nodded. He had his head propped on his hand, his face tilted a little so as not to look at him directly.

"I could have made her mine and she would have been safe, but... she wasn't... she wasn't a virgin. She... she wasn't chaste."

The young man's face changed a little.

"Are you sure it was her fault that she wasn't?" he asked, which was an odd thing to ask.

"Well, no, I suppose not," Catlin admitted, a little surprised. "She told me how it happened."

"She was forced?"

"She said an upright man broke her in when she was twelve and put her to work for him," Catlin said, "So I suppose it wasn't her fault. And she had no other trade."

"Was she a good woman in other ways?

Catlin thought about it. At least the waterfall in

413

his eyes had gone to a trickle. He trumpeted into the hankerchief again.

"I don't know, I think so, she was kind. She never laughed at me. She talked to me and listened to me. She... she stroked my head." His voice wavered and broke and he had to hold his breath against the pain in his chest.

Goodfriend smiled a little. "She sounds as if she was a good woman."

"But... but you don't understand," Catlin almost wailed to him, "She must infallibly be damned!"

"Why?"

"Because she was a... unchaste."

"And are you of the Elect? Are you one of these Puritans that follow Calvin?"

"Yes, of course. So by Calvin's logic and St Augustine's logic we are separated for all eternity. Either by her sin or by both our sins bringing us to Hell."

"Your sin of fornication?"

Catlin nodded.

Goodfriend looked up at the plain altar table and the headless saints of the old screen. He seemed to be thinking.

"Sir, if you will, may I speak my mind?"

Catlin could only shrug. The young man spoke quietly, in measured words.

"I fear that your undoubted sin of fornication was

414

by far the least of your sins. Your much greater sin was pride, in that you loved the woman but did not make her honestly your wife rather than fornicate – for pride's sake, not for any other reason. This is why Pride is named one of the seven deadly sins because it makes a gateway for other sins."

Maliverny stared at him, transfixed.

"But she wasn't the only one... " He protested. "There were others... "

And then in a long scalding flood of words it all came out, like the pus from a lanced abscess. And the details: how he had returned from Paris Garden, drunk and shocked at himself and utterly spent, heading for the sanctuary of Isabel's room and tripped on Kettle Annie's corpse after meeting Mr Enys. How he had been in fear of being found out as one of Kettle Annie's regular clients, back in the old days when he worked for Sir Francis and she was a prime source of information about the Papists in the Clink. How he had agreed to look for the murderer and worked only to hide the fact that he knew the women and how as a result of his delaying, Isabel herself had somehow been killed... And that was why he knew he was damned. He said it aloud, the thing the beating ugly voice kept saying over and over in his head. "So you see, Mr Goodfriend, I am damned. Infallibly. And logically. You cannot deny it. As Calvin teaches, God knew from the beginning of the world who among us would be saved and who damned and..."

"I must say, I've always thought that Calvin was a pathetic excuse for a theologian," said Goodfriend outrageously, "What a numbskull. I don't care how many Swiss Puritans think him greater than St Peter, the man could no more argue logic than a striped grey cat."

Catlin gasped with horror.

"Let me put it to you this way. Who made Logic itself?"

"Er... God?"

"Having made Logic, is God greater or smaller than it?"

"Greater?"

"Which came first? God or Logic?"

"God is precedent of all things?"

"And which of the two is omnipotent?"

"God."

"Ergo which is bound by which: is God ruled by Logic or is Logic ruled by God?"

Something fell back into place inside Catlin. Perhaps... perhaps there was a little hope? He blinked at the young man who had somehow smashed all he had always believed since he had read Calvin's writings as a young man. It felt very odd to have your foundations suddenly slipped out from under you and tossed casually away.

"Sir," said Goodfriend clasping his hands together

416

tightly, "I would only ask you to consider this proposition: that the only worse sin than Pride itself is spiritual Pride which is the worst of all because it leads us to think that we are so right, we need no forgiveness from God or can get none. And very ingeniously we argue ourselves into believing that we know the Mind of God and that we know how God would act. And yet in Isaiah chapter 55 it says, "let the wicked forsake his way and the unrighteous man his thoughts; let him return to the Lord that he may have mercy on him, and to our God for he will abundantly pardon. For my thoughts are not your thoughts, neither are your ways my ways, says the Lord.""""

Maliverny knew the verse but had never really listened to the words. "Do you really think that's true?" he asked.

Goodfriend actually laughed. "I hope so," he said, "I am as much or perhaps more in need of God's mercy as you, sir, as God knows. Only this can we know – we have, in fact, no knowledge of who is saved and who is damned. All we do know is that Our Lord Jesus Christ came to save all that will ask Him to save them."

Catlin said nothing. The way he was thinking now was too strange. Goodfriend grinned.

"So perhaps, if she repented, your intended is saved while you, if you do not repent, most certainly will be damned."

417

Catlin shuddered. He had always been afraid he was in fact damned, but it had never crossed his mind that Isabel might go to Heaven and he might not.

"But..."

"Did Our Lord not eat and drink with publicans, tax collectors and sinners?"

"Well, yes, but..."

"Did He not tell the parables of the lost sheep, the lost coin and the prodigal son?"

"Well yes, but..."

"So which do you believe? Calvin's tortured logic or Our Blessed Saviour's words in the Gospels of Holy Scripture?"

Catlin's lips parted. He was finding it hard to breathe. "Do you really think so?"

"I know so," said the young man, very seriously, "It's why I became... well, God sends His holy angels to help us and His Son to save all of us that desire it. Surely your betrothed desired it?"

Catlin frowned. Isabel had often said how she would not ply her trade if she had any other way of eating. And he himself desired salvation too. Only the idea that it was not a fixed certainty but might change made him feel queasy.

"But surely that's too easy?" he objected.

"Yes. Our Lord said that His way is easy and His yoke is light." Goodfriend had his hands out and open,

418

palms up as if he was receiving something into them.

At last Maliverny nodded once. The waves of misery had faded down to a distant thunder for the moment. Perhaps. Perhaps this man had a point. Perhaps somehow he could meet Isabel again?

"Sir," he said with a painful smile, handing back the now sodden hankerchief, "My name is Maliverny Catlin. You have helped me greatly with your wise words, Mr Goodfriend. Is there anything I may do for you?"

"Well... ah... yes," said the man uncertainly. "I am in a quandary. I am urgently in need of a place as a serving man or clerk or perhaps a tutor as I have... I have had a falling out with my previous lord. I was about to go to the serving man's pillar in St Paul's. In fact, I had best go there now or there will be no gallants left near Duke Humphrey's tomb. If there are any at all, thanks to the prentices."

"Very few, because of the plague's continuance." Catlin looked at the man. He seemed clean and well-set-up, his hands bore no sword calluses, so he was not a soldier returned from the Netherlands. He had spoken eloquently and with knowledge of scripture. "Can you write a good hand, Mr Goodfriend?"

"Yes, Secretary or Italic, as you desire. I read Latin and a little Greek as well. Alas, I have no letters to recommend me thanks to my dispute with my former lord."

"Hm. What was it about?"

The man coughed. "It was on a matter of religion, sir, I had rather not speak of it."

Catlin only needed to consider for a minute. "Well Mr Goodfriend," he said, "I myself have urgent need of a clerk and a man to carry messages for me . Would you be able to do those things?"

"Yes sir, I would."

"I can't pay you much, but I can give you board and lodging and perhaps livery," Catlin warned, his habitual frugality reasserting itself.

"That would be a king's wage compared to my recent living," said Goodfriend.

Catlin clapped his right hand on the man's right shoulder. "Then you're hired, Mr Goodfriend, and I hope we may have more conversation on philosophy. I urgently need someone to deal with Mr Topcliffe for me."

Goodfriend stopped for a second as if shocked, and then he smiled again. From the lines at the corners of his eyes, he often did that. "Sir," he said honestly, "I think my own prayers have been answered."

.

Peter the Hedgehog was breathless and sweaty from bouncing up and down in the middle of Fleet Street,

420

but full of exhilaration and rage as he danced in front of the mob. "E killed my sister!" he shouted again though his throat was hoarse, "He's the witch, he brung the plague!"

The women of the town were now close to the ranks of the trained bands of London who were starting to look shifty and frightened, especially as some of the whores were calling out to men that they knew as customers. Mrs Nunn was talking to Recorder Fleetwood who was standing in front of his men with the scroll of the Riot Act now stuffed into the front of his buff coat.

"We want the lawyer," shouted Mrs Nunn, "When we've got him we'll go home."

Her brother Gabriel stood at her shoulder, his own buff coat buckled up and a veney stick in his hand, a woollen statute cap on his head, pulled down over his blond hair and looking as if he had a secret under it, an iron cap to do duty as a helmet. Peter somehow felt safer knowing that Gabriel Nunn was there.

"Will you give him a fair... no, any kind of trial?"

"We don't need to," shrugged Mrs Nunn, "We know it's him."

"What will you do with him?"

Peter suddenly knew that Fleetwood was playing for time. "We'll hang him," he shouted, "He killed my sister! After he wapped her," he added.

"How do you know Mr Craddock killed your sister?" asked Fleetwood directly of him, "Did you see him do it?"

"Nah," sneered Peter, "Or I'd of stopped him, wouldn't I? I know he wapped her."

There was a look of distaste on Fleetwood's face. "The sin of fornication with a whore is not a hanging offence..."

Peter's head filled with blood and fury. "She warn't no whore before he wapped 'er, she was a virgin!" he shrieked, "That's why he killt her."

Fleetwood was standing solidly, his thumbs braced in the front of his buffcoat, quite clearly prepared to stand there and dispute all day if necessary. Suddenly Peter wanted to kill him too. And as he thought that, as if thinking it made it happen, a rock came sailing from behind them and hit Mr Fleetwood right on his helmet. It made a loud doiing noise.

He staggered and fell to his knees. As if he had been the keystone of a dam, the trained bands lifted their arrows and spears and the whores started throwing stones themselves. Peter stood and stared. He had seen where the stone came from and it came from Craddock's house, from an upstairs window. Skirts and men with veney sticks brushed past him and he stood staring at the house. Why would they throw a rock at their protector?

422

Suddenly James Enys rushed shouting something into the middle of the ruck and pulled Fleetwood up, stood him on his feet again. Fleetwood was stunned and googly eyed, and Enys started unstrapping his helmet. Rocks began banging against the bricks and wood of the shuttered house, there was a thrum as the archers shot their arrows over the heads of the mob, while women with buckets of slops threw them at the young men of the trained bands. Some got angry and broke their lines to try and catch the women. Suddenly the whole thing broke up into a succession of small fights and prentices were swinging veney sticks at each other as well as their enemies in the trained bands, running up the road shouting at each other. Nobody had actually been hit by an arrow which was a sort of miracle.

Gabriel Nunn was fighting at the head of the upright men, with Briscoe at his back, who was in his Sunday best for some reason. There was an iron purpose in Nunn for all the chaos. He plowed through the fighting with his veney stick in a businesslike way until he came to the door of the house. Briscoe hit it with an axe to more shouting from the whores.

James Enys helped Fleetwood sit on the edge of the conduit and splashed water on his face. He closed his eyes and swayed but seemed to be coming round.

"What...?" he asked. "My lord, I apologise..."

The mob was gathered round the lawyer's house like

423

ants around a sugar loaf, people were climbing the sides and the sound of Briscoe's axe was crunching steadily into the fine wood of the door.

Enys was pale with fear and had something that looked like a book tucked into his doublet. What was he afraid of? Afraid of the prentices and upright men breaking into the house while the trained bands gathered helplessly in bunches at the sides of the street? And he's afraid of me, thought Peter proudly, then he felt uncomfortable because Mr Enys's sister had been nice to him and given him a pie all to himself.

So he stood by Enys with his little knife and thought he would stop anyone from attacking him at least. It was getting late, the light was nearly gone. Some people at the back were lighting torches.

"Mr Fleetwood, sir," said Enys in a low urgent voice, "look at this please?"

Fleetwood coughed, shook his head to clear it, rubbed his eyes and squinted at the book Enys was waving under his nose. One of his men came near with a lantern he had managed to light. Ah, he had a slowmatch lit, perhaps for an arquebus. He took it and turned the pages. His face was already pale and it went paler.

"Whose is this? Mr Craddock's?"

"No sir, his mother in law, Mrs Ashley her book. Her daughter identified her writing for me."

424

There was a ragged cheer as Briscoe's axe went through the wood of the door and the Nunns shoved their way into the house, followed by some of Gabriel's men. Briscoe turned in the doorway with his axe, which he swung around his head. The mob behind him flinched back from it.

"You can stop there!" he roared at the other women and prentices crowding to see the lawyer's house, "If anybody's getting the plate cupboard, it's Mr Nunn!"

There was a babble of complaint and argument. Briscoe simply stood massively in the doorway. "You can try it on if you like, darling, " he said to one particularly shrill woman, who turned out to be the extremely drunk Eliza.

"This amounts to a confession," whispered Fleetwood. "She killed seven, not four."

"At least."

"Where is she?"

"She's got away by now, sir, I think it was she who threw the rock to make a diversion."

"God damn it!"

There was a babble and confusion. One of Gabriel's lads came running out the door and headed for where Fleetwood was climbing shakily to his feet again and buckling on his dented morion.

"Mr Recorder, Mr Recorder," shouted the lad, "He's done it already, he's topped hisself."

Fleetwood, Enys and Peter trailing along behind ran to the door where Briscoe stood aside to let them in.

The entrance hall with its elaborate highly polished banisters was dim from the shuttering. From the top post of the stairs hung something like a heavy sack, which turned and creaked. Peter sniffed: you couldn't mistake it, there was the smell of turds you always got with a dead body. From the way the head was angled, the rope had broken his neck. Mr Craddock's face was quite peaceful, considering.

Word was going back from the boy into the crowd, causing a general stir of combined approval, disappointment and triumph.

Fleetwood stared up at the body. Then he looked across at Gabriel Nunn and at Mrs Nunn. "It wasn't him," he said, "It was his mother-in-law."

"What?" snapped Mrs Nunn,

"Madam, if you want us to catch the woman, take that body out on a litter, show the women you brought that they have what they came for, even if it is in no way justice but rather murder, pure and simple, and tell them all to go home."

"How do you know it's murder?"

Fleetwood gestured at the body. Peter saw it at last. The hands were tied.

"We would of been blamed for that," said Gabriel shrewdly, "If we'd all got in together."

426

"Yes," said Fleetwood. "Will you see to it, Mr Nunn?"

"I will, sir. I'll untie his hands first though."

Enys had gone up the stairs and looked in the rooms. "She's not here and the back gate is unbolted. Mr Nunn, you might want to ask the lads pillaging the larder to leave behind any fresh meat."

Fleetwood strode outside again, the book in his hand. He had to read it carefully to make out the ugly Latin. Enys came up to him and spoke urgently.

"I believe I know where Mrs Ashley has gone and her daughter is there as well. Will you come with me."

Fleetwood nodded and beckoned over his usual four assistants, leaving Jenkins with Briscoe. Nunn was ably organising a makeshift litter from one of the other doors and had already cut down the corpse of the lawyer.

Peter stuck close to Enys. He kept as quiet as he could and hoped no one would notice. He'd heard what they thought, who had really done it and he was furious with himself for not realising before. Who else could be a witch?

He planned to be in on the finish.

Still, he couldn't resist shaking his fist as Nunn and his helpers hoisted Mr Craddock onto the litter. "Ha!" he shouted, "See what you get, you old bugger!"

"Shh," said Mr Enys, spoiling the moment.

"He won't get to Purgy will he?" Peter asked

427

anxiously as they headed across to the alley that led into Whitefriars. "I don't fink Mary would want to see him again."

Enys shook his head irritably and didn't answer. Fleetwood was striding ahead and they had to run to keep up.

.

Shakespeare desperately tried to focus his mind: he felt sick and hot, his heart was hammering and the world around him seemed suddenly made of colourful putty. The woman in front of him was constructed of parts that didn't fit together. Everything had gone horribly wrong.

It had been going so well to start with. He had lain on the wall until Mrs Ashley had let herself into the stone shed, then he had slipped down and peered through the window. Thin little Mrs Craddock was embraced in Mrs Ashley's arms with her head on the older woman's shoulder, weeping. He watched, fascinated as Mrs Ashley gave Phyllida a cup of some dark liquid and the girl stared at it and cried even more. She didn't drink though. Mrs Ashley moved out of his vision and he watched the girl, wondering if she would drink it and what would happen if she did...

"You're the bald player, aren't you?" said the cold

428

voice of Mrs Ashley behind him. He turned, to see her standing there with a small wheel-lock dag in her hand. It was wound and seemed to be shotted and loaded.

"Ma'am?" he had gasped, so shocked he couldn't move. There had been no hissing of a match to warn him.

"In there," she said, her face stiff and calm, "You shouldn't poke your nose where it isn't wanted. Go on. I'm probably going to hang or burn anyway, I can put you on the bill as well if you want."

It was the lack of passion that convinced him. He went the way she gestured, into the stone hut where young Mrs Craddock was standing, wringing her hands, the still full cup beside her on the counter. He was enthralled by Mrs Ashley's certainty as a rabbit might be enthralled by a man with a drawn bow or a dog, quite frozen with fear. She was only a woman but the dag gave her complete sovereignty. If you had a gun you didn't need a man's strength, just will power and from the look of her she had will in abundance and overplus.

He swallowed in a totally dry throat. There had been an insane part of him which liked that phrase.

"Mrs Ashley, I..."

"Quiet. Sit on the stool."

He sat. What else could he do?

"Phyllida my love, tie his arms to the stool."

The girl approached him hesitantly from behind and

he thought about grabbing her and using her as a shield.

Mrs Ashley brought the dag closer to him so she couldn't miss but not close enough so he could grab. Besides, his insides were melting with fear. As often happened, the part of him that was always a poet stepped back to watch what was happening with interest. You fool, Will thought to the poet, if I die, you do too.

No, I don't, said the poet smugly, I can't die. Haven't you heard of the soul?

Too late he thought of grabbing his expensive forty shilling poinard. She had already taken it out of its scabbard. The thin ropes went round his wrists and pulled tight. Did she know how to tie a good knot? Women generally did from all the embroidery and spinning they did. She wrapped the rope several times, passing it under the stool as well, made several knots so it didn't matter. He pulled at it experimentally and got nowhere.

"Phyllida, my heart," said Mrs Ashley in a grey voice, "I know you are sad and worried. So am I. Everything has gone wrong. And so we must do what I warned you about or otherwise we will suffer terribly in jail and then perhaps burn at the stake."

"I never asked you to kill people to find out how to fall with child," whispered Mrs Craddock sulkily.

Shakespeare shook with the cold selfishness in her voice.

"I never expected anyone to notice what I was doing," said Mrs Ashley, "They were only whores after all."

"Why didn't you use people with plague?"

"I did," said Mrs Ashley, "but they were all bloody and destroyed within, I could see nothing. So take the medicine, my dear."

The pale child wrapped her arms around her bony shoulders.

"I don't want to," she said.

"This is the only thing that will work. You must take this potion which will make you sleep like the dead. They will not bury you but lay you out for the inquest. By then I will be able to come and rescue you."

"What if you don't?"

"I will. Don't be afraid. I have measured the exact amount."

Shakespeare's wrists were burning as he tried to free his hands. Whatever plan Mrs Ashley had for escape, she would have to kill him to keep it a secret.

"Have you eaten today, Phyllida?" she asked, looking at the girl narrowly.

Something in her voice caught Shakespeare's throat, despite his rising panic, there was so much sadness and love in the voice. Phyllida shook her head.

"How could I?"

Mrs Ashley reached out, took the cup and poured

away some of the poison.

"Phyllida," said Shakespeare, his voice shaking,"If you take that, you will certainly die. Help me and..."

Mrs Ashley hit him across the mouth with the back of her hand. One of his dog-teeth went into his lip and started bleeding.

"Phyllida, my dear, simply take it, drink it down quickly so you don't taste it."

The girl took the cup and held it, looking at it uncertainly.

"Will there be bad dreams again?"

"No," Mrs Ashley was pulling one of the pots towards her. She scooped out something white and fatty with grey flecks in and then suddenly slapped Shakespeare again, slathering it across his face. He spat and coughed , it was goosefat with bitterness in it, the stuff went over his lips and in his eyes, some up his nose, it was disgusting. He sneezed and tried to wipe it onto his shoulder.

Mrs Ashley put her dag down on the counter. "Drink it," she said again to Phyllida, who held out the cup and smiled. It was empty.

"Now lie down quickly," said Mrs Ashley, "You don't want to see what I'm going to do to the player." She laid her cloak down in the corner by the fireplace and Phyllida lay on it obediently. Mrs Ashley sang softly to the girl as her eyes closed, an old lullaby, and stroked her hair. He watched the girl as she seemed to fold herself obediently into sleep and as her breathing became shallow, fascinated by this onset of death, wanting to know if you could see the moment when...

Shapes began to grow out of her and out of Mrs Ashley, square baskets and round wheels, golden spider's webs growing across his eyes. Mrs Ashley turned to him, suddenly huge and terrifying with a black hole where her face should have been. He was panting and couldn't get enough air, but he could see the knife flashing in her hand. Her fingers were made of knives. Something had happened to her, she had turned into Goody Mallow. Ah yes. She must have put on the orangeado woman's clothes again. Yes, there were her good gentlewoman's clothes folded in the chest, which she shut.

Of course. That was how she planned to do it. Nobody except Shakespeare and Enys knew of her disguise as the orangeado woman, she had every chance of getting away with it.

Except first she has to kill me, Shakespeare thought, and tried to fight the rope again but his muscles were turned to butter and his head spun. The devil in front of him leant down with her knife.

"I have to go," she said, lifted the knife, then hesitated. "But I'd very much like to know what's inside you, Mr Player. Where do your plays come from? Is it your belly or your heart?"

433

The warmth was filling Shakespeare's head. "From God," he said, struggling to make his bolster-sized lips move. "From God almighty."

The devil smiled at him. "I doubt it."

Play for time, said the poet, time is your only gold. "Why d'you want to know?"

The Devil's eyes glittered. "Why don't you want to know? Why don't you ask questions? You're all so dull and stupid: do you think you're made of meat? You're not. Inside you is a wondrous arrangement, more like clockwork than meat. Where is the soul kept? Men sow their seed inside us and babies grow. How? What makes one baby grow well and the other die? Where does the blood go when it comes from the heart, how does it get back to the heart? I know it's not a furnace, it's a pump, and I know that it travels round the body like water in a conduit but how? What makes the heart beat? I've watched it clench and unclench, it's a wonderful thing, but how does it work?"

The knife came closer to his eyes. "You might as well be blind, all of you. You look but you don't see. If only to God I had been made a man and not a woman, I would have gone to Padua to be a physician and I would have been the greatest physician ever known, I would have studied these things. My father taught me to read and write Latin but all the same, when I married, I had to obey my husband and leave off all studies and learn

434

to make confectionary." She spat the word, as if it was bitter like an orangeado.

Play for time, said the poet, let her speak.

"But... why did you have to kill people... why not wait for them to die?"

She smiled and the smile was deep in the black hole in the centre of her face which was growing to cover her whole head. "No," she said, "Our bodies move when we are alive, everything stops when we die. It's the most wonderful sight in the world. When I first saw it I was only a child..."

"How?" Shakespeare whispered, unwillingly fascinated. The words were spilling from the woman as if from a bursting wineskin, as if they had been fermenting inside her and must be allowed to drain, or perhaps an abscess...

"I saw into my mother," she said, "When my mother died in childbed after three days of labour. She begged him to do it, she begged him to cut her open..."

"Wh... what?"

"My father studied medicine in Cordoba, you know, he was a physician but he also learnt surgery. So when my mother begged him to cut her open to save the baby, he gave her hebenon to quiet her and laudanum to ease the pain and he cut into her belly to find the babe and I saw. I peeked through the window and I saw. I saw the blood, I saw the entrails moving like snakes, I saw my

435

mother's hysterum pulse and clench, full and swollen with the babe. I saw the mystery of what is inside us and when my father cut into her womb and took out the babe and the afterbirth, it was blue and unmoving and then as my father wept, the babe opened his eyes and cried and went from blue to red – and how and why those colours? He cried and my mother heard and smiled and died in blood and snakes. Then everything inside her stopped."

That was when Shakespeare knew that this woman was made of parts that did not fit and that there was a black hole in her head. The rest of the world was gone to putty and all he knew was what she was saying to him and that he must keep her speaking and speaking for the sake of the poems in his head, which were the only things that mattered and he could not allow them to be killed though it didn't matter if he himself died.

Mrs Ashley's face was pulsing to and fro. A ghost paraded past her, wringing its hands. Mrs Ashley clasped her reddened hands as well. Every finger was a glistening steel knife.

"So when my own babe could not have a child and was dying with sorrow for it, I decided to find out why and learn what not even my father knew, how a child grows in the hysterum of a woman or indeed an animal and what makes it do so. I began with dogs and cats but they were very different from what I had seen so I found

436

people dying of plague and opened them. Whatever plague is, it destroys the innards, it was all a mess of blood. Then I opened a young girl that I knew had not borne a child although she was an evil little bitch that stole my daughter's husband from her. I could hardly find her womb, it was so little. Then I found myself a grown mature woman that I knew had borne children, gave her hebenon in an orangeado and opened her. Hers was lumpy and filled with noxious matter. Then there was the old whore, French Mary, and the same with Kettle Mary – they were old whores, I thought nobody would care at all. There were two country girls between that no one missed for I caught them just as they came to London to seek their fortunes. They were saved from whoredom at least. And when the old witch Harbridge accused me of being a witch and said she would tell the Recorder, I had to kill her too."

Shakespeare nodded. He was wondering where the grinning faces of the dead women were coming from. Keep her talking, he thought, she's a woman, she likes to talk. Keep her talking.

"It was clumsy, I had to throttle her as Eliza had stolen my hebenon when you and your lawyer friend found us. Then I thought I'd look inside but I didn't have time to find the womb before I was interrupted by that stupid woman's shrieking, Mrs Bailey. I'll have to kill her too now, which is a nuisance."

"And Isabel?" Shakespeare croaked.

"I had to kill her to get my hebenon back. I left it on the bench and Eliza picked it up. The stupid bitch was using it as hair oil. I'm sure she had some interesting dreams."

She looked fondly at the girl lying on her cloak and then her eyes narrowed. "I wonder what men have inside them?" she said and reached for Shakespeare's doublet.

Out of pure fear that had been rising in him all the while, despite the poison, he wrenched back and kicked out and caught her on the knee. That tipped the stool back, it skittered on the flagstones and then tipped. He landed with a thud on his back, hurting his hands and with his legs in the air.

"Convenient," said Mrs Ashley, rubbing her knee with the hand that had no knife in it. "Let me see..."

She loomed over him, pulled up his doublet and at that moment some kind of little demonic imp jumped from the window ledge and cannoned into Mrs Ashley from behind, screaming something incomprehensible. He clung to her neck like a monkey and stabbed over and over again with a little knife at the woman's neck with its ruff.

She screamed as well, grabbed the imp's hand and wrenched the knife out of it – it didn't seem to have hit anything vital, though blood was spilling down her

438

woollen bodice.

The imp dragged off her linen cap, tore at her hair, she whirled around with Peter the Hedgehog still clinging to her while Shakespeare tried desperately to wriggle out of the way. Now there was blood spilling from her ear where Peter had sunk his snaggled teeth into her. Phyllida Craddock still slept, hardly breathing and Shakespeare lay on his side, wrenching at the ropes that tied him, kicking out with his legs to push himself to the side of the room where he thought Mrs Ashley's knife might have landed. He rubbed his face over and over on the floor, bruising his nose, panting and gagging with the foul fatty stuff on his face and lips.

An axe thudded into the door, the light made a tinging noise as it sparkled off the bit of blade showing between the very clearly delineated woodgrain, it was pulled out, disappeared, thudded again and again, the boards shattered and a large hand appeared, lifted the bar.

James Enys burst through just as Mrs Ashley managed to pluck Peter off her back and throw him against the range and then advance on him with her hands out to throttle while he kicked and squawked desperately. Through it all the woman's face was grim but unmoving, as if still frozen.

Enys crossed the room in two strides, caught up the open jar of henbane ointment and brought it down

439

on the back of Ashley's neck, hit again before the jar shattered in a shower of rainbows. The witch dropped to the floor with a grunt.

Phyllida didn't move. Shakespeare thought the whirling ghosts in the room were fading now. They must have come from the vapours of hebenon, said the poet at the back of his head, but how odd that all eight of the ghosts were now laughing.

Mr Enys bent down to him and Shakespeare flinched at the knife in his fist, but then he cut the ropes on his bruised wrists. He struggled to sit up through the fleeing coloured chaos of the world.

"How did she take you, Will, are you..."

Shakespeare shook his head, trying to clear it of vapour. What had he been talking about with the witch? It was going, it was running out of his memory like sand from a sieve. "She had a dag..." He croaked.

"What?"

Enys spun to see Peter scrambling to his feet with tears and snot smearing his bloody face and the wheel-lock dag in his hand, overwhelming it. The other hand was hanging uselessly. His whole arm trembled as he pointed it at Mrs Ashley who was trying to climb to her feet, Shakespeare thought the witch was probably perfectly safe and in no more danger than anyone else in the room, given the way a bullet could bounce around walls made of stone. A strange figure that had followed

Enys turned out to be the Recorder of London in morion and buffcoat. Mrs Ashley was on her hands and knees, shaking her head slowly which was covered in fat and blood, and trying to get to her feet as if none of her muscles were working right. Good, thought Shakespeare, incoherently, see how it feels.

"Peter," said Enys steadily, looking straight at the gun which was frankly more likely to kill him than the witch, given the way it wobbled in the boy's grip. "The kick will break your wrist."

"She already done the other one," sobbed Peter, "Don't care anyway, so what?"

"You'll be saving her from burning for petty treason and poisoning," rumbled Fleetwood behind them, "Is that what you want, Peter?"

The boy's nostrils flared. "Burning?" he repeated.

"Justice," said Fleetwood.

"Witches hang, don't they?"

Fleetwood nodded once, heavily. "Witches hang, but she poisoned and killed the head of her household, Mr Craddock. That is petty treason and for that she burns."

Peter's face twisted. "Good." He gave Fleetwood the dag with a surprising little bob of a bow, then suddenly went white, his eyes turned up in his head and he crumpled.

Fleetwood's men came past and manacled Mrs Ashley who was mumbling to herself. They held her up

441

between them.

"Mrs Ashley," said Fleetwood gravely, "I am arresting you in the name of Her Majesty the Queen for the crimes of murder, poisoning, petty treason and witchcraft."

She shrugged. "I only killed the whores to know what was in them," she slurred, "The rioters killed Mr Craddock. All I wanted was to help my daughter." She was breathing hard through her nose, blood on her shoulder from the cuts to her neck and the toothmarks in her ear. She looked down at her daughter was was either still in her drugged sleep or dead, there was no visible breath.

"Look after Phyllida," she said, "poor child, she never understood..."

Then she looked blearily up at Fleetwood's granite face and pressed her lips together.

In the narrow alley outside, the crowding whores of London cheered as she was brought out stumbling between the two men, her head hanging. Enys helped Shakespeare to his feet, shaking and queasy with the vapours from the poison. He leaned on the man's shoulder and felt the strength of him holding up his weight and then his body remembered that this was a woman and started to gather itself together a little.

"Brandy?" enquired Enys.

·

The whores were out in force in their striped petticoats and low bodices, though most wore some kind of shawl or veil over their dyed hair, out of a certain sense of respect.

Maliverny Catlin stood upon the bankside scaffold with his back to the new theatre that was rising next to the Bearbaiting ring. Work had stopped on it months ago for lack of money, but the scaffolding was still there and there were urchins and prentices hanging off every one to see the notable witch burn. There hadn't been such a thing for decades, the cost of a square foot of ground in the area around the scaffolding was rumoured to have gone above two shillings and a man called Henslowe was going around with two large helpers to collect it.

Catlin was very fine, wearing a new white falling band, his black satin doublet gleamed. He had newly been named an elder of his chapel and had paid a great deal to preach this sermon and avoid doing penance for fornication. His new secretary, Goodfriend, had helped him draft it. He felt he needed to make a point. "Brethren," he said, "I am come to speak to you on the terrible and horrible tale of a woman that put herself above God's creation, a woman that dared to trouble her brain with trying to understand the workings of God's creation, a woman that broke all the righteous

443

commandments that she should be subordinate to man as Eve was to Adam and..."

Three women by the scaffold stairs, stood quietly, ignoring Catlin's well-wrought words. Portia Morgan was wearing a veil to hide her face and the slender and now widowed Mrs Craddock stood bare-faced beside her. On the girl's other side was little Ellie Briscoe, a very determined look on her face. Mrs Craddock was leaning on Portia's arm and Portia could feel her trembling.

"We can still leave, nothing has happened..." she offered.

Phyllida Craddock shook her head. She was in black widow's weeds and they made her pale blue eyes look almost white. There were dark circles under her eyes.

"I have to be here for her so she knows I lived."

"How...."

"She always intended I should and she was always very clever with drugs and poisons."

Portia said nothing. Phyllida had come back to life a day and a half after the arrest of her mother, in a bedroom in Fleetwood's house. Several hours of careful questioning by him and by Portia Morgan herself had found plentiful tears, but no sign she had known anything of her mother's activities. Fleetwood had decided not to arraign her.

Her mother's trial for petty treason had been swift and easily decided. She had pleaded not guilty, as it happened. But there were plenty of witnesses to the fact that Craddock's hands had been tied when he supposedly hanged himself and there had been grease on his face. Her other murders were taken into account but in fact were not relevant to the men of the jury. The petty treason by itself was enough for her to burn.

And so the whores were gathered together in a group, their striped petticoats rustling. There were even some false nuns from the Clerkenwell convent. Normally they would have been competing for trade but today they had come to see their enemy burn.

"...in such defiance of God's law, such a hideous crime..."

The cart had appeared at the end of the street, with a boy trotting ahead of it, by the two Shire horses' heads. There was a drummer as well, playing a slow hard beat and on either side of the cart were Mr Pickering the King of London's men, beggars and upright men, roaring boys and bravos, forming a loose guard. A Fool in patches and tatters danced slowly among them, his face painted white and red, waving a pig's bladder on a stick. Mr Pickering had asked Fleetwood for permission to form the guard and Fleetwood had given it, reckoning order would be better kept that way. Behind the cart came Mr Fleetwood and his men, relieved not to have to hold back the whores.

Mrs Ashley stood in the cart, bolt upright, her hands

chained, in her shift which had the marks of the turds and bones that had been thrown at her. Her head had been shorn, her face was stony, frozen in contempt. Her eyes passed over Portia and fixed on her daughter, Phyllida Craddock. There was a tiny nod.

Catlin flung out a hand. "See, see, the wicked Jezebel!" he shouted, "Yea behold upon her face the wickedness of her impenitence..."

"Oh be quiet, you foul little man," said Mrs Ashley loudly and clearly, "You're only here because I killed Isabel, the whore you should have married, you whited sepulchre."

Maliverny Catlin stared and gobbled at her, and Portia was glad of her veil to hide a grin. After all, what had the woman to lose?

Some of the whores elbowed each other, while the others, led by Eliza, screamed and shouted at her and drowned out what she said. Then the Fool climbed onto the cart and danced around the woman, then shoved a gag in the woman's mouth, strapped it on tight. The crowd laughed and yelled approval. But Portia saw Mrs Ashley's jaw work as she chewed on the leather, swallowed. Something in her face relaxed. The cart lurched on to stand by the scaffold and Mrs Ashley, suddenly fainting, was half helped, half dragged onto the scaffold where they chained her tightly to the pole and piled it up with faggots of wood.

Portia felt her gut tighten. She didn't know how much of this she would be able to watch. In fact she had gone to see Mr Hughes the hangman with every penny she could find in her chambers and the result of pawning her new sword. He had shaken his head at her regretfully when she asked him to strangle Mrs Ashley first. "The whores have paid me," he said, "They want to hear her scream."

So she had gone back and got her sword out of pawn and come as herself to see the end. In some obscure way, she felt she owed it to the woman. Shakespeare, it seemed, was not so steadfast as he was nowhere to be seen. Mrs Briscoe stood perkily, staring up at the scaffold. Young Peter was there as well, she saw, as he crawled through the legs of the crowd on one arm, the other being in a sling. He had a large piece of left over cake from Mrs Briscoe's churching in his teeth. He came up to them, grinning and pulling bits off it to eat. "I love cake," he said to her, "This is good, innit, Mrs Morgan."

She didn't answer. She was staring narrowly at Mrs Ashley. The woman's head was down, her face was reddening, she was still chewing at the gag in her mouth and...

Portia looked around for the Fool who had climbed up to put the gag there and couldn't see him, wondered who it could possibly have been. Then she looked at Phyllida who was watching carefully as her mother sagged against the pole she was chained to. There was something quite smug in the expression around the eyes.

Ah, thought Portia, and wondered who the girl had found to do the job of putting a hebenon-smeared gag into Mrs Ashley's mouth. It was a good idea and somehow very fitting.

Catlin was still preaching but had lost a great deal of vigour and whores were answering him back now, twitting him about Isabel and Eliza herself pulled her bodice down and offered to take Isabel's place. One of the other whores shouted at her for being unseemly. Catlin ended somehow and stepped down from the scaffold, his face flaming with embarrassment. Whyever did the man do it to himself?

Fleetwood was standing on the scaffold now as the upright men circled it to keep the people back. He read out the indictment and sentence in a loud steady voice, but there was no mention of witchcraft. Her Majesty the Queen disapproved of such things, although she had her own soothsayer at court. Then Fleetwood stepped away as Mr Hughes approached with his assistant, each holding two torches to light the pitch-covered brushwood in several places.

As the smoke rose and then the flames, Portia could see Mrs Ashley sagging against the pole she was chained to. The whores were disappointed for there was no screaming. She might as well have been dead if she wasn't in fact. There were angry complaints at the anticlimax and somebody shrewdly shouted for the Fool.

Portia watched Phyllida watching her mother burn and saw no tears, no sympathy. Yet she was there. It had to count for something. After all, by her account the woman had only wanted to help her daughter have a child although if Peter the Hedgehog was right about Mr Craddock, she could have gone a very much simpler way about it.

Portia sighed. She hated Mrs Ashley for what she had done and she hated what was being done to her. The flames crackled and consumed the figure, while the smell that came from the fire was a disgustingly pleasant one of roast pork.

"Phew," said Shakespeare, standing beside her, "It worked."

"What did?" Then she saw that there were traces of white paint on the sides of his face although he had changed out of his patches and tatters and there was no sign of the bladder on a stick. "The gag greased with hebenon?"

Shakespeare nodded. "I felt sorry for her," he admitted. "I don't know why, considering she was going to have my guts out in the light of day. I wish I could remember more of what she said but... She'll burn anyway in Hell." He smiled crookedly. "At least this way

449

my ears are not offended by her screams although no doubt the whores' ears will be offended by their lack."

Portia watched him narrowly through the mesh of her veil. On the whole she thought she preferred the velvet mask. The player courteously offered her his arm. "Mrs Morgan," he said, with a very serious expression, "Do you think your brother would be offended if I asked you and your gossips to bear me company at the Cock tavern for some brandy and the daily ordinary?"

For a moment she was honestly confused and then embarrassed. And what about her pocky face? But then he knew what it looked like, he'd seen it often enough when she was James Enys.

Ellie Briscoe shoved her in the back. "I'll come with you, Mistress," she said, "My mother in law is looking after the baby."

Phyllida was turning her pure pale face aside. "I'll stay here," she said in a distant voice. "Until she's all gone. I'm sure Mr Fleetwood will escort me back."

"Well... er... no, I don't think my brother would be offended," Portia stammered, "He always speaks well of you, Mr Shakespeare." Bald Will grinned in pure mischief so she added, "Although he warned me that you have a terrible reputation as a skirt-chaser."

Shakespeare looked suitably offended but she took his arm anyway.

They left Mrs Ashley there, left the heat of the flames

450

and the cheering whores and headed for London Bridge with its hat shops and drapers. As respectable women they couldn't possibly go into any of the notorious stews and alehouses south of the river but the Cock was just about respectable enough.

Behind them the fire danced and the whores of London cheered in triumph as their killer burned for killing her son-in-law.

James Enys and his sister, doubtless accompanied by Mrs Morgan and her brother, will return soon. In the meantime, readers who have acquired a taste for Elizabethan intrigue may care to visit Sir Robert Carey at www.poisonedpenpress.com

Sir Robert is the creation of the novelist P F Chisholm. Readers with a taste for more modern intrigue may notice a certain resemblance between P F Chisholm's biography at Poisoned Pen Press and that of Patricia Finney at www.patriciafinney.com

Even more books by Patricia Finney may be found at www.climbingtreebooks.net

Lightning Source UK Ltd.
Milton Keynes UK
UKHW010627080920
369553UK00002B/305

9 781909 172500